Shadow's Ember

Shadow's Ember

DELUSIONS OF A CYBORG SAVIOR 1

Nathan Helmly

Clovercroft Publishing

Shadow's Ember

Published by Clovercroft Publishing, Franklin, TN
www.clovercroftpublishing.com

Cover Image by KAdala S.R.L.

Edited by Ann Tatlock

Cover and Interior Layout Design by Suzanne Lawing

Printed in the United States of America

ISBN: 978-1-956370-84-3 (print)

This edition includes a drawing before most chapters which were envisioned in color, but later printed in grayscale.

If you would like to see the drawings in their original form, scan the QR code above, or visit:
gifthammer.com/shadows-ember-drawings.html

CONTENTS

Prologue . . . 13
Midnight Attack . . . 25
Morning Haze . . . 43
Family Matters . . . 55
Insurgent . . . 63
Aftermath . . . 75
Outcasts . . . 87
Rematch . . . 105
Something Else to Strive For . . . 117
The Scarred . . . 137
House Call . . . 161
Upgrades . . . 173
Rescuers . . . 185
Scent of the Sea . . . 201
Confrontation . . . 209
Cleansing the Sacred Vine . . . 219
Gladiators . . . 229
Bitter Losers . . . 239
Showdown . . . 249

Desert Viper 259
Setbacks 269
Under Siege 283
Coldfront 293
Skykeep Tower 305
Heart of the Keep 313
Where It All Started 323
Genocide 339
Intervention 347
Epilogue 363
Postscript 369
Acknowledgments 375

Maker's Log #55021: Biomining.

Every time I walk past this garden, I think about you. It makes some irrational part of me hope that, just maybe, you're smiling up there somewhere as you watch me.

I keep imagining a proud grin on your face… of yourself for coming up with these brilliant gardens, and of me for managing to not mess them up.

Now, your idea for mineral-mining plants has turned out better than you'd ever hoped it would. Our machines have turned into farmers too. Whole villages are growing up around each of your little experiments. These plants feed us every mineral and metal I could ever want now. More than just the few simple necessities we used to wish so hard for.

Sorry, I have to pause and stretch. Pruning back a chromium sapling here while I talk. It gets tedious to keep doing every couple weeks, but if I don't the whole thing will end up poisoning itself and stop soaking up any sunlight. Then there would be no more of these infinitely useful little nuts it grows.

I think you'd have found it beautiful, if only you could see it now.

If only…

<HEAVY SIGH OMITTED>

I dare not think of that again.

Keep pressing onward Avoma.

PROLOGUE

All right, settle into your bed while I go stoke the fire, sweetheart. Now, where were we? Right.

The great and magnificent Onok didn't grumble as he slid his hand along the bumpy stone veins of the tunnel. Elders of villages *never* grumble, in fact. It's not very heroic for someone who's taller than both of us combined and commands one of the five great elements. Maker built this whole island with those powers, and then gifted one to each of his first, strongest, and most heroic creations. So, no, Onok does *not* grumble. Ever. Thoughts drifted through his circuits as he considered his plan again. Yes. It was sure to work this time. Onward he marched, feet padding as silently as he could manage while the rough stone walls ground away at the metal in his fingertips.

Onok didn't even complain when the shadowy depths started to make him feel blind. Yes, that's even more surprising than it sounds. I know your eyes haven't adapted to it yet, but Onok doesn't see light and shadow the way you, or even I, do. Normally, the shadows themselves are what he sees. It comes with being the Elder of Shadow, you see.

Of course we *all* have a little darkness in us. Yes, even *you*, my little candle. It's in there, right beside your fire. You just haven't unlocked it yet. But Onok, now, he doesn't just have a *little* darkness. He IS the shadows, and Maker made the shadows to be part of him. Onok watches over us all, same as all the Elders do, but *especially* him, the Elder of Shadow. Just remember that the next time you're scared at night. Onok can always see—wherever the shadows settle.

Except for today. Because, you see, as pure as he is, he was about to meet something even bigger, even stronger, and even more purely black than him. And before the great hero Onok became *Elder* Onok, *this* creature was the master of all the island's shadows. So like I said, the fact that he couldn't see in a nice, comfortably dark, dank place was surprising. It didn't surprise him, though. He was down here for a reason, and so he knew this might happen.

Why? I just *told* you why. Pay better attention, Tirak, and get your finger out of your nose! No, you'll just have to keep listening until it comes up again.

Patience.

Onok gave up trying to bend the shadows to his will and let himself feel the currents move. Yes, you can feel even the shadows themselves shift around like the swirls of a campfire, if you're the hero of shadow. Raw stone crunched softly beneath the plates of his bare feet. No, it didn't clank and thud because he's not as clumsy as you are, dear. Aw, don't worry, you'll learn how to sneak *far* too soon.

Don't give me that innocent, confused look. You know exactly what I mean, young cybri.

Onok sighed as the heavy gear behind his neck clicked forward. The violet glow of his readied shards faded a little. *Click!* The glow dimmed further. Another click and he reabsorbed the last of his power, the shards disappearing into the gearbox between his shoulders. He needed every splinter of it he could get in order to be sure, but . . . *yes!* He could feel the shadows ebb and flow like ripples of water in front of him. It was leading him deeper into the caves.

What? No. Keeping his shards ready for a fight wouldn't do him much good down there. You see, something was waiting for him.

Shush, don't scream, Tirak. We don't provoke the island when we travel its jungles as guests, or else it might turn against us. We aren't even *at* the story's monster yet.

That thing, Onok knew it was strong enough to steal his beloved shadows right out of his fists. He knew, because that's exactly what it did the last time he snuck down here and tried to spy out its home.

It had writhed and pulsed in the middle of a huge cavern like a giant, lightless heart. Veins wider than his legs spread out in every direction, eating away the stone and leaving tunnel networks so long that we still haven't mapped their farthest ends. Some go beyond the island's three capes beneath open ocean. An appropriately titanic monster indeed for our titanic hero.

After a long time of walking, and at least a few new bruises on the less metallic parts of his shins, the air started to smell damp. Some of the chill was gone too. Onok knew he was getting close now.

No, even with bruised knees he didn't cry one bit. Elder Onok is the greatest hero across our whole island. And heroes don't cry. *Especially* not when they scrape their knees.

The jagged stone disappeared without warning around Elder Onok. He must've entered some kind of cavern. The casings of his fingertips had already been scraped almost to bleeding, but he still wished he had that familiar touch again to orient himself. For just one moment, he hesitated. Should he back up a step and find the wall again?

Then, he heard a distant gurgle.

Calm down. I'm still not at the monster yet.

Instead, it was *water* being squeezed through rocks too narrow for it to flow comfortably. He focused on the sounds vibrating against his ear disks as the sound echoed and bounced off a thousand surfaces.

The cavern must've been *HUGE!*

The longer he listened, the more Onok could hear about his surroundings. He couldn't see, but this was almost as good. Somewhere far to his right, the echoes became much more hollow. That had to be an even deeper chasm. He decided it would be a bad idea to go that way. Even the island's greatest heroes don't like spraining their ankles.

Behind him, Onok could pick out the edges of the tunnel he came through. A few columns of rock were here and there. All he needed to find now was … *there!*

Okay, okay, I'm sorry. You're just too jumpy for me to resist.

Onok's ears noticed something strange straight ahead of him. No, it wasn't a growl. It wasn't a bark either.

It was *nothing.*

No, really, I mean it. In a cavern that was alive with tinkles and echoes, there was only one patch of dead stillness. One spot of emptiness that absorbed any sound that came its way.

That is, until that empty spot let out a roar that shook the walls!

But Onok didn't come unprepared. An Elder never goes anywhere unprepared. Even when they can't conduct their element, you wouldn't want to dual someone whose sword weighs twice as much as you do.

The sword he drew had a dark blade that was at least as tall as I am. Just like how your dad's favorite blade is tinted slightly red, Onok's was as pure a black as the metal in his shoulders and legs.

Onok almost tried to call up some energy before he remembered how stupid an idea that would be. Why? Tirak … I've told you at least a dozen times now. Nobody can conduct an element that someone stronger is already conducting.

And Onok was wayyy out of his league. But a hero doesn't back down once his mind is made up. The blackness before him began to churn on itself. That unseeable *nothing* was, in fact, a thing after all! And Elder Onok had just made it very, *very* angry.

Tentacles exploded from its surface. Onok had to dive to his side in order to dodge the first exploring feelers. As a master of darkness himself, he knew all too well what would happen once one of them felt him. He rolled into a crouch and searched the emptiness for snakes of that vague extra dark. And good thing he did too! One writhed just beside him!

He backed away cautiously, dancing between the slap-clapping of the monster's arms. How would he ever get out of this?

He shook off the worry. This was his island. He would simply creep as close as he could to the thing's body and—

A sickening squish echoed beneath him. For one horrifying second, Onok felt a squeezing, squirming mass between his two toes.

The monster cried out as much in pain as in surprise. How had such tiny food snuck so close to its grand presence? It couldn't see, but it had been feeling the air for him and everything!

He was still too far away, but Onok didn't hesitate to strike. His elemental sword didn't do him any favors against the creature, but few things can ignore a hundred sacks-worth of sharp metal. One tentacle thudded to the ground and grew stiff.

Arms shot toward him from every direction, but the beast had once again underestimated our greatest hero.

Limbs began to litter the space around Onok as he swung and danced with the skills of an expert warrior. Yes, even more expert than your father. Onok has been the best swordmaster since before your dad was born. No, that doesn't make him old, love. Elders age differently than you and I do.

Yes, differently than Dad does too. Now peace, Tir. Don't you want me to finish this story? Yes? Then you have to let me *tell* it.

Tentacles bled and squirmed underfoot, but Elder Onok's battle was far from over. Some say he defended that spot for a whole day without either of them gaining a single finger's distance. So far beneath the ground, we'll never know for sure how long it was.

But as the fight went on, he began to feel his strength fading. There was no way he could overpower this massive creature on his own. What had he been thinking?

No sooner did he doubt himself than a tentacle as thick as his shoulders *slammed* into him! It cracked like a whip, instantly bruising his skin and even tearing a few armor plates right off his chest. Elder Onok was flung backward.

He sailed. Then he fell.

Then he fell some more.

Then he fell *even more!*

Where in Maker's name was the ground? he wondered.

Of course, that's exactly when he struck the floor of the pit he'd been knocked into. Hundreds of heads above him, the monster pounced down. It had been so unmoving and lazy till then that Onok had assumed the thing was no more capable of walking around than a plant.

Just think about *that* the next time you stand under the shade of a thirty-head-tall tree. Just look up and imagine it more than black from root to leaf, leaping at you like a tiger. But where was his *sword*?

Onok stumbled backward as it approached. It was his second biggest mistake of the whole day.

It was also the second most important thing he had ever done.

Something smooth and cold rolled underneath. Before he knew it, Onok was flat on his back yet again, and a particularly pointy rock was making sure his shoulder blades knew it. Even his gearbox dented slightly. He ignored the damage. It would only heal.

Meanwhile, that hard thing he had stepped on bounced away with a peculiar *pling-CLANG*. Had that been his weapon? Or … maybe just its handle?

He didn't much like that last thought.

All the while, that monster was falling toward him. Its body was truly *huge!* Nothing else on the island has come close since, except maybe Mount Fulkana itself.

No, I promise. Those were Elder Onok's own words!

He decided that he had no choice. Onok leaped for the metal object that was still humming its clear tone. His hands closed around its cold shaft as the ground began to quake with the monster's landing.

The unfamiliar handle was clearly not part of Onok's sword. He twirled its surprising weight once behind him. It was almost half as tall as he was, and had something bulky at one end, much like the end of a miner's chisel might have. It crackled with a familiar energy of its own too. Not powered by Onok, powered by *itself*!

Out of options, Onok hurled the object like a spear. If it didn't somehow wound the beast, then maybe it would at least distract it for him.

And that was the biggest mistake Elder Onok ever made.

It also turned out to be the single most important thing he's ever done.

To his dismay, the chisel passed right through the shadow's hollow form and snapped against the wall behind its head. No screech of pain followed. He wasn't even sure the monster had *noticed*! He was just about to turn and run when a much deeper snap rumbled through the cavern.

Dust exploded from the wall, coating monster and hero alike as a zig-zag line of energy traveled up its surface. The fissure jumped the gap between the cliff where he had first been standing and the ceiling high above.

White-hot light exploded from the newly bored hole in the ceiling as the noonday sun shone down. Blinding white struck pure dark, and for one fateful second, our hero could just *barely* see the shape of the depths' terror that had plagued him down here beneath the island for years!

Then, like the smoke of wet campfire, the monster evaporated away before its one and only weakness.

Exhausted, Onok flopped onto his back and welcomed the darkness as it hugged him close. Released from the foul beast's grip at last, the shadows welcomed him as their rightful master. He watched the once-blank cavern come to life before his eyes. Beautiful violet crystal buds cast a twinkling glow from the ceiling, fading only around the rift where a much more powerful light still blinded his eyes. Breathing out a contented sigh, Onok let his body unravel into a haze of wriggling wisps. It felt good to slip into his Second Nature after holding back like that for an entire fight.

He picked up the chisel that had saved him with reverent hands. It had fallen from the wall and rolled back to him again, as if even it wanted to call him its master.

Elder Onok looked at the flowing water and beautiful rock and made up his mind. An idea was already forming, even then.

"I think I'm going to call this place my home."

~~~~~

Tirak's circuits kept on racing while his mom's energetic voice trailed off, her story finished for the night. He let her pull him into what she liked to call a "fond mamabear hug" while they watched the campfire crackle. He wanted to squirm out of any more embarrassment, but truth be told it was kind of a cold night. A breeze played across his back, and he found himself nestling more tightly into her side. *Completely* against his will.

Across the pit from them, the fire cast brilliant shadows across the canvas and wood walls of his family's wagon. The little home that held all their possesions in the island. The longer he watched, Tirak could start to imagine he was seeing Elder Onok's fight against the Chasmheart monster play out in the shapes those shadows cast. A log popped loudly, sending a fat spark up into the air just as he imagined the final blow cracking the cavern's ceiling open. That glow was the daylight shining through and slaying the beast. Inside the back half of the wagon, the canvas ruffled slightly. Dad was probably rearranging all the crates back there again.

"All right, Tir. Now settle into your sack and try to sleep," his mother encouraged as she dropped the storyteller tone.

Despite her words, neither of them moved. It was too cozy to stay right there. He thought about the story, and couldn't help furrowing his brow.

"So, if that ca-vuhn belongs to Elduh Onok, then how come so many fire people like us live thewe?" Tirak asked.
~~~~~

Stupid tongue. When would he grow into it like Mom promised?

"*Ignii*, sweet," Mom chided, pronouncing it with that stupid ee-eye ending he could never say right. "Be proud of the name Maker gave our element. But to answer that, I'll need to tell you a whole different story about the time Elder Hakhoz tried building a city that sank in lava. It was very kind of Elder Onok to let our people share his city, but … his rule is why so many of us don't stay."

"You mean, you and Dad are outcasts?"

"No. No, not outcasts. We just … prefer to live out here on our own. Ugly things happen when the elements mix together too much. It'll make more sense after I tell you about the adventures Elder Hakhoz had."

Tirak was tempted to try and pronounce their Elder's name again to see if he could make that weird guttural kh sound his mom used. Why was it such a big deal to say it with a simple K anyway? His own name was perfectly fine like that. He decided to spare himself another motherly giggle at his expense and kept silent.

But that didn't protect him from motherly *affection*. She pulled him into another bear hug and wouldn't let go no matter how hard he struggled. He tried his best to avoid letting her kiss him, but of course it did no good.

He grimaced. He was almost thirty already; that was a whole two *years* old! Only another eight months and he could start apprenticing with his dad as a traveling warrior, like a real grownup! Kids as big as him certainly didn't still need goodnight kisses.

"Okay, okay… phew. I'm serious now, Tir. Time for bed."

She gave him one more squeeze, then laid him on his sleeping sack like he was still a child. His dad's arms appeared on either side of her as she tucked his blanket around him. Like two King snakes trying to attack with his red and black plating colors.

The two best faces on the whole island stared down at him together. Especially his mom's with those flecks of yellow and gold that made her cheeks look so pretty during sunsets. Flecks that he shared too, though she always said his hues looked much more handsome with the way they were tempered by Dad's reds.

"All right, bud, settle in and try to sleep," Dad said. "We'll be back on the road before sun-up. Your mom and I are going to squeeze in a little sparring practice, and no, you can't join. We won't be far into the woods, so just call out if you need us."

A coarse hand stroked his cheek. Tirak returned his dad's smile. He would have pits in his hand plates too when he grew up. Every awesome warrior needed a few scars and pits to be proud of.

Tirak closed his eyes and listened to their feet crunch away in the gravel. He wasn't all that tired, but Dad would get mad if he didn't at least try to sleep. He drifted off before he even knew it, content knowing that this little patch of the island—the clearing he and his parents made along the road each night—was always a safe place to be. He slept peacefully, even when a wet snout crept out of the bushes for brief sniff next to him, because he knew this would last forever.

Maker's Log #85342: The very last island.

You can see I tried to capture each of the four primary biomes along with our island's overall shape. You already know, I'm sure, but each one is subdivided into microbiomes that follow an overall trend: northern desert, southwest jungle, & southeast glaciers all tied together at a volcanic center. It's split into three radial capes that follow the surrounding ocean's circular current. The vortices it causes near the center of each bay can get pretty dangerous, even for Biri's water prowess, so I would warn never to fly too close.

Yes, our little slice of paradise is indeed quite—

Yes, Korma… I KNOW I'm bad at drawing.

And yes I KNOW Limna isn't actually that big of a village!

<SILENCE>

Well if you hate the way it makes your mountains look so much, why don't YOU draw the next copy?

You keep talking about HOW MUCH BETTER your view is up in the sky. Maybe put all that buzzing around to use for once.

Oh, great… my notebook is still recording isn't it?

Prissi, cancel that note and turn it off, won't you?

<ACKNOWLEDGED. CONNECTING RECORD TO INTERCOM … >

Gah! No, you little rust bucket! Grrr… come HERE!

I swear, every year you gizmos get worse and wor—

1

MIDNIGHT ATTACK

Tirak ran his hand along the rough grains of his family's handmade wagon as it rolled along beneath him. The jungle road rocked and jostled him just as badly as the last time they'd come this far into the southwest peninsula to see the water Cybrii. Hopefully, they would stop and rest for the night soon, but Dad had always talked about how much he didn't like the beasts in this area, so maybe they wouldn't.

He flexed a scrawny arm that was quickly building up some really tough-looking muscle as he picked at a loose splinter. A piston engaged with a hiss as he put a little more oomph in and tore the piece away. Better to have a small gash looking ugly than a needle point catch something and tear it. His mom gave him a flick across the forearm.

"Stop that. I thought you were still listening. Do you want to hear the rest of it or not?"

An eerie chatter wafted through the blackness outside the wagon's window and interrupted his answer. Tirak shrugged, then nodded. He knew them all by heart now after octets of months spent listening to each one. But it was still fun to hear the way she told them. She smiled, smoothing out a few hairs atop his head and started back in.

Tirak watched the dark underbrush roll by, and could imagine they were the cold, stony walls of Onok's cavern, just like in his mom's story. More sounds crept out of the darkness to join the first cry. Soon, a dozen chilling voices echoed an ugly song together through the night air. Tirak couldn't help edging away by instinct, deeper against his mother's side. Her hand combed through his hair, fingers skimming the glassy ridges of his memory cores. If only she'd let him grow it out a little more, then the cores wouldn't stick up like a glowing red mohawk.

"The Maker gaped at the high, craggy ceiling above them as they entered the cavern at last. 'Onok!' He cried, 'This is incredible! How in my great creation did you even manage such a thing? Look! The way you carved new seams out for the wellspring into … wait. Is that supposed to be my mask?!'"

Tirak rolled his eyes at how silly his mom sounded when she was trying to put on a deep, manly voice in stories.

"Onok looked down sheepishly and gripped the beautiful Biri's hand a little tighter. It had been her idea, but Onok didn't want to put her on the spot. 'Oh, it wasn't all that hard … Most of the place was already like this. Biri and I just touched it up a little where a gap wasn't big enough, make it more homey and all.'

"Maker continued to gawk and press him about each little detail. In their haste to explain the process, Biri showed Him the chisel Onok had found that first day.

"The air went deathly still. Maker's sunken eyes looked back up at the hero; twin mixing pots of sickness and rage.

"'Onok,'" She slipped into that awful Maker voice again. "'Where… where did you get that spear? Throw it away! Get rid of it right now!'"

Tirak lurched away at his mom's sudden intensity. Her eyes had become cat's-eye slits, a wild craze filling them. She hugged him once the moment passed.

"Yep. Onok was as scared as you were just now. He had never known the creaky old Man to react angrily at *anything*, and he still remembered smashing *three* separate holes in Maker's home when he'd first been born and ran away."

Tirak tilted his head up. Had he heard right?

"Nuh uh! He couldn't be *scared*. Onok's a hero."

She squeezed his waist in a silent laugh.

"Oh yes. Even heroes get scared sometimes, love. I guess not everyone can be as bold as your father *all* the time …" His mom sighed.

She rested the flat of her free hand against the rough-sawed wood behind their heads. She was wearing that dreamy expression she got whenever they talked about Dad for too long. The mushy, stupid one.

He didn't *really* mind though. After all, he'd met a few friends whose parents weren't like that, and their lives all seemed *awful*.

He stuck his hand into the leather pouch tied around his shoulder and rummaged through it by feel while he waited for the expression to wear off. His fingers brushed a warm lump of metal, and it reminded him of how chilly it was that night. He pulled the new favorite locket out and opened it. A red glow hugged his face on all sides and drove away that chill completely. Dad said the jagged shard inside was called "Trueglass." Similar to the crystals his parents grew in their gearboxes, but more pure. More ancient. And … it was basically money. And it was all his now. His hands trembled at the precious birthday gift. He stared into the glowing twist of heat and warmed his hands against its sides.

His mom cleared her throat and put on her "Maker" voice again, this time hissing through clenched teeth as if she'd just bitten her tongue.

"That … *thing* is a weapon of *putrid* destruction! It's a relic from … well, from long ago in my time. We called them Disintegration Staves. Only a monster that wanted to see its friends turned into little meat clouds would ever touch such a thing."

She let the image sink in quietly for a few seconds while the wagon lurched its way over several rocks and roots. Tirak's teeth rattled hard. Huge tangles of ferns were growing thicker around them every minute, and he wondered when they would have to get out and push their stuff the rest of the way to the water people village. The brush was even starting to drag against both sides of the wagon at the same time.

He had hoped the nights would get more pleasant once they'd left the foothills behind. But instead, all they'd done was trade the awful mountain chill for a jungle clamminess that was trying to choke him from the inside. Mom had said it would only get worse once they reached Limna. He wondered if they were called water people, maybe not because of their elemental power, but instead because they didn't need to breathe. Who actually *could* breathe in this oppressive swamp air? He tugged his shirt away from his neck and purposely distracted himself with Mom's story.

He could almost picture a black cloud of blood, with that barely visible purple glow around the edges. In his mind, it began to condense like a sticky rain and plop to the ground. The wet splats sounded just like the game his parents would bring back to camp and gut together before cooking supper.

Gross.

"Onok looked down in horror. He could see it now. He could feel the hate crackling in that purple lightning along its tip. How'd he ever thought something so destructive was a *chisel*?"

This story seemed to be going all wrong. It didn't even make sense, no matter how many times she told it. Why would Maker be so mad at them for creating things the way He did? He just couldn't keep quiet.

"But, but! Elder Onok never used the chisel to hurt anything, cybrii or creature!" Tirak protested.

He caught himself on the last word, his voice cracking. Had that been too loud? His mom's face was turned toward the window, but he could see that thin reflection of her pupils in the crystal. He winced. Yes, too loud for sure. He hated it when she looked that worried.

More quietly, he added, "Even the Chasmheart he fought was an accident. He didn't think he could hurt the thing. Plus, it was the light that killed it ..."

She turned back toward him, her eyes their normal round shape again. She tapped a hardened orange finger on his nose.

"Yes, you're right, love. And … that's exactly what Biri pointed out too.

"She said, 'Maybe, love, it doesn't matter how evil a tool is. *It* was made to destroy, but You turned it into something creative.'"

Tirak frowned. Was that supposed to be an answer? It still didn't explain why it made Maker so mad!

"Onok watched her speak, more enthralled by the colors of her armor that reflected Maker's little flameless torch than by what she was saying. Two shades of blue, one like the deepwater far out beyond the shore and the other as piercing as that salt spring we took you to a few months ago, wove between skin as pink as a sunburn. He wondered how he'd ever convinced someone so wonderful to love him."

Mom turned her head up toward the ceiling and smiled as the wagon rocked from several more bumpy stones in the path. It sounded like one of them had even launched Dad a little, judging from the solid bump overhead.

"Onok reached out to embrace his beloved Biri, and they shared a kiss like—"

Tirak clapped his palms over his ears, striking the rims of his drums painfully.

"*Moo*-oom! Why do you always have to add the mushy bits?" he hissed.

She smiled down at him again with a twinkle in her orange eyes, brushing another hand through his hair.

"The 'mushy bits' are part of the story too, love. One day, you'll grow up and start to appreciate them too. You know, when I was about—"

His mom gasped.

Out the window, two eyes glowed a hungry red. A howl pierced the air nearby. Tirak trembled as the beast locked eyes with him and began to growl.

Except, no. That sound was coming from *beside* him. Mom reached a steady hand toward the wooden panel above their heads and gave three soft knocks. Tirak was amazed to see her throat quake as her growling dropped an octave lower. Any second now, his father's single knock would reply …

A red-and-black paw smashed a hole through the wood.

It reformed into a metal fist and disappeared again. Above, a canine voice let out a wounded yelp. The wagon rocked violently a second time.

His mom screamed Dad's name, reaching for the door's latch.

"Wait, Mom! Don't we need to run? You said fighting beasts angers the island."

She nodded to herself, her lips moving in a soundless whisper. Tongues of fire began to leak from her fist. Tirak had watched them spar often enough to know what was coming. Her voice had held its guttural tremor as she answered him.

"Sometimes, Tirak, the island decides to be angry no matter what we do."

Fangs sprouted as she spoke. Her lips split into distinct halves as pointed ears rose above her head. She planted two metallic hind paws against the far wall and waited for the creature to return.

"When that day comes, a cybri needs to be ready to fight tooth and nail for what he loves."

Claws soon scraped against the wood again.

"A small chance we all live is always worth more than a large chance I survive the rest of my life without my mate."

A damp paw found its way into the window.

So Mom struck!

She exploded from the wall with a leap that left an afterimage in Tirak's eyes. Her punch landed with a blaze of light and tore the wagon door clean from its hinges.

She rode it out into the open air, landing with a distinct *squish* onto the hard packed ground.

Tirak stared wide-eyed as she slid to a stop thirty legs away. The beast didn't try to get up again from beneath her, but she hadn't stopped to check anyway. The whole line of brush beyond the open path was churning, boiling. Packs of the creatures belched forward from the vine-crusted ferns.

The wagon rolled Tirak to a gradual stop a few moments later. More clashes rattled the roof above him. There must have been more that circled around from behind and were now attacking Dad. One of them shrieked as the tip of a blade pierced down through the ceiling.

Mom was weaponless, but she held her own just as easily. She always preferred her bare fists to one of Dad's weapons. As Tirak watched, she spun sideways through the air and brought her toes down on a skull. It caved in as the rest of the beast collapsed to the ground.

A claw swiped across her leg! Her yell jolted Tirak; he had never seen her face like that before. As he watched the purple-black blood trickle down, it dawned on him that his parents might actually be in danger. They had never faced a challenge they couldn't overcome, but Tirak began to wonder if this was something new.

"A cybri must always be ready to defend those he loves." Her voice echoed in his ears.

He reached into an overturned chest and gripped one of his Father's smaller blades. More and more of the things were gathering from the woods. His parents wouldn't be able to fend them all off alone. It was his duty to help them. He leapt out of the wagon with a war cry, bringing the sword down on a smaller beast as he landed. It stumbled, and he had just enough time to bring the weapon back around into a clumsy version of his father's favorite finishing strike.

The next few… moments—or maybe hours—were a blur of snapping orange jaws and flashing steel. Tirak barely noticed that the pack was thinning until it had vanished entirely. His parents shared an uneasy, exhausted look.

"Why did they stop? Did we scare them off?" Mom asked.

Dad's hands were already flying, gathering sticks and random materials around him.

"Hellhounds don't get scared. Both of you, get back in the wagon, and we'll try to hold them off from inside. Ironically, they don't like fire. Especially fire they can't conduct themselves."

"But what good is that going to do us, m'love? We can't hold them off forever."

"Dawn is only three hours away. Maybe four. If we last that long, they'll leave us alone."

Tirak thought Mom looked unconvinced, but she pulled him into the wagon's cargo area anyway. She began digging materials out of crates and reinforcing weak-looking windows or gaps in the otherwise sturdy walls. They had it looking like a wheeled fortress in only minutes. Mom kept working, but Tirak soon found himself idle, biting his lip.

"Tir, go help your father build that fire. He can't stack wood and light it at the same time."

He obeyed. In no time at all, they had an impressive line of fires encircling the western half of the clearing. As it spread, the bright clusters became an unbroken wall against the night itself. His father's hand ignited to kindle the next pile of sticks, but stopped short. His head was angled high into the air, his ear a soft triangle above his head instead of its usual flat disk shape.

"W-what's wrong, Dad?"

"I don't know. It feels … darker than usual." Then he gasped. "The stars! They're gone!"

A low rumble vibrated the domes of Tirak's ears from behind. As he watched, the glow of the fires waned, then disappeared entirely. He could still feel their intense heat, but somehow he couldn't *see* them anymore. He couldn't think what could possibly cause such a thing to happen. Dad took one step toward where the wagon might have been.

The rumble grew to an earsplitting rush of wind, and suddenly Tirak was on his side. His shoulder had dug a trench in the dirt almost as deep as his hand. Wind howled against his ear domes, sounding high-pitched and screech-like through the trees. Like a mournful wail. Tirak could imagine it belonging to one of the magical banshee creatures from Maker's fairy tales.

And even quicker than they had gone, the lights returned. Tirak's stomach churned. Dad was just stumbling back to his feet, and beyond him lay … what was left of the wagon. The front cabin area was flattened and shattered. Its animals lay in a twisted heap, off on their own. Whatever was left lay on its side. A singular intact wheel spun idly in the air.

Dad groaned and fell onto his side again. Tirak rushed over to him, begging to help. Dad pushed him away and pointed at the wagon.

"Tirak! Listen to me. Go find your mother in there and make sure she's OK!"

Tirak knew that look in his eyes, and knew better than to disobey him at such a moment. He reached the safety of its walls just before the howls returned.

"Mom? Are you in here? Do you need help? Where—?"

A hundred bodies began to slam into the walls. Tirak felt his footing shift as the whole wagon began to tilt again . . .

. . . He woke up to the sound of a struggle. His head felt foggy. He tried to push himself out of the mud, but something heavy held him down. Even more worrying, he couldn't feel his leg at all! His thigh throbbed worse than the dark itself, but … but he felt nothing beyond it.

No, that wasn't true. He wiggled his right two toes and sighed in relief. Then the implications set in. That had worked … so why couldn't he wiggle anything on his left leg?

Wood scraped on wood, and a sharp edge suddenly dug into his neck. His remaining breath was squeezed out by a cry of pain. It took him a long, agonizing minute to press a gap into the mud and let himself breathe again. He froze as he heard a snuffling somewhere not too far away.

"No! Leave him alone, you brutes! Fight me instead!"

A heavy rock cracked against the splintered floor of the wagon, right in front of his face. An un-cybri-like voice screeched and fell silent under the bite of a sword. The clashes became more and more frantic. Soon, the air was filled with an indistinct clamor of growls and snaps.

~~~~~

A rod whistled through the air and cracked loudly against the yellow plates in his cheek. The blow made him stumble against the uneven footing of large, foot-polished cobbles. Stupid foot. If he had been knocked to the right he could've recovered just fine. Tirak braced for more jeers from the other trainees waiting their turn along the courtyard's wall. They always got a kick from seeing "the cripple" try to practice like he was one of them. Except no, Tirak remembered that it was just the two of them here today.

"Keep your defense up, boy. Don't get distracted. A warrior of the Guard never gets surprised."

He wiped his offhand on the stained, coarse tunic that had been white earlier in the day and quickly reset his stance, feeling the smooth cobbles through the armor in his toes. His left had never quite lost all of its numbness since… that—

Red-hot fangs snapped in front of his eyes. Growls seemed to fill the air again. Why did his face feel so hot?

He shook his head again, but it just wouldn't clear. Sloppy. He'd been in a weird mood all day, but that was no excuse. Tirak blamed his new caretaker. The guy wasn't normally so demanding, and Tirak normally wouldn't let a tiny bit of fatigue wear him down so much.

He supposed it was just going to be a weird sort of day.

"Sorry, Onok," Tirak muttered.

He moved the shield back into place and tightened his grip on the training staff. The memories had been plaguing him nonstop. Tirak
~~~~~

tried to blink them away and focus on the giant pile of ebony armor he was sparring against. Onok rumbled with his signature chuckle. Like a boulder slipping its way down a stone slope.

"You can just call me 'father,' you know."

Tirak glowered at Onok through broken images of glowing maws dragging away his real dad's body. His head twitched as he imagined hearing that hollow snap of bone again. Curse the stupid mountain, why wouldn't he realize the kinds of thoughts he was digging up? And that stupid toothy grin, too!

"All right, I won't force you to, either," Onok rumbled with more laughter, "Now, *prepare*. Left. Top. Jab. Spin. Jab. Reset."

Tirak's arms fell into the steady rhythm of Onok's voice. His annoyance fueled his movements, flaring each empty strike into a spike of raw anger. He repeated the steps of their practiced dance again and again, always ending with a flourishing spin to strike the imaginary opponent that was sneaking up behind.

Their staves clacked and crashed in a mockery of his parents' final stand. Each blow wore him down a little further, made his vision swim a little more. And the closer the tears got, the more frustrated he became.

He couldn't lose control; a warrior was better than that.

"Don't get sloppy, Tirak. Calm. Keep your stance firm. Stay cool."

"I know, Onok!" He barked through gritted teeth.

Oh, so he was supposed to stay *cool*, was he? Because he was a *fire* cybri? He couldn't help feeling like that joke was at his own expense. He tried harder and harder to keep his attacks and parries in control.

"Slow down, boy. Stay in control."

"I... *am*!"

He swung a well-aimed blow at Onok's shoulder, just to help the point sink in. The maddening Elder somehow managed to dodge at the last minute. Maker curse him.

"Things will never be quite as easy once your Second Nature finds you, boy. Keep—"

The city's torches flared painfully bright for one prolonged heartbeat. A piece of his mind noticed the cavern's high ceiling was perfectly visible, too. The once-faint glow of crystal pockets up there glowed like sunlight. Every sense seemed to blaze to life as if for the first time. An overpowering smell of sweat, blade oil, and rusty metal from the training ground. Then, an intense heat filled his chest.

Tirak looked down. Red embers swirled up and down his arms like an army of bees. He glanced back up at Onok, fear clutching his throat. Before Tirak could think, flames exploded outward in a bubble that swallowed the both of them. The blast was over in seconds, and Tirak sank to his knees. To his horror, it had left a cloud of black mist where his new father had stood.

Images of a dark forest flashed before his eyes. As cold panic crept into his veins, the cloud began to boom out a hearty laugh. Onok's body coalesced a few hands away from where he had been a moment ago. He stepped closer, and Tirak sobbed a faltering apology as powerful arms wrapped around him.

"Hush, my boy. No harm was done. All is well."

Tirak looked up at the burn marks across his dad's arms and face.

"B-but, your face!"

Onok smiled back at him and waved a careless hand.

"Ah, these will disappear in a couple hours. You should have seen some of my worse scars."

He grew a little more serious and gripped Tirak's shoulder with humorless pressure. With his other, he brushed a few flakes of ash from Tirak's shoulders.

"This was important. You needed to see the consequences of your power firsthand. You've been out here tempting fate all week by picking fights behind my back. There was a reason I barred you from sparring. Maybe now you'll be a little less brash against the other trainees. Take your lessons a little more seriously, hmm?"

Hearing his reprimand stung. Tirak slumped his shoulders and muttered something noncommittal. Onok's grip softened, cupping his neck rather than trying to hold him in place.

"You really are close to being a great warrior, boy. And … I'll admit I may have planned things for today of all days on purpose. I knew what I was getting into and I knew you couldn't hurt me. Good thing I don't have to follow my own city's laws, isn't it?"

He chuckled idly to himself before noticing that Tirak had begun to bounce with newfound energy.

"All right, I made my point, didn't I? Now run along. I think you have some friends to brag to."

"Okay. Can you teach me some more about my Nature after that?" Tirak bubbled.

"Ha! You may find you have to discover it for yourself, boy, but I can certainly try."

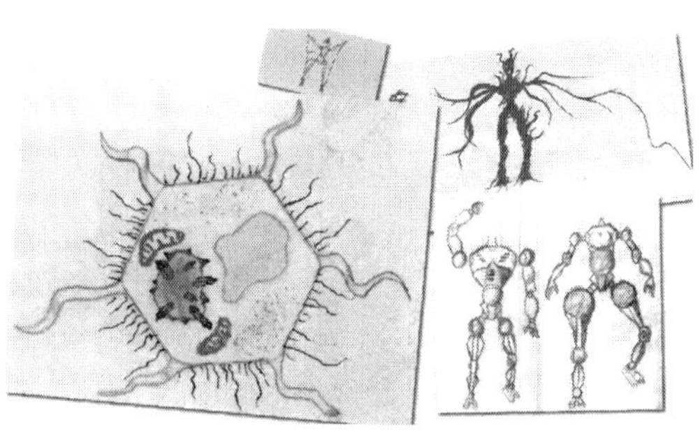

Maker's Log #85911: Cybrii, the children of Darkness.

My earliest designs were going to be purely robotic. I still have the old parts lying around here too. But they just kept failing. Stress fractures, weathering... you name it, one of them broke to it.

Worse, they weren't ALIVE. Not one. But the question kept bugging me. It had happened once, so why not again? I'd SEEN it. Machines CAN live. I tried to layer lab-grown muscles and animal parts onto the frames, and it made them a little more life-LIKE... until they started to rust. But they still weren't LIVING. I had no clue what I was missing.

Finally, I dared to try the stolen shard of my ancient enemy. It granted you their powers, but then ... something more too. IT gave you your life. Tempered by my teachings and love, each of you was born as something wholly new. No longer any one of your three origins. More than that, the Dark blood in your veins can reshape even pure metal like it's a wet rag. You were built to take even the toughest punishments. I couldn't stop you from breaking, but I found a way to let you always bounce back again. But your blood comes at a cost too.

Remember, my children: walk in my light, even at your darkest moment. You don't have to be the villains you came from. You CAN be better.

Your Elders were my first prototypes, one for each element. Yet somehow those five worked so well while the rest of you turned out pitifully weak. They age normally, but you Cybrii have lifespans like gnats! After years of fighting with biological nuances, I settled a truce with a quarter lifespan. It worked, but it meant you needed a way to not spend more than half your lives as children. I had a stroke of what I can only call pure genius. A simple, two-step system to fix all the problems that threatened to exterminate your species (heh, auri pun): Remote data downloads, coupled with an elemental killswitch until your fourth birthday! Talk about a hands-down coolest sweet-sixteen gift ever (or, more like 25th if you also take brain maturity into account). Even a naturally born Cybri is eloquent within their first few days.

And, that's how I reforged the Darkness into humanity's last line of defense. A piece of animal, a piece of me, a machine's bones, and a little touch of Shadow to bind it all together. Those old superhero filmshows would've loved my result. Five whole races of element-wielding cyborg wolverines? Yeah, pretty sure that would've been a "box hit" in ancient days.

Oh, I also forgot to add a glossary in case somehow I end up no longer being the only living person in the solar zipcode, so I'm going to go ahead and break my rule by appending new glossary words and details about the Cybrii as I think of them. Yes yes, it corrupts the scientific value of dating and paginating these journals, but keeping info organized is far more important.

Units of measurement:

- *8 Fingers make a Hand (convenient, because Cybrii are four-fingered)*
- *1.5 Hands make a Foot (varies Cybri to Cybri)*
- *8 Hands make a Leg*
- *2 Legs make a Head (The most common unit Cybrii think in)*

Cybrii *[sib'-ree-eye]: Or, Cybri for singular. Don't ask me why they hate the letter 'S.' The old terms our company used for the cybernetics department are too clunky for them, so the name they call their people eventually got shortened to match their elemental names.*

Lifecycle*: I had to compress the cybri lifespan into roughly one fourth the typical human's in order to raise their population levels high enough before the Darkness breaks through my barrier. One unanticipated re-*

sult is that years are a much more abstract concept to them, more like decades are to us while a month in their minds is more comparable to a year. The differences are perfect, but just about everything with them is accelerated, so I guess it makes sense.

Octets*: Cybrii don't like to think in base ten. I force them to when I can, but they hate number conversions just as much as I do. Our impasse has resulted in borrowing some interesting colloquial words for their base-eight numbers. The most common and important of which is "Octet" instead of simply "eight." They count on an octet of fingers, a year is two and a half octets of months, a month is half (essentially) <SOFT GRUMBLING INCLUDED> an octet of days, and so on.*

Elements*: Rome must have rolled in its collective grave when I introduced my Cybrii to Latin. Guess what they came up with when naming their five fundamental elements? The fire cybrii call themselves Ignii, Aurii for air, Limnii for the water ones, Terrii for earth, and Umbrii for shadow. It's official. Someone else finally tied you for terrible name ideas. Though, in their defense, I'm pretty sure Biri or someone came across one of your old research notebooks and just stole those words since they're almost identical to what you called the crystals.*

Shadow*: yes, I said five fundamental elements. Why is Shadow an element? Don't ask me. They dissolve into a useless soup whenever I try to design them without it in there. Could it ruin the whole plan? Yes, and I'm trying not to think about that.*

Elders*: These were my first few <INSERT: SUCCESSFUL> prototypes at making Cybrii, one for each of the classical elements and one for pure shadow. I was a little too ambitious with them, and now their age and colossal size makes all the newer generations look up to them as leaders. Each element's village ended up forming around its corresponding Elder.*

Word endings*. They use -a [ah] suffixes for places, -i [ee] for singular nouns and possessives, and -ii [ee-eye] for plural. I tried convincing them to bring back conjugations for adjectives as well, but no, they just use -i for everything that doesn't fit the other two use cases.*

Glass / Trueglass: *The cybri name for newtonian-bending crystals that their bodies can grow and absorb—wait, why am I explaining this to you of all people? You were always the expert on that subject, and if someone else gets hold of this somehow and doesn't already know, then they don't deserve to. Let's just say I've taken the idea a lot farther than using Kudzu to farm the stuff. I think there's some kind of difference in their minds when they call something Trueglass, but I don't really understand it. Either way, "Glass" is how they power whichever elemental power a Cybri is born with.*

Maker: *Oh goody, my least favorite topic. So… don't get too upset, okay? Look, it started when the Elders asked me where life came from. Turns out, a few centuries doesn't make that talk any easier to have with your kids. Now, they all call me "Maker" with a VERY uncomfortable tone of reverence. I wish I could make them stop too.*

2

MORNING HAZE

Tirak yawned as he stirred another helping of red sandglass into the kettle he was brewing. He needed the extra kick today. He needed it most other days too, but not every day was the anniversary of your parents' slaughter.

His mind dodged away as soon as it nudged that thought.

A day off. Yeah. He should focus on that. No drills with the other Umbra Cadets to be on time for. He still needed to check in with his courier boss in the city's lower tiers, but they were ignii. Way more laid-back about nonsense ideas like "rigid schedules." Hopefully, they wouldn't pull him in to be extra muscle on any jobs, though. Those were getting … unpleasant, and he had other things to do today.

A smile crept across his lips. Kaleek was even more demanding about schedules than work was when she had an idea in her head. This was one appointment Tirak had zero plans to be late for. One more day of getting to completely dunk on his little sister and still pretend it was "practice training"? Yeah. No way he would miss it, even if someone offered him the whole island and the ocean around it too.

He paused to wonder what her powers would do to her after they set in. Would she really be able to control *both* elements at the same time? He had never heard of someone doing that before. And most importantly ... *would it make her go feral like everyone said?* Somehow, Tirak doubted it. Kaleek had already been a feral brat since day one. A feral brat that he loved fiercely, of course. He didn't know anything about hybrids—no one really did—but the idea didn't even make sense. Why would one extra power triple someone's inner darkness like they claimed?

Tirak tapped his Shadowsight to find a spice jar that was hiding near the back of a cupboard above the gloomy stove. Shadow was already a second element that everyone shared. Wouldn't a second element make their shadow weaker instead of stronger? If anything, Tirak's sister was destined to become the purest saint that ever walked the island's shores. Now there was a thought. Tirak caught himself before he could snicker out loud.

In the end, though, all this theory crafting was just an effort to distract himself from the unbroken chain of noises on the other side of the room. This was a ritual for him; his safe place before the day shoveled another heap of dung onto his head. He would wake himself up with glass-tea, yawn over the kettle, and roll his eyes at dad's newest attempt to "chat."

Which reminded him: it was about time for another eye roll now.

"...and so instead we'll pick up breakfast sticks—her favorite, you remember—on our way to the arena so she can pick out which weapon and equipment she wants to use in tonight's graduation. Which, that will take up most of the morning, of course."

"Mhm," Tirak nodded absently.

He kept stirring his small pot. It was so close to boiling.

Dad had been droning on and on about their plans for Kaleek's birthday ever since Tirak woke up. As if last month's party hadn't been overblown enough. He wondered how much of the fuss was just another attempt to cover up her half-breed birth. Onok was always coming up with ways to dote on her, and always expecting Tirak to just go along with it all. Onok certainly never did much to make *him* feel special.

"She'll have to join the rest of the graduates to participate in the ceremony after that—"

"Assuming her Nature doesn't awaken tomorrow, you mean," Tirak corrected.

Onok scoffed.

"Of *course* she'll awaken today! *Maker's own* never find their powers late."

Right. She was so much more special because Maker had built her by hand just like the first generation. Not a lowly natural-born like the rest of them. Like *himself*. Tirak wanted to throw in his earlier offer to bet on whether the Second Nature she awakened would be a sea turtle or mosquito, but … he valued eating dinner for the next month a little too much. Onok had kept talking right on through his thoughts. Wait, what was that last part?

"…wear something nicer than tattered pocketshorts for a change, or I'll cuff you both on the ear. He's one of the city's most important citizens, and his mate-to-be is no small girl among Biri's staff either. This is a *very* important wedding for all of us, *no matter how long* it goes into the night. Hmph, it makes me happy to see him pick a mate from outside the village. People need to get over the idea that Biri and I broke things off for such a trivial reason. We didn't. She just … has her own village to lead. And … I …"

Tirak nodded, thankful that his back was still turned. That way Onok didn't have to see the confusion his face must have been radiating. But he didn't continue. Wait, silence? That was new. Tirak turned just in time to see Onok sag into a chair by the kitchen table. It groaned and flexed under his mighty bulk. He … looked depressed.

Great. Tirak couldn't handle *this* again too.

"It's okay, Onok. She can't hate you forever."

Tirak said it not because it was true—it *wasn't*—but because he knew that's what Onok *wanted* to hear. Eldress Biri was a female. Of course she could find a way to go on hating forever. But Onok brightened at the encouragement, and soon he was back to all his planning.

Seriously though, what wedding was this, and when had Dad sent someone to train under Biri? Dark, how had that tempest of an Eldress not spat in the poor girl's face? Assuming she was another Umbri at least. She had to be, right? An Igni wouldn't have lasted *two days* in that swampy village.

Well, he wasn't going to get an answer now, so Tirak shrugged inwardly and made a mental note to ask Kaleek about it when they met up later. Either way, the invite was a surprise of its own. Onok had never really mixed his home life with his role as Umbra's Elder before now. Sure, people knew about "those two oddball kids" that hung around his manor, but nobody really knew him. And his sister? Well, most people thought of Kaleek as just "that half-breed monster." A pet that only someone as powerful as an Elder would keep around. Birthday parties were always an especially sore point for her because of that. It was pretty hard to invite friends over when you didn't have any worth inviting.

Oh, right! Planning the day out.

"...She'll probably want to explore the market before that–shop for a spear or something with you, if I know my Kal. But that probably won't take more than an hour."

Tirak plastered on a grimace, but hey, that part didn't sound all too bad. If only it was going to happen...

"Onok, can't we just have a *simple* party for once?" Tirak asked.

Onok scoffed and gave him a stern look.

"My little girl will only turn four years once in her life! We *have* to celebrate the day she becomes a full-grown lady."

He stopped and gave Tirak a stern look.

"You're on duty again today, *aren't* you?"

Tirak shrank down.

"Um... *yes*?"

Onok sighed and pinched the bridge of his wide nose.

"I'm serious, boy. I can tell your officer you have the day off and he'll understand. The guard always has someone else they could call. You work *too* much."

"It's not guard duty, Onok. Somebody needs a courier package before noon. I already told you."

"The courier companies listen to me too," Onok offered. "And it's important to remind the girl she matters to you. You're her big brother, boy. It would make Kaleek's day if you change your mind."

"I'm *fine*. I'll hang out with her later."

"When?"

"*Later*," Tirak enunciated.

Another prolonged sigh. Onok stood up and started pacing.

"Why I bother at all is beyond me. Anyway, as long as none of the guild advisors corner me in the market, we can all swing by ..."

Tirak silently tipped the coffee into a mug and walked outside to the balcony. He sank into a fur-covered armchair and stared out at the orange glow of their city coming to life. With a bitter sip, he relished the wakeful strength that washed through him and settled back to watch the townscape while his mind drifted free. From his vantage atop this cliff, he could see almost everything. He wondered how long it would take Dad to realize he was talking to an empty room. That made him chuckle. Probably an hour.

Tirak slammed his fist against the railing in frustration. Why was *everything* about Kaleek? Was it really so hard to even acknowledge his existence with a simple "Good morning. How's it going, son?" Even just once?

Well, no.

For one, *Onok* only knew how to call him "boy," over-enunciating it as "*bow*-why" with that stuck-up umbri accent. Tirak guessed he didn't recognize anyone but Kaleek as his family. Probably not even his original umbri villagers.

His hand twisted into a balled-up paw as his thoughts drifted further away. Metal and skin melted and flowed into new patterns. Fur began to sprout in patches. He didn't notice.

Why did he bother sticking around this ridiculous excuse for a family anyway? They both just ignored him, *used* him, *tortured* him with reminders of the *real* parents he lost … and, of the siblings he might've had. Sure, Tirak was sixty and birthdays didn't matter anymore, but Onok paid attention to the tiniest milestones in Kaleek's life while he went ignored. Did either of them even *remember* both kids shared a birthday? He and she were even a nice, whole octet apart. Tirak's huff came out like a growl. That giant fool and his twin-element freak, both of them. They just—

He stopped himself, sighing out a ragged breath. Pointed ears melted back into the hairline atop his head. His jaws lost their panther-like muzzle, but his eyes remained narrow slits as he opened them again. When he pulled his hand away from the rail, the metal beam traced a jagged, deformed line that glowed softly red. That … could have ended badly. He wrenched his mind back toward the sleepy morning and the sights of his pretend-dad's underground village.

But other memories kept sneaking their way in. Before he had noticed what his hand was doing, a dented locket had slipped out his shorts and sat open in his palm. Broken facets of what used to be Igna's emblem shined red against his face from inside. The whole left tongue of flame was completely gone, and cracked lines ran through the pieces that he had glued back into place. He saw hungry eyes and snapping jaws in every little glint.

No. He couldn't let his mind drift that way either.

A light breeze wafted over his back and made his sleeveless shirt ruffle, sucking fresh air from the surface tunnels behind him and over the cliff's edge. It would filter through the terraced neighborhoods below, then funnel toward the river's outlet at the lowest level of the cavern. The town was split into three wide layers of disk-like terraces, two of which were visible below him while the uppermost just barely peeked out around the walls on either side of him. His level. The rich, umbri level. Windows slowly ignited here and there, joining the cavern's imitation of sunrise as their hearths were rekindled for the morning meal. Most of what he saw were ramshackle ignii homes. All the umbrii neighborhoods where hidden from sight up here, on "Top Tier," where they wove artistically between various market streets, rock gardens, and all *sorts* of uselessly decorative nonsense.

The only exception was Onok's neighbor. For the Elders of Shadow and Fire couldn't rule as equals if they didn't live side by side, here at the precipice that separated the Umbrii from their lessers down below. Tirak wondered if Elder Hahkoz ever felt cut off the way that he did. They were the only two Ignii Tirak knew of that were allowed to live up here. As if seeing the rest of the island were a privilege too good for the smelly fire types. No, no, that wasn't fair. Ignii could visit the rest of the island any time they wanted to ... provided they were fit enough to climb the dangerous collection of rock spikes and fraying rope ladders from Bottom Tier up to the Aura bridge. Easily two hundred heads high. Then, all they had to do was survive the frigid mountain weather until they could hike back down to a more livable climate.

Perfectly reasonable. Of course they had no need to take one of the shorter, straighter routes. Those were for cybrii who actually mattered.

His thumb idly traced the ridges and fingerprints embedded into his mug's metal surface. It wasn't a pretty piece, but it held water and didn't wobble when he set it down. Sure, he could have asked Dad for some disgustingly fragile piece of glassware, but he preferred having his own skills to trust.

...Even if the thing *did* lean to one side a little. He was going to fix it one of these days. Maybe he should risk paying that girl Sara another visit at the forge. She hadn't seemed to mind teaching him how to use the bellows and tools *last* time.

The disks of his ears vibrated. His attention snapped back. He heard it again. Someone was throwing pebbles at a window. It was close by, but that was too far away to be for him, unless … curses. The gang sent *that kid* again.

Tirak sighed and gulped the rest of his mug. Chewing on a few undissolved bits of sandglass, he swung his legs over the railing and shimmied toward the side of the house. Best to intervene before the pimple-faced messenger got caught "vandalizing the *esteemed* windows of Elder Onok" and had to explain why a dirty ignii was way up here.

Before he got there, he passed beneath one open window which had a length of white cloth fluttering in the morning draft. A coarse hem fluttered past, just barely missing his head. His heart stilled for a deadly second, before thundering onward again.

His sister's gown hung from a hook next to her sill. A breeze was sucking it out the window. It was true the things looked like rough-grit polishing rags. He grimaced, remembering how his own had felt on his shoulders eight months ago.

He dared a glance over the windowsill and breathed out a sigh. Kaleek was still sound asleep inside. His hand found its way to the satchel tied around his neck, to where a perfectly tailored set of warrior's leathers were rolled into a neat bundle.

"One more day, Kee, then we can torch that torture device together. Throw it down a mineshaft where it belongs. I promise," he whispered.

Kaleek looked peaceful, nestled deep into a half-dozen furs without a care. One arm hung out past the edge of the cot. A pale, almost white forearm sat at the base of deep blue fingers. It was one of those rare times when she *didn't* look consumed with worry over being a horrible freak.

He grimaced at the sight. Those colors really did look gross together.

It was even worse whenever she tried to wear an outfit with Umbra's colors. Black, purple, blue, *and* teal-pearl-whatever-she-called-it? Yuck.

A sudden wave of fondness burned away the impulsive thought. No. He shouldn't think like that. His sister had never asked for her elements. Ugly or not, he wouldn't give her up for anything on this island.

Unfortunately, it didn't look like Tirak would get a chance to wish her a happy birthday. He leaned a small shardpouch on the lip of the window for her to find later. Then, after scrawling a quick note in charcoal across the sill, he moved on to deal with the idiot who was trying to get himself caught.

Sorry, Job came up. See you this afternoon when I kick your butt.

He grinned to himself. Let her panic for a few heartbeats over who might be spying on her at night. He was going to enjoy getting one last chance to knock her flat before her powers had a chance to awaken. Things would be way too fair after that. Girl was tougher than pure steel and eight times sharper.

Maker's Log #89906: "The Underworld"

Umbra City is a truly incredible creation.

Covered in a dome of rock beneath the ground, it's a cavern that's split into three flat tiers, as if weathered by limestone and water. Rather, I think it was a result of the bile from that massive landsquid Onok killed some years back. Whether acid or lime, though, I suppose the effect was still the same.

When the other Elders picked their home to settle above ground and started looking after the early batches of Cybrii, Onok chose to stay down there. He's made from pure darkness, so I suppose it makes sense, but it sure makes it awkward to visit him. Every time I walk those tunnels, I can feel myself dying again. My mask reacts to that gloom poorly. But that reaction is unique to me. The Cybrii all seem right at home, whether their element is shadow or even air. The city's relatively central location has made it the popular hub of commerce for this fledgling society.

Don't worry, Limna is still my favorite by a long shot. Nothing can compare to your gardening genius, but Onok's little "Underworld" is nothing short of a testament to the power these Cybrii wield together. If these children of mine had overlapped with our own people... I'm not sure we would've stayed at the top of the foodchain.

The galaxy is safer for it, I guess.

For now at least.

3

FAMILY MATTERS

Just as Tirak expected, a scrawny boy with maroon and black armor was throwing pebbles against the walls of one bedroom after another.

"*Pssst!* Wrong window, Pimplewart. Are you *crazy*?"

The boy's cry of surprise was way more satisfying to see than it should have been. Somewhere on the street, the stuffy voice of a guard picked that moment to pipe up.

"Hey! What was that? Did I hear something breaking over there? Elder Onok? Are you all right?"

The accent was definitely umbri. Tirak guessed it was either the obnoxious guy he had shadowed yesterday, or maybe the new graduate from the day before who still hadn't learned the difference between a joke and a stab wound. Whichever one it was, if he came and looked over the hedge, then he'd either recognize Tirak or immediately try to arrest two filthy fire criminals. The first option was probably worse.

Tirak nudged the kid and pointed to a gap in the back wall, where a stone had knocked loose ages ago.

"C'mon, I've got a shortcut that goes down below."

The opening led them back to the edge of the cliff, where a narrow crack beneath the porch was just big enough to squeeze one's way into.

The almost two-hundred-head climb was a little tiring, but it wasn't all that long in the end and it hid them from prying eyes. Tirak liked to think the daily exercise was part of what gave him a leg up on most guys his size.

The boy's wheezing gasps beside only reinforced that fact. Tirak stretched casually until a joint in his back made a satisfying pop.

"See, kid? You need to do that *more* often. Maybe you should add it to the daily routine until you can even knock big ol' Hod onto his back."

The boy grumbled and gave him what was supposed to be a light punch on the shoulder. Tirak stumbled until he had managed to catch a hand on the wall beside him. Stupid bum leg. He would never admit it if asked, but it was just as tired as his friend sounded.

Soon, they were wandering free through the smokey lower streets of Umbra as the pipsqueak filled him in between complaints about his arms. Sure, the air stank with a mixture of street sewage, animals, and glass forges. But to Tirak's nose, that smoke was the sweet scent of family. He rested a hand on the boy's shoulder and grinned at a pair of passing guards. They were fellow ignii, but they still wore Umbra's emblem. They were still the enemy.

Tirak kept his grin wide and forced himself to relax. They needed to look more natural and disappear into the crowd. In that case … what to talk about?

Oh! How about the kind of topic an older brother would bring up? Something that would make the kid squirm.

He tossed a few fire shards and a violet flake toward one street vendor he recognized and picked a few breakfast buns off a skewered stack as they passed. Tirak took a large bite out of one and dropped the other into the wide-eyed kid's hands. Wiping a sticky palm on one leg of his shorts, he threw the now-clean arm around his friend's neck in a brotherly, conspiratorial gesture.

"So, did you ever ask out Talli?" Tirak asked.

The sagging shoulders told him all he needed to know.

"No…" Pimplewart mumbled.

"I'm telling you, kid, she's into you even if she doesn't act like it. You should just ask her. What's the worst that can happen?" he pressed.

The boy laughed nervously.

"Well, she could turn me down, then tell her friends about how ugly little 'Pimple-Wart' tried to kiss her or something. I could become a joke to my whole city-tier … or worse, she could find out what I am and report us all!"

"Nahh." Tirak yawned. "She wouldn't do that. Her dad's an old brand too, you know. Besides, who cares if we're Goldenhearts? That's a badge of pride anywhere but Upper Tier."

Tirak gave him a soft punch on the shoulder.

"See? You should go for it. She's pretty cute," he teased with singsong inflections.

The boy's eyes widened.

"H-He's a…? Oh *Maker*… that just makes it even *more* awkward! What am I gonna say? 'Yes, sir. I'll go beat up that shopkeep right away, sir. By the way I have a huge crush on your little girl'? Yeah. No thanks."

Tirak shrugged and kept walking. He waved to several familiar faces. Haggard mothers tying up soiled laundry to dry as if they'd been able to clean it down here, kids playing a game with splinters of fireglass, lifeless forge workers on their way to a new day of slave work. They were all family down here. Life was tough, but that was just what the island threw at you.

Pimplewart caught up after a couple seconds.

"B-but what about you? I heard you were gonna make a move on a glassforge girl, *Sara*."

A cough lodged itself in Tirak's throat. The boy's eyes waggled. He knew exactly what he was doing. Did *everyone* know about that? Tirak had only told a couple of drinking buddies.

"S-Sara?! What, her? Nah. Shot down instantly."

This was bad. He needed to stop talking. How in the island could he get out of this?

"I didn't even get past a stuttering 'I-'. I think she's one of our dear Elder's *extra* devoted followers. The ones that get all weird about any kind of abnormal that burns outside the fire pit, if you know what I mean. And I've *always* been a misfit."

Tirak rapped on his bad leg and felt nothing. The boy's eyes were drawn to the cavity where muscle still refused to grow.

"Either she hates me cause I'm a Goldenheart or she hates me for becoming an Umbri's cleaning boy to make ends meet."

The boy kept prodding him for details no matter how much Tirak tried to deflect him. His cheeks were getting flushed. How was this turning against him so quickly? In truth, he had never asked the girl. The comment had been an idle dream, not a serious plan. He cringed at the idea of trying to juggle a relationship along with all his secrets.

Time to change the subject. Tirak lowered his voice.

"Hey, so what's all this about? What does Blade want us to muster for this time?"

The boy grew serious at the mention of their boss's name, his voice suddenly more hushed.

"I honestly dunno. Blade was just all mad and wanted absolutely *everyone* at the den for a meeting. I… think it has something to do with that green fish you caught snooping around the market last week."

Tirak bristled at the slur. He couldn't help feeling like it was directed at Kaleek every time he heard it used.

"Don't throw that word around unless you need to."

"Why? A fish is a fish, plain and simple. Doesn't matter to me if she's kinda pretty," Pimplewart scoffed.

He could hear the clueless bravado in the kid's voice, but so many other members—ones older than both of them combined—talked exactly the same way too. All it did was encourage spite.

"Listen, kid. I know a lot of firebrands get all uptight about anyone that's not igni, but it's not helpful to go around insulting everyone just because we can. But that's all beside the point. You think Blade's planning a hit on her or something?"

Pimplewart shrugged. "Dunno. Probably."

"Why, though? When did we start having beef with anyone but the Umbrii?"

The kid wouldn't say anything more. And, given his age, Tirak guessed he didn't know. He grunted and let the matter drop.

"Hey, Tirak? Did you have … the dream again? You're always so grumpy when you do."

The question cut through Tirak like a glowing dagger. Like it always did. His shoulders deflated. He had to fight back an image of glowing red jowls biting at his head.

"Yeah … and look, before you ask: it's not just that. Today's just … *not a good day.* You know? It would have been their anniversary if … if it hadn't been for yesterday. And *NO*, I *don't* want to talk about it."

"Oh, wow. I'm sorry, Tir. Did they really get eaten defending you from a pack of hellhounds?"

"Yes …" Tirak hissed through clenched teeth.

It was getting hard to see where he was walking. Red fangs flashed in the corners of his vision.

"Wow, they must have really cared about you."

"Hey, Pimplewart? Shut up."

He leveled his strongest glare at the kid, which would have been a little more intimidating if his voice hadn't cracked halfway through. In the end, their silence for the remainder of the journey was less to do with how intimidated Pimplewart was and more with their being thirty paces from the door.

Maker's Log #92105: Goldenheart Graffiti.

Elementalism has always made tensions run high between Umbrii and the ignii refugees that share Onok's "Underworld."

Lately, though, something more than pride is triggering it. Some new gang has been causing those pressures to skyrocket. According to Onok and Hakhoz, their members seem to be ignii, but no one claims to have seen them.

They strike from the shadows like some kind of vicious Robin Hoods. A storefront or a cart will suddenly be vandalized, or some poor soul will be doubled over, beaten up, but people keep saying they never saw anything suspicious. At most, a few accounts mention some hooded travelers.

But in every attack, this graffiti mark is left behind on a wall nearby, or occasionally on the person or vandalized thing itself. Its charcoal black silhouette with a yellow version of Igna's emblem over its chest has given the gang its name.

The Goldenhearts.

Some of Hakhoz's people are already starting to see them as heroes of equality, but I think I agree with the Elders. It's disturbing to see how easily they leap to violence.

I'm afraid of what they'll do if Onok doesn't smooth things over soon.

You've always been good with people, Bozrakh. Terra is such a model city, and yet your makeup is very similar to Umbra. If you have the time, please pay your friend a visit and see what you can do to help. I'm sure everyone would appreciate it.

Sincerely,

The Maker

Sign. Send. Close file.

4

INSURGENT

Hours later, Tirak followed a loose group of nondescript hooded figures upward through the city's layers. They shifted like smoke through the crowd. Up, through progressively busier, cleaner, fancier streets. Each thud of his foot seemed to echo Blade's scathing words in his head.

Today we strike at the heart of our people's oppression! With this union, our dear, dear, friend-of-the-people merchant SPITS in our face. A wedding tonight, he says? To what? To some FISH! That should be OUR sister by his side. The girl he had promised himself to! He wants to reject our sister without cause, the week before their wedding, and marry some outsider? Then we'll show him how the Ignii answer betrayal.

Tirak had his misgivings at first, but Blade's evidence had grown into a mountain over the course of the hour-long brief. He spat out a growing taste of disgust. So *that* was who Dad had been going on and on about earlier. The heartless umbri snake couldn't even wait *a week*! Worse, the spurned girl herself had been there. She had a maddening story to tell about how the merchant had tried to take advantage of her, then shoved her out the door after she wouldn't give in. Right into the arms of two patrolling guards. She had only just been released from the city dungeon last night.

Blade was right. This merchant needed to know the Ignii were a people to respect. He couldn't just push a girl around and do whatever suited him after making promises, just because he thought someone else was prettier. The male was sick. Needed to be put down. And if this new fling of his couldn't see through it, then maybe she did too.

More Goldenhearts seeped into the growing crowd. A cloud of emotion followed them through the colorful market streets, all the way to the front of an ornate clay-and-stone warehouse. A lot of people were already standing around. Tirak had never met the guy, but his trade network was supposed to be one of the island's biggest. He was by far the city's most renowned citizen outside of the Elders themselves.

The hastily built stage was still empty, but the merchant's address to the people was supposed to begin shortly. Tirak noted some of the stones were still settling into place, as if the grout wasn't yet dry. Yep, there was a trowel left forgotten to one side. This really was slapped together last minute.

The couple emerged on cue, wearing intricately sewn robes of a mixed purple-and-blue pattern. Tirak paused to admire the image they cut together. The vibrant colors should have clashed with each other, yet they somehow managed to complement the other half of the pattern while flattering both wearers. A perfect symbol of their proposed harmony between the limni and umbri trading industries.

He had to remind himself of how disgusting their union was beneath the surface. Not because he was mixing his elements—though some old-blood Umbrii probably thought so—but because of who he'd needed to scorn in order to pick up this girl.

A soggy fruit flew past the couple's head. Several voices jeered throughout the crowd. Tirak hissed, wondering why the fools didn't rein their hatred in better. But then he noticed the closest voice to him. It belonged to a distinctly *umbri* young male. Tirak hadn't seen onyx armor plates darker than his on anyone but Onok himself, and even the skin was almost indistinguishable from his armor.

"Polluter! The Elders won't let you weaken our shadow with someone like *her*!" another voice bellowed.

The merchant avoided a few more rotten missiles as he walked, future mate still in hand, until they both stood at the platform's amplifying center.

"Friends, friends! Why yell so loudly?" His voice projected across them all. "Are you really so afraid that one so small as I could threaten our great lord of shadows? Does anyone question the Maker's wisdom? You speak fears of mutants and half-breeds, as if you've forgotten that we are already all the elements in one. And all the elements have a little of us inside them too! Look at this charming young female and tell me, should we not rejoice that a once-diluted daughter of the sea will soon reunite with the only pure element? All of Maker's children have a taste of our lord's untainted shadow flowing in our veins, but only *we*—the Umbrii—know its full embrace. Do you really want to deny those of other elements from drawing closer to that embrace too?"

Tirak felt his nose twitch, lips curling in a repressed sneer. All of that *could* have been said about his last fiancée too, and he would've had a fraction of the uproar, *because she was an adored member of the COMMUNITY.* Who even was this new fis—errm … water person? And how had she so completely supplanted a girl this merchant had claimed to have *loved*?

The umbri introduced his partner and offered her the stage. Tirak had to admit, she was a pretty good speaker herself. As they talked back and forth together, the crowd's agitation began to evaporate, their anger clearly starting to burn itself out.

Good. Let the wasted ashes form a blanket across the true coals. The Goldenhearts were content to smolder there until the time was right.

An elbow nudged Tirak's side, urging him to move further into the throng. The Goldenhearts' layers needed to be ordered by each person's skill in aiming—the best shots up close to cover the two most likely escape routes once the targets started moving—and Tirak admitted feeling a little smug that it placed him directly beneath the center of the stage. They trusted him to nail his shots no matter which direction they fled. Blade himself was somewhere in attendance today. The plan was for someone in the back left to send the first bolt flying. It would give Blade room to pinch in from the right before any guards could react.

As the next lengthy speech began, Tirak's eyes drifted back to the fiancée and lingered. Up close, he could make out even more detail in their faces and in the stenciled artwork along the blue bands of her dress. Studying her face, he noticed a faint metallic scratch on her left cheek. The mark had healed a long time ago, but the placement reminded him of Kaleek's face.

As soon as he thought it, regret flooded through him. The female—still a girl really, and a cute one at that—*looked* just like his sister. Her two metal tones had a more greenish tint that was missing in Kaleek's, but she had that same pointy chin. That same expression of timid defiance that his sister always wore.

He began to feel uncomfortable. This girl could have practically been Kaleek's older sister. More dainty by a mile perhaps, but that just made it even worse. She might as well have been the very picture of defenselessness.

...And he was about to mug this girl and her fiancé? Who knew what else the older members would try? He tried to swallow a wave of nausea as his mind replaced the girl's face with Kaleek's. His blood began to pound. He couldn't do this. He needed a way out.

Tirak smelled a wisp of smoke, then the grizzled firebrand that was his pair gave him another elbow to the side.

"Cool it, kid. Wait for the signal."

Jolted, he looked down and realized the sleeve of his coat was beginning to smolder, heated by his own fist. He relaxed his hand and tried to pull it back into himself. A few eyes glanced their way. They probably noticed the smoke too.

The accident gave Tirak an idea, however. He tried to catch the limni girl's eye, but he doubted she would understand the warning in time. So instead, he waited for the speaker's gaze to sweep back this way. Concentrating, he made his eyes burn bright.

The merchant glanced over him casually, then froze mid-sentence.

Tirak watched the cogs turn within his skull for nearly a half second too long. The guy wasn't getting the message, so he reached up and put down the hood of his cloak. Streetlamps reflected clearly off the orange plates of his cheeks. The man seized his fiancée's wrist and bolted for the alley behind them.

Tirak saw where they were heading, and also saw the twin hoods that would soon block their way. By instinct, he took aim and fired a bolt. It sailed between the couple and their attackers with precision. It clipped one of their hoods, but no one would have thought it anything but a misplaced shot. Belatedly, the crowd sprang into action. The other members knew the surprise was ruined and flew into damage control.

"Goldenhearts!" their cry rang out.

A dozen more flames leapt from raised palms and streaked for the fleeing pair in a chaotic jumble. Bolts struck indiscriminately against stone walls, barrels, random street debris, and even a few bystanders. One bolt found its mark in the girl's shoulder.

Hearing her ragged scream snapped something inside of Tirak. He would do anything in his power to stop this from happening. He took off down the alleyway after them, leapt over people, danced gracefully around burning obstacles as they fell, and breezed past the other pursuers. He burst into the open training yard a few moments after the couple, but stopped short when he saw Blade blocking their path with a squad of backups. Setting his jaw, Tirak sauntered forward.

The self-important leader raised a hand and smirked. It began to crackle with hungry orange flames. At the last moment, Tirak's own glowing hand snapped forward and shot a bolt of his own. Flame and hand collided just as the second bolt was fired. Nudged off course, the leader's shot flew harmlessly down another alley.

Furious eyes locked onto him.

"Back off, boy!" The leader pointed wildly. "This isn't your prize!"

Tirak closed the rest of the gap and stepped between the couple and his leader. He raised his fists in defiance.

"*Really*, boy? You gonna go soft over this lil speck of blue? Unless it's the guy… I promise, *neither* one is worth dying over. Now get. Out. My. Way."

"We've all done dirt for you, Blade, and you always promise it'll 'help the cause' in the end. But this is too far! You're about to make half the island hate us. Just who is that going to help?" Tirak hissed through clenched teeth.

He could sense the others circling around him, blocking them in. He wished he could just stand there and convince Blade, but Tirak knew he was running out of time. Between words, he whispered a silent prayer to the Maker.

All he needed was a gap to push the couple through, then he wouldn't have to hold back. Neither one looked like a fighter, but he could be their distraction. Sweat beaded along his back as he thought about Blade's unnatural strength. Tirak didn't think he would join in personally, but if he *did*…

He spotted the target he was hoping for. One of Pimplewart's friends had been guarding a back exit and now formed part of the fence around them. The kid was a complete pushover, more of a cutpurse than a real fighter, but he got away with it because he knew how to lie.

The circle was stretching thin at that end while everyone began to focus on his argument with Blade. It had been a long time since someone had crossed their boss, and they seemed eager for the chance to remember why it was a stupid idea. Perfect.

Tirak struck mid-sentence, breaking eye contact with Blade only moments before his tongue of flame flashed across the boy's face.

Harmless disorientation was followed up with a kick from Tirak. Metal met metal with a satisfying crunch that sent them both flying away from each other. The boy sprawled onto his back, while Tirak flipped over the two lovers' heads.

He dropped lithely to his hind paws, behind the couple. His feet were wide, flat, and cold red metal in a heartbeat. A solid hand on each back sent them stumbling out of the circle before anyone had quite caught up with what was happening.

Anyone, that is, except for his former leader.

Steel whistled past the dome of Tirak's ear as he dodged to the side by sheer luck.

"Run! Just run!" Was all he could yell.

He wiped a nick on his jaw as he turned to gauge the glowering faces all around him. Faces he had once thought of as brothers.

"Blade! They're getting—" a lackey started.

"Leave them. We'll catch up."

Tirak glanced at Blade in surprise.

"Oh yes. There's nowhere they can run in this city that I can't reach. Once these fine fellows here kick your face in enough, we're going to rip them out of whatever hole they try to hide in, then I'll let you watch while we finish them off anyway."

Blade tossed a dismissive hand into the air as he turned on his heel.

"Do whatever to him, boys. Just make sure he lives long enough to be conscious when we torture those other two."

Someone's fist swung from Tirak's left. He ducked and grabbed the arm as it passed. The fellow and his slightly graying head made an excellent battering ram against two of the others with just a little encouragement. Tirak followed him with a quick volley of punches that downed another and a flourishing kick to a third member's stomach. He heard the poor guy's balljoints crack as he fell back.

Tirak danced to his feet and assumed his normal fighting stance again. They all backed away.

But their fear was short-lived. Orders were orders, and *no one* told Blade "No."

Tirak wove between the next three attacks as his muscles reenacted Onok's merciless drilling. Between practicing nonstop for twenty months and his new internship with the patrol guards, he was all but untouchable.

His breath was starting to come heavy though. He was good at this, but he knew he couldn't keep it up forever. Especially not when he had to lose them all at some point and still make it back here for *another* fight with Kaleek. He mixed an occasional flash of fire into his attacks to keep them off balance. It wouldn't hurt an igni, but all eyes were the same.

The trick wouldn't keep working like the first time, of course, but Tirak was an apprentice of the Guard. He had no shortage of others to pull from.

One of the younger lackeys—a mostly pleasant guy about his own age that Tirak had drunk with a few times—lunged for him while others frantically started grabbing wooden poles. He grimaced as the admittedly too-proud nose crumpled under his fist. Ways to apologize later immediately started darting around his circuits. Maybe he should let the nose heal up first…

No time! Someone on his left started forming a fireball in his own palm, as if he was trying to steal the flashbang idea. Tirak sniffed. A casual forearm across his eyes was all he needed to keep from letting it blind him while he gauged the next strike coming in from his right—

His wrist cracked backward across his eyes with a sudden jolt. His vision shimmered with static and he fell on his bad leg a little too hard.

That wasn't good. He dove to his side again, shaking his head to clear the fuzziness quicker.

A hand clamped around his ankle before he could go far.

Crack!

Wood shattered against his shin plates. A lucky miss.

Tirak slipped fully into his Second Nature, but even the smooth paw bulged just a little too much to break free. He cursed.

Panic began to sink in.

But it didn't last long. A sharp pain in his stomach blew that panic right back out again.

"That's for Hod, you darkspitter! Yeah, how do you like it *now*? Sure feel good when it's you, don't it?"

Agony flashed across his back as two more kicks fell. He heard a sickening whack as loose splinters fell from one of the shards he'd readied in his gearbox.

A halfhearted tongue fizzled on his fingertip as he fought to ready another reserve.

He was already starting to get low on power. Not good.

A foot swung in as more of them closed the gap around him. But the kicker wasn't paying attention to his balance. Tirak caught the blow and twisted, hard.

The cry sounded agonizing as the fool fell backward into several others. His foot was pointed sideways. Or, more backward than anything. Tirak groaned. Why wouldn't they stop already? He *knew* these people. Most of them were friends of his. They were brothers. Why did they keep forcing him to hurt them?

Onward the dance went, and Tirak still had his part to play unless he wanted to see his own head become a nice salad bowl. His good leg was free now. He forced out a grin between his knees at whoever was trying to hold him down. A quick blow to that face and he was free again.

He flexed his crystal gear. A fresh set of three clicked into place behind Tirak's head. Time to turn things around. He planted his hands behind his head and arched his back for a flip onto his feet.

Another foot took him right in the spine.

Tirak yelled out a fresh curse and tried to roll toward the attacker. Hands grabbed his arm before he could deliver his next punch to the male's kneecap.

Another hand clamped itself to one leg, then his other. He tried to lean out of the way as a boot slammed toward his face, but by now only his weak arm was free. Tirak let out a desperate explosion as it connected.

Several hands loosened, but it wasn't enough.

"Hold him!" one of the others slurred though a loose jaw. He threw in some kind of slur about his parents while at it, followed by, "...give that prettyboy face some rearranging. Keep hold'a that gearbox!"

More hands began pulling on him. His shoulders felt like they were about to pop from its socket. Several kicks bruised his side. Then, one shoulder really did pop loose as Hod slammed his heel down again.

Tirak's head cracked against a protruding cobble and began to swim. Absently, he noted it probably meant one of his cores had cracked. He wondered why Maker left those so exposed. Didn't His own race keep their processors deep inside their heads where they were safer? Seemed like a real flaw in His design.

Another blow to his already weakened nose fractured, then shattered it. He screamed as splinters of it dug into his face. His eyes were already screwed shut, so he couldn't tell whether he had just been blinded or not. An even sharper snap echoed through his skull, and he felt his jaw drop open at an angle.

More kicks fell.

Tirak's world became pain.

Nothing else. Only pain.

Until oblivion came to his rescue.

Maker's Log #88207: A pre-element girl wearing her graduation robe.

My first experience with this little tradition was some years back when paying a rare visit to Onok, Hakhoz, and Biri. The simple outfit isn't much to look at: a starched white with a smudged charcoal stencil of the island on its centimeter-thick canvas. Feels like sandpaper to me.

But apparently I'm what caused it to start?

After the disaster of building the Elders, I rebuilt my assembler machine to suppress each Cybri's elemental powers for their first few years. Turns out robotic toddlers wielding fireballs and rocks are just as terrifying as you'd expect. And the only downside is a minor weakening to their incredible healing abilities, scaling it back to the average human's. As long as they protected their children from any GRAVE damage during their first four years, there should be nothing to worry about.

The change can still be explosive when their powers "awaken," as they call it, but each village seems to have developed a whole ritual around the days leading to up the switch from child to a conductive adult. It's one aspect of their fledgling culture I can't claim MUCH influence on. However, many of them claim to have met me in their last few milliseconds before the killswitch is broken, citing vivid hallucinations of caves, dark monsters unlike any across the island, and a glowing, ethereal ver-

sion of me. I can't say for sure, but I think the remote data syncs may be playing some small part in this.

It's been on the backlog to investigate and fix for a while now, but honestly they don't seem to mind. Onok's people have started calling it "The Tutorial" like it's some kind of religious experience. Hah!

Each village has its own twist on the ceremonial week too. Aura sends their kids out to forage in the peaks and survive the avalanche their eventual airburst causes. While Onok's little Umbra cave? They like to turn everything into an arena contest. That's one ceremony I can't stomach watching. Kids shouldn't have to fight things as big as that without any training…

5

AFTERMATH

Tirak stared around himself in confusion. He was … nowhere? His surroundings felt like a room, or at least something enclosed, but he couldn't actually *see* a roof. Nor any walls. Nothing but an uneven haze that drifted around him and a singular beam of light cutting through it, lighting the center of the space. A kind of endless infinity.

He stepped into the pool of light, drawn by the existence of at least *something*. How had he gotten here? His arms were wrapped in bruises and cuts. His breathing would only come in shallow, painful gasps too. His chest wouldn't move *at all* anymore! It felt welded together from the inside, like his middle was nothing but a large hole. Hadn't he been trying to protect something? Something about his sister, right?

She had a name, he just needed to think of it again … Kaleek's face popped into his mind with a jolt of terror. He needed to find her! Stop her from— She … She was about to …

Why couldn't he remember? She was in danger, and he needed to find her. Quickly. He *needed* to get out of here.

A sound like a dozen overlapping voices interrupted his thoughts.

"Enough of all this prattle. You're playing games. You avoid our questions. But we do not get distracted. We are eternally focused."

Something was very wrong with Tirak's mind. It felt like it was moving at a pace of its own, jumping between random memories of his life even while he tried to wrangle it back under control.

"We will ask you again: what are you? You are like us, so why do you fight us? And where is he who masks his face?"

Tirak found his tongue forming a response while he searched for the source of the voices. If he could find them, maybe it would let him find an exit.

"What am I? I… I don't know what else to say. Like I told you, I'm just Tirak. One of Maker's Cybrii. He made us to share His island, and to use the power of the elements to protect it against the threat of the Darkness."

"Cyb. Ree. Eye… Elements… The Darkness. Explain to us," the many voices demanded.

Tirak nodded to the air. He had paced in a wide circle, but never seemed to move from the center of the room. It was as if that single ray of light held him locked in place.

"Uh, of course! I'm trying to get to that. Just be a little more patient and I'll tell you all about it."

~~~~~

The first sense that returned to him wasn't the *PLINK!* of blood dripping off the wall. It wasn't the chill that glued his hand to the cobblestones, nor was it the uncomfortably sweet smell of charred flesh. What his mind fixated on instead of that was a paradox: if he was a child of fire, then why was his body covered in burning pain? The stinging of unseen needlepoints wracked his unprotected side. It felt warm, but not like the gentle kiss of a campfire's tongues. His side was burned—was probably still burning—with an unforgiving menace in its bite. He tried to swallow a lump that had his throat sealed and grimaced as the strain pulled his jaw in three different directions. He would've screamed if only he could.
~~~~~

Only then did he start processing the rest of it: the scrape of something hard rolling by, the chill of ice, the smoke and blood in the air. In his mouth. His fight with Blade and the other Goldenhearts flooded back to him.

Was… was he even still alive?

Tirak knew he should keep silent. He knew he shouldn't move around in case someone was watching. But as his jawbone and throat reknit themselves, he couldn't help releasing an earsplitting gasp against cold stone walls. A low moan followed, which morphed into a curse as soon as he sucked in a second lungful of air.

A few cracked ribs screamed with pain, and… well actually, his whole *body* hurt like darkness itself. A series of echoey pops announced his chest was dutifully realigning itself, and the sharp jab it sent through him each time was almost enough to make him black out again.

Finally, Tirak forced a swollen eyelid open. Just a sliver, but all he needed was to figure out where they might've dumped him. He expected to see a lightless cellar's moldy walls or something. Instead, it was an open space. Rectangular, with an occasional window awning. Wait, awnings on the *inside* of a room? An uneven stone floor, by the feel of it. And far too many other bodies for him to actually see what the floor looked like. He shuddered, realizing for the first time how many people they murdered each day.

What in Maker's island had he been involved with all this time?

He tried to raise his head, but a sharp pain was followed by a numbness that spread through his chest.

Okay. Nope. That was a bad idea.

Since he couldn't move yet anyway, Tirak continued to lie and look around. As he did, his mind drifted away from planning toward what he had just lost. Not the leftovers of his nose that were working their way out of his cheek at the moment. Tirak would recover from that in a few minutes, tops.

Instead, his thoughts focused on his friends. Blade was a lost cause, but most of the Goldenhearts were good people. That betrayal in their eyes behind raised fists cut into Tirak. He pressed a flap of his shoulder against bare muscle and waited for the wound to heal without noticing what he was doing.

He knew the other Goldenhearts had also seen what he had. They had no business pulling off some of the hits they did. Those others may not have snapped like Tirak just had, but they saw. They didn't want to kick innocent girls' faces in any more than he did.

He nodded. Yeah, he should lean into that. They might even be sore after having to beat him up like this. Several of those guys in the alley had been brothers to him. The fight must have been just as hard for them. If he could just talk to some of them one on one…

He decided he should start with innocent-faced Pimplewart. If anyone had nothing to do with this pit of bodies, it'd be that kid. Even sweet, little Kaleek had more dark secrets than him.

Tirak pushed himself up onto one arm and finally dared to take in the rest of whatever room they had thrown him into. Body parts were everywhere! A fat black drop fell from a wooden beam, making a splat as it hit a spare head. He turned away from its youthful, agonized expression. The blood was all but suffocating. Metallic. Acrid. Rotting. A lot of it was so fresh it still glowed faintly purple.

Blade *needed* to pay for all of this.

The room had more openings leading out of it than he expected a body pit to have. Seriously, who would go out of their way to add windows to such a place? And what kind of building would use cemented cobbles for flooring? Unless…

He raised himself a little higher. A purple crystal glimmered from the faraway ceiling of Umbra cavern. So, he was outside. And why did the place feel so familiar? A courtyard, its corners filled with barrels and crates anywhere a body hadn't been thrown.

With a start, Tirak realized he was still in the alley behind that merchant's warehouse. And to think he and Kaleek had been about to hold their last practice duel here before her awakening came!

That thought froze him.

He looked back to the dismembered head, and noticed for the second time how similar its owner must have looked to Pimplewart. It… it wasn't, *right*?

He forced himself to look beyond the head, to another body.

A body wrapped in a soiled white dress that had been utterly torn to shreds. Burn marks covered the dress. Its coarse material as thick as a finger was the only trait left he could recognize it by. That, and a smudged image of the island drawn in charcoal on its front. Blue armor on a petite shoulder and arm. Her jet-black hair pulled into a warrior's tail.

Tirak's heart snuffed out.

"Kaleek!" he cried.

He leapt to his feet, and was beside his little sister's corpse in seconds.

A dull stare had frozen itself to her grey face. Rigor mortis made her lungs heave in a mockery of breathing, spewing puffs of white air from her lips.

Muscles in her chest flexed, making it rise as if…

Wait. She really was breathing!

He cupped her head and held it close. Her eyes darted back and forth in an expression of numb pain. The kind that normally belonged on the very lowest of beggars.

"K-Kee?" he practically whispered.

"K-k-killed them… I-I killed them," her lips muttered.

Her eyes continued to twitch, staring past him as if she wasn't conscious. He stared around the alley as meaning sank in.

Hatred flashed to a boil in his veins. How *dare* the golden-hearted pigs put his sister through this?! How dare they so much as touch someone wearing her graduation dress?

He began to shake her, wishing she would snap out of it.

"Kal, *look* at me!"

His shaking became more violent—or no, that was his own hands trembling.

"Please, tell me you're all right..."

He leaned his forehead against her, hope beginning to evaporate again. What had happened to her? Here was the one person he'd seen be fazed by anything. The fact she never took an insult lying down was exactly why she was so much fun to trash talk. She always just found a way to get better and keep punching back. Who even was this shivering husk in his arms?

"Never again, Kee. You'll never feel powerless again. I promise it..."

At the same moment, Kaleek's eyes snapped into focus on him. She opened her mouth, and he hoped to see that lip curl into a thankful smile once again. Instead, the power of her scream made the ground disappear from his feet. Wind rushed past his ears as he spun head over heels.

Before he knew what had happened, Tirak's shoulders were propped up against the wall that his head had just smashed a cavity into. In front of him, a massive, blue dragonfly was reforming into his sister as she shuffled back against the far wall.

She was panting—hyperventilating, he realized.

He tried again to approach, warding off any further blasts of power with the most soothing voice he could muster until he was seated next to her. It took all of five more seconds for her head to end up buried into his shoulder, sobbing violently.

It was a long time before she calmed down. Eventually she just ... stared despondently down at her once-beautiful dress. Eh. He reconsidered the "beautiful" part. Graduation robes were all the same glorified grain sack, sewn together with thorn branches. But, they did have a *presence* to them. That clean white, with one stark symbol of their home across the chest. Now, soot and oblong holes seemed to mark every handbreadth of its yellowed surface. Tirak felt awful for her. As bad as his own burns were, hers had to be unbearable. He squeezed his eyes shut, hoping desperately that nothing worse had been done.

If they *had*… Tirak began to see violet, and imagined what he would do to any Goldenheart member he found. If they had, he was going to make the streets run black before he was done. Kaleek let out another sniffle against his chest.

Tirak let her calm down while he stared at the gore surrounding them. The two siblings clung to each other like that for a long while.

"So, what happened?" Tirak finally asked.

Just when he thought she had ignored him, wet eyes dripped with their blue light as she looked up.

"I-I don't know. It all happened so fast. I got here to warm up, and they were all kicking you, saying the most awful things."

The lid finally unsealed, Kaleek unfolded the details of her ensuing fight for their survival. She had apparently thought it would be easy to take them all after training with him so many months. Then, she started losing ground. She grew desperate, and then her powers awakened.

No one had been ready for the detonation of air and water that followed. Her least of all. Tirak shook his head and looked around at the buildings painted with carnage. The ice had all melted by now, but all that extra liquid running down everything just made things look all the more… drippy. Nothing else needed to be said, and she eventually fell silent.

Sometime later, deep drums echoed through the streets. The arena's weekly invitation for the city to come celebrate. Kaleek jerked her head up, almost smacking him in the chin. Her pupils were two dark pinpricks sitting in the center of glowing saucers.

"No… not yet!" she whispered hoarsely.

Tirak snapped out of thoughts that had been spiraling into darker and darker places. She was rigid in his arms, the grip of her fingers biting into his skin.

"What's wrong?"

"Don't make me go there, Tir. They're all going to hate me."

He was having trouble following her thoughts.

"What? Why would anyone hate you? You'll do great in the arena tonight. You've been training to prove yourself like this your whole life. All the rest of those kids are just pretending to be warriors compared to you."

She shuddered and looked around. Tirak felt his voice trail off as the contradiction dawned on him. Sure, *nobody* could hate her, including all these dead Goldenhearts around them. Okay, fine. *Some* crazy zealots could hate her, but that wasn't true of normal people.

Tirak blinked as his eyes fell on Pimplewart's decapitated head. Black blood still dripped out of the neck, casting a purple hue to what was left of the agonized expression it wore. His vision began to swim. These were normal people. Misguided, sure, but… He shook himself. Kaleek had been saying something that he couldn't hear.

"…best I could hope for anyway. Maybe I should turn myself in and just face the consequences. Dad will understand… won't he? I can always wait till next month for the ceremony, or maybe people will forget and I won't have to go to one at all!"

"Kal… Onok rarely ever deals with civic issues like this. It'll be members of the guard that investigate this whole thing. If some hardcase gets put in charge, there's no telling what could happen to us."

Instead of sagging her shoulders, Kaleek's face brightened.

"But *you're* part of the guard! You can talk to one of them and make them understand!"

He laughed dryly.

"I'm just a cadet that shadows them sometimes. And besides… we only have so many laws for a slaughter like this…"

He leveled a mirthless stare at her. She had to know what he meant: none of the laws had pretty consequences in store for her. She was still hesitating. If he pressed her, she might give in.

"The ceremony really is your best bet. By the time a guard finds this mess, nobody will suspect a random girl proving herself in the celebration arena. We can talk to Onok tonight if things are still looking bad and let him figure it out. You have nothing to fear. He would never let something bad happen to his little girl."

She barely even acknowledged him with a signature glare. He gave her hand a reassuring squeeze.

"But what if..."—she waved her hand around the sticky courtyard—"*this* happens to me again?"

"It won't, Kal. Cybrii only have one reawakening. Now that you have your elements, *you're* in control of them."

She squinted at him, unconvinced.

"Even if it doesn't, what if they come after me in the arena? Two of them were my age. They know I have to participate tonight. It's *hopeless*! Anyone who sees me wearing this rag will know I'm supposed to be at the ceremony, and if I leave it off some guard will see the burns and start questioning me."

She buried her head in her hands.

"Can't we just hide. Run away? I don't want to be in Umbra anymore. I... I want to be free."

Tirak barely heard the last few parts. His mind was still stuck on her previous statement. Rags. He felt stupid for not thinking of it sooner. She looked back up at him and frowned at the grin that was starting to split his face. He reached a hand into his precious satchel and pulled out a tight bundle.

"Who says you need those rags anymore? There's a spring-fed channel one street over from here. You can wash yourself up before anyone notices, and this will hide the rest."

When she didn't respond, Tirak pressed the gift he'd meant for a happier moment into her limp hands. He noticed Kaleek's eyes widen just a fraction, her fingers tightening around the thing she'd been begging Onok to buy her for months. Despite the circumstance, his heart began to lurch with pride, his throat choking on a traitorous tear of joy.

"Just trust me a little, sis. I think I have a plan to get through tonight and out of the city before anyone can realize what happened..."

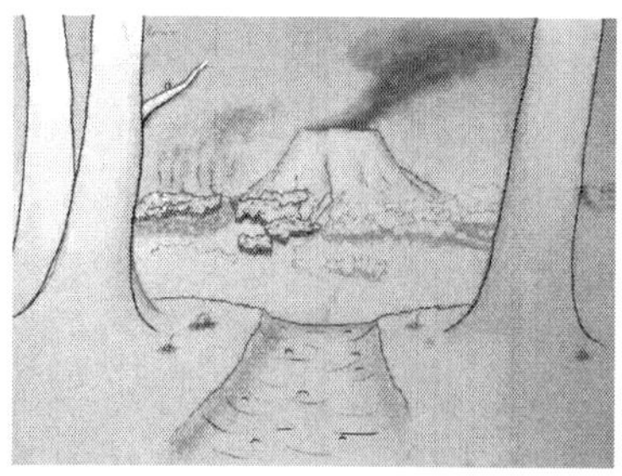

Maker's Log #91003: The Rainforest and Jungle biomes, as seen from the southeast peninsula.

I couldn't help stopping to sketch this one day while I was returning from a visit to my relay tower in the mountains. Korma was as uncomfortable and reclusive as ever up there, the few times I came across him, but thankfully those exchanges were all short-lived.

Flighty as a bird, that one is.

As for this view though... the mix of colors between the tree trunks around me, the last remaining dustings of snow, the orange glow of new lava flows cascading down Mount Fulkana while it offgasses a dark plume, and the indescribable greens of the jungles beyond it... a pen just can't do justice to all the facets of contrast that the eye can see. Even through the yellow tint of these stupid protective lenses I'm forever cursed to wear... Truly beautiful.

Just, not as beautiful as you.

Every time I look at one of the inhabitants here, all I can see is your necklace, those gems gleaming their distinct colors across your wonderful, tan face.

Gah... why is it I can only find the courage to say such things now, long after it's too late?

6

OUTCASTS

Pain stung Tirak's cheek as he waded through the muck-filled shallows of a creek. He tried to ignore it. All around him, a high canopy of flat-leafed trees cast patches of light across the water's surface. It made the atmosphere here feel not all that different from Umbra's caverns. He gritted his teeth, determined not to shed another tear for the home he and Kaleek had gotten thrown out of. One difference was for sure as he stared down for any sign of motion: Tirak hadn't had to deal with this much sunlight, rare as the trees made it, in years. His eyes wanted to water any time they drifted past one of those dots of shimmering misery.

Tirak's face prickled with the threat of another flareup of pain. He had to focus. He couldn't let himself get distracted. That was just an itch, it didn't really—His hand reached up by instinct before he could remember not to scratch the spot. His finger collided with a plate of metal that hung a couple fingerwidths in front of it. The pressure forced a spike harder against his cheekbone. Tirak stopped, gasping. Coolness trickled down his cheek, confirming the scab had ripped open yet again. Agitated patches of raw skin rose to the chorus of their neighbor's agony.

He hissed a short curse.

It took a long pause between his careful steps to force down the searing itch. He told himself that he just needed to let it heal. A few of the steel scabs were already starting to flake off. It was a good sign, but it was only making the itches worse. His face felt stiff too, pulled in unnatural directions by the heavy multi-piece mask. Some pieces were carved from wood, but the rest was "lightweight" metal.

Tirak decided it was easy to call anything light as long as you weren't trying to suspend it off the skin of your face.

He needed a distraction, desperately. So, he glanced upstream to where his sister hovered over a similar spot. Her own hideous mask showed inflamed skin around its edges, from where she'd been scratching it even more liberally than he had. Otherwise though, she looked every bit like the predator she was in her new dark brigands. They were dyed in Umbra's colors. Layered over top of them were panels of leather sewn between bonesteel plates that shimmered a dark plum.

The mask somehow only managed to add to the image. Its designer had twisted it into a crude imitation of an avian face. It gave Tirak an unsettling feel of being hunted every time he stared at it for too long. It had been etched, after being welded on of course, with a pattern of sweeping lines which was then inlaid with Umbra-purple steel. It completed the mask's presence with a feather-like appearance. He noticed a dark bead trickling down her temple. Was that because she constantly disturbed the wound, or maybe she needed him to grind off a few more burrs? He had the perfect flat stone for that back at camp.

A rumble in Tirak's stomach matched the pain in his face, reminding him where his attention was supposed to be at that moment. He knew that creature had to be lurking around here somewhere. He'd seen it poke at the surface too many times to be a coincidence. It *was NOT* getting away again. He wasn't going to spend another day starving.

He focused on the water again, trying to look past the reflection his own torture device. His mask's empty, laughing face seemed to mock him from the water. Even its tongue stuck out through the exaggerated grin. That unrelenting itch kept causing his eyes to swim. Would he ever get used to the pain?

Something dark and red moved beneath the crystal surface.

Excitement coursed through Tirak. He hurled down a blunt spear and let out a battle cry. The thing did a better job catching itself on his legs than he'd done to spear it, but it was strong! He dove his hands in before the stunned creature had a chance to react. They clamped around something large, slippery. He heaved, but it shot from his grasp easier than a pleasant memory. In its wake, a line of needle points scraped across his chin. Also like a pleasant memory.

A fish broke through the surface, spraying water across him. His heart lurched with panic. Sure, he'd prepared for this by building a wall of stones around the shallows, but he knew it would never contain something so big for long. That one jump had been enough to launch it within fingers of the deep water. A stack of rocks next to him wobbled and fell. He saw Kaleek storming toward him from the corner of his eye and thanked Maker she'd noticed.

"C'mon, Kal. Help me!" he yelled.

A bright tail flashed as the fish prepared another leap for freedom. Tirak lunged first. When its head collided with one of his hands, he strained to keep it trapped between his palms. Good thing it didn't have teeth… *probably.*

The huge body writhed and twisted beneath him. The shallows became a churning storm of bubbles and mud. Even after wrapping his legs around it, the thing was slippery enough that it *still* threatened to squirm its way out.

It gained inch after painful inch.

"Kal! It's getting away… do something!"

"H-how should I help?"

Her voice came from somewhere close above him. If he'd had the energy to spare, he would've rolled his eyes. Really? Someone who could conduct water didn't know what to do right now?

"The… water! Use your power!" he shot back between gritted teeth.

He continued wrestling. Nothing happened.

Tirak looked up, but immediately regretted his mistake. The fish took advantage of his split attention and launched out of his loosening grasp. It exploded from the water, but its angle was wild and unplanned. It slapped down, not against open water, but into a carpet of moss that covered the bank. A bulbous eye immediately started rolling back and forth in search of the lost stream. A wiry, steel fin dug into the soil to help it search the unfamiliar environment for a way to escape.

Tirak pounced again.

His claws sank into the hard, scaly flesh. He hadn't even felt the change happen, but a surge of anger, fear, and hunger was enough to confirm he was using his Second Nature again. Grey fangs protruded as he let out a growl. He dug one leg deeper into the soft mud. The fish had been just about to flop its way past the wall, but now that he had a firm grip on the thing, it wasn't getting away.

Then he felt the world starting to tip sideways. A spear of panic shot through him as he saw the water rushing up to his face. Hunter and prey crashed into the open water together. The fish's tail whipped at him as it began to swim. It dragged him for several paces until he could plant a steel backpaw into the algae-slicked riverbed. He heaved with all his might. He knew that if he lost his grip for even a moment, it would be gone forever.

He dug a single claw deep into its head, right behind the eye. The torrent of motion finally went still. He panted, waiting to see if it would make another play for the water. Steam rose from iridescent scales as the creature's body instinctively tried to burn its attacker. It made a pleasant warmth against him. Blood dripped from the creature's mangled back.

As his chest rose and fell, his mind began to catch up with the mistake he'd just made.

The water began to churn farther out, several innocent logs beginning to drift toward him in the lazy current. His careful stick wall hadn't just been meant to keep the mouthwatering fish in.

Tirak launched off the riverbed on a powerful kick, his body rising halfway out of the water.

He was too late.

He cried out in pain as something powerful and toothy clamped itself around his leg and twisted. A loud pop rang out as it effortlessly pierced through a plate that ran the outside length of his shin.

"Kaleek!" he screamed.

The next moment, his head was sucked underwater, water pouring down his open throat. He kicked and tried to cough.

Neither worked. More water rushed to fill the bits of air he still had inside, and his clawed hind paw glanced off something leathery and bulbous. His dad's stories ran through his head as Tirak struck again and again. He knew it would all be over as soon as it decided to start rolling.

A mudkroc's biggest strength is its use of fear. Ignii are their weakness, Tir, but that won't help you if you panic. They use their earth conduction to hide and keep their skin untouchably slick, but they cook as easily as anything else.

This was the worst time he could've been caught like this, his body shaking with the effort to muster even a single crystal into his gearbox. It clicked a step forward behind his head.

If one bites you, then smile, son. It just handed you the key to victory.

He'd lost all sense of direction in the green abyss, but he didn't need it to begin forming that shard. He poured all his focus into it, searching his body for any last trickle of power to suck up. He shivered, feeling even his body heat start to disappear.

Something yanked on the prize his hands were clutching. He held fast. A coil of pleasing warmth curled around his body, snaking down his leg. Bubbles prickled against his shin as the feeling collected just above his knee.

With a mental command, the heat left his leg and shot between several gaps in the mudkroc's teeth.

Its body went rigid.

Water rushed past his head, then Tirak exploded into the light for the briefest moment before slapping back down against the surface. He watched abstractly as a fountain spewed out of his mouth.

His mind was growing numb. It was shock, he knew, but he found himself helpless to do anything as the current pulled at him. He just needed to rest. Maybe his leg would heal after a few more minutes. Or maybe something else would eat him first. He barely had the strength to care. Once he'd healed a little, he could swim to the bank and find his way back to camp where Kaleek would surely be waiting.

Yeah. That would work.

Hands reached under his arms and heaved. He heard a small grunt. Weight fell from him as something broke loose from his leg. With a feminine yell, Tirak felt himself thrown onto a thick bed of moss.

He shook himself out of the stupor. His sister stooped over him, her hands braced against her knees. Streams of oily blood flowed down his leg. Tirak winced as he shoved his thumb into the hole halfway up his shin before it could bleed him dry. They panted in silence for the next few minutes as the wound slowly closed up. Metal armor twisted back into shape with one last pop.

Kaleek put a hand to her mouth and gasped. Tirak didn't want to follow her gaze, but he already knew what was coming. There was no point in ignoring it. He stared at the once prized catch and felt his heart sink. At least half of the fish was gone, stolen by that cooked carcass. Most of what was left were bones and guts. Hardly any meat at all. His eyes trailed the river downstream, to where a circle of brown vultures flew beyond the next bend.

So much for a full belly today…

An hour later, what was left of it was sizzling next to a few succulent friends over their campfire. All of them were either red or blue. They had no need to eat anything that wouldn't recharge them. Elemental game seemed plentiful enough, after all. His teeth ground against each other as he checked himself. Plentiful, if they could just *catch* any of it.

Since Kaleek was still being her recent chatty self, the two of them ate in complete silence. She picked at her plate slowly, but Tirak's own was polished clean all too soon. He eyed the fire again. Those bluish minnows were far more numerous, but he hadn't served more than a few of their scraps for himself. Going hungry was still better than getting element poisoning.

Tirak stared down, mouth still watering for more.

"We could've eaten a lot better if you'd just helped when I asked," he grumbled before he had thought better of it.

He winced as soon as the words were out. Kaleek's fork went still. An uncomfortable silence sat between them. He dared a glance and found his sister staring away.

She started mumbling something, but all he could hear was the phrase, "...any less than we'd eat back home..."

His jaw clenched together. She was right... *technically*. But out here they had been exhausting themselves for days on end, both physically and elementally. He still felt like he could barely muster more than a spark or two. He resisted pointing out that flaw in her logic. She wouldn't listen anyway. In her mind, their powers *were* the whole problem.

He needed a different tactic.

As he watched her pick at her food with continued disinterest, Kaleek's hand snuck to the side of her face and began scratching at the edge of her mask again. He wanted to chide her before she accidentally reopened her wounds, but he knew better. It would probably just make her scratch it harder out of spite.

The perfect idea came to his mind.

"Yeah, I can hardly stand it too," he said in the softest tone he could.

It worked. Her hand dropped, and she looked up at him with a sheepish expression.

"I… I still can't believe they did this to us. I thought they just *told* people not to take it off. How sick do you have to be to go and weld stuff to somebody's face while they scream? Seriously. Did the guy have to smile like he was enjoying it the whole time?"

Tirak nodded. The guard captain had been pretty brutal. He'd earned his nickname as "The Butcher" long before either of them was born.

"Yeah. If I ever find the person who told me Igni can't be burned… I'll have a hard time trying not to prove how wrong he was."

"Tirak… please don't talk like that. It's not funny."

He looked up at his sister, one eyebrow cocked. She shifted uncomfortably. Relenting, he extinguished the tongue of fire he'd been holding between thumb and forefinger. He could feel the fish starting to infuse his body with fire again. That breed must have been able to store a whole lot of power for its size.

"What? C'mon, not like we've been afraid of an edgy joke or two before."

"There's more than some edge to it when you say stuff like that now."

"You're right." He grinned beneath the mask's even larger grin. "It's got a point too."

He tapped the sharpened point of one of his welded studs for extra effect.

"Tirak…" she complained.

"Fine, sorry. Forget I said anything. But hey, just think. Soon we'll be in Maker's Grove, before the Man himself, receiving His pardon. I bet He'll cut off the masks for us. Things *will* go back to normal. And that's not even the biggest part of it. He's sending us on a *quest* after that! A *Quest*!!"

His sister seemed not to hear him at first.

Eventually, she replied in a dull monotone, "What's the point of trying? Maker's just going to think we're lying, like everyone else. Maybe He'll sentence us to death instead…"

"Come on, Kee. You can't think like that. Have some hope, won't you? Not everyone's as big a bigot as Onok and Hakhoz are."

Tirak sighed. He had to redirect this elsewhere before it fell apart any more. He leaned back onto his palms and looked up at the light that was filtering down through the treetops. He forced a content smile onto his face.

"You know what I find helps a little?" he asked.

She looked up at him, an eagerness creeping into her eyes.

"What's that?"

"A cool splash of water from time to time," he said, his smile returning.

She narrowed her eyes and immediately became more sullen.

"No."

"O-okay, sorry! I'm sorry!" he said, then sighed. "Look, Sis. You can't hide from it forever. You'll just end up hurting someone again if you do."

That one worked. Her eyes began to bug out.

"You-you said I couldn't explode again!"

"Not *explode*, but, well… You already know that's not the only way to hurt someone."

He made a point of pausing to give her chin a gentle pinch. It was one of the few parts of her face that was exposed beneath the ugly crow's beak mask. She winced at the purple bruise that was still healing. A small part of his brain wondered at that. In what world would a simple bruise take days to heal? Not even hours, *days*? Something about the beating his gang gave her must've really taken a toll.

She was looking at him with one eyebrow cocked higher than the edge of the mask's socket. Right.

"Uh, besides," he continued, "it's just like the old story about Biri and Dad. Just because something's good at hurting things doesn't mean we have to use it for that."

He opened the fist that he'd been clenching in front of him, releasing a burst of fire in the shape of bird mid-flight. As it flew, he conducted it through the air, making it circle back toward them and start spinning around Kaleek's head.

She stared up in wonder, mouth open. A hand reached out to try and touch the ball of orange light. Just before the firework exhausted the last of its heat, he made it shoot away and released his hold. The bird broke apart with a tiny pop, splitting into a hundred fizzling tongues of fire. Each one winked out just as quickly as it had appeared. Like little sparks in the air.

Silence hovered around them for several seconds. Even the screeches of birds across the treetops seemed to die down.

"Tirak… Th-that was so beautiful. Can… I make things as amazing as that too?"

He grinned widely at her. She'd just taken the bait hook, line, sinker, *and* spear shaft. He shrugged.

"I dunno. I've never conducted water before. You'd have to find out for yourself."

She hesitated, looking like she was straddling the line between clamming up again and nodding. He produced a bowl of water and set it down in front of her.

"Do you want to try?"

Tirak didn't give her a chance to say no. He scooped up both of their plates in one smooth motion and started walking toward the riverbank to wash up.

Behind him, he heard the soft reply, "Darkness curse you… but, yes."

Tirak worked slowly, trying not to look interested in what she was doing, nor look too busy with straightening up the camp. The last thing he needed was to risk distracting her and completely undo the whole morning's work. The smoldering cook fire was next, something his sister thankfully hated doing. He picked through its ashes one ember at a time, piling them up in a thick cradle of insulation to simmer until night fell again. Even though a snap of his fingers could turn any stack of logs into a blaze, he was still flagging from exhaustion. He hadn't been this starved of his element since his awakening. Every ounce of energy he saved was another fish he didn't have to spear, or crystal-pelted rabbit to snare.

Something sharp bit into the side of his finger. He yelped, yanking his hand out of the ashes. Black leaked from the side of one finger, where plain skin ran between two pads of metal. What in Maker's name had that been?

Sucking on the cut, Tirak grabbed a stick and dug around in the spot again. Something light and crystalline made a clink after a few stabs.

He frowned and scooped ashes away, this time with a little more care. The cut would only take a few minutes to heal, so he ignored it while he worked awkwardly with his good hand.

Tirak closed his grip around the shard as its meaning began to dawn on him. He wiped its flat edge on the grass, and found a piece of translucent glass glittering back at him. He could see almost straight through it. Only the even, faintly teal glow did more than the chips and scratches did to obscure the world beyond.

One of his mother's earliest stories came back to him.

This had to be a piece of airglass, from the ancient days when Maker had first risen up and defeated the island's shadows. Their fight had shattered the sky itself, turning it always foggy and gray.

Whole fields of these airglass splinters could be found all over the island, anywhere the rains or an unfortunate camper washed away the centuries of dirt that had covered them. Apparently, they were camping in the middle of one right now.

He turned the sharp splinter over in his hands, wondering if they should move to a new spot today. Then again, why? This field alone likely stretched over a mile in any direction. He dug a little farther, and found a handful of the shards along with some clear trueglass.

His eyes went wide. This… this was a small fortune! Unlike the elemental stuff, trueglass could actually melt from heat and be formed into all sorts of useful things. It was just like the sandglass that an igni forge could make, but it was never cloudy, never dissolved in the rain.

Glancing at his sister's forgotten plate, he noticed Kaleek hadn't eaten any of the white-shelled creature he'd found. Given the ugly thing's roasted head, he really didn't blame her, but food was food out here. He knew she wasn't just being picky.

She was still terrified.

He watched Kaleek stir a puddle with her toe as an idea spread through his circuits. The puddle's surface rippled, rising into the air like a winding snake as it obeyed her will.

But, she had more than one power now. How much more could she do if she just tried? He crushed the brittle airglass in his hands, careful to keep it between the plated sections this time, and dumped them into a lopsided mug. A crack in its side started to bleed a drop of liquid, so he made a mental note to smooth the metal out again later. Too much to do, and not enough energy to fuel it all…

He walked over to Kaleek and pressed the mug into a lump of moss between them.

"Tea?" he asked as he sat.

She barely thanked him with a mumble, but at least she picked it up. That was thanks enough.

"There, uh… might be some sugarthistle sludge at the bottom still. Completely edible though!"

Kaleek didn't respond, but neither did she pour the mug out. An absent-minded sip put his mind at ease. The clump of water in front of her continued changing into new shapes as she nudged and poked it. A worm, then a leafy vine, then something like a chasmheart, even a bird raised on one leg. On and on it went.

He cleared his throat and nodded toward what she was doing.

"That's pretty incredible, sis. How in the world did you make that flower even grow veins on its leaves?"

A half-formed deer collapsed to the ground with a splash. Kaleek scowled and tried to move away. He put his hand over hers, begging her not to leave.

"Kal, come on. You can't keep giving up. Your powers will *literally* never leave you."

She hadn't ripped her hand away yet, so he picked it up and gave it a squeeze.

"Remember the story about Onok and the chisel that carved Umbra. Nothing has to be awful. You don't have to use your powers to ruin."

Her scowl deepened. She turned her face away.

"I already have used it to ruin people..." she muttered.

"And I'm *alive* because you did!" he insisted. "And I can promise you at least two other innocent people are alive because you stepped up when it mattered most."

Her mask tilted toward him just enough to eye him with a sideways glance.

"Why... why *were* those guys beating you up anyway?" she asked.

He bit his tongue. No. He couldn't let her know about that. He'd already lost everyone else.

He couldn't lose Kaleek too.

"No, don't change the subject. *You,*"—he poked her in the arm—"are incredible. I think you were made to be a warrior. Yeah, you had an explosive outburst, but they *asked* for it when they backed you into a corner like that. Don't let one mistake keep you from becoming what you've always wanted to be, Kal."

Kaleek snorted.

"Why not? Dad already made sure it would. We can't go back home. Even if we do this ridiculous quest and Maker pardons us, that fire gang will have a target painted on our backs for the rest of our lives."

"And who says Umbra is the only place that needs warriors?"

"If you're about to convince me we should move to Aura after this, no. They hate outsiders, and I'd be the least welcome person on the whole island."

"Come on, that can't be remotely true!" Tirak pressed.

This hadn't been the direction he was going, but Kaleek's depression was getting the better of her again.

"Think what you want. We're never going to find out," she mumbled.

Tirak sighed. This wasn't the right battle to fight. Time to get back on topic.

"That wasn't what I meant anyway. You remember what my parents used to do, right?"

"Uh, lay around dead?"

It took Kaleek a moment to realize what she'd just said. But Tirak had felt its bite right away.

"I-I didn't mean that."

He tried to wave the joke off, if only his throat hadn't discovered a rock hiding in it. Water filled his eyes that wouldn't blink away. Wow. And she was the one who wanted them to be less edgy? What a hypocrite.

"Tirak, I'm sorry. Come on."

"Forget it," he managed to croak and turned away.

"Tirak… I do remember. Look, they were wanderers right? Traveled around, training people to fight and guarding them for pay, or something? You told me how they always felt proud that they were serving Maker the way He originally wanted us to. They served the needs of the island instead of just filling the pockets of only one Elder's village."

The butchering of their legacy was somehow even worse than the thoughtless joke. Tirak swallowed the lump and forced his feelings back down into their rightful place.

"C-close enough, yeah… They walked free from any village's rules. They stayed on good terms with all of them, but they kept moving around. Always practicing, always growing stronger. They …"—he had to pause and swallow another lump—"They lived a life that would be perfect for us. You still want to be a hero like the Elders, right?"

Kaleek nodded, thoughtful.

"Or greater," she added.

Tirak leaned in, picking up one of her hands to hold between both of his.

"Then you need to start where *they* did, and learn to use what you have. What happened, happened. You had no idea what you were doing. You were just trying to protect me and it happened to be the wrong place at the wrong time. That never has to happen again. No one's ever heard of a cybri losing control again after their awakening. And no cybri ever became a heroine by ignoring their most useful skills. I've never seen anything as powerful as what you did back there."

Kaleek tensed, and started to pull her hand away.

"I… *no*, Tir. Something about it just—just felt wrong. Please just drop it. I can't stand using air. If I run out right now and never recharge it, it still won't be soon enough."

"That's fine. I won't make you charge that half of your powers. Just promise me you'll give them one more try," Tirak pressed.

She tilted her head back and forth, clearly searching for another protest. He struck before she could brandish it.

"And nobody's around here to get hurt. Don't you see? And I already know how to duck, so don't worry about me either. There. is. *Nothing*. To fear."

He pressed until the cracks had widened too far to resist. She finally gave in.

Maker's Log #43061: Your happy place still thrives.

A Mudkroc is floating down the river past me, doing its best to imitate a log despite the glowing tan spines running down its back. It's blissfully unaware that I'm even here. I have nothing to interest it with anyway. Still creeps me out whenever I lose sight of one. How are they so good at hiding?

Sorry, you don't even know what those are, even if you've guessed. Supercharged crocodiles that eat Anium. They're every bit as terrifying as they sound too, which is exactly what I grew them to do. What the oldworld crocs did with algae, mine can sculpt the mud itself into whatever camouflage or attack they need.

Sigh.

I'm sure you'd hate me for desecrating the lush jungle you once fell in love with, but it's still as hardy as ever down here. Know that I had no choice but to introduce the changes that I did. Something had to guard your precious garden beds, after all. Don't judge me too harshly, my light.

A whole ecosystem has built up across the island under my watchful eye. It coexists in near harmony with the old creatures, and sometimes both the biological and the cybernetic feed on each other.

The circle of life has become a figure eight around me. A beautiful Celtic knot.

And tying it all together are your gardens. You saved us.

...And then you didn't live to see it for yourself.

7

REMATCH

Tirak buzzed around his sister energetically, helping her set up all sorts of challenges to test what her powers could do. It took Kaleek a while to stop looking like a kitten stiff with fright every time he forced her try a sparring move with it. Neither of them knew much about conducting water, so Tirak took things as slowly as he could with her. Once she could actually parry and make a few attacks, he started to mix in a few ways she might be able conduct shadow and water at the same time. She shied away from even that small change at first. Tirak had to lock a shadow shard into his own gearbox before she even began to consider it.

Only after Tirak showed her how even he could burn a vine with invisible flames, she realized it wasn't such an awful thing.

Seeing him do that was a good reminder for Kaleek. In a way, all of them were halfbreeds. Every village but Umbra could use more than one element. She wasn't wearing her shoulder-cowl, so nothing stopped him from seeing the moment a single new shard locked into place on her gearbox. Pride flooded his chest as he saw its purple glow bleed around the edges of her neck.

"Here, lets start simple. I'll show you how I mix my elements to burn that vine over there without any flame you can see."

He raised his hand, and a lush, green vine began to writhe and pop, turning black and breaking apart as if it had been dropped into the heart of a bonefire, which, it had. He stepped back and nodded to his sister.

"Your turn. Try to put the fire out without letting me see what you're doing."

She squinted and frowned, but nothing worked. A mist of shadow formed around her left hand while the other drew a ball of water together, but the jet that shot out was perfectly normal. Kaleek's next test was to turn a puddle between her feet invisible. No amount of grimacing or black tendrils poking into its surface worked. Grumbling, she lifted the whole puddle into the air as a sphere and tried to make that go invisible. It kind of worked. Actually no, it didn't work at all. What Tirak thought was the edges starting to change turned out to be the ripple of a stale breeze.

Frowning, Kaleek concentrated harder and brought the ball back toward her. The moment it touched an outstretched fingertip, the sphere turned black as pitch. Both siblings gasped. Before she could recover, the ball fell to the ground with a decidedly viscous plop! They stared at each other in disbelief.

"What was that!?" Tirak hissed.

"I don't know!"

Kaleek was beginning to grin.

"Could you do anything with it?" he asked.

"I… don't know."

She dipped a toe into the thick mass.

"I… I almost can't *move* it anymore. But it feels—kinda soothing?"

The next hour of trying didn't get them any closer to figuring out the weird mix of powers. Then, with significant coaxing, Tirak *finally* got her to spin a single air shard into place on her gearbox. Blue, violet, and pale teal shimmered beautifully through the hairs of her messy braid. He gave his sister a reassuring nod as she raised a hand that was quickly becoming encrusted with frost.

A spike of ice shot out faster than either of them could track. It drilled straight through leaves and underbrush alike. Somewhere farther off, they heard it shatter against something solid. Tirak leaped for her and wrapped his arms around her neck.

"You did it! Great Maker, that was cool!"

Her amazed smile hung there, then faded slightly. Her eye cocked sideways toward him.

"Was that another pun?"

"Huh? Oh. Uh…"

It was a pretty good one, if only he'd noticed before blurting it out. Kaleek shoved him away and rolled her eyes. She started to shake her hand free of the still-growing frost spikes, but Tirak convinced her to keep trying more things.

Once it was obvious she would turn a few spikes on *him* if he pushed any further, Tirak decided to move on to something else they needed to do. He led her back to the campfire and they started separating out the glittering fish bones and other scraps of metal from the refuse.

"I think it's time we both had a real weapon of our own, don't you?"

"No… please. I'm going to go insane if I have to knap even *one* more spearhead!" Kaleek begged, despair creeping into her voice.

Tirak followed her gaze toward a pair of crooked spears, their blunt stone heads stuck into a pile of sharp chips and failed tries. He laughed.

"No, no, not at all. I've been collecting our leftovers for the last few days. All these bones pile up quickly. Should have enough to make a couple knives by now. See?"

"But …" She frowned. "Won't we need, like, a forge or something? And tools? And…?"

"Answer:," he interrupted, "rock, rock, and… rock. Also some mud."

He led her several paces and pointed to a squat, makeshift kiln he had spent the last night forming.

"The only trouble now is drying it out. I could fill the bottom with some coal and light it, but the whole thing might crumble if I heat its walls too fast. That means the kiln could take at least a week to be ready on its own, and that's only if we don't get another rainstorm. If only someone could leech away every drop of water and instantly dry it…"

Tirak grinned at his sister.

"Fine…" she grumbled.

She rested a hand against the dome. After a few moments, Tirak watched what looked like a hundred tiny worms of water squirming their way out of the soil. They crawled toward her hand, growing bigger until they became one unbroken chain of water flowing in a tight spiral up her arm. Tirak breathed out in awe yet again.

"That… is going to come in handy for sure."

He got to work on the knives right away. He started to wish he had spent more time around the forge shops in Middle Tier. He could think of one pretty face he would have loved to learn more of this stuff from. He blinked away a stubborn, smoky tear. No use. He hadn't lost that chance. You can't lose a chance you never had. He had to just focus.

"Thankfully, this is something I'm already good at, so it shouldn't take too much power. You know, since somebody hasn't had much real food lately to let him recover."

"How many times do I have to say sorry before you stop holding that over my head?"

"Until you don't leave me hanging like that and almost get me killed," he retorted.

Kaleek tried to stick her tongue out at him, but the bladelike beak on her mask reminded her how bad an idea that was. She sucked the cut back into her mouth while Tirak let out a good-natured chuckle and returned to the job of superheating two bowls of metal.

Sweat poured from Tirak's forehead when the sun changed course and started drifting toward the ground. He set down his hammer-rock and was forced to admit that the blades weren't getting any better with time. He'd simply have to cut his losses and pull them out for a final round of shaping while they cooled. Even with some encouragement from his conduction, the setup was too primitive to consider details such as putting a proper temper on their edges. These would have to do, he supposed.

He carried a dagger in each hand and dropped them into the river to cool. After a violent few minutes of hisses and sputters, one of them faded to a dark, uneven blue while the other never quite lost its red after their glow had vanished. He offered the first of the new weapons to his sister.

"These will get us by for now. Pretty sure I burned what little charge might've been in them. The metal was pretty diluted to start with anyway. Next village we visit, we should buy some pure bonesteel swords that match our elements. Those are a downright *dream* to swing. Till then, at least these can actually survive a few scratches."

He felt his way across his new knife as he listened to himself adopting a trainer's voice. A soft glow returned to the dagger's edge as he spoke. He couldn't help showing off a little every now and then.

"Nothing beats good old-fashioned discipline and practice in a fight, but a bonesteel weapon can become like an extension of yourself in ways that plain metal could never match. You're going to have to learn to feel that with this weak dagger until we can find you a better practice weapon. Pure bonesteel helps you focus the charge in your attacks, making them far more powerful than you could ever be on your own."

He opened his dreaming eyes and lunged at Kaleek.

The blade arced down toward her head. She screamed and tried to dodge out of the way, but too slowly. An edge dull enough to be called flat scrapped across her shoulder and chest, and he knew from experience that it would leave a nice long bruise across her skin. But a ritual is a ritual. He wouldn't take that privilege away from his sister.

"OW! Are you spitting shadows? You just cut me! What's wrong with you?"

He tapped the knife edge-first against the side of his mask, showing it hadn't left a mark.

"We haven't sharpened them yet. Now, defend yourself!"

He laughed and aimed another jab at her arm. This time she executed a perfect roll beneath him, regaining her feet inside an opening where she could strike from. He saw the smile curling her lips and knew he was on his way toward losing. Blade ground against blade as he quickly pivoted, just *barely* catching her attack.

With a brief sense of shock, he noticed a trail of flat mud behind her feet. She had just used her conduction!

If he kept pushing her onto the defensive, maybe he could coax her Second Nature out of hiding too. That was another thing they needed to learn about. Another thing Kaleek needed to get used to before it made her lash out by accident.

He made another swing for an opening along her side, and again she slid out of the way just in time, faster than should've been possible with her unwavering poise. She had even disarmed him in the scuffle. Another skid mark across the ground proved she was cheating.

He tried to sidestep her next swing, but his feet felt like they were being dragged through molasses. Metal clinked against his forearm before he could pull it back. His sister grinned.

"Got you."

"Oh ho ho, so *that's* how we're playing, is it? Fine then."

A red crystal clicked into place behind his shoulders, then evaporated with a blink. Power burned across his arms.

He pushed himself into a roll as he used a flash of heat to free his feet. His dagger was still a head or two away, where he had dropped it in his surprise. Stupid move on his part. Onok had trained him better. The ground steamed in a line beneath him as he dove into a roll for the weapon. Everywhere he touched became dry and cracked.

A knee to her side. A fist against her mask—*Ow*, stupid him—the butt of his dagger into the top of her shoulder.

Each hit sent off a small puff of fire. Tirak began to smell the burn of flesh as he landed hit after hit. In his head, he yelled for Kaleek to get up. She would never grow if she didn't embrace this now.

A pincer snapped at his next attack… and caught it midair!

Tirak looked down at what had been his sister just a moment ago. A bulbous head with deformed half-globes sticking out of either side stared back at him, its body a twiglike collection of carapace. Sharp mandibles clicked at him. He could see sections of her mask retracted halfway into the new face. It… didn't look comfortable. Two wings sprouted from its back and blasted him with air.

He tumbled head over heels, catching himself on the second roll. His hind claws dug into the dirt as his paws melted back into their normal shape. Feline Natures were certainly useful. His eyes searched the desaturated clearing. Now, where was she?

The thought had barely flashed through his mind when he registered the screaming. An instant later, he realized his face was in agony. He doubled over, clawing at his face but finding his mask warding his hands away. He pulled them away, covered in blood.

His voice gave out after another second, and he realized he had been the one screaming. What had *that* been?

The blood was still dripping into his eyes too. He was blinded by the oily mixture, and his mask made the stuff impossible to wipe away. Kaleek was sure to strike again at any time. He was all but helpless.

No, not helpless, he remembered. When using his Nature, his eyes were almost irrelevant. He could hear things ten times faster than his eyes could register.

He tried it… and regretted the choice no sooner than his face had begun to shift. Searing pain ripped through him a second time. He staggered into his normal form, helpless while he waited for the wave to pass. It finally clicked, why the villages welded a mask on anyone they deemed too dangerous to keep. They wanted to deny him his own Second Nature.

Well, Tirak was going to figure out a way to use it whether they wanted him to or not. Still gasping, he searched for any other way he could steal back the upper hand in his duel.

Something big clicked in the bushes on the opposite side of their clearing. Dust blew into the air as a blurred streak of blue shot toward him. Tirak tried to dodge, but too late. *Anything* was too late against whatever Kaleek had become.

She slammed into him. Blood sprayed across his face, and now he could see up close what his own mask must've been doing to him. Her face was only half formed around the foreign pieces, leaving open wounds that dripped steadily. She began to pummel him at least as hard as he had done earlier, her face flashing back to normal somewhere in the middle of it all.

By the third hit to the head, his drills began to kick in. Instinct raised his arms. He caught one blow, deflected a second, and pushed Kaleek away before the third could land. He hooked the blunt dagger out of her hand as she fell.

Not daring to give up the advantage, he committed to using both weapons and leaped for her. Frost puffed in front of her and both daggers were caught on something flat and glittering.

"Checkmate, bro."

His sergeant's voice yelled the moves in his head as he let go and dove for her legs. She stared him down, eyes taunting to try again as a manic grin spread its way beneath her mask. Her lips split into separate mandibles as the smile kept on widening.

This fight was getting out of hand. He needed to disable her before either of them actually got hurt. Should… should he let her win just to end things faster? Hah. Yeah, right.

His arms snapped closed around empty air right before the dust cloud slammed into him. Kaleek was gone again.

She descended on him an instant later, and they began trading swings back and forth. She was dodging much more expertly than he had expected her to. He felt a little stab of pride as he saw how well his training had paid off. She was finally using every element, and getting better at it by the second!

Finally, they connected. Heat blazed against humid ice. A dense fog shot out in every direction, swallowing them completely. Tirak gasped in surprise, and then choked on the sudden humidity. Their fight broke off. He tried raising his hand to his face, but he couldn't see it until it was only a few fingers away.

"Holy Maker and all His machines…." He gaped. "Kal, we need to remember this move for the future!"

"Why does everything have to be a move?" Kaleek groaned.

He let the silence linger for a second. Two hazy blue rays turned toward him.

"Just… don't give it a cheesy name."

"Don't worry," he assured her. "We'll call it Smokescreen."

His sister groaned. He'd nailed it.

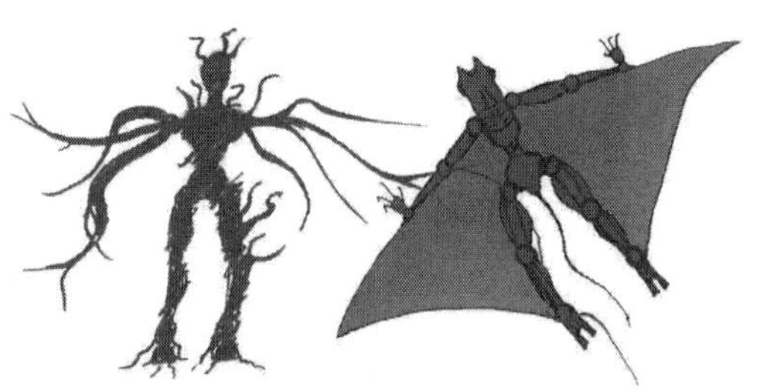

Maker's Log #85997: Sketch of Onok & Biri adopting their Second Natures.

Second Natures are without a doubt the most bizarre aspect of cybri biology to me. When I designed the first few prototypes—er, the Elders, I mean—I certainly wondered if that side of their genes would come through somehow, but this ability to melt even their toughest metal components and reform themselves into animalistic terrors is completely beyond anything I expected.

After a few years of testing, I'm fairly confident the trait is a byproduct of their power source. Two hundred years, and I still know next to nothing about the things.

Sigh... this was always YOUR specialty. It's times like this when I miss your presence the most. All these years, and yet your missing light is all the more precious to me.

Erm, sorry. The Natures. Right.

Every Cybri's Second Nature stays the same once they unlock it along with their elemental conduction. What's interesting though is that each cybri element seems to have a very specific range of Second Natures associated with it. Fire Cybrii always take on the shape of furred mammals, while Earth types have a strong reptilian trend, and so on. Each of the elements has Nature forms that just make sense.

...Except for the Umbrii that is. Shadow still doesn't make sense as an element to me. I don't know how to describe those except, "tentacled night terrors." Sorry, Onok, but your people truly are horrifying. I can't say it any other way and still call it the truth.

When donning their Nature, a Cybri seems to respond on instinct more than logic. It's as if even a part of their brain gets consumed in the transformation. At the same time though, the reflexes and traits they gain are truly superhuman.

Seriously. My mask had to regrow my whole arm after giving Biri a completely benign insult during one experiment. I never even saw her claw lash out! One second, it was by her side. The next, by her face, and I was bleeding all over the floor. Even more strange, the wound seemed to burn HER as much as it did my arm's remains.

8

SOMETHING ELSE TO STRIVE FOR

A new voice coughed as it approached through the icy cloud. A feminine figure stepped into view, waving a hand in front of her as she went. She was choking on the frost as much as Tirak himself was.

He watched the female stab a spear into the dirt, close her eyes, and spread her hands to either side. A column of air suddenly turned clear around her. The emptiness seemed to billow upward as the haze vented away, drawing in fresh air toward the three of them. Ripples of heat made her appearance swim. Everything quickly settled, then she stepped out from a circle of charred grass.

Tirak's voice had lodged itself somewhere deep inside his throat. Metallic scars twisted all across her face. And yet it had a slender, stunning build. Orange and yellow armor patterns ended in a pair of naturally woven shorts whose rips and stains spoke of a long time spent wandering the jungle. Not filthy, and anything but unkempt. They were just... *well used.*

She gave him a quick look-over before wiggling two feline ears at him. She had, without a doubt, the prettiest face Tirak had ever seen.

Strong, confident, her beauty not marred in the slightest by the lines of struggle cut into her face.

"So. What're you kids up to?" the lady casually asked.

He was smitten instantly. She raised an eyebrow and looked him over a second time.

"Oookay… Tryin'a play the silent type or something. What about you, girl, are you anywhere as talkati—"

A weapon sang past her head and paused there. Its never-sharpened edge glistened a dull blue.

"What do you want with us? Who are you?" Kaleek growled. "A-and what's wrong with your face?"

The newcomer put on a calm smile.

"Here's a tip, sweetie. Maybe don't threaten somebody 'less they deserve it. And make sure ya have a *real* weapon, first."

"Answer the *question*!" Kaleek demanded. "If you don't, I'll, I'll…."

The taller female sighed. If Tirak had to guess, he suspected the expression was somewhere in the ballpark of "annoyed."

Her hand slapped the dagger away before Tirak even saw it move. A hatchet appeared out of nowhere in the opposite fist and came to rest against Kaleek's neck, its back edge forward.

"And don't give 'em a warning unless you know you'd win. Y'see this? This is a warning because I know I could take a pipsqueak like yerself any day."

Kaleek set her jaw, then dove into a tight roll for her weapon. She lunged at the stranger, but came up short, unable to move. The hatchet's blade was biting against his sister's mask. She spent an unbelieving moment scrambling for purchase on the sandy dirt, but couldn't overcome the humiliating posture this fiery queen had forced her into.

"And *this* is a threat, because you tried to attack anyway."

Tirak finally swallowed the rock in his throat.

"W-wait! We're just trying to fend for ourselves out here. We don't mean any trouble. You… just kinda surprised us."

The lady spared him a look and smiled. He felt his insides churn a little further.

"There we go. That was so much easier. Glad this little tempest has such a good boyfriend t'keep 'er in check."

She holstered her weapon just as quickly as she'd drawn it. Kaleek toppled off balance from the motion, but the lady clasped wrists with her before she had a chance to faceplant. She was lifted onto her feet like the two of them had been the best of friends all along.

"Name's Rekke. And yes, I know what my face looks like. Got chewed up by an animal when I was little. So. What brings two light-weight kids into my territory?"

Hard, knowing eyes measured them both with a firm stare. They'd never stopped measuring, really. Tirak watched uncomfortably as they roamed across the whole camp. They held a shrewdness that warned him not to—wait. He *knew* that stare! That posture. His trainers had taught him *that* exact expression to use whenever he needed to ask villagers who had taken whose shardpurse. He glanced to where she had come from, and on second glance, the spear that stuck there was no plain hunter's spike, either. That bladed, bonesteel head was made for killing. What was this female? He had watched her keep a complete awareness of everything around her, even in the middle of that stunt with Kaleek. Was she a guard? A scout? And if so, what was she guarding out here? Why didn't she wear any village's colors?

Kaleek cleared her throat with some discomfort.

"We, uh… we're just passing through."

Rekke raised an unamused eyebrow at them.

"Wolf dung."

She sighed and gestured to ask if they could sit.

"Let's try it this way. How 'bout some firejerky? Sorry kiddo, don't got anything blue fer ya, though."

"I wouldn't want it anyway." Kaleek said with a sneer. "And no. You should leave."

"Ah, c'mon. Let a gal sit down fer a bit. Been walking my beat all day."

Rekke crossed her legs beneath her and sat without waiting for permission. She dangled a juicy strip of dried meat in front of Tirak's eyes. Spices and red scales stuck from its surface. His stomach rumbled.

"So, what'll it be?"

Tirak snatched the piece and sat across from her. Beaten, Kaleek huffed and dropped to the ground next to him as well.

"Good choice. Now, lemme guess. You got masked, what, a few days ago at most? So, that means yer on yer way to see the old liar over the hill, and ya think yer so impossibly innocent that he'll he'll just snap his fingers 'n roll back time like nothin' never happened."

Tirak swallowed a lump. The way she had described it made their plan sound foolish.

"Well… yeah, we think have a pretty strong case. I actually am innocent. Just spoke up at the wrong time and got caught up in the whole thing. And Kal isn't a murderer. She got blamed for defending herself… and…"

Rekke's impassive, knowing expression made the rest of the words die on his lips.

"You kids are good as dead." She said.

She bit off another chunk of meat and passed the rest of the strip to Tirak.

"Y'know, if ya need another plan… Well, nobody says you gotta do what those stuffy Elders say. You don't *have* to go all the way to that grove."

"Yes we do! We're supposed to—" Kaleek tried to interrupt.

Rekke raised a hand to cut her off.

"Nobody *important* says you got to. All the villages want is to keep people like us outta their hair. So… I live a few days' walk from here. Got a campful of people back there that prove my way works. Life's rough, but we're happy there. Why not come check it out, maybe buy a… *real* weapon or two."

She eyed the blunt dagger Kaleek was still clutching and smirked. Tirak mulled the idea over in his head. It wasn't a bad one. After all, they *did* need some better supplies… and cooking gear perhaps, and—

"No."

Tirak blinked and glanced at his sister.

"We owe it to Maker to go see Him as soon as possible. He *is* expecting us. We owe it to our Elder, too. Maker already has a quest we're supposed to go on once we get there."

Rekke's ears flattened against her head. A disgusted hiss escaped her teeth as she rose to her feet, spun on her heels, and walked away.

"Pfft… of *course* it's another pair of suicidal fools," he heard her mutter.

Tirak stared after the female in shock. She was at the edge of the clearing before his mind reengaged again. Something inside him screamed that they shouldn't let her go so easily.

"Wait… wait!" he called.

Rekke cast a glance over her shoulder, one hand lifting a fern branch that was at least as tall as she was. One pointy ear boring into him with its attention. It was a distinctly feminine pose. Full of poise and all that stuff his mom had always talked about.

"Can't we at least offer you something to drink? Uh, some tea maybe?" Tirak asked.

The lady snorted in obvious derision. The ear twitched above her head, completing the expression.

"Kid, don't treat me like a lost kitten. That's what *you two* are. *Yer* the grinning fools running off to your own deaths at that pretender's hands. Trust me as someone who knows what they're talking about: starving to death out here is the better fate anyway."

Tirak's circuits still reeled from the dump of new thoughts she had just unloaded on them. What had she just called Maker? How was one death better than another? And how on the island was she so overconfident about everything? So many questions.

"P-pretender? Wait, that's not important. Please, just call it a way for us to apologize for our rudeness if you want. Can we pretend none of that happened and start our introductions from right here?"

Her flat stare was anything but convinced.

"Or, uhhh… maybe call it an excuse for you to correct all our misguided ways?" Tirak tried.

A lopsided smile finally cracked her lips, spreading its way across half her face.

"So he's humble as well… All right. Show me whatcha got, then I'll give ya an abridged version of 'The history no village will ever admit to you.' Catchy name, no?"

She winked his direction. Tirak pounced at the chance and started hurrying to reboil their pot. There were just enough leftover sticks he could mix with the coals to rekindle their small cookfire. For Kaleek's part, she continued to stare the older female down with crossed arms and an unabashed glower.

Tirak turned to the newcomer again and cleared his throat. Why was it so scratchy all of a sudden?

"Uh, it'll take me a few minutes to relight this. You could probably start telling us your history lesson while we wait… If-if you want… of course."

He couldn't shake the feeling that he was staring down a tiger as he looked into those bright orange irises. They were even narrowed into slits just a little. Rekke rolled her eyes, then a fire burst to life next to Tirak's face with a Fwoosh! He stumbled back, his numb leg catching on a root and landing him hard on his backside. It earned him a small cackle from both girls. Blushing hard, Tirak returned his attention to what had become a full blaze. He started reassembling the crude branch contraption they used as a spit and carefully suspended a lumpy pot from its middle. Behind him, Rekke's voice finally started talking.

"Based on yer attitudes, I'm guessing you already know what the old hermit *does* to criminals that beg him for 'judgment.' So the fact yer still headed that way tells me either yer delusional… or idiots."

Her ears were slumped, unimpressed. Nearly aggressive.

"Actually," Kaleek started, "we're going because Elder Onok wants us to—"

But Rekke hadn't paused to invite comments. "He doesn't spare anyone. Ever. Forget what the 'civilized' villages claim. Nothing—and I mean nothing—is truly tame outside them village walls. And that hermit you worship is the most sadistic creep of 'em all."

Kaleek huffed.

"Come on. The Maker might be stern, I don't know, but He can't be *that* bad. Look at this island! Look at *us*! Someone as bad as you say can't *possibly* make things that are as beautiful as *all this.*"

Kaleek waved her hands toward the jungle around them. A wicked smile spread across Rekke's mirthless face.

"A *very* wise observation, sweetheart. Yet I've watched him rip kids apart with his hands because they *annoyed* him a little. So you tell me: s'that sound like someone full of 'love, care, 'n beauty' like yer villages preach?"

She gestured a hand toward her torso of bare armor and skin, and Tirak noticed for the first time that she had scars on far more than her face. What he had taken for vents beneath her ribcage… Those had to have been some truly deep cuts to only heal back that far.

"Not all these come from a judgment mask, y'know. I come from a whole camp of examples that prove what that sadist's '*help*' looks like. Tried to reintegrate a bunch of us back into productive society or some nonsense. Cybrii like me are the result."

Tirak handed mugs of tea around when Rekke's voice grew quiet. She nodded her thanks his way and smiled briefly. Her ears drooped all the way down to her braided hairline. Watching such a wounded expression twist that tough, beautiful face nearly tore his heart apart.

The wetness in her eyes made him yearn to make her life better. And still she wasn't finished.

"He started off with a really good show of pretending to care. Showered us with gifts and little trinkets to make our lives better. He didn't ask us to fix our ways right out of the gate, but a lot of us were wary of him anyhow. After a few months of us not responding as sickly thankful as he wanted, his intentions became obvious. He grew a little demanding at first… then he cast his disguise off faster than he did us 'unresponsive belligerents.' The… massacre was…"

Rekke shuddered, her voice trailing off.

"I dunno why I survived, to be honest. Shouldn't have. Few others did."

Rekke took a sip of her tea during the long pause, and her eyes went wide. She turned toward Tirak, expression intense, yet hard to read.

And she proceeded to spray the contents of her mouth across his mask.

"Are you *TRYIN'A* poison yerselves?!" she screeched. "That berry ain't a sweetener, hon! *Dark*, you two really *are* stupid, ain't ya?"

She stormed off, leaving them both speechless. Should he try to go follow her? But she reappeared before long, waving something wildly in her hand. A leafy branch slapped his mask and would've fallen into his lap if a few of the sprigs hadn't gotten pinched between several plates. He fumbled the thing out of his face for an embarrassing second while her words continued to rain murder around him.

"This! You see it? Memorize it! Then, *never*! Pick one! A-*gain*! Absolutely stupid…"

And with that, his and Kaleek's chance to show off their survival skills devolved into an afternoon of scoldings, mockery, and at least a few slaps across the back of their heads. Rekke kicked the pot of tea off the spit and let it smash against their makeshift shelter. With a pitiful groan, that became a lump of leaves. They could hardly tell it apart from the rest of the forest floor once the dust had settled.

Rekke paced the campsite for several minutes, fuming. When she returned, she declared that leaving them now would be criminal. She was going to teach them at least a *FEW* basic survival skills, and depending on how well they did, she might even be able to offer them a cozy little camp of scavengers that could shelter them until they learned how to do anything besides commit suicide.

Tirak wanted to say she was being unfair, but his tongue was still too numb to reply without slurring.

Once, she had caught him trying to speed up a task using his unfinished knife. Rekke confiscated both weapons in a heartbeat and promised she would only return them if they managed to prove they wouldn't cut an arm off by accident. Now that really was being unfair. She hadn't even seen their sparring match earlier that day.

But, once again the slurred tongue kept him from earning an extra slap across the head.

She started them with the basics. As soon as they were about to go insane from stripping coarse, fanlike plants into fibers with their bare fingers, she started teaching them how to make strings out of them. From there, Rekke must have taught them a hundred more types of knots than Tirak had ever thought were possible. She tested them on the details of each one with ruthless attention. And whenever they were off balance enough to let their guards down, the lady would fire in a question like a dart between armor plates.

"So, where'd you meet yer girlfriend, Tee-rak? She's such a cutie."

"Ew!" was all Kaleek could say from her place several legs away.

"Kal's more of a… sister. We're not anything like that."

"Oh? And where did you two come from then? I didn't realize any villages were okay with an igni daddy becoming a fish f—"

"Terra," Tirak blurted out, already familiar with Rekke's flavor of word choice. "And we aren't real siblings. Her parents took me under their wing, is all."

Daylight began to fade. Tirak's stomach growled, and he wondered silently when they would take a break to go hunt for supper.

Apparently they wouldn't. More hours passed, but when Rekke finally commanded them to stop, she sent them straight to bed. The two of them looked around stupidly for a bed, but she made it clear they would be spending the night curled up on the ground. Rekke had produced a mattress of dry ferns from seemingly nowhere, but she gave Kaleek a switching across her shins when his sister tried to walk toward the collapsed shelter and its half-decent bedding.

Tirak's stomach kept up its complaints as he fell asleep, as well as each of the few octet times that he stirred to roll from one sore shoulder to the other. He was hungrier than ever when morning dawned. Even his nose kept trying to convince him the smell of frying meat hung in the air, just waiting for him to take a bite.

Tirak sat up and realized he wasn't hallucinating at all. A deer—yes, an entire deer—hung from a spike of metal that spanned a brand new cooking spit above a fire pit much wider than he remembered.

"C'mon and eat. Get your strength back," Rekke invited once she'd noticed him.

He hesitated, searching for the trap hidden inside this new lesson.

"What, you're not gonna make us catch it ourselves and starve for another six hours?"

She scowled. Tirak knew it was an unfair complaint, but he was tired and his head was beginning to pound from its shortage of fire energy.

"Lucky I *ain't* making you, else you'd starve for sure. But this lil' feast ain't a gift, hon. It's a down payment. And don't think for a second I won't earn back every ounce before I let you sleep tonight. So, *eat.*"

She grinned maliciously at him, but the bargain was somehow comforting. It was straightforward, with no tricks. Tirak could appreciate that. He dragged himself toward the fire and gratefully accepted a plate of food. Yes, they had *actual plates* now. They were little more than a flat basket woven into triangles, but they kept the food off the ground no matter how small the chunks were, and only Kaleek's misshapen attempt kept falling apart.

Despite the female's gruff attitude and sharp words, there was a kindness to everything she did that filled Tirak's heart with gratitude for the chance that had led her to them. Had either of them even thought to return her thoughtfulness yet? She deserved to hear it, even if she ended up scowling to keep up appearances.

"Thanks, Rekke," he started quietly, "I don't know what we'd have done without you swooping in to save us. Your skills are really amazing. You don't know how… cool it is to see such a competent female as you out here."

She straightened up and eyed him with a wary expression. His chest tightened. Thinking back, maybe that sounded a little flirty. Had that been a bad thing? Was she trying to figure out if he meant it, or…

"You got a problem with me?" she asked.

"W-what?"

Tirak opened his mouth, about to laugh his nerves away. That *had* been a joke, hadn't it? Then he noticed her arm rising to ready a backhand.

"N-no! Completely serious. Sorry. I just meant… You know… You're really good at all this stuff, and… um, sorry if I…"

Her fingers snapped at him.

"See? That. Right there. Even when yer stumbling over your feet to apologize, it looks like you're mocking me for being too sensitive."

He tried to explain himself, but Rekke's face only grew more stern with each fumbled word.

"Look, just stop, all right? I *want* to believe that what yer sayin is sweet, hon. But, then I look at yer face, and… I just can't help but think it's all a big joke to you. Seriously. If you plan to make *any* meaningful connections, *rip* that silly thing off."

"I *can't*! Its pieces are welded into my face!" He sighed. "Not yet at least. If I do that, there's no turning back… *is* there? I should at least *try* to do what my Elder asked first, and try to rejoin the village before I give up, right?"

Rekke clearly *didn't* agree.

"Sure, go ahead 'n speedrun yer way to makin' the girl watch a monster butcher you for sport," she said flatly.

Tirak was at a loss for words. He shook his head sadly and left it at that.

"Huhhhh… fine. If ya won't take my advice, at least drop yer gaze so people can't see that stupid grin when you talk. *And don' speak nuthin' my way* til you change your mind. And if you even ask me one more stupid question, that mask's won't be the *only* tongue I cut off. *Got* it?"

With that, she turned her back on him and continued tending the pot of roots they had all gathered yesterday. The conversation was clearly over. His shoulders slumped as he sat there in silence. He already felt the loneliness creep back in as he watched her ignore him. It grew like a wall, its pointed shards facing inward toward him. Tirak had half a mind to reach up and start ripping the pieces out one by one.

A particularly large, dirt-caked tuber landed in front of him.

"Something else that'll help is pulling yer weight. May not help you seem any less arrogant, but it'll at least earn ya a reason to let it show."

Exhausted, Tirak tried to get up and do what she said, but… couldn't. He just needed *power*. If nothing else, he needed to feel fire against his skin again. He remembered his parents stoking the family's coals by hand each night. He reached his own hand forward without thinking. It began to warm, bringing him a little relief. So he stuck it in a little deeper. He seized one of the burning logs and held tight.

And suddenly, the fire was inside him. Tirak shook as a buzz washed over him from his arms to his legs and back again. The campfire dimmed to a single curl of smoke. It rose like a black tail in the air, hung there, then slowly fell back to the ground.

A palm cuffed him on the head.

"You put that back this instant. I'm not wasting my energy to re-light it again if you're just gonna steal it."

Kaleek stumbled back from the creek looking as groggy as he felt… or, come to think of it, he didn't feel so bad anymore. He didn't feel great, but the headache was gone just like that.

"Put what back? Tir, stop trying to flirt with everyone."

"Hey! Come on. I do *not*."

"Little twerp just stole my cookfire from me," Rekke added into the mix.

But when he looked, her face wore a smile. Not a cruel one either. Did… wait, did she look *proud* of him? He felt a pleasant flutter squeeze his chest.

"He… what? Ew, wait," his sister stammered. "Is that supposed to have some kind of… *meaning*?"

Tirak frowned at the two girls and wondered just what they'd been talking about yesterday.

Rekke cackled with laughter. "Yer learning, sweetheart! Not this time though, no. Big bro here finally figured out why I've been keeping you two away from elementals."

"Huh? I thought you said they were just hard to find."

"Nah… unless I let you exterminate them all, that is. Tirak just found a better way. Show her, hon—Wait wait! No. Silly me. Relight *my* fire, feed it a *lot* more logs first, then show her."

He did as asked, remembering to keep his head down and avoid antagonizing Rekke. After piling the fire high with fuel, he spent the painful ounce of heat he had stolen to kindle a small spark. It took a while to fan into a full blaze, but it beat trying to use flint sparks. He pulled a few choice branches back out and built a smaller fire near the first one, then stuck his hand inside. Kaleek gasped as she watched the fire eat through all its fuel in seconds without growing even a bit brighter. Ripples of heat flowed around his hands, seeping into his arms as it traveled in a spiral.

She rushed toward him, sliding the last few feet on her knees and stuck her own hand into the center. She yanked it back out less than a second later.

"Ow! That's *cold*!" Kaleek yelped.

Rekke started laughing.

"Fool move, girlie! Could'a told you that myself. As you can see, conduction ain't just about moving yer element from here to there by draining glass shards. Your elements are *part* of you. They seep into yer body as long as you ain't too full, waiting to be used. Don' ask me how it works. All I know is we're good at nibbling on little bits of energy around us and turning it into glass. Once stored, it's ready to be used again when we need it."

Kaleek wrinkled her nose.

"You mean Waterglass is… my poop?"

Rekke put a hand to her chest and made an exaggerated gasp.

"How un-ladylike! We'll make a half decent Scarred outta you yet, sweetie. But nah, don't think of it like that. Think of it more like… well fingernails, I guess. Little bits of extra steel that keep growing until we're able to shape them into something useful. Seriously though, girl, 'poop'? You can do a lot better than that—*need* to do a lot better if you want to be respected out here. Guys are gunna keep punching you down until you prove they won't win."

Tirak didn't like the direction this was going. He knew from his Goldenheart brothers more than enough of the language Rekke was talking about. The less of it his sister learned, the better off she'd be. They didn't plan to get in the way of many people between here and Maker's Grove. It was a good time to turn the conversation around toward something useful.

"Scarred," Tirak thought aloud. "That's what your camp calls themselves, right?"

Rekke paused midway through a statement. The glare she shot his way burned an angry red.

"I thought I told you not to ask stupid questions. Asking me something I've already answered is *downright* stupid."

Kaleek's soft voice moved in to defend him. Maker bless her brave heart.

"Like it's *so* hard to forget, Rekke. You hardly said anything about them. You've told us ten times as much about Mak—"

Rekke's hand shot into the air.

She spoke, her voice stern, "Stop. I warned you once and I hate repeating myself. We're not going *anywhere* until *you* get something straight, sweetheart."

"All right, all right, I mentioned the Guy by accident. I get it, I'll try not to—"

"*Stop*," Rekke stressed again, her voice just barely short of a shout. "Just stop. Before you visit my village and shove yer whole foot into yer mouth, you two *need* to understand this."

She unfurled her legs and gestured for them to follow. The fire fizzled out behind them, its heat streaming toward their tutor's outstretched arm. Kaleek obviously had some retort burning a hole in her tongue. Probably something along the lines of not caring if they did visit her camp. It took Tirak more than a few sharp nudges to keep her from saying it out loud.

"Walk with me," Rekke demanded, "This is clearly somethin' I need to beat into yer faces til it makes it through those stupid masks."

She stormed into the underbrush in a seemingly random direction without saying more. The siblings had to sprint a few paces in order to not get left behind. Only when they had caught up did Rekke continue speaking.

"When he first came across my people all alone out here, that little demon did a good job of hiding what he was. He was arrogant, sure. Confused why we would cut ourselves off from the village fools and hang out in a messy jumble of elements. But he pretended to care too. Offered to help any of us reintegrate with the villages if we wanted to. My ma pushed me to join the group. I was born out here, y'see. Back then, parents tended to make sure their kids looked just like themselves so we wouldn't sneak off."

The sky seemed to darken through the treetops, growing even more grey than usual as they walked. An occasional drop of water began to fall as the last tall fern and vine-draped tree gave way to a stale, green bog. Tirak licked away the first drip that leaked through his mask. Bleh! When had he started sweating so heavily? That one drop had been downright *rancid* with the stuff.

It wasn't until Kaleek lurched back and started sputtering too that he realized it was the rain itself. Salty… rain? Rekke hardly seemed to pay it or their reactions any mind, pausing only just long enough for them to stop coughing and catch up to the next little mound of solid earth that she had leapt to. Rotting trunks and mossy boulders rose out of the water around them like grave markers. It lent the place a creepy feeling. Even the trees that hadn't been choked out yet seemed to be crying with every salty drop. Rekke's own voice had grown soft, vulnerable. A whisper of her normal confidence.

"But you've had some knocks already yerselves. Y'know it's hard to trust again after someone stomps on ya. Most of us were happy right where we were, and told our gracious new benefactor exactly that. He explained over and over that it wasn't his plan for us, that we had important jobs to do, and mumbled his nonsense about ancient enemies."

She stopped in front of a gnarled trunk that was already half rotted. Tirak watched her place a reverent hand against a metal plate in its surface. The whole place had an air of reverent sorrow to it. The sky had become a constant grey drizzle as they approached too. The rain lent tear ducts to every rock and every stump so that they could cry forever. It stung Tirak's eyes and found its way into his mouth the longer they stood there.

"My cousin was the one who joked that we'd rather give ourselves to the Shadows than keep dealing with the villagers' scorn for us. When he heard that, the pretender's little act lifted as surely as if he'd taken off his silver mask. My cousin was with the first group that was going to reintegrate. Instead, he got reintegrated with the ground on the spot. You know what the worst part is? He stood there afterward and tried to apologize for lashing out like nothing big had happened. Covered in fresh blood, he tried to explain himself as if it had been perfectly rational for him to do it. 'The kid was beyond rescuing and would've ended up harming the Plan' and all kinds of snake dung like that."

Rekke's thumb rubbed a thin layer of moss away, revealing a rusty skull's forehead underneath.

"Someday, I'm going to get a chance to find that f …." Her voice drifted into a long string of whispered vulgarity. Most of it seemed anatomy related, with a heavy mixture of mutilation added in.

She looked like she was in agony. Trembling for his life, Tirak rested a hand on her shoulder.

"I'm so sorry, Rekke."

"So you see? Y'might throw that innocent name around and think nothing of it. But every time y'say it, you prop up the lie that he was right to do all this to us. You imply my people—all of us banished—*deserve* to be tortured whenever he wants to."

She lifted her head to look at them both. The redness at the edges of her eyes were from more than the glow of her irises. She sniffed.

"Well. Now you know how stupid you are for hoping to find any redemption in that grove. He doesn't deal in forgiving mistakes, and he certainly don't try to right injustice. This island has no shortage of monsters." Rekke let out a harsh laugh. "I'm related to my fair share of them, but… that place yer tryin'a get to hides the worst of 'em all. Y'see now why I want you t'come our way 'n settle down? You've got nuthin' else for you out there anymore. If y'want a new family, we're here for ya. We understand ya like no one else's gunna. We're not all as ruthless as those villages ya come from."

"I thought you said nothing out here is tame," Kaleek said.

Rekke chuckled. Her voice sounded scratchy from a river of with-held tears.

"Oh, we aren't tame, sweetheart. We just aren't monsters like those village folk. Ignore what the overprotective Elders have been telling you. There are good folk out here that won't bat an eye at judgment masks. You can still live yer whole lives out here and be happy. Dark, but I mean it when I say they'll even help you cut those off, if you want. I remember wearing one for a little while. Worst month of my life."

Maker's Log #87723: An outcast proudly shows off her self-inflicted scars.

An unhealthy fascination with animal forms and their darker tendencies, these social outcasts break my heart to see more than anything else my children get up to. I try and I try, but they see even my best intentions as hateful. I honestly don't know how to relate to them anymore. Am I really getting that old? I guess a couple of centuries can do that, huh? Two centuries. Wow. Have I really held the evil at bay so long? Sleep well, my love. I don't know how much longer I'll last.

Er, what was I saying? Right. Scarred. They seem to get a twisted pleasure from pain. The one pinnacle rule that unites their fractus camps is the rejection of village laws with a violent removal of their own masks. Rather than try to hide their crimes, these gangs make a point of doing as much damage to their faces as possible. On one of my earliest visits to them, I found a child with cheeks so mangled he couldn't even chew food. The disgusting paste he'd scoop into his mouth would leak back out before he could swallow so much as half of it. Yet while he withered right in front of me, the boy adamantly refused that there was anything wrong with him. I… didn't have the stomach to go back after one day, he… was nowhere to be found.

What could possibly drive such a choice?

I did go back, but… my heart wasn't in it anymore. We'd butt heads over every little thing. They were clearly a lost cause. I decided to go back one last time, I'd persuade any of the younger kids I could, and then never return. Most of them were too little to have been masked anyway. Plenty of families in each village that would take them in, LOVE them. They didn't deserve to grow up in a filthy mudpit.

Worst mistake I could've made. I arrived just as they were getting ready to cut open a little girl's face for their twisted "adoption" ceremony. She was too young to heal wounds, barely old enough to stand. I tried to stop their priest. Tempers got hot fast, and soon it was just us. Me. The girl. But… someone had given her the knife. SHE HAD spent the whole battle stabbing herself, and crying. It—

<CRYING> Sorry. I… HATE reliving that day. All that and weeks spent regrowing my infected hands, and I still didn't save her. I made myself a liar, and it gained me nothing. <SNORTING> Some pacifist I am.

…Avoma's log, cycle eighty-seven thousand, seven hundred… SOMETHING since the catastrophe. Twenty-five maybe? I'll check the charts later. Maybe someday I'll figure out what that means in earth days.

9

THE SCARRED

A fog of dreams assaulted Tirak's mind. Fury boiled in his veins. Kaleek tried to hold him back.

"Come on, boy. You know how unfair that is."

Maybe it was, but in the middle of staring down Onok, Tirak found he didn't really care. What did "fair" even mean anymore? He made sure his so-called father knew as much too.

"Really? You want to bring up *fairness* after that mockery of justice you put on in the arena? I'm done here."

He started to turn his back on the infuriating fellow, ready to walk away into the infinite gloomy jungle in front of them. It would still be under Onok's reign until daybreak, but he wouldn't follow them too far away from his stupid cave.

"Tirak... *son*."

The single word might as well have had the whole weight of his dad's shadows inside it. It couldn't have held him in place any more surely even if it had. Just like his powers too, the word had a softness that Tirak couldn't ignore. A softness that could overpower all reason.

"I must be my people's leader above all else," Dad continued. "But that doesn't mean I love you two any less. You don't know how much worse passing this judgment has hurt me than it did yourselves."

A corner of Tirak's lip curled into the start of a sneer. For a moment, he had almost believed he actually meant something to Onok. Him. Not just the idea of a son. Tirak had lapsed for just a moment and forgotten that Onok was a legend, a hero. And heroes all shared the same true love. That single, ever unfaithful mistress.

Power.

"…I was thrust into such a hard place, don't you see? And so suddenly too. I had to decide not only what was right and wrong in the span of a few moments, but I had to figure out what the people of Umbra *thought* was right and wrong, and who would be the least offended by any decision. It's not that I didn't believe you two *at all,* I just couldn't be seen favoring my children over what the city needs. I won't apologize for my judgment. I would do it again if given the choice, too… because I know you both are strong. And as painful as it might be in the moment, I knew that you two would always know that your father loves you. So you two were the only ones who might be offended the least in order to appease the rest of the city. You can't deny that what Kaleek did was heinous."

So it was all about Onok. Of course it was.

"Uh-huh. And you figured that Kal was worth the trade in order to be rid of *me*."

Anger flared up in Onok's eyes. Anger that was more than matched by what Tirak knew his own showed.

"You know that isn't true, boy."

"*isn't* it? I've always just been 'that boy' your daughter dragged in. The little damaged Igni she made you look after. I've never even been a person to you."

Onok stared aghast at having been called out. Whether he tried to put a hand on Tirak's shoulder next, or poke him in the chest, or… Tirak never found out. The weight of it forced him a step backward.

A step onto the leg that enshrined his parents' lives. He ended up in a dusty heap, flat on his back.

Onok muttered something with a croak in his voice as Tirak picked himself back up.

Tirak didn't hear it. He was already walking. The only thing he did hear was the shrill sound of Kaleek's voice ripping into Onok with all the viciousness Tirak had wanted to use. The girl could be rather elequent when she wanted to. A single glance back showed the selfish Elder melting into an almost literal puddle beneath his daughter.

~~~~~

The urge to sniffle lurched him out of his sleep. Tirak stretched in the sticky pre-dawn heat and sat up. The details were getting fuzzy already, but the dream's emotions hung heavy on him, and his nose continued to feel wet.

Tirak looked around and took in his immediate surroundings. He had ended up squeezed between the two girls all night. Those close confines, on top of the jungle's oppressive humidity… Between it all, he had slept fitfully at best. Not that he minded. Rekke really was an intriguing lady to be around. Still, he *hated* feeling sweaty. Especially this gritty, salty sort of sweat. The constant mist drizzling on them didn't help, either. For a Maker-cursed reason Tirak couldn't begin to fathom, it added to the salt instead of washing it away.

Who'd ever heard of salty rain anyway? Tirak remembered his parents telling him about the Weeping Forest once, but he had always thought it was another one of Maker's fairy tales, like glass megacities and Uniform-corn horses.

Tirak tried another futile time to wipe his face clean. He stopped, remembering what Rekke had been teaching him to do the last few days. He really was stupid. Someday it would become another reflex for him, but until then…
~~~~~

He closed his eyes, concentrating on the air he felt around him. He separated it in his mind from the heat that was bothering him. Then he drew that latter part toward his chest. When he opened his eyes again, the air was rippling like the top of a chimney. For a few seconds, the awful warmth intensified. Then it faded.

He felt cool, finally. His body shivered. Okay, maybe a little too cool, actually. His hand, more damp than ever, tried to pull his shirt tighter around his chest. It clung to him, dragging uncomfortably across skin and snagging on corners of armor, soaked through.

Fanning himself didn't work either. Moisture continued to bead up across his armor. His skin felt no less damp. He stared down at his clothes, absolutely dumbfounded.

A haze was beginning to obscure his toes. Yes, an actual cloud of mist was pooling around them. Tirak had never seen anything like it. What was going on?! Tirak wasn't secretly part limni too… was he? Why was he controlling water—

And, he was beginning to cough on his own condensation. Another voice coughed next to him. No, no, no. He needed to fix this before Rekke woke up!

"Tirak…?" His sister groaned.

Then, the voice he dreaded hearing. "Aw, sweetheart. What the Dark are you *doin*? It's freezing! Y'know, there are *far* better ways to help someone get a little—"

"I-I didn't mean for it!" he cried, leaping to his feet.

The mist kept sinking toward the ground instead of following him, but a new pool was already growing around Tirak.

"This place is so humid I'm dying! How do I make it stop doing this?"

"Golly, I have no idea." Rekke's voice was laced with mockery. "Maybe stop *causing* it."

She got up and wrapped Tirak in a warm hug. Warm as in a wave of heat flashed across his skin. His face began to sting with the not-quite-forgotten pain of the branding iron. Water steamed off them both with a chorus of hisses and sizzles.

"Better?" Rekke asked quietly.

He nodded. She… had her arms wrapped around him. He should say something, right? Before his brain completely shut down? He knew he needed to.

"Y-yeah… Thanks," he forced out.

The female gave his hair a playful tussle with her fingers.

"Y'still got a lot to learn about fire, kiddo. Better brush up before you need to do something like that on purpose."

Tirak's cheeks flushed with embarrassment, but the ribbing was already over… after one final pat on his head, of course. Rekke walked away and started whipping the morning into shape around her. Efficiency was in her every step. He counted off the days as he jumped in to start helping her, then grinned. Today was when she had promised to let them visit the camp of outcasts she kept telling them about. They would *finally* be around real people again… and then there was the unspoken offer to let him and his sister stay forever; to join up with them.

He still wasn't sure how he felt about letting someone snap off his judgment mask piece by piece. No choice but grit his teeth and bear it, he supposed. Rekke said that not even a single person had been kicked out since they had founded the camp. No one lived in fear that they might do something wrong. No one worried about whether they might lose everything tomorrow and be forced to invent a new life for themselves. That kind of safety would be more than worth the trade.

Not just safety, *healing*.

Soon, Kaleek joined them and took over hauling water up from the stream. Tirak was grateful for a break to sit down and pound tubers into a sticky hash paste instead. He watched her trudge sluggishly to the water's edge. She stared down, her posture blank except for a sullen frown. With a burst of motion, she threw aside the bucket and stuck her hand into the surface.

Tirak craned his neck a little higher, and must have caught Rekke's attention. She turned to watch as well. He nearly called out to ask if Kaleek had found anything when the surface began to ripple and swell.

A crystal-clear column rose into the air, wavered, then tilted sideways. It grew toward them with rapid purpose. The farther its head got from Kaleek, however, the faster it churned. It was practically foamed white before it reached even halfway to them. The head split into a spray of glistening beads and fell like rain. The effect cascaded all the way back to the edge of the stream before his sister could get control of it again.

Water slammed down all around her, playing havoc with her clothes. He blushed and looked away as her heavily layered shirt started to ride up her back.

Rekke didn't look away, though. A frown turned into an unreadable half-grin. It wasn't that the sight was *immodest*, per se. After all, Maker had designed them all with modesty built right in. It just wasn't polite to look when someone felt the need to wear clothes. But Rekke wasn't one for politeness, he already knew.

For Kaleek's part, she was wholly focused on the failed goal now. A new mound of water built its way skyward, and this time the air began to warp and shiver around the column too. The serpent curved sideways with even more grace than before. Tirak felt his eyes rise up his forehead as its clear surface started growing spines. It slithered its way toward their cooking area and deposited itself, bit by bit, into the much larger basins they would drink from, cook with, and even wash up with today. Every last drop found its place with precision.

"Say, girl. That pattern on yer back is quite fetching," Rekke called.

Kaleek was shaken out of her trancelike focus and realized they had both been watching. She hurried to adjust her shirt and cowl.

"Aw, don't worry about that. I don't even bother with a shirt half the time. That color though… bit pale to be limni, ain't it?"

Kaleek's whole body went rigid, eyes wide inside the sockets of her mask.

"Yer a hybrid," Rekke finished the accusation.

She laughed as his sister shrank down further. Droplets shimmered in the air as they leapt from her in every direction. Instead of falling to the ground, they hung in a line in front of her. They formed a shaft in seconds, a sharpened point facing Rekke. Frost turned it solid a moment later. Kaleek's face was turned upward, anger burning a vivid blue in her eyes.

"Tell anyone else, and I'll make sure you never have a heart to heal with again."

"Oh, ya poor thing, I didn't mean it like that. In fact, I think it's all the more reason you two'd fit in nicely with my camp."

Kaleek reeled as if the statement had been a kick to the face. Barely a heartpump passed before she nudged the icy arrow tip forward again, doubling down with her glare.

"So it's lies now, too."

"Look," Rekke sighed, "I better not go into it yet, but you might practically be worshiped. Air 'n water, huh? Sounds like a pretty strong combo, if ya ask me. Gonna have to watch my back around you. Y'might jest snap up all the boys before I even get a chance."

True to word, Rekke didn't explain any further, but that didn't stop her from telling them about everything else to expect in the Scarred camp as they dug into breakfast. She kept on talking even as she began commanding them through breaking camp for the day.

A particularly interesting topic started when Rekke's ears came up again. She kept twitching them above her head, purposefully drawing attention toward them. Okay, that was it. He was dying to know now. If she gutted him, it'd be worth it.

"So, are those natural?" He gulped and tried to back his way out of the question when she whirled on him, "N-no no I mean, uh, were you born with them, is all. They look so pretty, so they can't be defects. They have to be part of your Nature, right?"

Her expression relaxed. Had he just managed to say something that didn't make her fly into a fit of rage? That would be a first in *days*.

"Ding ding ding. Boy's got some brains in there after all. Must've been hiding somewhere down in yer left thigh I guess. All them scars must make it hard to think most of the time. Yer right, though. I'm using my Nature right now, and I appreciate you noticing its *undeniably stunning* beauty. If you've figured out anything about me by now, I'm sure it's that I love control. So, this is a little game I play."

Kaleek had outpaced them a few steps, tracking some new prey animal in the trees. It left the two of them side by side. Rekke leaned in even closer, close enough that Tirak could hear the purr vibrating under her breath as she whispered softly enough that only he could hear.

"Not only is it a hard balance to hold, it brings so many extra... games with it. You've noticed the way you can react when yer Natural, right? The way everything feels so much more alive that way?"

Tirak nodded, remembering some of the fights where he had used it. The memories rarely ever made sense when he played them back. Just a powerful sense of hate, or joy, or determination, or...

"Holding yourself halfway into molting is almost as strong, but you stay almost as smart too. It's absolutely..."

He let out a shiver as Rekke traced a finger across the back of his neck. He could practically feel the rumbling purrs in her chest through the few fingers of air between them.

"De-licious... Try it sometime. You'll see..."

Suggestions that brought color to Tirak's face aside, the three of them were soon on their way. The conversation moved right alongside them, winding and curving in new directions in the same way the crags and underbrush changed their path. Kaleek and Rekke were hitting things off better than ever today, too. They spent most of the trip chatting in low tones, only occasionally roping Tirak into the conversation. The lady claimed to be intent on "toughening the pipsqueak up some," and the topics kept his sister in an almost constant blush.

A scent of smoke eventually reached his nose. With it came smells of bread, roasting meat, and other, less pleasant things that all announced they were finally getting close. Tirak had just convinced himself they might not be as close as he thought when Rekke's hand rested against his back. She shoved both siblings out into an unexpected clearing without as much as a warning. Two guards stood in front of a spiky wooden gate, the face of each more twisted with grey scars than Rekke's was. Both of the guards immediately kicked a spear up into waiting hands as they came alert. Two metal tips were leveled at the siblings' chests. Rekke sauntered past before any of them—siblings and guards both—had quite caught up with what was happening. She nudged the spear tips downward and effortlessly shoved open the gate doors. To Tirak's eyes, she stood framed by that entrance like a queen from Maker's legends, beckoning them to enter her domain.

"Welcome to the village, kids!"

Kaleek's hand slipped into Tirak's as they followed inside. Several burly looking sentries nodded toward Rekke as they passed. Their heads almost seemed to bow with the gesture. Tirak suddenly eyed the female as he rethought everything he knew about her. She must have been far more respected around here than she was letting on.

"Down, boy!" Rekke called out.

Rekke was just slapping away an unseen claw that had been reaching for … Tirak jumped when he noticed a corner of Kaleek's skirt between the creep's fingers. He tried to rest a protective arm on her shoulder and huddle closer, but his sister shrugged him off.

"It's all right, Tir. I'd be looking for anything else to touch besides myself, too, if I were him," Kaleek said loudly.

Guffaws followed them for several paces. Tirak knew a glare must have been burning into the backs of their heads, and couldn't help a glance over his shoulder. Instead, he saw the sentry wearing a look of surprised amusement. He gave the trio an appreciative nod before they rounded a collection of tents and he disappeared from view. But before they did, Tirak noticed a few heads turn and start whispering intently.

Curious, Tirak eyed his tour guide's beautiful ears and wondered if he could imitate those features. Maybe that was how she always knew exactly where the two of them were when she wasn't looking. He trailed a little behind the other two. Just enough to let him focus on that feeling of change that drew out the animal inside, without either girl noticing. His Second Nature crept toward the surface like a starved kitten. It sensed no danger, no reason to emerge, and that made it hesitant to go further.

He tried to force himself into the change, but it shrank away. A few more seconds of coaxing, and finally he felt it start. Fur sprouted around his eyes, and a sharp hunger replaced the almost comfortable grumble he'd ignored all morning. Light and shapes became less focused, and a thousand smells and other senses started to overwhelm him.

No no no, this was all wrong. Too much. He backed off the feelings and mentally stroked his Nature until it had all but retreated again. Only a third, hypersensitive ear remained, tucked carefully into his hairline where it would hopefully be hard to notice.

Tilting the ear back toward the camp's entrance, he could once again hear several guards making fun of the humiliated pawn. A few colorful statements were thrown around about the "new girl," but all of them were tempered with warnings not to try it.

"Rekke doesn't bring in pushovers," he heard one of them say.

And then, too many voices between them made the air an impossible cacophony to focus on anymore.

Tirak began to choke on a sudden flood of relief, anxiety, and pride. Kaleek had practically knocked them all flat! But were they afraid *enough*? Or had she just become a fascinating challenge to them? How closely did he need to watch Kaleek's back for her now? Halfway through the jumble of thoughts, his eyes brushed across a girl who was stretching sheets of cloth out to dry. She gave him a smile-filled wink.

Fire burned in his cheeks. He caught himself taking a half step toward the alley-like gap between tents. What was he doing? He shook his head and let go of his Nature. This was way too dangerous to keep playing with. How did Rekke not go crazy doing this *every day*? Still… Tirak could see the appeal of it too. The memory of everything he had just felt lingered with him long after his Nature had retreated. It was intoxicating.

Tirak turned back toward the girls. Rekke's mouth moved for several seconds before his mind had caught up with what was happening. His sister nudged him and repeated the question.

"Tir? Hello-oo… You mind if our babysitter dumps us on some family for a while? She has something else to attend to that's just sooo important she can't be bothered."

"Hey, watch it, Twerp," Rekke shot back. "I still have time to tell the leaders you aren't Scarred material and get you kicked out."

The words sounded harsh, but then, her casual grin showed there were no teeth behind them.

Rekke deposited them at the entrance of a slightly larger than average tent that bubbled with giggles and the stern voices of two haggard parents. The accents even seemed igni. To Tirak's happiness-starved ears, it sounded like the myths of afterlife inside.

A round face poked out of a window-gap-thing and stared at them.

"Mama! Aunty Rekke brought some weird people again!"

Rekke rolled her eyes and gave the little disembodied head a light shove.

"Wo-oah! AAAH!"

A crash sounded from inside the next second after the head had disappeared.

"Hekol!" a young and motherly voice yelled. "No climbing on the cupboards!"

A stout, female head with only a few thin scars highlighting it poked out of the tent's real door and beckoned them all in with hospitality in every worry-line. She and her mate instantly started busying themselves to make the three travelers feel at home, though Rekke stayed just long enough to tell them about her adventurous last few days.

"So," the father said, joining them on a wide dining rug and crossing his legs. "You two're thinking about whether to settle down here? Can't say it's a bad place for it. Better than half the villages, really. We have our occasional spats between families, but we all care about each other at the end of the day."

"Plus, the both'a ya sure will turn a lotta heads," the mother tacked onto her mate's implications.

"Ooooh, I bet Siwa would *love* you, Tirak. She's always making eyes at the older boys. She's my big sister, by the way."

The boy's mother finally managed to hush him with a growing chain of harsh words, but her smile had a *certain smirk* to it too.

"Th'boy ain't wrong. Our girl's a pretty thang, and no I ain't just sayin' that cause she's mine. And she's sure to fancy *you*. She's out checking traps with the other gals right now, but I won't shoo you away if ya wanna stay for dinner."

She topped the suggestion off with a wink. Tirak took it all in stride, deflecting the comment with a good-natured smile. The jokes made it feel just like "home" among the families of Low Tier. And the uncomfortably serious edge to them was even more so. Ignii were nothing if not forward.

The longer they all talked, the stronger Tirak felt tempted to just stay and forget about the "Maker's Quest" Onok had sentenced them to. And why shouldn't he, anyway? Umbra hadn't ever held anything for him besides the Goldenheart gang. And Kaleek? That cave had *less* than nothing to offer her. A couple of friends she despised and that was it. So what if she wanted to be "the island's greatest heroine" or whatever? Let her become that out here.

The two Scarred parents had spent the last few minutes warning them about some of the more contentious topics and people to avoid around camp while Tirak pondered. The latest warning dragged his attention back in. They had said something about an "Eldest One"? Surely that couldn't have meant Elder Biri. She already had her own village to look after.

"… though when you get a group of everybody *else's* castoffs, it's only obvious you'd get a high number of crazies. Most of them are benign. Really, Jak 'n Floki are the only two you gotta avoid."

"They have no idea who that is yet, love," the female reminded her mate.

"Oh right, well I can point them out at the next meeting we bring you to. Anyway, the rest of the leaders are actually pretty understanding. They know us common folk don't care about the Light & Dark mumbo jumbo and just wanna live our lives. Other than a little induction ceremony to officially join us, you don't have to worry about any of the worship stuff if you don't care for it. Lots of us don't."

The father must have noticed Tirak's attention only now coming back. Kaleek's posture, meanwhile, remained distant. She did her best to ignore the conversation by drawing different shapes in the furry carpet that spread from end to end of the tent. The male cleared his throat.

"Anyway… I didn't mean to drag the conversation down with that boring stuff. I really am serious though when I say that's all the worst you have to worry about around us. We're nice folks, and I don't mean this little cluster of tents neither."

Tirak nodded at his words and nudged Kaleek. She glared back at him for smudging one of her lines.

"What about you, girl?" the dad asked. "I can think of at least three really nice boys you could meet, if you're interested."

"I don't need a boy."

Her words were laced with ice. Tirak and Hekol's father both looked awkwardly between each other, the latter forcing out a chuckle to smooth over the room's tension.

"Er, okay. I mean, if that's the way it is, we could also introduce you to a few—"

"People just get in the way," Kaleek spat. "I'm not stopping until I've put every other Elder to shame for masking me. They'll all bow out of respect once I'm the greatest heroine the island's ever seen."

And there it was. If he was being honest, Tirak was a little surprised to hear her say it out loud too. He had always known she was driven, and a bit of a recluse, but surely that was just because Umbra never had any other water types like her? Or not, he supposed. This was something more. Did she think *he* was in the way too? Maybe he should ask her sometime when they had a quiet moment.

"W-well, a heroine still needs a cute darling waiting for her back home, right?" the dad kept trying.

Kaleek snorted harshly.

"You can drop the flattery and lies. I'm fine knowing the whole island hates me. I don't like them either. It's not going to stop them from respecting me."

Okay, yup. Tirak *definitely* needed to have a chat with his sister about some things, and soon. The surprised silence stretched on for several minutes. But small butts start to fidget when things get too quiet, and Hekol was no different. Sure, he knew there was a tense, pointedly grownup energy hanging over the room, but Tirak could see him care less and less with each second. Soon, his eyes brightened with some new topic to spring on them all.

"You know what makes heroes look even more tougher? Scars! *All* the biggest and best warriors I've seen have them. Did you know, Onok's *whole right arm* is nothing *but* scars, and look how tough he is! Lots of people around here are warriors too. You'd fit right in!"

"I don't *want* to fit in. I'm going to make sure I'll stand out forever," Kaleek growled softly.

Even his mother tried to cut in, "Hekol, sweetheart, let's not jump to conclusions about…"

But the boy didn't hear. He had obviously been bridled for long enough. His own torrent of words was deaf to anything outside of his own mouth. His mother stepped away and left her guests to their enthusiastic fate.

"Mama says you can only hang out with the warriors if you join and get your face scars like the other adults. She says it hurts a lot, but

I don't mind! I can handle a to-ooon of pain! Besides, nobody ever complains about it afterward, so it can't be *that* bad. I'm gonna join the moment Eldest One says I can! You guys are *sooo* lucky. I bet you're old enough to join any time you want! Shoot. You could probably do the scarring ceremony *tonight*! You totally should if they ask you!"

The matron of the home reappeared from the next compartment over, carrying a wooden tray spread with all sorts of food. As she handed bowls and serving dishes between everyone, she held her gaze on Kaleek.

"That reminds me… Rekke told me yer a rather special girl. She said you have some wind in you, but… clearly your armor is mostly blue…"

The little boy began to bounce on his knees, jostling his food until it started to spill.

"You're a hybrid? Twin elements? You really really are? Wowww! I've never met one before. Is it true you're two times more powerful than anyone else? What kinds of things can you do with two powers? Aunty Rekke says the more power someone has, the easier they can give themselves to the dark masters. I can't believe you're so incredible!! I wanna see you do something *reeeeeally* cool! Can you show me? Canyoushowme?"

The longer the boy talked, the less intelligible he became. But his energy shattered the last of the moment's tension. Kaleek opened her mouth to answer several times. It was soon clear that he wouldn't give her the chance. The four adults began to chuckle as both parents took turns trying to calm their son down.

The reaction had taken Tirak by surprise though. And by the way Kaleek's cheeks were blushing around her mask's edges, the same was true for her too. Since when did anyone get *excited* to meet a polluted, two-element… well, *freak*. Sure, there were the bedtime stories about the romance between Maker's first and last Elders, but everyone knew that was just fairy-tale love. Biri and Onok hated each other now. No one was *actually* stupid enough to spit in Maker's face and start that kind of family.

Or, apparently some were.

The mother finally wrangled Hekol into an arm lock and got him to quiet down… *enough* to hold a conversation again. She reached out a hand and gave Kaleek a caring prod.

"It's true. Hybrids are practically legends out here. I've only heard of a couple before, but both of them went on to lead whole camps of their own. Hybrids have a way of catching the master's eye. Their strength makes them perfect vessels for heroics."

Kaleek was staring at her, a thoughtful frown slowly creasing her face like the cracks that it spread between the segments of her mask. The matron must've noticed at some point and stumbled on her words near the end. It took her a hesitant second before she could finish the thought out loud. Kaleek's mask turned her storm-filled face into a muted, impassive thing that stole the breath from anyone who gazed into it for too long.

As the couple continued trying to explain things—and Hekol interjected his own hyperactive two shards on every topic—Tirak wondered what could be bothering his sister. He had to admit to some curiosity about this master that was some kind of opposite to Maker, but Kaleek had been acting standoffish since they had entered the camp. The talk of power and fame was obviously appealing to her, but still she acted like someone was trying to slip poison into her soup.

Kaleek's teeth began to screech as they ground against each other, metal on metal. She was shaking with frustration. Tirak reached a hand toward her shoulder, but just at that moment, a familiar voice cut in from behind them.

"Well Dark, kid's got a better sales pitch than I do, don' he? Gonna put me outta business at this rate, Hekol."

Rekke leaned against one of the posts holding up the tent's entrance, casual as always. The boy bounced to his feet and was hopping around her in the blink of an eye.

"Aunty Rekke! Did you ask them? Did you ask the leaders? How many more months till I get my scars?"

Rekke laughed the question off with an appropriately vague answer.

"C'mon, kids. Leaders said it's all right to show you around as long as you still plan on joining us. They already talked it over with Eldest and everything. And guess what, Hekol?"

Rekke crouched down, hands braced on her knees to reach the boy's level as he went statue-still. A mischievous gleam was in her eye.

"I was able to pull some strings, and Eldest said he *might* just let you join early along with Miss Kaleek and Mister Tirak here. The Master wants you at the ceremony tonight anyhow."

Something in the corner of Tirak's eye caught his attention. Hekol's mother was just wiping away an odd expression. Had that been concern? The grimness of a mother seeing her children grow up, perhaps? Whatever he had seen, it was already gone. As for Hekol, he turned into a small fire tornado of excitement at the news… minus the actual fire part. The orange and red, mixed with the candlelight, still made the effect pretty believable.

Kaleek pushed herself onto her feet, naturally interrupting the previous mood with her cloudy attitude.

"Sure, let's go. Why not," she answered Rekke. "Anything as long as we aren't sitting around."

Tirak flashed an apologetic smile toward the hospitable family.

"Uh, sorry, but we probably *should…*"

The dad laughed. "Hah, don't worry! Go on and give it all some thought. You've got time. Just don't stress it and I'm sure you'll make whatever choice is right for you."

"Thanks. It was nice meeting you. I really mean it. And uh, maybe I can take a rain check on that dinner with you all sometime?"

"You're welcome any time, Tirak." The mother waved them off with a laugh.

Satisfied that the mother's meaningless flirtation had been answered and courteously postponed, Tirak felt safe to forget that any of it had ever happened. It was good at least to know the Scarred weren't some alien culture of their own. Ignii were still igni, and parents of young girls still looked out for them with all their hearts. A good place, all in all.

Rekke's brief second tour went by in a flurry of tents, fire pits, and more faces which all bore the same twisted grey markings as the ones they had already met. The place was practically a small village of its own. The tightly packed rows of tents more than making up for the clearing's small size. Everything looked rugged, but in a surprisingly comfortable way. Sure, these people might not have all the finest catches from the deep water off the coast, or all the same trinkets that he was used to seeing, but Tirak had been fed up with those sorts of luxuries and comforts for a long time now anyway.

Most of all, Rekke kept flashing him those looks. Those half-hidden smiles. All he really wanted was to know what was going on inside that beautiful, yellow head.

Her lips moved as they stopped near another tent, where a much older couple waved to them and smiled.

"So what do you kids think?" Rekke asked.

"It's… incredible!" Tirak admitted. "How did I never know about your people before?"

"We're all the same people, hon. We Scarred just aren't allowed inside villages, and I take it you've never really left Terra before."

"Actually, my parents lived out of a wagon on the roads when I was little. Mostly around Limna too. I…"

He started to realize what he was saying. Cold sweat threatened to condense on his skin. Had he really just given up their whole cover story? As if his blunder hadn't been bad enough, Kaleek had to go and call attention to it.

"*What?* No you didn't, your parents were… wait, what? Why don't I know about that?"

Well, with *that* reaction, she might as well have screamed that they were lying. Wait! Confusion. That was actually good! They were both kids, there was no telling whether they knew what their theoretical parents had been up to before they were born. He could still work with this. Rekke's eyes already seemed a little more suspicious than before, however. But how did Kal really not know about that detail? Shouldn't she have picked up on his slip into the truth right away?

"Yeah, didn't I tell you about it? Ohhh… now I remember, you were what, four moons when we moved to your street. I keep forgetting you're a *lot* younger than me."

A pink tongue shot at him from around her mask's beak-knife. Thank the Maker, it looked like Kaleek was playing along now.

"Okay, okay cool it, you kids. Or… dry off, Kal. Or whatever expression you fish use. Look, I'm *sure* your life history is fascinating, kid, but frankly I'm on a schedule today. Would love to hear about it some other night, but… well that brings us back to my question: You've seen what it's like here now. Am I going to start seeing you around here after today, or are you really going to keep chasing that fool's errand?"

Tirak looked at his sister. He hadn't needed much convincing after that family had greeted them near the gate. *Her* face, though… it was a riddle of uneasy thoughts to him. What could she possibly not have liked about the Scarred? Was it their unfortunate name? She had never been one to shy away from earning a good scar in the past. In fact, she still wore that old gash across her eyebrow with pride.

"If we did…" she started quietly, "we would never be able to see Dad again."

Tirak scoffed. *Onok*? Was that really what she was worried about?

"How is that a bad thing? He had his chance and shunned us. Don't forget: it's *his* fault we're here at all."

"I dunno, Tir. He's still our—my dad …"

Her voice trailed off, and something in her expression told him his argument was slowly winning in her head. Rekke rolled bored eyes at them.

"Welp, I can't stand around here forever. We're welcoming some camp kids into the fold tonight if you want to join us. If you decide not to meet Eldest One with them, even to wait a week before deciding, I'll have to show you outside. Don't worry though, leaders said I could stick with you outside a few more days if yer undecided. Talk it over, and either meet me under that huge tree or make sure you aren't inside when the gates close."

Hmm, that was a new name to Tirak. He knew of the Maker and the village Elders. This "Eldest One" couldn't be Maker, given how much they hated him. Could He have some dark twin that the stories never talked about? The Darkness was something else, wasn't it?

"Yeah, Kal and I will do that. We'll see you in a bit."

Kaleek glared, but didn't contradict him. Clearly, it was decided. They looked awkwardly between each other for several minutes, each waiting for the other to start talking. In the pause, Tirak noticed some other family observing them from their tent nearby. He hadn't known what he expected from a camp full of criminals, but three toddling children dancing around their parents without a care in the world hadn't been very high on the list.

The couple greeted them from a distance with warmth in their smiles. The mother yawned and stretched against her companion. Suddenly, Tirak felt a yearning for a life as simple as that. He felt a small tear form as, for a moment, his mind replaced their faces with his own and that of a certain glassforger's daughter. He imagined those kids with Sara's golden hair, her orange glow in their eyes. But… no. Even if he was allowed back into Umbra, one day, he had probably burned that bridge. She would never be able to stand him, now. Well, he could settle for such a life here, instead. They had walked almost the entire camp, and no one looked out of place or ignored. Everyone was *part* of something here, *together*. Surely, there was a place for him too. Rekke had sworn as much. He wanted that.

He supposed that wasn't fair though. It wasn't the same, but Kaleek and he had always been there for each other. Had always been ready to lean on each other. And now more than ever. Now, with strength in her toned muscles and her outfit and posture yelling confidence at the top of its lungs. They were their own kind of partners, weren't they? But they could be part of something more too…

"Well, let's go become a part of something again."

He took a few steps toward the direction Rekke had pointed out, but Kal only lagged behind, tugging against his arm. They continued on anyway. She would come around after a while. Everyone else was already walking this direction too. It only made sense to go along with them all. Nothing could go wrong.

People seemed to join a stream of bodies as they approached the center of camp. Surely the villages couldn't have banished so many others. And Rekke had said this wasn't the only camp that followed the Scarred's way of life. Tirak itched at his shoulders. The salty rainfall was constant here. Who had ever heard of such a thing? He had always thought the Weeping Jungle was just a myth.

Kaleek lagged even farther behind as they neared a massive willow tree. He paused, waiting for her to catch up.

"What's wrong, sis?"

"You mean besides their disgusting faces?"

A few nearby cybrii chuckled as they passed, but Tirak glared. It wasn't like her to be this rude. Onok had taught them both better.

She sighed, continuing, "Something just feels… gross here. I don't know! I can't explain it, Tir. Can't we just go? I really don't want to stay."

"Whoa. That's pretty unfair of you, Kee. Everyone we met so far today has been nothing but nice to us. Didn't you like Hekol's family? And Rekke? I thought you liked her. It's probably just the salt that feels gross. We can live on the farther edge of camp if you want. It's much more fresh over there."

Kaleek gave him a sideways glance. She opened her mouth a couple of times to say something, but kept stopping short, chewing on her tongue instead. Should he just push her to say it, or…

"Do you *really* think she's interested in you like that? No offense, bro, but she can do way better than you with all the looks she gets. She's clearly just fishing for more gullible recruits."

"Um… okay, *ouch*," he said. "Second, whatever gave you that impression? You know I'm here for you, sis. Nothing matters… til we…"

He trailed off beneath her emotionless stare.

"You're seriously going to stand there and deny it? Bro, you're more obvious than a construction sign. You've been shooting 'I'm blushing now' glances at her for the last three days."

Tirak didn't respond. Maybe she was right.

"It's more than that, Tir. Look at the faces around us. *Really* look at them. I… I don't know how else to say it…"

"All right, I'll try to look. I'll keep my eyes open. Let's just catch up with Rekke and decide what to do when we get there."

Kaleek didn't look convinced. For a moment, she didn't budge either. Maybe it was just the tree that was spooking her. It *did* have a slightly creepy, twisted shape to it, he supposed. The rotted burn marks twisting up its hollow core didn't help either. Combine that with the dancing torch lights underneath its woven root system, and he could see how a younger girl like Kaleek might feel uncomfortable. He reached out for her hand.

"C'mon. You've faced worse challenges than this, Kee. Let's face this one too. It'll be worth it. Just watch."

She let out a long, conflicted sigh.

"Promise?"

"I promise," he said.

Maker's Log #30910: A wrecked mech leaks coolant onto a field of jagged glass that shimmers teal-white.

Did I do the right thing in drowning us all? Should I have stayed my hand when I had the perfect opportunity to wipe them out?

I did it for you, my Light. They deserved so much more for your sake alone. But… every day since, I've asked myself, "Was it really the right thing?"

The hate I felt that day makes me shudder. If I had been just a little stronger, I would've cast aside my mask then and there, even though it would kill me. You don't understand how sick it made me to see my own carnage. I keep thinking how many innocent lives I must have ruined along with the rest. Surely some of them weren't monsters. Yet all of them are equally dead now.

How can I ever repay such a debt as that? Do I even deserve to try?

No, Avoma. Stop thinking like that. You're not the only one you're fighting for. Her friends—void, YOUR friends—are still down there.

<SIGHING>

Still. A single thought back to that day is enough to make me remain a pacifist forever. I'll never lash out like that again.

10

HOUSE CALL

Tirak numbly flipped to the next page of the little journal he had picked up. He wasn't taking in much of what he read, but he also hadn't realized it yet. The emotional whiplash of the last few days still made him dizzy, and grounding himself on each bizarre new thing his eyes fell on helped him stay upright. Collections of alien-looking trinkets were each organized all around him, each into their own little shelf of wood. Column upon column, row after row meandered this and that way around the room.

How long would they have to wait for the Maker to greet them?

He glanced at the ceiling again, trying to distract himself from the bitterness inside. The sight above him worked. He shuddered. Surely all that loose dirt was going to collapse, crushing him and Kaleek without a moment's warning. But no, it wasn't dirt, despite the twisting, turning tree roots that grew out of it and overlapped one another with no order to them whatsoever. It was a clean, polished stone that rose in a dome. Or Tirak assumed it did. It was honestly hard to tell between all the mess.

Even more strange, dozens of little yellow shards grew right out of the roots' smallest ends, lighting the room with a comfortable glow.

Comfortable as long as he didn't try to see with shadow vision, that is. The crystals weren't all that bright, but when he had tried to switch his vision to see into a poorly lit corner of one shelf, the pain had felt like a boot to the nose.

As for the roots themselves, they were just as clean as the stone. He had no doubt they were still perfectly alive though. Something about the study felt like a blinding yellow version of Umbra city. Everything ordered in a perfect chaos.

The feeling made him powerfully homesick.

Tirak flipped the page again and finally noticed something that caught his eye. A field of airglass shards with some kind of robot coated in moss and flowers in the middle. It was beautiful. He could almost imagine it was the same place he and Kaleek had camped, long before the rainforest had grown over it. Had the island's legs always been split into the biomes that he knew so well? Tirak realized he had no idea.

His eye stopped on another detail. The writer seemed to be talking in overly poetic language. The kind of stuff a guy only uses when he's trying to impress someone he likes. He flipped back to the front cover and re-read it.

To my love, my light when the rest of my life is dark.

Sleep well. I'll keep working until I bring your dreams true. Or else, until I'm asleep next to you.

Great. So it was some mushy nonsense that the Maker was into, not a journal after all. Light forbid, maybe the Old Man even *wrote* it. He screwed his eyes shut and gagged at the mental image of his creator getting frisky. But there *had* been some interesting details in its pages. Ideas that Tirak had never heard of before. The book found its way into his satchel before he thought twice about it, and he started browsing a new shelf.

His casual kleptomania made an image of that little Scarred boy pop into his head again, of him stealing a berry from Kaleek's plate. Tirak stopped and had to blink. His eyes were starting to swim.

Why had he thought about Hekol again? A new wave of sickness washed over him, and before he could help it, Tirak stole a glance at his sister. The poor kid... He had been such an enthusiastic little fellow.

How could Kaleek still be so relaxed after what happened? Killing him hadn't affected her at all! Their escape was a chaotic jumble in Tirak's head, but that one scene continued to play and replay as vividly as his parents' death had.

He watched again as a feeble priest held out a jagged razor to Hekol's palm. Kaleek screamed and tried to yank the kid away. But... but she had panicked at just the wrong time.

Oh Maker. So much blood. The color black was *everywhere*! That rotting, metallic scent again. No, Tirak had to stop. That was in the past. That bridge had burned. He still had his (*murderous*—no, stop that!) sister. That was all that mattered.

He looked around to a new shelf. One trinket here was a pool of sand dotted with stones. Fine metal ridges peeked out of the sand's perfectly combed surface, drawing an outline of the island. Next to it was a sheet of metal stamped with some kind of language. Surprised, Tirak realized he could read it. It told the World Making story that every child knew. How an old hermit had fought back the evil Darkness, then used a stolen fragment of it to create warriors of metal that would stand after he fell. He knew it by heart, but... This version was different somehow. It seemed... more dry perhaps?

Tirak's attention broke when he heard a rush of air somewhere behind him. Long. Drawn out like a hiss.

He glanced at Kaleek, who was only a few shelves over, but she hadn't noticed yet. The rest of the room continued to sit undisturbed too. All except for a life-sized costume whose silver mask rocked back and forth in the unfelt wind ever so slightly. It was a captivating piece once Tirak noticed it. It would've covered a face completely, a trap door for the mouth and smooth pieces of yellow glass set into the eye sockets. Wearing it must've been a death sentence… a thought which made him shiver as soon as it crossed his mind.

Wait. *Unfelt?*

The brief hiss ended. The nonexistent breeze no longer made the mask swing. It was looking directly at him.

"I already *told* Onok not to send anymore of you here!" the statue complained in a muffled, unnatural warble.

Kaleek let out a girlish shriek. The kind that Tirak would have never made, even if he hadn't been looking directly at the source when it spoke. And since he had been looking, he definitely didn't make any sound remotely like that. The statue turned around, supported on a stout cane, and started shuffling away toward a door that now stood open. It waved a hand indifferently when Tirak tried to call out after Him.

"I told him, I won't kill even one more of you. Not even if they bring the Darkness itself down on us all! Go back and tell that fool Elder to cut it out. I exonerate you, or whatever mumbo-jumbo you need to hear… And tell him he's late while you're at it!"

The door started to slide shut behind the Man. Tirak needed to act fast! He doubted they would get another audience with the deity.

"He's *not* late! Elder Onok sent US to take his place!" he yelled.

The door clicked into place, and silence fell on the room while they waited.

"Uhhh… should we go after Him?" Tirak wondered aloud.

Kaleek's answer was to bolt for the doorway. She skidded to a stop, looking for a handle to pull on. But instead, it slid itself open again with an obedient hiss.

They followed it hesitantly into a more comfortably lit hallway of the same polished wood and root-crossed ceiling. At the opposite end, the Maker was hobbling at a completely unfair speed. He disappeared through another door on the right. The siblings crossed the distance in seconds and waited for this door to reopen as well.

A cozy room of intricate furniture—most of it covered in thick, spongy-looking fabric—opened up to them. And only *half* of it was a complete clutter of random sentimental items and half-assembled devices this time. Maker was already settled deep into a ridiculous chair as wide as three or five normal ones, poring over thin white sheets of bark with His back to them. Tirak found a laugh slipping out before he could control it.

"What in Maker's name kinda chair is *that*?"

The Maker turned silent, unamused eyes toward them as they approached.

"I really don't wish to be rude, son, but I need to keep working on this. Unless, you have something more important than the survival of our whole island and everything we hold dear?"

"W-well, sir. Y-you see we were told to come see you…"

"Ah. Right. You'll be wanting some kind of written pardon, I guess."

He snatched up a blank sheet and scribbled a handful of lines across it that *almost* looked like words.

"Here. That should cover whatever…"

"N-no, sir. We… were told you needed—That, um."

Tirak swallowed. Why was it so impossible to speak in front of his Maker? Stories from his youth churned in his head. He could almost imagine the Man snapping two fleshy fingers and dissolving them both on the spot.

"Fine, then. Why don't you come sit down and tell this old man what convinced a couple of young Cybrii with *far* better things to do with their day to come and waste their time on a boring old hermit like myself?"

The question caught them both off guard.

"Um, w-what do you mean?" Tirak asked for them both. "You're *The Maker,* sir! …Aren't you? You aren't just some dusty old male."

Kaleek had gone completely silent around the unfamiliar person. He wondered if it was something about the mask that covered His face, and the way it reflected the color of their own masks back at them. Whatever the reason, it was up to Tirak to take the lead.

The Maker just stared back at them, making a few slight wheezing noises. There was a squint to the eyes—could He be laughing?

"Well, you see, sir… Our dad told us we had to come obtain a quest from you—even before the masks were involved, you see. But now they are, so there's that too now. And…"

"Eh? Wait, *whose* father, exactly? And what does a Judgment mask have to do with anything? I already convinced Onok to hand out his own tasks rather than bother me. In fact… I honestly can't remember when an Elder last sent me someone for a judgment. Ah, but that's not the point, now, is it? You said one of your two's dad sent you here instead of doing whatever balowney Onok gave you?"

Tirak felt himself growing flushed as his head raced to answer the barrel of questions dumped on him. Also, his circuits completely failed to register that word toward the end, but something about it gave him a strong meaty impression.

"W-well no, sir, it's not like that. We—our—I didn't mean *real* dad…"

"Well, what is it like, son? I swear, you're more tongue-tied than a schoolboy who just tripped over his first crush."

The Maker's chuckle was more than obvious now.

"So…" Tirak tried to clear his head and focus. "The two of us are both adopted… well, *were* at least until we got banished… and we got sent to you first of all becau—"

Kaleek's soft voice slipped like an arrow between his words as she leaned forward, partially blocking Tirak. "Elder Onok sent us to answer your summons for the greatest warrior as our punishment. We are here to do whatever you bid. And if we fail, we are to remain exiles forever."

Kaleek finished the curt statement with a respectful nod, then shot a satisfied smirk at Tirak. Annoyed, he opened his mouth to regain some control of the situation, but Maker clearly had other ideas. He blinked quietly at the two siblings, eyes darting between him and Kaleek from deep recesses in that silver face. His mechanical voice made a rough coughing sound. Laughter, maybe?

"He sent me a child… to take the place of a full Elder," the Maker said with a flat tone.

Tirak bristled.

"I'm not! I've been working a full decade," he protested.

Maker tilted His head, and something like a snort echoed out of His mask. He nodded for them to sit in the plush triple-chair across from Him.

"Ten months is still a child, son. You realize how many *thousand* moons I've seen? So, those slackers convinced two… gullible upstarts to come instead of themselves. *Hrmph*, well that's a shame. Isn't it?"

"Huh? What part is, sir?" Tirak asked.

"I was kind of hoping to see Onok again… not just a couple of young miscreants. My plan isn't going to work without the five elements' *masters* at its helm. They're our most powerful by a mile, and I need them to become tenfold stronger still. There's just too much ground to cover if we start from nothing with two like yourselves. Less than nothing, it seems, since you're the only ones from any village to answer the call. But let's not worry about that! Onok sent you, didn't he? So he must have *some* faith in your abilities."

Maker scratched the chin area of His full-plate mask. How did He even switch to His Second Nature with that thing? Maybe humans had Natures similar enough to their regular form that it didn't matter? The rest of Him *did* look pretty fleshy already.

"Still… This plan was going to be impossible enough if we started with the Elders. And with Korma dead at that… There's just too much ground to cover otherwise. Ah, where are my manners? You've got to be wondering what this is all about after spending the whole trip here thinking about it," Maker said.

"Actually, sir, we don't know anything about your quest. Dad—Elder Onok didn't really say much about why we had to come here. He just said we'd been summoned."

"Well, no," his sister corrected. "He *did* say You summoned the greatest warrior from each village, and, well… we *both* got picked because of the way we were banished at the same time."

"What? When did he say *any* of that, Kal?" Tirak asked.

The Maker's friendly laughter cut off any further argument.

"All right, all right. The important part is that my little surprise isn't ruined yet. Good, good… Well, why don't you both follow me further downstairs, then? Seeing how young you are, it'll probably be best for me to start with a little history lesson."

Not waiting for their answer, the figure began walking toward *yet another* door into the room that Tirak hadn't noticed. It was beginning to scare him seeing how many secrets this place held. They could get lost down here with just one wrong turn.

"Oh, don't worry about that, sir! Tirak and I have grown up listening to the island's histories over and over."

"History? Hah! I doubt that, missy. More likely, you heard a bunch of fantastic myths about how I made the world. No, what you're going to need for your quest is the *real* history behind our little home here."

Tirak followed in silence as they continued. Every corner they took awed him in new, unexpected ways. Even this far down, the walls bore the same unbroken wood surface as they had seen lining the upper levels. The sides met the ceiling in an unbroken archway, the obviously living wood looked polished by the magic of time. He needed little convincing about whether he was in the presence of his Maker. Rekke and her clan could go chow on dung patties.

A series of turns led them into tighter, more utilitarian hallways of square corners and rough stone.

"Now, I promise to go into the details in a moment, but to start things off…"

Maker paused to heave open a pair of heavy doors. Lights grudgingly snapped on inside, glowing to life as if waking up from an especially long sleep. Every wall had shelves and rows of benches braced against them, all covered in hundreds of trueglass tubes and shapes of every type. Pipes, dials, and all sorts of gizmos stuck out of the walls at just about any angle they pleased. More lamps flickered around the edges, slowly illuminating the thing that consumed the entire middle of the room.

"You kids—well, all of you, really—just so happen to be my mortal enemy."

Maker swept His hands to the side. The center's lone feature was a glass vat that rose from floor to ceiling. A greenish sludge swirled inside, taking on a faint purple glow that rippled across the surface, like something that had rotted long ago and never quite realized it.

It looked like… like the outlines of a thousand arms climbing over each other to break free. Once Tirak noticed it, the violet outlines were unmistakable. His hand rose to his mouth by instinct.

"Diluted down of course, but that's the beautiful trick of it all. You're my big gamble to get out of this mess. I'm sure you've heard the street market tale of how I 'stole a dragon's scale' and crafted the first Elders. Well, it's kinda true, I suppose. A little embellished, but the basic idea is correct. You inherit most of your traits from the Darkness itself. It, along with some structural additions of my own, is why each of you is grafted from flesh and metal both. True also is the idea that I couldn't tame the Darkness without combining you with the island's animals. You get your Second Natures from that lineage, which is also why each tribe has a unique range of natures …"

It took Him many hours to explain the difference between truth and tale to them. It took so long in fact that Maker invited them to stay the night. There were whole wings of guest rooms and white, uninviting places He called "medical bays." They picked a set of beds and watched while a small swarm of robotic drones dusted them off and changed the thinnest blankets Tirak had ever seen. Maker kept on talking throughout it all, despite all of them growing too tired to think straight anymore.

"So, you see. Your people always joke about the dark hearts inside you, calling each other villains. But it's true. You were built from villains, but…"

He raised a solemn finger in the air.

"That doesn't have to stop you from being heroes. People change with the right encouragement. That's my philosophy. Once you're all strong enough, you can twist the Darkness' own powers back on itself and save us all. Sleep well, children. I have some upgrades to show you in the morning."

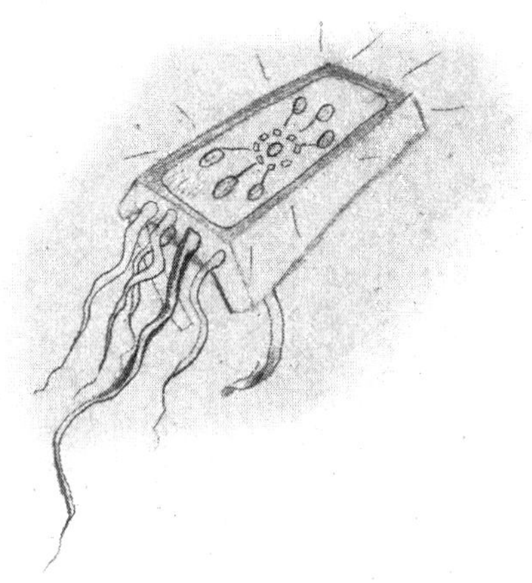

Maker's Log #92181: Mass Transfusion Bracer #001.

I can breathe a little easier for the first time in decades. I can't believe I actually did it! Take THAT, professor Rob. I TOLD you Triune State Theory was more than just another whackjob idea! If it was nonsense, then tell me how I just watched a biological computer crystallize a TERRAJOULE into a bead of glass, then emit it back out as light. We've been approaching the question of whether light is wave or particle all wrong for a millennium! And just like your assistant thought, Anium crystals prove it.

Light isn't either one. IT'S INFORMATION! The Laws of Conservation were only HALF right. I can totally 'destroy' energy if I want to, and light does this all the time. Yes, you can only make energy or matter change forms... UNLESS YOU USE MORE THAN ONE INGREDIENT! Once you start looking at Mass & Energy as not just two sides of a coin, but THREE sides of a pyramid, the job becomes simple.

In the old Asian wars, we learned that atoms could turn into HUGE amounts of energy by splitting them. And even Glass Age crazies tried to stop it, we still get most of our power by doing the same thing carefully. Then with computers, we learned you can create ALL SORTS of information if you sacrifice a ton of energy. But all along, we've only been missing the right tools to do the same with any of the three at will. THAT'S how these crystals grow!

Sure, this violet Anium burns me whenever I touch it. And before you ask, that static you hear is definitely the machine shop and NOT my own breathing after I cut off another spoiled finger before it rots. Yeah... I'll be fine. Mask'll take care of it in... still another hour? Wow.

Sigh. Must be getting old. Bizarre that this tech can repair anything about me for centuries, but not this crystal stuff. Not even a scratch. I still don't understand them, but hey, when has that stopped science?

Anyhow, that's not important. Shadows are coming. So obviously, the best solution is to get my own army of Shadows to start stuffing themselves on all the power they can. I sent the invitations what... two weeks ago? Surprised that at least Biri hasn't shown up yet.

Eh, oh well. Gives me more time to build the next batch before I lose another finger. This'll turn into a riot if they learn what these bracers can do, only to find out it's the only one I've built yet.

11

UPGRADES

Tirak focused on keeping his breathing calm as he watched Maker fuss over his arm for a few more minutes. All he needed to do was not hyperventilate. That was easy to do. Yeah. Tirak could manage that. The slight bleeding had stopped a long time ago, but He kept the damp rag handy anyway.

"Good, I don't see any more signs of rejection. Your body seems to be grafting the device in quite well. Er, the pain wasn't too bad, I hope?"

"I barely even felt it," Tirak replied.

Tirak's arm flexed as he turned it over to get a better look at the flat bracer. It felt weird when that happened, like something else was controlling him. A bluish screen flickered to life in response. It wasn't all that different from that wristwatch device Maker wore. Sure, he supposed it was ten times larger, and Maker's didn't have braided chains of raw muscle embedding themselves directly into His skin... but still. Basically the same.

This... was completely normal.

"Wonderful! I knew it would adapt properly to match your DNA. Your body should start to see it as just another part of yourself over the next few hours. Until then, let's get you used to your new abilities!"

Maker hopped off His round stool and led them through another confusing twist of halls and doorways, this time mostly made from a smooth, painted rock and steel. Tirak and Kaleek both found themselves staring at the bracer whose tendrils were still writhing, burrowing their way deeper into his forearm.

"So, uh… What abilities *did* you just give me, exactly?" Tirak asked.

"The short version is that I gave you a way to eat all the elemental power you want."

Tirak cocked an eyebrow. Couldn't he do that already? Rekke had taught him how. The traitorous… He shook his head. Maker saw none of Tirak's mental exchange, of course. The judgment mask would've made it impossible for his face to show anything even if Maker had been looking.

"I realize that doesn't sound like an answer at all yet, but all in good time, my boy. In good time."

A set of double doors opened out into a cavernous room nearly a tenth the size of Umbra. For just one room, it was *huge*. Floodlights cracked on in rows down the length of the high ceiling. An echo sang across the floor as Maker clapped his hands. Sections of the floor opened up and vomited an assortment of crates, tables, and objects that Tirak could only begin to describe. He and Kaleek stood with mouths gaping. Maker on the other hand walked forward as if nothing had happened and began picking through the nearest table.

"Just a word of caution first: I designed this with the Elders in mind, so it may be especially hard for someone of your size to get used to. Best to take things slowly until we build some confidence, yes? Now then. Let's show you what your new bracer can do."

An hour later, and he had gotten pretty used to the new tool. Or, well, that's what Maker claimed. To Tirak's eyes, the floor around him was littered with the failed attempts to do anything at all with the bracer.

His one moment of excitement came when he thought it was starting to work. Kaleek doubled over with laughter once he realized it was just glare from the ceiling lights. Sometime later, she joined in with Maker, throwing more bits and scraps. He rubbed the back of his head and groaned.

Who was going to tell her that his face wasn't the target?

"This is stupid, Maker! What's the point?"

Maker rubbed the bottom of his mask with a fleshy thumb.

"Frankly, I don't know. It's like flexing a muscle you're not used to, I suppose."

Another involuntary ripple through his arm made Tirak's skin crawl.

"Yeah, in more ways than—OW!"

He stumbled, nearly slipping on a rust-colored bone. He aimed a glare at Kaleek, who didn't look anywhere *near* remorseful enough. Her hand tucked itself behind her back. A well-aimed heatbolt sent her scrambling away, giggling all the while.

"I'm telling you, something just isn't *right* about this. The stupid thing doesn't *WORK*!" Tirak finished.

His last word was punctuated by a loud bang. Static swam across his eyes for a long, silent second. It took several more until his ears could hear more than a few muffled flutters. That was dangerous. If he'd been in a fight, a pause like that could've killed him.

"There you go! You see? You just needed to feel it out a little. And get it onto the right setting, I suppose. Hmm… I shouldn't have made that so sensitive to gravity, should I? Well, with that success, let's keep going!"

Maker drew a handful of small wing bones from His storage chest. The pearly frost-blue shimmer implied they must have belonged to some auri hawk from the southwest mountains. He wasn't even going to stop and talk about what Tirak had just caused?

"W-wait, Maker. What just happened?"

Tirak stood in a circle, maybe three legs across in total, of perfect emptiness among all the clutter that had been thrown at him.

"Did I just explode?"

"Stop getting distracted, young man."

Maker clearly wasn't going to stop and chat now. He readied His arm for an overhand toss.

"And what are *those*? I can't eat them."

"Oooh, do it, do it! I'll grab the chum bladder for when you puke," his sister chimed.

She disappeared behind a table before Tirak could shake a burning finger at her. Maker's eyes were squinted into another grin, as if saying, "I was waiting for you to say that."

"Just focus on tagging them all for the interface. Don't worry about actually absorbing them. Igni scraps just happen to be a little harder to come by. You know, my kind doesn't handle volcanoes all that well."

That sounded dumb. The Man had *made* Mount Fulkana; how could it possibly threaten Him? But Maker reminded him this was the wrong time to think about such things by throwing the half-dozen bones into the air. It proved hard to track them against the backdrop. Some of them were as small as Tirak's fingertip, but he tried his best anyway. In the end, he could only spot one or two before they all clattered to the ground. He felt frustrated, Maker had said it like the task would be no big deal.

"I think you missed one."

He shot another glare at Kaleek as he picked up the bones and gave them back to Maker. They reset and tried again. Three more tries, four, and again they clattered across the ground accusingly. Was this some kind of test to prove whether he could complete the quest? Was he failing? What did that mean if he was? His thoughts drifted back to Rekke's village, ruefully this time. That ceremony had been a little twisted, sure, but those people were *happy*. Kaleek gathered the bones for Maker again, but Tirak felt ready to give up. What good was it to keep embarrassing himself? The pale bones were arcing through the air before he could call off the practice. Reluctantly, he reached out and tried to focus on them all. He marked one in his head, then briefly saw another. It wouldn't do any good anyway; he simply couldn't look at so many invisible things at the same time. By the time he found one and looked away for another, he had lost the first. He was just milliseconds away from failing again—

FLASH!

Again, his vision swirled with static and color. No noise met his ears.

"What…? Tirak you did it!" Kaleek yelled.

A body piled onto his shoulders, hugging him. His eyes finally started to recover, and sure enough, there were no bones in sight. He hadn't even remembered tracking where they all were, but somehow he knew exactly where to look to know that each one was gone.

"W-what happened? Where'd they go?"

"You ate them, dummy! Do you feel sick yet?" his sister teased.

He began to brace himself. He could almost feel the nausea starting to build. Maker's wheezy voice chuckled again.

"You're right, Tirak. In a normal situation, eating something that carries an air charge would go right through you and do no good. Considering how potent it was, you'd probably even feel sick. These bracers were originally going to operate the same way, but I made a discovery on the first prototype that sent me along this path instead. Try it again, please."

He pulled out an assortment of pieces next. Every element except for fire. He had easily twice as many pieces as last time.

"The bracer will help you track the pieces. Its nerves are tied into your own, creating a direct interface to your brain's circuits. Focus on the general concept you want from it and it'll handle the details for you. Now, begin!"

A stream of purple energy snaked out from his forearm as Tirak focused on the fragments of bone that were scattering into the air. It blinded him again. Silence choked his ears as he blinked the colors away.

An excited whine slowly built in his sister's throat as Kaleek bounced up and down on her toes.

"Ohhh! What does it feel like, bro? Can you shoot water bolts now?" Then she gasped. "Or a fire tornado?! We're not going *anywhere* until I see you make it shoot lightning!"

"Kal… Kal! Slow down! I don't know how to do any of that," he objected.

Blessedly, Maker's raspy chuckling voice redirected her enthusiasm back onto the right path.

"Very well done, young man! You'll have plenty of time to practice that more before I send you off, and there's lots of elemental bits and bobs to find around here. I've been stockpiling for five Elders to show up, after all! But that brings me to the next feature you'll need to learn."

Both siblings perked up their ears, and Tirak molted Natural ears on top of his head for extra effect. It took a confused moment, but he earned a laugh once Kaleek noticed them.

"Yes, very mature. But your next lesson is this: *finding* elemental energy! The bracer has search and scan functions, in addition to the absorb setting that you've already used. Try the first one now, and when you find the little treasure I've hidden somewhere in this room, I want you to tell me its exact composition before you absorb it."

Tirak felt his eyebrows crawl up his face.

"It can *do* that? Wait! Composition? You mean the thing'll have more than one element in it?"

Maker nodded and stretched His hand toward the room. The message was clear: get to work.

An incredibly productive afternoon later, Maker waved the two of them back over to discuss His plan's next steps. Tirak felt himself bouncing on the edge of his toes with all the new energy coursing through his veins. His sleeveless shirt and pocketshorts even felt a little tighter on him than he remembered. Had he bulked up a little from eating all those elemental trinkets?

The Maker noticed Tirak's wavering attention and brought him back into the conversation. The plan was pretty straight forward. Almost disappointingly simple, even. Maker told them about three sources of power that were hidden near each tip of the island's capes. He called them "relay towers," and He wanted the siblings to visit each one and eat all the power they could. That, and make sure the villages were all prepared for battle. The Darkness was already tainting the edges of the island with its influence. Their news of the Scarred proved that, or so He said. So in other words, power, people, and then a whole lot of waiting for the fateful day to come.

Satisfied that they understood the gravity of their quest, Maker commanded the room to return to its clean emptiness with a clap of His hands. He pointed to the door, urging them on their way with haste. But when Tirak turned to follow his Maker, he found Kaleek blocking the doorway, her eyes a glowing storm that swirled behind the fragments of her mask.

"I'm not going *anywhere*, Maker. Where's my bracer?"

"Oh! I didn't realize you were hoping for one as well, child. I uh… I do apologize, but Tirak's is the only working prototype I have at the moment."

"But—but *I'M* the hero that Elder Onok sent you! Not him! You said you had five of them waiting for the Elders! Give me one of those!"

Maker's head shrank into his shoulders slightly, abashed. Kaleek noticed the reaction and narrowed her eyes.

"What aren't you telling us, Maker?"

"Why, nothing at all, child. I do intend to make enough bracers for all the Elders. For everyone, if the universe stays the Darkness' hand long enough. But unfortunately, I ran into a setback recently that left me unable to do much work. You may have noticed my hand, after all…"

Kaleek didn't stop glaring. Tirak looked down to Maker's side with some confusion. All four fingers were there, like normal.

"You look fine—and stop calling me 'child.'" She said flatly.

"Oh. My apologies. I figured you knew about my kind."

Maker held up his left hand and wiggled a *fifth* finger that they hadn't noticed.

"Um, gross? But I don't see why an extra finger has to stop you. Dad chose ME to be Umbra's champion! So get me a bracer too!"

Maker pinched the spot between his mask's eye sockets and released a mechanical breath.

"It's not that simple, child—"

"Stop calling me *CHILD! Ka-LEEK!* My name is *Kaleek*!"

"It isn't that simple," he continued, only mildly put off by the interruption. "It will take me at least a month to rebuild the tooling, and we probably don't have that kind of time left before the Darkness sends its Shadows down upon us."

"Fine then," she spat out. "Give me Tirak's!"

Tirak jumped. What had gotten into his sister? They were competitive sometimes, sure, but this kind of envy was completely unlike her.

"That wouldn't work, Miss Kaleek. His body is almost completely grafted with it by now. It's a part of him. It can never re-key itself to someone else again. Not without killing him that is. As you can see with my own mask, it's a problem I never quite figured out."

"Kal… just let it go. I still need you, with or without a bracer. The *island* needs us both. We don't have time to waste on arguing."

"Well said, young man! We—"

Kaleek growled stubbornly.

"We're not leaving until I have one too. You said that's the only *working* one, right? Well, show me where the broken ones are! Fix one of *them*!"

Maker took an instinctive step toward a different doorway than the one Kaleek was barring. Her eyes widened. Through the crack of an opening, they could see a tumble of machinery and tools that could only mean one thing: A workshop. Maker didn't have a chance to blink before her skin had molted into her Nature. She had crossed half the distance before either of them moved, slamming the door shut behind her without breaking stride.

Maker and Tirak broke into a sprint to catch up, but they were too late.

Tirak's hand was almost around the handle when the screaming started.

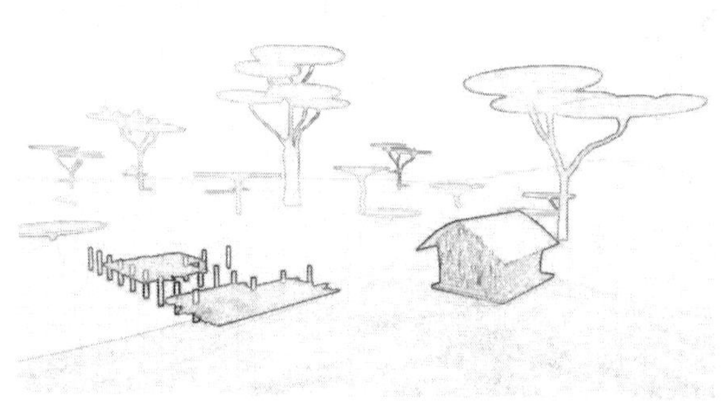

Maker's Log #89007: Anium Cultivation Pond #01, now "Limna."

Our Electrium garden was one of the first to become wild as soon as it stopped supplying an entire city's worth of machines. What had once been beautiful grew like a cancer until it was all but unrecognizable. It pained me to watch the place fall apart and slowly sink into the bay. I started finding excuses to ignore the service alarms that came from that peninsula's relay station. Then before I knew it, it had been a century.

Imagine my shock when Biri first dragged me out of my little home beneath the grove and took me to the very place I'd been avoiding. She had already put months of work into cutting away the rotting leaves from a dozen of the plants, nurturing the new growth that sprang out of its self-fertilizing mass. The air was still absolutely putrid whenever the wind stilled, but with my mask's filtration, I hardly noticed.

The result was STUNNING. Waterlilies bigger than buildings. Leaves wide enough—and probably thick enough—to land a helo on. I actually did park my old lander on a few of them. Up until the Limnii children started to live there in fact. I wasn't eager to become known as some sort of flying magical god to them. The Elders' fervent worship of anything I did was already bad enough.

And yes, you were right. The extra cellular support from Limnium was absolutely worth the extra complications. Keeping it separated from the Electrium buds was the hardest challenge I remember from our time together, but look how it paid off now. I'm sorry I cussed you out as much as I did. I think deep down, it was because I knew you were right all along. Seeing it now, these beautiful monstrosities would never've been able to hold up under their own weight without that touch. I hear it's even become a staple food for many of the Limnii.

Hah, the classic fight between burger or salad seems to be even more universal than just our own little race. If it's any comfort, I'd gladly share another salad with you...

I—

I...

<TRANSCRIPTION INTERRUPTED>

12

RESCUERS

Tirak tossed a dried strip of fruit to his sister as they pushed their way along a road that had gone months without seeing traffic, if not *years*. Maybe the footfalls of an occasional hunter at most. He held onto yet another stubborn branch, keeping it from snapping back, and let his sister pass safely under its thorny claws. She gave him a grateful smile as she stepped around him. The bandaged arm was obviously still troubling her.

"So we're sure about our story, right?" Tirak asked.

Ahead, Kaleek nodded.

"I think so."

She kept walking, as if they'd done all the planning in the world.

"And that story is…?" he asked, testing her.

Kaleek huffed.

"We're madly in love, but we're shy about that fact. We grew up together because our parents were business partners—"

"Ran a seaside forge together," he corrected. "It sounds more empathetic that way. Yours harvested the glass shards and bonesteel, while mine were obviously smithies."

"Right, right… aaand, their uh, 'Ocean-quenched steel'"—Tirak grinned when she got the name he'd insisted on right—"became popular in our little suburb. Once you and I grew up, people started to frown at how much time we spent together, so we struck out on our own."

Tirak nodded.

"Good, but we want to look like we're avoiding that part until they force it out of us. Even platonic mixed couples tend to get weird looks."

"*Dark*, bro! You think I don't *know* that?"

Tirak raised his hands to ward off another argument.

"I didn't mean…"

Kaleek held up her good fist, motioning for him to be quiet. They stopped and listened to the forest. Something did seem off that morning, but the fog draping this way and that made it impossible for him to put his finger on what. When no other sounds came, they cautiously continued on. Whatever the disturbance had been seemed to be gone. Hopefully, they would get their first glimpse of Limna soon. Whatever else was out here with them would soon be "in the rearview mirror" after that, as Maker had said.

"But how did we get these masks?" he prodded.

"Um, you said we should stick to the rotten fruit basket against Mom's rival, right?"

Tirak tapped the corner of his mask.

"No, the inlay is purple, not yellow. We need to go with the fumbled burglary one."

She sighed.

"I just don't like that one, Tir… it makes us sound like villains. We want to come off as endearing, not make them all reach for their shardpurses."

This time, Tirak was sure he heard the noise too. He could have sworn it sounded like a whimper—maybe a female's voice—and someone else trying to shush them. He silently unsheathed his weapon, and saw ice coalesce into Kaleek's hand from the corner of his eye.

"Hello? Is somebody there? We come in peace!" he called out.

Instead of answering, a female shrieked. The sound was swallowed by a crash of water and several voices erupting. They were cries of alarm, not attack. Kaleek and Tirak charged forward into a clearing and found themselves up against the water's edge. Bubbles still churned a few heads away from the bank, toward which a male—obviously limni—was stretching his arm. Several more held him back from falling in.

"Talisa!" the fellow cried.

A black spot moved under the water.

The situation became clear to Tirak's eyes. A dock and several huts sat nearby, each one partially smashed. Some kind of water beast had just snatched the man's daughter, or wife or… someone. And it was dead set on making it out to the deeper water as fast as possible!

Tirak sculpted a flash of heat beneath himself and rocketed into the air. Wind became a howl across his ears as he quickly caught up to the moving shape. So far, his angle was on point. As long as the thing didn't veer to either side, he would come down right on top of it.

Or so he hoped. The water had disappeared from view instants after he launched away. This stuff was thick as mud!

Tirak broke through the top of the fog and gasped. Limna stretched out like a garden of flat, leafy disks piled on top of each other. He started to fall, and shook himself out of the stupor. He looked around frantically for any sight of his target.

The retreating inkblot rushed back into view beneath him. He tucked his legs into his best attempt at one of Kaleek's dives and crashed into the surface. It still felt like an octet or two of fists had just slugged him in the gut, but this time he didn't feel so disoriented. A monster of legs, teeth, and fins loomed in front of him. Its mouth seemed to sneer, and in the process it let go of something sea-foam blue. The girl didn't hesitate to shoot away despite her bleeding legs.

Despite his sister forcing him to practice, Tirak was no swimmer. He held his stance firm anyway, bracing for that impossibly big maw to chomp down. Fangs seemed to snap closed in slow motion. His mind raced. He couldn't have done anything different. He was doomed.

But then, the thing lurched back and roared. It began to thrash violently. A hiss grew to a deafening pitch before Tirak noticed the steam bubbling off his blade. It must have cooked the thing's mouth! He kicked his legs to catch up, hoping to use this chance to end its life.

It turned out he didn't have to. Something struck the water's surface and pierced through the beast. As the cone of air collapsed on itself, it left behind a thin rod of ice. Kaleek's hand pulled him out of the water a moment later. The female they had just saved was already bobbing and screaming hysterically nearby. Kaleek dragged the both of them back to land and dumped them onto the broken dock. She took off at a sprint without glancing back, before Tirak even had time to empty his lungs, let alone catch up to her. So instead, he helped one of the locals tear pieces of the female's flowing dress into strips and bandage the teeth marks that covered her leg. It was several minutes before any of her babbling became coherent.

"Where's my baby? Save her! You have to save her!"

She pointed frantically across the water with her only unhurt arm. There, Tirak saw his first real glimpse of a Limna neighborhood. It was… even more plants? It looked like any typical waterlily from this distance, but it had as many as eight or sixteen flower buds that had been carved into homes and it towered maybe thirty—or fifty?—heads high into the air! Or, no. It was many, many bundles of the plants all woven together. Its first platform alone sat higher than any cybri could jump. Many more slimy creatures squirmed around its surface, occasionally falling into the water.

And in their churning center, a tiny girl with the same colors as this female was fighting for her life. Fighting without powers, he saw with a chill. Tirak supposed his and Kaleek's made-up story could wait a little longer.

This was going to be fun.

~~~~~

Or… It turned out to be boring and yet hair-on-ends stressful all at the same time. Kaleek never returned after she had charged off toward the girl. He caught glimpses of her fighting some kind of sea dragon whose front half was at least three buildings tall. And so, the job of making sure *everybody else* actually stayed safe behind her fell on Tirak by default.

He tried his best, but he couldn't look in every direction at the same time. So after the third or fourth injury from smaller predators snapping at the group's members, Tirak drove everyone inside the sturdiest building he could find and guarded the door himself. Only one monster tried the windows after that.

All in all, it worked out pretty well. But it left them waiting for hours.

Tirak slowly felt his sanity draining away. If that short teal kid tried to sneak out the door even one more time…

A large body thudded against the roof where he and several dozen villagers were huddled. He waved them back frantically.

"Get back, get back! It could be another one. You, do any of them fly?"

An inky blue-black tail inched downward outside the window nearest him. Kaleek's head popped into view soon after the braids, cresting below the top edge.

"Nope! Just when they're underwater. Coast is clear, by the way. And I mean, it's *REALLY* clear! That last monster splashing down made some serious waves. Washed a whole bunch of stirred up gunk right out to the bay."

She swung down, flipping upright to land on four nimble toes.

"Rest of the monsters didn't stick around after that. So when'd you start cowering in here?"

"I was not—there was…" he scoffed.
~~~~~

"Yeah yeah, don't care. Come on. I talked to some grouchy old lady two pads over who sounds important. Pretty sure she hates my gears, but we saved the village and all that, so she promised to ask Eldress Biri if we can stay in the village a while and help out. We're supposed to meet her on the top leaf of that really big stalk over to the north."

Kaleek dragged him past dozens of faces that all wore distant, shocked expressions. Few took any notice of them until they'd made it most of the way up the first massive tower he had seen. He caught Kaleek's smiling face and grinned back. It started with a few calls of praise, and turned into a cheering band of followers the higher they rose. For the first time since it had been welded on, Tirak felt like the people around him didn't see his mask.

At the top platform stood a building that Tirak was not prepared to witness. Calling it a home would be as much of an injustice as calling it a shack would. The dome-shaped structure had downright mind-boggling proportions. He thought the neighborhood platforms on their way up were impressive—and being able to walk across leaves thicker than a cybri was tall certainly *was*—but *this* thing…

The palace—for that was the only thing it could possibly be—looked much like a flowerbud as well. Rich green, with leaves folded tightly into each other to form a smooth, living wall all the way to its pointed top. Round window holes had been drilled about a quarter of the way down from its tip, and a curved doorway looked more *grown* than cut. Although, someone had gone back over it to attach a decorative awning of bamboo and cloth across its top.

Tirak tilted his head back again.

…And the whole thing had to be more than twenty heads tall! He stole a peak backwards and felt his stomach drop out as he realized just how distant the water was beneath them. Just how many hundreds of heads high were they?

"Don't tell me you all were here trying to beg my help while the rest of the village was busy fighting off that leviathan," a voice said from behind them.

It sounded annoyed. Tirak thought it sounded feminine, but something about the pitch, its power… it was different from any he had ever heard before.

"I swear, if I find out it's *your* faults such a beautiful creature is dead…" A sigh interrupted the voice's tirade, "Absolutely useless… I expect it from the males, but you lot? I thought I trained my government better than this. Don't tell me you're all getting too *old* to fight."

Faces went pale all around Tirak as everyone turned. As for the gray-headed "Old Grouchy lady," her unbroken chain of demands for Kaleek to explanation herself vanished into a wonderful silence. Her face had gone red as coals.

"E-Eldress Biri!" a younger assistant next to the grouch squeaked. "W-where… where did you go?"

Tirak's eyes took in the stormy-looking Elder, then snapped back to the girl who had spoken.

No… It couldn't be, could it? His heart dropped, and Tirak found himself praying to Maker that he could be wrong, but… that shade of green was just too similar. The slender frame. *And her excessively formal dress had stripes of purple and black running down the sides!*

That blend of Umbra and Limna colors dredged up memories in Tirak's mind that he thought he had finally buried. His could feel the welding iron's touch on his cheeks again. He wondered if the girl had recognized them yet. Or, no, Kaleek should be safe, but what about him? He hadn't really stuck around the couple long enough for either party to get a good look at each other. Hopefully he had been nothing more than their unrecognizable savior. If they'd had time to ask around though… Would it be a good thing if she recognized him, or not?

Better to avoid the chance completely. Tirak scanned the crowd for signs of her umbri mate, and sighed in relief to find him nowhere in sight. Filing that concern away for later, he tried to catch up with what everyone was whispering around him.

"You presume to ask her something so disrespectful? Quiet, girl! You should already know she would've spent all day out at sea, healing the storm's damage and helping soothe the displaced depthbeasts," the grumpy spinster rebuked, after getting her own reddening face under control first.

And so began the siblings' interrogation. Eldress Biri grilled them with questions for hours. Tirak understood the distrust that had to have come with two obviously competent fighters showing up on her doorstep with outcast masks, but her complete and total suspicion of them both—especially of *him*—was beyond justified.

Of all things, Biri and her counselors seemed to be more upset about the dead sea monsters than anything else. As soon as he heard one of them lay into Kaleek for *that* of all things, he was about ready to walk away and accept his life as a homeless wanderer. Maker curse them all if they insisted on being that unjust! He tried to defend his sister a few times, but… the *daggers* they all stared into him whenever he tried. One of the advisors had clacked a metal collar at him, and somehow Tirak didn't think the gesture was a joke.

The females eventually seemed to come to some sort of compromise, after the Eldress had finished confirming all the different "useful" skills Kaleek didn't have and why there was no need for two troublemakers to "help." Tirak simmered inside, having to listen to the… *very unflattering thing* he wanted to call her out loud, belittle his sister right in front of him. All he could do was slip a hand into Kaleek's and give her an encouraging squeeze. She responded immediately, drawing a little closer to his side. It made that protective feeling inside him flare to all-new heights.

~~~~~

Once his sister had been sufficiently insulted, the crowd dispersed faster than he could keep up with. Before he knew it, Tirak found himself walking one of the calmer boardwalks down by the water. Small
~~~~~

boats glided from dock to dock between the village-sized plant stalks in a hypnotizing dance.

Kaleek's hand slipped back into his again.

"Wow… that was brutal," she said with a quiet voice. "Y-you don't mind, by the way, right? We need to keep selling the story as much as possible, and this quirky love thing was the only thing to get any positive reaction. The sooner they start trusting us the better."

He glanced down and smiled, then tilted his head against the top of hers.

"You know I'm never going to push my little sister away."

"Ew, gross."

"Hey, *your* idea, remember?" Tirak whispered back.

A comfortable silence settled between them while a much larger cargo barge slipped by. Tirak's eyes settled onto the young males that were pushing it along with conductive rods. Collars and chains tethered every single one of them to a central pillar. Wait. What? They were limni just like everyone else he had seen up till then. What was different about this group?

The boat's captain seemed to notice his attention. She called out to them across the water.

"Ho, girl! Careful not to give your boy too much slack there or he'll turn on you. Give one a hand and he'll take a leg."

Kaleek held to him more tightly, and the captain dismissed them with a disgusted grunt. She cracked a whip at the male nearest her.

"W-what was *that* about, Kal? Why does everyone seem to look down on males here?"

Kaleek shrugged.

"How am *I* supposed to know? Not actually from here… remember?"

"Right, sorry."

The odd boat faded into the sun's sinking haze. That captain's strictness reminded him of another point they'd been grilled on earlier, though.

"Hey, what about that curfew they were talking about? Do you think the Elder was really serious about that?" he asked.

"Oh, deathly serious."

Tirak looked down at her in surprise.

"What?" she asked. "Would you want a couple of known criminals wandering around at night? Come on. I don't actually know what we consider sunset around here, and I'd rather not get it wrong on my first day."

He grinned as he followed her up a swaying rope ladder. She was already starting to feel like a part of her people again. Good for her. That show of crocodile tears she'd used to tug on the crowd's hearts; it had been masterful. Even he had begun to worry there was some truth behind the story. Maybe she really was desperate to reconnect with her dead family. Thinking back on it, Onok never *had* told him how he had found her. Just an offhand comment that one time, and it had sounded too unbelievable to be true.

Deep down, Tirak hoped for her. Even if the tears had been fake, he *knew* what it was like. The questions had to be eating her alive whether she admitted it or not.

They settled into a cramped guest hut that sat directly across from Eldress Biri's massive home. It was another of her requirements for their staying in town. The only place they were allowed to sleep was within sight of the village's lawgiver. Tirak watched his sister cast a longing eye out the window as the last of the light continued to fade into the forever-hazy horizon. The boat traffic between the towering plants below had dwindled to a trickle. He could only imagine what was going through her head right now. To be so close to her people after waiting her whole life, only to be isolated again like this. Mere legs away from what she had to be dying to have.

A knock sounded at the front door, startling them both out of their thoughts. Sharing a confused glance, the siblings moved toward the front room to see who it was. Tirak began to pick out a muttering voice as they got closer.

"...youngsters. Can't even have the decency to come to me. No. They expect an old sailor to drag his plated backside all the way up 'ere where he isn't welcome."

A less obnoxious voice answered it before Tirak had his hand around the door's rope handle. "Don't take it out on them, Gramps. They didn't know we were arranging this for them."

Tirak yanked the door open—earning a small squeak from the second person—and only afterward considered whether he should glare or raise an eyebrow at the intruders.

His voice caught in his throat. The worst possible outcome was playing out right in front of him. That female he had rescued in Umbra *really had* recognized him, and now here she was, a tough-as-nails sailor to guard her as she began to interrogate them about the attack Tirak had been involved with. His eyes flicked toward the back window. Could he fit through that if he jumped?

Pushing past him, Kaleek asked, "Hello? What do you want?"

"Hullo you two! I'm supposed to introduce myself and tell ye my boat's fer hire if'n ye need un fer 'oh-fish-ee-ull beez-nus.' There. Surely *that'll* satisfy the ol' hound and her pack?"

The last part was said to the gruff male's companion instead of the two of them, and by the emphasis he put on the word "hound," Tirak got the distinct impression it was a conscious stand-in for something else. A rebellious thread opened in the back of Tirak's circuits, and he decided to name the weathered sailor "Captain Crabcakes."

A blush had crept across the female's slight face.

"Grandpa!" she hissed. "You can't *say* stuff like that anymore! If you weren't such an important resource to the Eldress, you'd already be out on your ear."

"Ah, what of it? That hound wouldn't know what to do without me, so stop yer worryin'."

The girl rolled her eyes and turned to address the siblings. She adopted a much more regal, official air before opening her mouth again.

"My deepest apologies for his behavior. Yes. The Eldress' council of advisors has decided that if you are to be assisting the village with your... *missions*... then it would be prudent for you to have a way to facilitate your travel while you operate under any sort of official capacity, especially considering you are likely not familiar with Limna village. Fear not. Gramp—erm, *Sailor Hasa* here is not only licensed to operate without supervision, he is completely licensed to supervise other... *undesirables*."

The girl's eyes lingered on Tirak's mask as she stretched out the last word. His mouth felt dry, his throat cold. What did she remember? Did she know, or did she think he had been just another kidnapper? He watched her finger twirl through a purple tassel that hung from her loose, flowing sleeves.

Also, wow. Tirak shifted his opinion from "official" to "officious." That had been a mouthful. Did they have to train to sound like that? He felt himself bristle beneath the mild terror that had wrapped itself around him.

"Look, thanks but no thanks," Tirak blurted out. "We can figure it out ourselves, so get lost. Oh, and maybe try a little courtesy next time—at least to your own family if nothing else. He's your grandfather, isn't he?"

The advisor's assistant pinched her nose between two aqua-green fingers and sighed. She had been a hair away from exploding only a moment earlier. Clearly, she had inherited her double-sided personality from her grandfather.

"Look. Speaking candidly here for a moment: I understand how strange our world must be to outsiders like you. But the sooner you get used to them, the better. If you don't learn to be more respectful around the other villagers, you're going to find yourself collared."

"What?" Kaleek scoffed, and Tirak mentally thanked her for sticking up for him. "But Tirak is a visitor to the village! What kind of hospitality would it be if we started going around shackling our guests for simple misunderstandings?"

The assistant raised an eyebrow at Kaleek.

"'We'? *You're* as much an outsider to this village as your boyfriend is, Miss Kaleek."

"That's enough, girl," the sailor rebuked.

Now the assistant *really* started to look indignant. She stamped her foot on the springy floor.

"You can't talk to me like that!"

"The Dark I can't!" He held up a hand to ward off an approaching fight. "Kili! Go on. I'll stay and make sure our guests don't go tangling themselves up in any of your pretty hairs. Go calm your waves with that shadow of a husband."

The sailor awkwardly scratched between his memory cores as the almost-fragile girl stomped off.

"Forgive the lass. She's still a bit wound up after her wedding, and she gets that stormy temper straight from the Hound's milky… eh… I shouldn't say that. Forgive all a' us. Eldress Biri went through a pretty awful nightmare a few years back, and I don't think any of us have really recovered yet."

Tirak shared a curious look with Kaleek. No, she didn't know anything more about it. Or, maybe she did? That glance to the side as they turned back toward the sailor … They chatted with him for a little longer, then the sailor bid them goodnight after promising to meet by the western dock in the morning and disappeared into the night.

A guard poked her head in later that evening and looked almost surprised to find them still there. She nodded awkwardly at them and disappeared. No one else dared bother the two "criminals" after that. Tirak sighed and decided to leave a candle burning in case any other guards did snoop throughout the night. Might as well make their job easier. Nothing either of them could do to stop it anyway. Even the windows had no mesh or curtains to shutter them with.

The next day was going to be backbreaking if that morning had been anything to go by. They would need all the rest they could get. Tirak felt his lids getting heavy as he pulled Kaleek closer to him—

even in here, she insisted they needed to keep up appearances as much as they could—and he began to wonder whether they would get to go on any cool patrols soon.

Or maybe learn a new skill. Building things sounded fun…

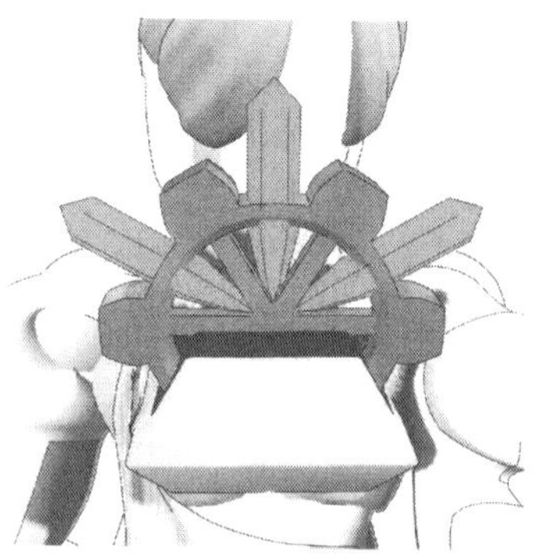

Maker's Log #86185: Cybrii Element Conduction Gearbox.

Wow. Truly, wow. I finally convinced Biri to show me what her elemental transmission box looks like up close. I'm staring at it spin whie writing, and… tahnk the void for spell check I guess. In concept, I built this thing. But seeing it working for real… it's a whole nother experience.

I'll go back through and attach what diagrams I can to help clarify. (Hear that Avoma? Don't forget this time, dummy)

The gear is TECHNICALLY more of a cog, I suppose. But it connects directly to the body inside their core. Elemental energy is part of a cybri's physical makeup, THANKS AGAIN TO TRUINE THEORY, ROB! And this gearbox is able to interface with that to pull power from their bloodstream. The six hollow channels are coated in a special catalyst that helps the dissolved power quickly crystalize into place or re-absorb it back into them again as needed.

It's a complicated system that any of my engineering peers should've raked me over the coals for, but the fact is, cybrii need it in that form to use the power with any sort of effectiveness. Don't ask me why. Yes, the dissolved crystals are just very small and suspended in the cellular jelly and whatnot, and yes, they CAN use the power in that form to SOME extent. But for some reason it's infinitely more potent when purified like this.

With the gearbox, a cybri essentally can equip themselves with an ammo belt of up to three crystals. Those are the ones exposed alng the top edge of the gearbox. While a cybri uses those, they can begin prepping another set inside the box to replenish the in-use ones at a moment's notice. Hopefully they'll never need to have more ready to use than that.

I can't see why they would.

13

SCENT OF THE SEA

Weeks slipped by as life settled into a pleasant routine. By day, they hunted down nests of deepwater creatures and put down any that couldn't be tamed. And by evening's twilight, they explored Kaleek's ethnic home. It took frequent walks through any public garden or street corner they could find to keep up their appearance as wayward but innocent lovebirds.

Not that Tirak really minded. He hadn't spent this much quality time with his sister since those first few days. When a much smaller Kaleek would bring every little trinket and adorable creature around to his bedside until he was able to walk again. Not a day went by that he didn't remember he owed her his life, and not just for dragging him out of that splinter pile.

What ever happened to all those fond memories of getting lost around the tunnel networks outside Umbra city, anyway?

He supposed he was to blame. Once he'd started to win a little favor with the Goldenhearts, he just hadn't had time to spare anymore. He fanned his back paws out and gave a mighty kick to catch up with Kaleek. Not too close, though. He still wasn't sure how she felt about people using their Nature around her after they'd escaped the Scarred camp.

Having her back in his life now, though, he found that the more evenings they spent together, the shorter each one felt. A few minutes of laughs followed by the unbearably long slog of hunting for monsters in a watery silence each day.

But another one was finally over now. They poked above the water almost nose to nose, Tirak sputtering, Kaleek giggling. He glared at her. They'd wrapped up a hard day of eradicating a nest of invasive pests a couple of hours ago, and the two of them had immediately seized the chance to enjoy a calm sunset with some fun. And yes, even with magical bracers, water was definitely still her element.

"I–" he started.

"Deserved that? Yeah…"

They came to rest treading water close to each other. He felt his heart lurch a little as a wave pushed her against him. Her face wore a strange expression as they broke away, and he was pretty sure that was a blush she was trying to hide by keeping her head tilted down. Not quite sure what he was doing, he leaned in closer to her again.

SPLASH!

Saltwater burned his unprotected eyes for several heartbeats.

"Ow! You slimy little fish…" he exclaimed, sweeping a hand out to get her back.

"Fur-brained kitty cat," she spat back, grinning.

Sibling rivalries ensued. The low-stakes fight was refreshing, but they were already exhausted. Eventually, floating on their backs amidst a truce, they watched the sky adopt a shade of fire as a pink sun nudged the horizon.

"Sure is nice of ol' Captain Crabcakes to let us take the boat out on our own."

"*Tir*. Be nice."

"What? That was being nice! The jerk practically insulted your whole lineage when we first met him. He doesn't exactly have that many redeeming qualities."

Another splash of water missed him that time. If accused, he would have denied any water conducting had been involved. Her eyes said she didn't really *disagree* with what he said, however.

And then they were close again. She bumped against his side, and had that same unreadable expression. His mind raced for a way to make this moment last. Following a stray idea, it settled on his experiments with Nature form. That would surely be interesting to her.

"Hey, Kee. Follow me," he whispered. "There's something else I want to teach you."

He reached for her hand, but somehow managed to miss and brushed her waist instead. His touch made her visibly shiver. He pulled forward as cautiously as possible before things got too awkward and found her wrist. Good enough, he supposed. She let him pull her back to the boat and even gracefully accepted his hand as they climbed up. He led her to the center of the deck. Sitting cross-legged on the rough planks, he motioned for her to follow suit and took hold of her other hand.

"Now, I've been practicing what Rekke said about our Natures affecting our emotional senses. It really works! It almost worked too well in some of our last fights. I nearly flew into a rage at some of the beasts until I got it under control again."

Kaleek blinked at him, her body completely still.

"You've… been changing into your Second Nature? Like… *regularly*? Tir, that sounds dangerous. Wait! What about your face?"

Her hand traced the edge of his mask with an incredibly empathetic touch. Tirak moved his feet to show her. She jumped when she noticed their shape.

"Just parts, and always subtly," he assured her. "I eventually figured out how to keep my head normal, but it's also stopped hurting so much the more I've used my whole Nature."

Kaleek nodded. She had been using her Nature in combat far more often than he did, so she must have noticed it too. It probably meant they were forming calluses that would never heal, but survival had to come first.

"In fact," he continued, "my feet have been paws all day. Turns out, the extra reach makes it a lot easier to swim. A-anyway, that's not the point. The point is it really changes how you think if you use it for more than the rare few-second burst of fighting skills. It does so much more than make your reflexes sharper. You should try it! Even if you mess up and start bleeding, we have no shortage of water around us. It'll be easy to rinse off."

He waved a hand toward their tranquil surroundings.

Some unseen thought warred against her will behind those crystalline eyes. She began to tremble.

"Tir… I don't know."

"It's—Wow, I made it sound awful, didn't I? Once you get the hang of it, it's *really* amazing! We can start slow. It'll be fine; it's perfectly safe. Here, the first part is just getting yourself to *stay* in your Nature rather than popping in and out."

She relented and closed her eyes. He watched her concentrate, then leap into her Nature faster than he could blink. The change almost threw him onto his back. He held fast to her hands, and just barely managed to keep from tumbling over. Whatever else happened, Tirak *refused* to let his face show any surprise.

"Good. Just hold it like that for a few minutes and the initial rush will fade, letting the other feelings take its place."

She struggled. But this was a time for him to shut up and be patient. He reached out a hand and gently wiped away a few drops of black that drizzled past the rim of her mask. That look of concentration never left her face—even when it stopped looking very face-like—so it was best to let her feel out the right balance on her own.

"Okay, now see if you can relax it just a little bit, until just a few hints of you are left Natural. It'll start getting easier to focus."

She did so. The first few attempts snapped her almost completely back to normal before she would catch herself and careen fully back into her Nature. Dozens of changes later, she settled into a much more gradual fade.

"I… I think it's working!"

And it was. Her eyes were a little unsettling, and her hands were still more like carapace pincers than anything, but she was mostly normal. Tirak gave the pincers another encouraging squeeze.

"It's an… interesting combination to go with, but it's an amazing start!"

The words were barely out of his mouth before he heard the insult they might imply. She frowned, then began to droop. He panicked as several of her eyelets started to glisten with moisture. He had to salvage this, *quickly*!

He chose to rely on her animal senses rather than trying logic. That would be the more powerful argument given the situation, and… who knows? Maybe he would finally get to find out if she had been having any of the same feelings he had. His thumb stroked an even more delicate than usual forearm. He gave it an extra squeeze to draw her attention there.

"Hey, but how does it *feel*?" he whispered.

Her face cleared instantly. A massive grin split her face, radiating warmth, joy, and maybe a little of something else back at him?

"Amazing!" she breathed.

He leaned in close. His other hand still rested against a carapace cheek, damp with a few flecks of her blood. That face, strange as it looked, radiated sheer beauty into Tirak's eyes.

"So… um. D-different question. What about, uh… Can I…?"

She didn't seem to follow his meaning at first. He could see a war of thoughts inside her, but sensed the longing underneath it all.

Yes. It was the exact same longing that he felt.

As her mouth opened to answer, he let the toes of his forepaw drift upward and cup her cheek.

"Yes," she gasped.

Kaleek closed the gap to kiss him. It all finally clicked into place in his head. This. This right here was what he needed to protect. This was what he had been searching for his whole life.

Maker's Log #85045: ~~A surprise visit~~ Not a failure!?!

I… I have no clue what to say.

I just had. THE MOST. Bizarre afternoon. With a manta ray… and a ***tentacle monster****. I haven't left my little hovel for, what, fifty year-equivalents? AND NOW THIS???*

…

Sorry, I've erased this 3 times already.

Not only am I ***not*** *ripped apart limb from limb, but… THEY CALL THEMSELVES FREAKING ONOK AND, well I guess the female ray had no name for herself. But, but still! As the old records say: pog!*

But once she told me about how she awoke from her animal stupor, and then went on to tame her friend Onok, I realized she was my very first success. My first real creation. The name jumped to my mind immediately. It's something from an old fairytale tome my grandmother read to me from time to time. Niv's Message? Something like that. Had a whole language to it and everything, but she insisted it was infinitely better than trying to learn the original Tyrants Tongue it came from. No kidding. There's a reason that whole period is a dark mystery in history.

Heh. Rhymes.

Put simply, Biri fell in love with her new name ***instantly****. I can't say it's the most creative name in the world, but hey it's true. She'll always be my creation.*

I… this changes ***everything****! I told the couple about my vision for a warrior people, and Biri and Onok have already given me enthusiastic promises to help tame any other prototypes they find. At the mention of* *shepherding children along the hero's path, they volunteered even more animatedly. The way those two act around each other... I wonder if it's more of a... special, friendship between them. Eeugh, how would that even work—NOPE nevermind I just remembered. Gross!*

Hmm... that might throw some interesting wrenches in what I'd planned, but I don't have the heart to even consider discouraging them. For mechanized nightmare monsters, they are downright adorable around each other.

Is it childish of me to see in them a little of ourselves, my Light?

14

CONFRONTATION

Tirak stirred as sunlight began to reach around the window's circular edge and lick his face. He cracked an eye toward the guest hut's ceiling and stretched, bumping the massive bundle of blankets that he assumed was Kaleek. He couldn't tell, of course, but she was probably still sound asleep, pressed up against the wall on the opposite corner of the hut's only bed.

She had locked up soon after they shared that kiss the other night, but his mind had never been clearer after that moment. A smile split his lips as he watched her roll over again.

She just needed some time to sort through her feelings, he knew. She'd come around soon enough. Once she let herself open up a little, they could be together for real. It would be one less lie to keep track of around the Limnii.

Tirak wasn't left to his thoughts for long, however. A heavy fist began pounding at their door. Kaleek shot upright, a dagger condensing into her hand out of the humid air.

She saw him watching her and glared back.

"Visitors Kaleek and Tirak. Mistress Biri demands your presence!" a voice called through the front door.

Their eyes found each other again. Kaleek went pale.

"You don't think that poacher said something, do you?" she asked.

It wasn't impossible. They had run across some mangled carcasses on the way home yesterday and went to investigate. What they found was a limni trapping and skinning the beautiful pelt off of Kaleek's favorite species of organic. Needless to say, they "reminded" the guy about Limna's poaching laws and made sure he didn't have any tools to keep doing it. He had been pretty furious at them afterward. How could someone blatantly breaking his Elder's laws really be *that* self-righteous? He seemed like the type who'd be petty enough to spin their short fight as some kind of attack.

"Maybe she just wants to congratulate us on a job well done and send us on our way…?"

Neither of them believed the lie.

The guard whisked them across the platform after allowing the absolute minimum time for them to get ready. Hands shoved them through a gaping portal and slammed the heavy leaf-doors shut behind them with a springy *THUD*. There was nowhere to go but forward, so they followed the entrance toward three shallow steps.

Water plinked as they stepped into its ankle-deep surface. The warmth of it soaked between their toes, surprising Tirak. Water was never this warm.

They found the Eldress alone between a row of bookshelves, rummaging through a stack of books. The towering silhouette never turned to meet them as they approached. They stepped through the pool with care.

"Did you know," Eldress Biri's voice echoed, "less than three percent of Cybrii leave their home village for longer than single-month trips? That's not including the scourge of fiery brutes, like certain ones in this room, of course."

Tirak bristled. That kind of elementalism was why so many hated the Goldenhearts. What was an *Elder* doing spouting that same kind of filth? He bit back a protest. Silence seemed like the wisest bet here.

People like her would twist anything into a weapon against him if given the chance.

"What is even more curious," she continued in an almost bored tone, pulling down a new book, "are the statistics for village-to-village migrations when you separate them by element. Tell me, little heroine, do you know how many children of the sea have found their way to Bozrakh's cracked old dust bowl of a city?"

Kaleek glanced at Tirak, swallowing audibly.

"Um… I only knew of my parents and me. We, uh, didn't get out much…"

She looked like she was going to say more, but really, who could be expected to keep an even cool with a storm cloud like her looming over them?

Biri was standing next to them in just two graceful strides. She ran one finger down Kaleek's shoulder.

"Such smooth skin, too. Quite unusual for a girl who spent her childhood baking under that awful desert sun, the sand pitting her flawless armor…"

She grinned at their silence, a predatory blue shine to her eyes.

"I've been speaking to the sea, you know. One fish told me a most curious little tale about two little children from a dark cave. It said these two siblings were cast out of the cave by their own father—an incredibly tall and ugly shadow—and were given new faces to wear. One was blue… and her brother, red and gold."

Tirak's tongue became caught in his throat. She knew! She knew everything! Of course she did; she and Onok had once been the two closest cybrii across the whole island. He felt stupid that they'd ever even tried. Had she known all along and just wanted to see how long it took for them to slip up?

"Now, I wonder who that sounds like."

The accusation hung in the air between her and them. Light from the ceiling's portholes began to dance erratically on the floor.

Kaleek's voice was almost a whisper. "C-could be almost anyone…"

A quick movement at the corner of his eye drew Tirak's attention. A face ducked further behind a massive living pillar. He was "hidden," but there was no mistaking that opulent V-patterned robe and blackened face. The assistant girl's mate…

"You! You backstabbing little worm…" he growled.

Tirak wanted to say so much more. He *wanted* to launch himself at the self-important, ungrateful umbri in one powerful leap and give him a real mouthful. He took a small step toward the edge of the room.

"Leave him alone," the Eldress snapped. "You will not harass a friend and family member of my city. Come forward… *both* of you."

It took a second to fight down his rage. Even the best intentions could be used against him, he reminded himself.

Apparently the second had been one too long.

"I said, *come HERE!*"

Water exploded into the air around Tirak, wrapping around the balls of his ankles and wrists with a strength that defied all logic. Tirak was spun around to face the Eldress, her face burning with a rage of its own. His bonds undulated like glistening snakes as he was dragged behind his sister. Their unpredictable, gushing shape from moment to moment left him at an awkward slope to the rest of the room.

"*Now*, then. The two of you have been accused of harassing the cybrii of my village, stealing from them and from myself, and undue killing of Maker's holy creatures. What say you in your defense?"

She sneered as the siblings exchanged wide-eyed glances.

"Like I thought… Assistant Sokku! Bring me the mask etcher! I, Eldress Biri, first of Maker, pronounce these two liars before me *criminals* of the worst degree! They are unfit to live among my cybrii, and shall be marked as such!"

"Come on!" Tirak shouted. "You aren't even going to let us defend ourselves! Show us some—*oof*!"

A massive shimmering ball expanded in front of Biri's hand and shot toward him before he could finish his tirade. Water surrounded his head on all sides, turning his senses into a muddy blur. As quickly as it had happened, the mass retracted. It allowed Tirak a tunnel of air that focused solely on the imposing Eldress.

The rest of his twisted bonds dragged him forward until he was eye to eye with her. Fanged mandibles clicked on either side of her mouth, opening and closing as she tried to form words. She… she was actually losing control.

"Filthy *boy*! Know. Your. Place. Your duty is to obey. Nothing else!"

She pushed him a few paces back with a backhanded wave, turning toward wherever Kaleek had gone. His lungs screamed in pain as water began to fill them.

"And *you*, girl. How *dare* you step into MY presence with a *grin…*"

The mad Elderess' voice trailed off. Tirak caught one bloodcurdling scream before the bubble of water resealed itself.

His eyes went wide in fear. She was going to kill him. His body started to shudder as the fight for his life began. He tried to swallow. He tried to blow it back out. He tried to vomit. The water was more solid than metal. His lungs quickly began to burn for air, more out of fear than actual need. The world began to darken around him, and the ringing of pressure against his ears grew stronger and stronger. The corners of his vision fuzzed… like crystals spreading.

A small thread in his circuits wondered why death would look that way.

Tirak felt his body pitch sideways and smash into the edge of a table. Spikes of pain shot through his head. The globe prison shattered around him! He called up some fire and flashed the remaining ice to steam, coughing out the scalding brew.

"What did you just say?" The Eldress' voice hissed.

Kaleek's voice shot back at her between the crashes of a battle his eyes were still too unfocused to track. "You don't get to terrorize every male across the island just because of what one monster did to you! You're supposed to be making an army out of these people!"

"Maker sent you! I knew it!" Biri shrieked back.

"I already told you that. It's not important. Just let it *go, Mom*!"

Tirak's blood froze.

"*You...*" A fearful malice dripped into Biri's tone.

Tirak snapped his head up in time to watch a whole new level of hatred darken the Eldress's eyes.

"You preach harmony," his sister screeched, half-consumed by her Nature, herself. "But you keep doing your best to *stomp* out nature! Can't you see what it's done to your village? Maker wanted us to be *warriors*, and you've turned your strongest into quivering wimps!"

Biri launched a wall of jets that spanned from end to end of the wide, now disheveled space. Every one of them froze in the air, the columns that didn't turn on their mistress fell ineffectually to the floor.

Tirak stared in awe at his sister's unshackled strength. A cloud was forming in the air behind her. She dove and leaped, trailing the misty stuff as crystals of deep blue and pale aqua spun in an almost constant circle behind her head. She was burning through more power than Tirak had ever seen her use.

Eldress Biri's legs were encased in ice, locking her to the floor. It didn't stop her from trying to throw attack after frantic attack at her small opponent. Water was beginning to even seep in through the doors outside. She was pulling power in to be her rescue, throwing globs of it at the whizzing blur that was Kaleek.

"Get it off! *GET IT OFF ME!*" she screamed.

Those too quickly built up into a wall of ice, and the three of them were soon sealed into a room inside a room.

"Stop it stop it *STOP IT!* Stand *STILL*, you little parasite! Stand still and die like you were supposed to!"

The words slammed into Kaleek harder than the few shots that actually connected. Tirak cocked his head. Why had that of all things gotten to her?

His sister's eyes flashed bright with color. Her hand went to her neck, to the clasps of the leathers he had given her. Then she stepped into a pool of light that streamed down from a porthole... and right into the Eldress' next attack. The protective shawl and vest blew free of her.

"Stop it, Mom!"

Maker's Log #88115: Anium substation #1, post-catastrophe.

Drew this sketch of the Limnium distribution relay today during my approach.

Or, as it's better known by Biri's followers: the Temple of Life. Yes, my little creations have all but taken over the place and turned it into their sacred hall to purity. They seem to worship the ideal above anything else. Sometimes I think that keeping their swamp waters clear and free of pollution is their single goal in life. They even managed to tame the spawns I've bred to keep unwanted eyes away from the tower. That… shouldn't have been possible. And it makes me worry that they'll end up failing to do their job one day when it's actually important.

I've heard a few of them call it the "sacred vine" too. A rather apt name, I have to say, what with how it's become so overgrown. I don't THINK it was one of my Kudzu experiments either. Normal vines don't grow that big, nor straight from the water either. The stuff obviously has Limnium grafted into its fibers now. Maybe my little sentry creatures picked up a skill with husbandry somewhere along the way…

Eugh. That's a terrifying thought if so. The gene splicing needed to grow something like that so fast… I thought I was the only one left who could do that.

Regardless, whether a mindless hive dweller or a jealous Limni, at least SOMEBODY is guarding the tower most days. I have more important issues to worry about anyway. Stuff with far more moving parts.

Which reminds me. Hopefully the Terra contraption will fly when the time comes… and hopefully there isn't too much of the city in the way up there either. Yeah, when averaged out it should be able to handle everything in its path. But what if it didn't break into as many chunks as my models said?

With MY luck, there's going to be a whole city block still up there, right in our path when we launch.

15

CLEANSING THE SACRED VINE

A crowd parted for them as the wide doors to Eldress Biri's palace flew open. She stood like a statue and waved for them to exit. Kaleek strode, her head locked forward with her chin raised in defiance. Her leathers were slung over one shoulder, hooked in place on one finger. Pearlish cyan showed in patches on her bare shoulders as she stepped into the sunlight.

"Disgusting…" Biri muttered as they passed.

Tirak stopped in front of her.

He set his shoulders and lifted his face to glower at her. But as he met her eyes, the lingering feel of water strangling him from the inside held him mute. His cheeks began to burn with shame. Finally, he dropped his head and followed Kaleek into the open air.

Their march down to the docks slipped past in a quiet daze. Before the sun had reached its high point in the sky, Tirak was already accepting a last package of supplies from stiff, formal hands.

He glared at the traitor. For another heartbeat, he wished he had never saved the ungrateful umbri's life. The fellow's wife nudged him and muttered some sort of apology before they walked away. At least she seemed a little remorseful for ruining their lives.

An elbow planted itself point-first in his ribs.

"Tir, stop it. You can't blame her for being suspicious of our flimsy story."

His teeth ground against each other.

"Sure I can. They didn't have to be alive right now. You and I didn't have to be kicked out of our home. If they knew who I was, then why couldn't they shut up and be grateful?"

"W-what?"

His blood went cold. He'd almost blurted the truth out loud.

"Never mind. It doesn't matter." He shrugged.

They finished casting off the boat, and several quiet moments passed while they focused on avoiding the intricate hazards between the docks and the edge of town.

"*No*," Kaleek's soft voice finally came. "I'm not letting you off this time. What was that supposed to mean? Why should they be grateful to us?"

He stayed silent. If he just didn't answer her, she would give up, right?

"…Tirak? Why *did* they recognize you? Dad was never one to show us off to the city. I can't even remember a single *dinner party* that you were around for. How. Did. They recognize you?"

Kaleek locked the rudder in place and turned to face him, crossing her arms. He looked out at the receding docks behind them, feeling her gaze bore holes into him. He could only hold out for so long before breaking.

"Didn't you ever wonder why those urchins were beating me up that day? Why *you* had to be the one to run in and… blow up on them?"

She shrugged.

"You got in the way of a robbery or something."

"Goldenhearts don't rob, they pillage. They don't murder, they *slaughter*. They were going to kill those two back there during a big speech. 'To set an example' or so they said."

She leaned in closer to hear. He knew his voice had gone soft against the backdrop of the waves.

"I was the only one stupid enough to stand up to them. I looked into that girl's eyes… and I saw your face looking back at me. I couldn't bear to watch something like that happen to you."

Her hand fell still on the ropes. She looked intently at him and frowned. He glanced away and blushed. She was going to berate him for getting mushy on her again and that he should drop the act.

"Why would you know what the Goldenhearts were planning?" she asked instead. "Were you staking out their operations, like a spy for the Guard or something?"

"No… Kal, I was…" He sighed, searching the horizon for a way to escape this explanation. "Until you found them kicking my face in, I was a Goldenheart."

He cringed at the sharp gasp his tucked-back ears detected. He knew Kaleek would never have approved of what he did from day to day, but… Bile rose in his throat, scalding it with acid. Maybe he should just throw himself over. Those eyes stabbing into his chest… No. No, he could bear this as long as she was here with him.

"Bro…? Are you going to tell me why? What do you mean you were one of them? The creeps are *monsters*! Everyone knows that! You're—you're kidding right? Those people *are* the stress that's been slowly killing Dad. Why would you willingly *help* them? Why would you undermine Dad like that, Tir?"

He forced himself to meet her colorless eyes. The whole world seemed a little more grey. Those eyes looked hurt, and more than a little angry, *but not filled with hatred*. He looked away, clinging to that knowledge with his life.

"It wasn't that easy. They weren't evil at first. They just offered a community—*a family*—to kids like… to orphans like me. It was hard to resist at a time when Onok only paid you any attention. Took me a long time to figure out what he saw in you."

He met her eye and winked. Rather than smiling back like other times, Kaleek glared.

"Ugh... nobody still believes our story, you don't have to keep pretending, you know."

She didn't understand that he was serious.

"What if *I* still believe it, Kee...?"

Kaleek stiffened. Her next words were slow, carefully measured out.

"Don't be gross, Tir. Let's get this quest over with... and agree to never talk about this again."

Pain gripped his heart. Terror. What had he gotten wrong?

"But... that's not what you thought when you kissed me the other—"

"*Tirak*! Stop talking before I rip the air from your lungs and let you choke on what's between your ears. And because you didn't *understand* that, I'm talking about a vacuum—complete *emptiness*."

That last word was forced out through hissing teeth. He felt his throat tighten up. Did... did he really disgust her that much? Whatever happened to *being there* for each other? To being like family? Or as he thought they'd started to agree, a little more than family.

The mid-high sun cast a grey, toneless glare down on them as a colorless jungle passed Tirak by. Was he the problem? Was it something wrong with him that made even his... whatever Kaleek was to him hate the very idea of his presence?

An uncomfortable quiet hung over the rest of the trip. Ahead, the old sailor swung his vessel around, pointed out the nearest entrance and a few submerged roots to beware of, then made wake for Limna as quickly as possible. They had soon disembarked and were moving through the Sacred Vine in silence, cutting down the hive creatures with barely three words between them the whole time.

Kaleek led the way through dripping hallways of vines, Tirak following and trying his best to cause her no extra frustration. The place was a hive of stinging creatures and eight-legged nightmares, but the two of them had spent the last few weeks killing—and siphoning power from—these things' betters around the bay. Other than something batlike in the corners of Tirak's vision, they were hardly a challenge. He couldn't shake the worry that something was guiding them, leading them toward a trap, but soon he and Kaleek were standing in front of a huge circular hatch door. Maker's script had been etched into the steel's surface eons ago, pronouncing this part of the temple to be what they had come for.

After working hard together to crack it open, a crescent of blue began to shimmer around its bottom edge. The door continued to rise, swinging upward away from them. The color of ocean washed over their faces as they stared at what was inside. It. Was. Beautiful.

He shared a slack-jawed grin with Kaleek, and Tirak noticed absently that even this display didn't match her own beauty. For a moment he saw that warmth flicker through her eyes again too. She *did* still care about him. He just needed to convince her it was okay to care. Okay for her to be more than a heroine of legends.

Immediately inside the door was a porous, grated floor that completely circled an enormous tube of glass. The column stretched from high into the infinite ceiling and disappeared into the depths of water they were walking across. Vertigo attacked him as Tirak moved farther away from the edge. The water wasn't standing still, it was swirling, swirling, spiraling toward the center, speeding up the closer it got to the tube. Deep blue shined from every inch of both the glass and the water beneath like a bonfire.

Two wriggling bracers raised themselves into the air, both screens already glowing with hunger. A series of flashes erupted from their arms, and Tirak's eyes went wide as a staggering rush of elemental power flooded into his bloodstream. He swayed, doing everything he could to stand upright under its euphoria. Had even the Eldress herself ever felt *this* much of it before?

A motion at his side caught Tirak's eye.

He turned, glowing hand ready to blast away another bug that might be sneaking up behind them. There was nothing in sight… *not even Kaleek*! He glanced down to find her lying in a heap, her forearm soaked in fresh blood.

Blood! Tirak let go of the energy flowing into his veins and rushed to help her straighten out. Her body was contorted with cramps, every limb fighting him when he tried to move one. He conjured a spray of water to rinse the blood away. Beneath, he found deep gashes and torn skin radiating out from her bracer. Each writhing chain of dark muscle ran the length of a chasm-like wound carved into her skin.

He panicked as he thought through their options. He desperately wanted to rush her back to the village and get help, but the blue lines on her mask reminded him they couldn't go back. Maker was counting on them to fix this, and the bugs would only be more fearsome the next time if they returned again later, but Kaleek would bleed out before he absorbed so much glass. He pounded his fist repeatedly against the floor in frustration, hoping it would clear his mind.

Scattered puddles splashed and rose in swirls with every impact. Each time, they hung in the air a little too long before falling. He stared at the effect and saw flecks of crystal swirling too. He didn't even realize he had switched his polarity, and he could have sworn those bits of blue crystal were floating on their own.

An idea! He absorbed a few more chunks with his bracer to give himself time to think, then executed his plan.

~~~~~

Days later, Tirak slumped against the boat's wheel, exhausted. He had ended up spending every one of the crystals he brought with them on keeping the boat out of that Darkness-cursed vortex. And the depthbeasts that it had vomited from its wet throat... Why had no one warned him about that? And what other dark secrets was Maker hiding from them all out here in the open waters? He hadn't slept in days, and the incessant sun was wearing him down.

No. He couldn't give in yet. He had to...
~~~~~

Numbly, Tirak dropped to his knees and crawled toward the wall of the boat, where their remaining supplies were all lashed down in a bundle beneath a crudely hung tarp. He waved several horseflies away from Kaleek's unconscious form and prayed Maker would wake her up soon. Tirak was no healer. He had no clue how to help her. All he knew was they needed to get to a port.

He raised himself over the boat's edge and looked out again. He hoped the currents wouldn't pull the wheel off course too quickly this time. He shielded his eyes with a hand and squinted. The horizon looked especially brown ahead today. The waves especially tall. And… they weren't moving anymore? Not just still and lazy. Like. Not moving… *period.*

His eyes went wide as they caught the first flash of a rooftop beneath the dunes.

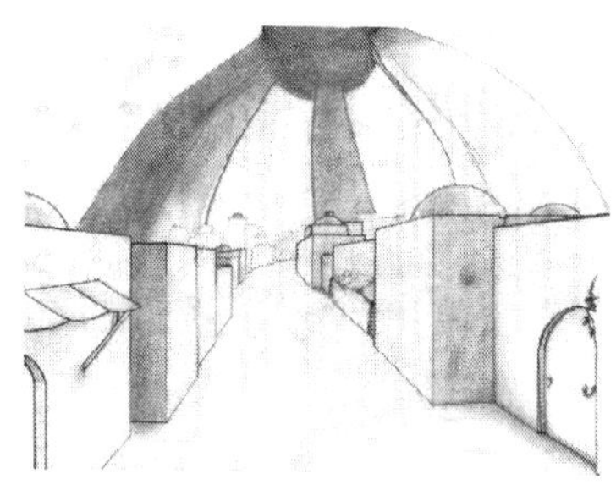

Maker's Log #90109: Terra City as viewed from Market street.

What? Oh don't mind me, I just have Prissi recording the sights while we walk. Tyrant... I thought this place was impressive back when it was just a sports stadium and sky elevator. Bozrakh. This is incredible! And the PEOPLE! You must have the lowest death rate across the whole island for the population to have exploded this much. It's even more crowded than my memories of home!

Huh, sports? Oh, just a sort of contest my people would watch each other play that involved using sticks to... You know what, I can leave that for later. I was never very interested in it and probably can't even explain.

I see the kindlewasps are surviving well up there too. Still no fatal interactions with your people yet, yes?

Perfect.

Oh! Why hello there. You're a cute one, aren't you? Any idea whose he is, Boz? Ah, that must be your mother's voice now, I imagine. Run along so you don't worry her. AND, why don't you tell her you met the Maker today. And He decrees that you deserve a sweet with supper tonight.

...

Ah, it's really wonderful to see how well your terrii are treating Hakhoz' children. The ignii deserve a good hug after that whole incident. I hope it doesn't turn him off from trying to build another one. That floating village design was SO close to being incredible. Plus, I know it has to be a strain on you and Onok trying to care for two elements now. Just don't forget that you ARE appreciated, Bozrakh.

16

GLADIATORS

Streaks of sand clung to Tirak's brow as he wiped the sweat away. Afternoon sunlight threatened to fry him alive as it sank into view below the rim of a mountainlike tower that overshadowed the whole city. Somewhere within fifty handspans, he heard a pitiful groan. Tirak couldn't help bellowing a laugh.

"I told you this would be fun! Aren't you glad I talked you into it?" he asked.

Kaleek coughed up a chuckle and grimaced. She had a hand pressed to her side, violet blood spreading between her fingers as the fresh glow faded black. It looked pretty bad. A thick, inky liquid began leaking from her forearm and covered the whole area. After a few seconds, a shiny layer of skin covered the otherwise raw and inflamed gash. That healing waters ability she had was *unfairly* useful.

"Oh *Maker*, it's hot out. Could you give me another splash across the face?"

Kaleek shook her head.

"Can't," she panted. "That was my last drop."

"Ah, being selfish as always. I see how it is."

She gave him a flat, unamused stare as her hands continued trying to keep her own blood from staining its way too deeply into the leather of her battleskirt. There kind of *was* a lot of it, huh? Eh, who was he kidding? Kaleek was tough as rocks. She'd have laughed if he so much as voiced the concern.

Tirak leaned back and basked in the mixture of harsh sunlight and roaring chants. They really *had* come close to losing this match. The other guys looked like their scars wouldn't be permanent at least. He still shuddered whenever he thought about their first fight. Thankfully that fellow had been Limni, so he could regrow those fingers like Kaleek was doing now, but his sword arm would probably never swing quite as straight again. Seeing her fight like that almost let him forget how close to death she had come. He tilted his head toward her with some concern. She was massaging her forearm again, even though she swore up and down that it wasn't tender anymore. Was that more blood she was rubbing between her fingers?

"How's the arm holding up, sis?"

She snatched her hand away and glared at him.

"It's *fine*. Same as the last five times. You don't have to keep asking."

"Sorry, I've just never seen you hurt that bad before. It's fine to have to recover, you know. And it's important to know how well it's progressing, especially if it's slower than you want it to."

"Whatever, *Dad*."

Typical Kaleek...

They peeled their backs off the sandy arena floor, passed through a shower of cheers and praises, and then reentered the surrounding streets completely unnoticed. The abrupt change was jarring, and Tirak felt his winner's high evaporating almost as quickly the farther away they walked.

The chants quickly became a murmur that was lost in the busy market streets. He shot a suspicious glance up at the other droning buzz that mixed with the street's sounds. Two of the things had their stingers locked in a vicious looking battle, sinking lower and lower in the air. He still couldn't understand how someone could get used to so many cybri-sized bugs flying around all the time; red eyes and glowing stingers hanging less than a thousand heads above them. It was far away, but not far enough that one of them couldn't swoop down at any moment.

He shivered, and forced himself to remember that no hive creature had bothered a villager before. Tirak whispered thanks to the Maker as he untensed. No more people to deal with at least. No rockheaded fan to smile at and talk to. He had almost feared that slimy earth Elder, Bozrakh, would have been waiting for them by the exit. Surely the creep was *just dying* to invite them on yet another tour of his proud city. Yesterday had been particularly excruciating. The Elder had only *mostly* ignored him, and Tirak in turn spent the whole time wishing he could slip away to find some peaceful solitude for a change. Yet the frustrating guy and Kaleek kept roping him back in just enough that it would have been rude of him to go.

What in the world made Kaleek latch onto such a buffoon? He was that type of person who managed to sound arrogant and insulting even when giving a genuine compliment (something Tirak had yet to witness him do). How was it *not* obvious that the Elder was hitting on her? It was disgusting. He was how many times her age? And at least three times taller too. Everything about him was wrong.

Well, Tirak wasn't going to stand around and watch it play out again. Not today! He and his sister had agreed to head out of town this afternoon and start scouting the next step in Maker's quest. He was beyond excited to leave the cramped streets behind. Today at least, it would just be the two of them again. They had already wasted too much time on useless—

"Oh how wonderful! Kaleek! Tirak! I didn't get a chance to congratulate you on your victory. That fight was truly incredible! What you did with the quicksand to trip those guys, Kaleek. I'm not sure I've even seen the great Biri pull off such a trick in battle before!"

The voice grated against Tirak's ears. Tirak felt his muscles tighten, his pistons press into their joints. He didn't even have to turn to know that a certain tan-and-brown figure was wading his way through the river of shorter cybrii toward them.

Nope. Nope nope nope. Something was definitely off about this Elder. No one could *accidentally* be that pretentious. Tirak opened his mouth and muttered his thoughts to her before the Elder could get close enough to see it.

"Oh please, Kal. I can't take another night of this. Can't we do something productive for once?"

For some reason, she just glared at him as if he had insulted her battle stance.

"And repairing the strained relationships between the villages isn't important to Maker's goal? Come on, Tir. Grow up and see the big picture for once. We need to be unified across the island before the Darkness comes."

"Right, because that's all he's looking to *unify*… Just tell him I have a friend I need to see, please?"

She gave him a confused look as he split away from her.

"A friend…? Wait, you don't even have…"

Tirak locked onto an unusual hood in the crowd again. There.

"Sure, I kind of do."

He didn't wait for Kaleek's reply. He guessed it had been interrupted by saying hi to the Elder anyhow. It didn't matter. Only one thing did: this shadow from his past. Tirak snaked along a crate-filled wall toward where he last saw that familiar tattered hood. It had been moving just about… *there*. He spotted it again, and this time it was suspiciously close to another hood. As he watched, the pair moved out of the stream of traffic toward a side alley. Probably some courtyard for a cluster of homes, but one could never be sure what else those dark corners might hide.

He turned into a similar nook one block away from the spot. A house of sunbaked clay here had the perfect construction for him to climb, with timbers jutting out like a ladder meant for a giant. In seconds, he was leaning over the spot where the two Goldenhearts had disappeared. He didn't want to lean out too far into view, but the alley below looked empty. Worried he had lost them, Tirak strained his ears.

"Blade won't be happy. Why didn't that kill the brat?"

"Don't ask *me*. I'm not the one who got distracted and lost the match. Besides, fish as slimy as her are tricky to spear."

Tirak nearly lost his grip on the ledge. They were talking about Kaleek, weren't they? This little adventure had just become *a lot* more important! Wait… did they just say that foul strike hadn't been an accident?

"Well, don't mess up again. Next time, Blade might just decide to replace his Terra captain."

The other voice snorted.

"Hah! You can find somewhere far better than my ear to stuff those useless threats. Why don't you tell that Elder to worry about problems big enough for him."

"*Hush*! You're going to ruin it all if someone hears us. It's not close enough yet that one bad step couldn't undo everything we've been working for."

"*You're* the one anyone is going to hear… now hang on. Before you go, there's something else Elder Blade needs to know about these two."

Tirak blinked. He had heard that wrong… right? He pulled himself back in to process those words. Blade… was an Elder? No, he wasn't. He was a little taller than normal, but he was still just a… But then again, Blade did have that way of talking about himself in the third person. Could he have been talking about someone else?

No. He didn't have time to get distracted. What had those two been saying?

"…something our fighter told me after their match this morning. Maybe he'll know how to use it."

"Oh? My my, so your spies really do have even more subtlety than speed. And what thing was that?"

"Well, you know how the girl is tied to Elder Onok?"

"What's next, are you going to tell me she's an orphan? Our whole city knows that."

"No… *she's a half-breed freak!* He saw it himself. She's no 'modest lady of the blade' like her fans think. *She's hiding another color beneath all those cloth wraps, and it's not just one either!* He'll swear that he saw one of her armor tones change from tan to sky."

This time, Tirak's hand really did slip from shock. Their talk about what Kaleek was had some effect, sure, but plenty of cybri in Umbra already knew her colors weren't… normal. It wasn't that. His eyes had scanned the housetops while listening, and there was *someone watching him.* Tall, huge even, despite the distance between them. By the time it had registered in his brain, the figure was gone. They had been heavily cloaked, but obviously an Elder from the height.

Who in the island could it be? Which Elder would be spying on him? It wasn't Bozrakh, surely. He had to still be talking Kaleek's ear off.

A spray of sand floated to the alley pavement below. Tirak flattened himself against the roof, cursing his own clumsiness. The voices cut off as his pistons nearly crushed his joints into thin plates from his effort to stay as far out of view as possible. Heartpulse after heartpulse passed in silence.

"What is it this time, Dagger? A pigeon? I swear, Maker made you more skittish than a half-starved kitten."

"I don't know… but I don't think we should stay here. This place could be compromised. The Sand Eel's eyes could be anywhere. A spy don't need to be Onok's friend to be a threat to us."

"Fine, we're done anyway. I need to get all this disgusting sand out of my gears. Dunno how you all can be happy living in all this filth."

"Hah, that's rich coming from *you*. I've *smelled* what it is *you* live in, so don't get me started."

"That's a low blow. You know it's not *OUR* fault the upper crust umbrii dump their trash on our heads…"

Their banter continued as it faded into the roar of the crowd.

A shadow passed overhead, and Tirak glanced upward out of instinct. His heart froze. A four-winged creature was diving *straight for him*!

Without thinking, Tirak dove away from the attack. Metal carapace dazzled his eyes, reflecting the blue-grey sky as it clutched at the empty rooftop for its prey. The creature settled onto four lanky legs and folded its wings into its body.

A segmented eye locked onto him with unnerving curiosity. It seemed to sweat beads of dark moisture.

Mandibles clicked.

"There you are, bro! I was looking everywhere for you! What are you doing all the way up here?"

Kaleek reformed into her mechanical shape and grinned at him. Tirak prayed to Maker that she hadn't seen the Goldenhearts leaving. How to explain that without looking like he'd fallen right back in with them again? Then again, what if she had seen? Something was off about her smile.

"Well, whatever, you'll just have to tell Elder Boz and I all about it during the hike as an apology for running off like that. And before you start, yes he's coming along, so play nice. The Elder knows the whole area better than anyone. He's going to show us around and save us all sorts of hassle."

Tirak started to wish it had been a hive drone attacking him after all.

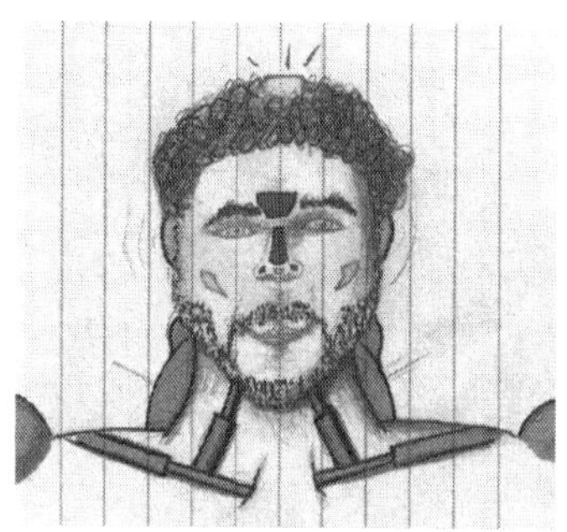

Maker's Log #85067: The first rescue.

Biri and Onok stopped by the grove again today. And, they had a companion with them this time! The fellow was almost as tall as Onok was, but had a shy, bashful expression as he stood behind them. Despite the lack of lizard limbs and a tail that could crush me with one flick, his brown-and-tan armor pattern with that dark golden skin gave him away instantly.

That's right, it was experiment #103! The second one I'd tried after Biri's escape and thought that maybe Terrium would make a better stabilizing base than water or fire had. I donned my insulating glove and shook his hand in greeting. The man... bot... lizard-thing (I really need to come up with a name for these bastardized Prox-Cies) was overjoyed to be welcomed in so warmly.

We chatted over tea for the next hour, and the new fellow really started to open up once he had gotten more comfortable. Charming just doesn't cut it when trying to describe him. He's an absolute treat to have around in any setting. I'm starting to see why it had been so easy for the couple to befriend him. I think I'm already upgrading him to that status in my own head, heheh.

I would've offered to let them stay the night, but Onok and Biri had a second bombshell to drop on me. He had spotted #102 lurking around Fulkana's lava flows! Apparently, Onok had even started making overtures to befriend the lion and didn't want to miss another opportunity tonight.

Hopefully it goes well… That one could be a real thorn in the side if it stays feral. I can't let it cut off my access to the reactor lab.

17

BITTER LOSERS

Kaleek pushed her back against the heavy stones of the stadium's wall and wiped her face. A spray of sweat dripped from her hand as she did. She looked exhausted, but as confident as ever. Tirak wondered how she could bear the heat so much better than he was, being a child of the flames and all that. He could barely keep his feet under him as he squatted down. The fans hadn't given them even a moment to breathe until they'd finally snuck out onto the streets. Out here, the only offensive sound for hundreds of paces was the metal-on-metal clanging of a work group doing repairs somewhere nearby. Maybe they were even wrapping up. Those sounds were starting to get further away.

"What do you think, sis, should we do some scouting along the coast? Maybe cool off with a dip?"

"Oh *Maker*, please yes," came her enthusiastic reply. "Does even Mount Fulkana get this hot? How does everyone else bear it?"

"No idea… Just let me finish catching my breath first."

"I am so sorry, sweetie. No. Can. Do."

They both spun toward the new voice. A hulking, square-built female loomed over them. A cruel light burned in her tan eyes as she cracked her knuckles. Her intentions were as obvious as her element despite the shadows that the narrow walls were casting on them. A mixture of terrii and ignii stepped out of hiding, weapons swinging loosely from toughened hands.

"What do you want?!" Kaleek challenged.

Tirak narrowed his eyes. Groaning inside, he pushed himself back onto his feet.

"You're Goldenhearts…?" he asked.

"Hah! No no. You see, *we* actually *own* this town. Anyway, it was nice chatting, but we're not here to talk politics. You and your disgusting girlfriend are throwing off our nice little hustle in there. The betting pools are *completely* out of whack, and it's costing us a pretty shard. So, now you get a choice: Give us back your earnings—plus half on top as an apology—and walk away, or we'll make you an example."

"Oh?" Tirak scoffed, a chuckle starting to bubble up. "I thought Elder Bozrakh owned—"

Pain blossomed across his cheek, a plate in his mask suddenly twisting inward.

"Example it is."

The blow had come from outside his view, but the female brick was readying her own fists too. Despite the splinters still spraying across his face, embedding themselves inside his gums, Tirak found himself mesmerized by the way dust flowed up from the street across Brick Lady's legs. It twisted around each one, seeming to harden and condense as it reached her arms. It was formed into distinct pebbles and stones by the time it all reached her fist—and that was about to be headed straight for his face!

He tried to duck to the side and found he was already tucking into a roll mid-air. A fist and two more rocks whistled past his eardrum. A blue shadow followed shortly after, flying the opposite direction. Kaleek must have caught on faster than he did and already thrown a water bolt.

No… *of course* she had thrown herself instead.

Princess Cinderblock stood there and grinned as Kaleek slammed into her and bounced back off. Water exploded in all directions from their collision. Kaleek recovered quickly enough to land on all fours, and for some reason, the female's grin was gone once the water fell.

Kaleek struck out a carapace foot with blinding speed. Eyes like saucers, the female's feet flew out from under her and sent her face-first into the circle of mud. Tirak cracked his knuckles and nodded to the nearest thug. He pounced.

He stoked a fire in his palm. Color faded as his eyes constricted. Movement at the edge of his vision made him pivot mid-jump. He caught a second thug's fist with his forearm and slammed his own into the opening. The tan thug howled in pain as flames exploded across his face. Tirak backed away and let the poor guy try to claw at his burning head. Two more crept toward him, making a *very poor* attempt to flank him.

Except... where was the first guy who hit him with that rock? Arms wrapped around him, squeezing him like boulders. Sand was condensing on the arms of the other two as they rushed forward. With only one arm free, he needed a way to react. He grew another fistful of fire, but the one holding him expected it this time and twisted out of the way. Tirak couldn't twist his neck enough to get a clear view.

Seconds left before he would get pummeled, he used the slight momentum to tap into just a little of his earth charge. The ground bulged under his foot. He used the leverage to attempt a backflip. The thug's grip was barely strained at all, but the other two were on him. With his height, he could use the one's chest for extra leverage to continue his arc. He was over top of the guy when the grip holding Tirak gave out with a pop. Two rocky fists connected with their friend's chest.

He landed on his back paws and laid into the thug's back. He roared in pain, but the roar Tirak bellowed back at them outstripped it. Singe marks were left in the abused shirt by the time he sent the group flying with a final kick. The other two were barely fazed, however. Tirak dropped to all fours and charged.

But these two must have learned. They dodged out of the way, and somehow snuck in a kick that sent him flying farther than he'd planned. He landed hard, rolling in the dust for several feet before he could brace himself. Dust was bad! He needed to get up before either of them got the idea to…

He nearly pulled his arm out of its socket trying to stand. The ground had clamped around it. He planted a foot beneath him and pushed with all his might. But before it could give, his foot started to sink too. He looked up in a panic. One thug was approaching him with an old metal pipe while the other kept his hands planted in the ground. The pipe-wielding kid didn't look all that strong, but then again, he didn't need to be when his buddy could conduct the whole area beneath Tirak. He was trapped, pressed into a defenseless ball.

Cold blue popped against the second thug's head. Diamonds glittered in every direction through the air. He dropped with a quiet "oof" and fell motionless. Tirak was suddenly free, just a little sand clinging to his foot. The sound made the remaining thug halt in his tracks. They both looked to Tirak's left. Kaleek's exposed arm was raised, cold frost still steaming off an ice-blue forearm. She grinned from her perch atop the unconscious Cinderblock.

The thug's eyes widened.

"You-y-y-you're a half-breed!"

Kaleek glared at him. Tirak actually chuckled. This kid was about to learn not to call *Kaleek*, of all cybrii, that word.

"I'm gonna tell the whole city about you! You'll never be able to hide! The whole *island* will find out what you are and hunt you down, you freak!" he continued.

She lowered her arm, clutching at her chest instead, trying to cover up the offensive armor even more than it already was.

"Yeah… yeah! You're about to be hunted by *every village*, little girl. You must be really messed up in the head to waltz into our town and try to take over the whole tournament games when you have a secret dark as *that*."

He spat to punctuate the statement and stepped closer to Kaleek, obviously angry. She… simply stood there, cowering. Tirak's eyes narrowed to slits as hatred built inside him. How dare some filthy brute talk to her like that?

Not realizing what he was doing, the gear in his back began to rotate. Power rushed into his veins as a fresh shard hissed into place. The orange armor of his forelegs took on a light brown cast. He slammed a paw into the mud. Sand flowed in a spiral up his arm.

He reached out and seized the insolent bug by its feet. It froze in place, confused why it couldn't pace its circle around Kaleek anymore. Tirak crept up behind it and loomed. He grabbed a shoulder and spun it around, making the creature cry out in fear and stumble further into his grip.

"Tirak?! Oh *Maker* what did you do?"

His sister could wait till the prey had been dealt with. It stared up at him, terror written across the sorry thing's face.

"*No*, n-not you too! You're *both* monsters!"

"You're going to forget you ever saw us," Tirak growled.

"W-w-what? No I won't, our boss *told* us who we had to attack! I can't lie to him!"

"Yes, you will. I know you, scum. You're the bottom of the food chain in the wrong profession. You fought your whole life to hear even one scrap of appreciation. One little sign to know that *someone* accepts you."

A feline rumble echoed in Tirak's throat with each word, his head dripping blood now that his Nature had taken over. His food quivered on its knees.

"So look at us. Get this into your head. We're feral, and we don't give up. You can't stop us. No one can. Your boss is going to hear you scream this tale and call you a lunatic. Probably kick you out the gang for lying about why the crew was so incompetent. *And then,* when you're all alone, I'm going to hunt you down and eat you, piece by piece."

He lifted the bug up by its shoulders to finish his point. It screamed in a terror visceral enough to be agony.

"...And nobody is going to come to your rescue when I do."

"Owww! My leg... my leg!" it moaned.

"Tirak! Stop it!"

Tirak spared a glance for his sister. Her eyes were lidless orbs behind the slits in her mask. She still smelled like fear.

"You made your point, Tir. Put him down... *please*."

She cringed away as soon as she'd finished talking. She was... scared of him?

He looked back at the kid trembling in his paws. His boyish face was bloodless with terror too. Tirak's grip loosened. What was he doing?

The boy whimpered as Tirak dropped him, retracting the claws that were piercing his shoulders. He glanced away before he could be forced to watch the pitiful landing on a leg that now hung uselessly outside of its hip socket. Tirak was going to feel sick in a few more heartbeats, so he decided he had to make use of his last ounce of strength.

"Fine. Tell your boss: no more of these tricks. As you can see, we're not afraid to play dirty either."

A tremor threatened his hand as he snatched his sister's arm and pulled her away from the groans and battle debris. His legs barely carried him far enough into a side alley to not be seen before he collapsed, back pressed into the wall. He welcomed the jagged sandstone that cut grooves into his skin. He deserved it.

"I... could've handled that a little better, huh?" he heard his own voice ask, raspy and shaking.

Rather than answer, his sister stared holes into him. The silence hung unbearably between them.

"C'mon, say something at least, sis."

"How *dare* you?"

Tirak winced.

"How *DARE* you use what I am like that? Don't ever mock me again. You hear? It's one thing for *them* to say things like that. I thought you knew better. You better feel ashamed of yourself."

And he did. As he listened to her turn and storm away, Tirak absolutely did.

~~~~~

Above them, a figure cloaked in faded black layers from head to toe watched. A street thug had just left behind his groaning gang members. The observer wasn't concerned about being noticed. The ones who weren't dead were still too incapacitated to notice them. Even the two children were far away in their own heads.

They turned from their perch and dove toward a lower rooftop. Silently, they melded into the shadows one street away from the carnage, disappearing.
~~~~~

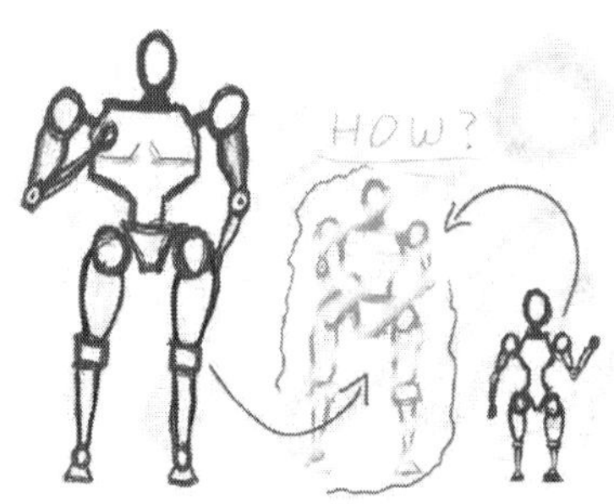

Maker's Log #92001: Genetic Decay & How to Combat Elemental Weakening.

Gene decay is no theory at this point, and my cybrii children seem a hundred times more susceptible than we ever were. Already, I've noticed the latest couple of generations are weaker in every way compared to the synthetic-born gens.

I thought the discovery of natural births would revolutionize their growth and ensure their integrity, that they would become self-sufficient. The first part came true, certainly, but… these kids don't hold a candle (or a wave or pebble or breath) to their grandparents. And I'm not just saying that because I'm some old codger. I mean, I am that by now, I guess, but I've watched their whole species develop. I've MEASURED the difference age-for-age between all six generations.

What IS it about that third, animal piece of the composition that makes their bodies so unstable though? The Elders don't suffer from half the problems they have, and their size should only exacerbate any design flaws, not solve them. The only explanation I can find is that their makeup only contains a fraction of the animal DNA supplementing the Anium-Darkness blend.

Thus the problem. It's too late for me to rip pieces out and recode the children now. But if there was some way to introduce Elder DNA to the general population, it might slow their decay enough.

Or, it might even reverse it entirely and become the compound scaling I'd originally hoped for.

There's no telling what the Darkness has been doing the last few centuries up there. They have every advantage. No resource shortages to worry about out there. Down here on this last remaining island, Humanity and the Cybrii are all we have left.

Maybe I could slip some coding proteins into their food, target one trait at a time until the third or forth gen from now has recovered? But no, they don't eat bulk processed goods I can tamper with…

I'll have to put a pin in this for now. Hopefully some idea strikes soon though. I don't know how many more generations they can survive for.

18

SHOWDOWN

Little else interesting happened over the next few days. Fewer and fewer champions were willing to offer them matches after their ruthlessly efficient showing up till then. So, he and Kaleek got some chances to scout the area around Terra city. Finally.

Unsurprisingly, there was little to see around the sand dunes that covered most of the peninsula. He hoped they wouldn't have to travel all the way back to the badlands near Fulkana to find the tunnel entrance Maker had described. He had warned them the tower's supports stretched miles into the ground at an angle to support itself, and that some of the easiest entrances were accessed from a cave or underwater, but this seemed excessive. Did He expect them to excavate a whole channel of sand until they found a door with a sign saying "Open me?"

And as for Kaleek? Kaleek took a while to forgive him after that street fight. It confused him. She had always been touchy about people making fun of hybrids like her, but come on. They'd both been exhausted already. Could she really blame him for leaning into that hated stigma if the moment called for it?

Girls...

But little of that mattered now as the two of them nervously cinched their gear tighter and checked each other's buckles. Up the stone ramp in front of them, the snake Elder's amplified voice drummed up the crowd's chanting to all new levels. Tirak grimaced, doing his best to ignore the popping rumble of noise as his ears gave up on processing the volume.

This was going to be it.

Tirak finally remembered to stop holding his breath, then gave Kaleek an embarrassed chuckle over the awkward gasp.

"I can't believe Bozzie convinced them to jump us straight to the finals like this," she said.

"I know, but it's not like anyone else was gonna fight—wait. When did the Elder become 'Bozzie'?"

His sister's cheeks blushed on either side of her mask's knifelike beak. She lifted her chin a second later, defiance in her eyes.

"Don't even start. He's a *good guy,* Tir. You'd like him too if you didn't keep looking for any way you can to insult him."

He set his jaw.

"I still think he's—"

But she cut him off, saying, "I think you could learn a lot from Elder Bozzie. Y'know, like actually being nice to people."

When had this become about him again? The announcements cut in before their fight could grow too heated. Thank Maker.

"Aaand coming up to face their final contestant are the fire-and-water duo we've all come to know and love! Damned to a hopeless mission, they're desperate for a win today…"

They both nodded to each other and started marching. The Elder was drawing out the last syllable of Tirak's name as they crested their way into the sunlight.

Tirak may have hated the suffocating crowds, but their roar reminded him once again why he let Kaleek talk him into the arena fights as they walked beneath the high archway. Cheers fell with flowers and ribbons around their heads. Lots of cybrii of both genders seemed to be eagerly vying for their attention. They began chanting something impossible to understand.

Kaleek turned to him and yelled to make herself heard, "I guess we should give them a show!"

He took her hand in his and began filling his reserves with fire. Kaleek's leather shawl began to ripple lazily behind her neck as her own gearbox clicked into place over and over. Twin columns erupted beneath them, one of azure water and one of blinding flame. They flipped through the air in a high arc. He even got to wink down at several adoring fans in their bench seats.

Silence spread across the arena like a wave as they landed hard in the middle of a dust cloud. Kaleek pushed it away with a hand wave, letting them emerge in a final, impressive stance. But the crowd didn't seem to react at first.

He stared around in confusion for three or four heartbeats. Then, Tirak saw the three churning pools of sand that surrounded them. A new surge of cheers made the previous noise seem like a whisper.

The disturbances began to move toward them. Tirak immediately began trying to recall what types of animals could do that. They had assumed the final test would be against other champions, but whatever this was seemed like it could be even worse. He frowned. Something was odd about the space between those swirling circles. If they were animals, wouldn't they either be clustered much *closer* together, or else spread more evenly apart? The crowd began chanting something in unison, and this time he thought he could pick out the syllables "el-der-ling" among it.

The nagging thought clicked into place. He spun around in time to see the ground beginning to glow in the missing spot. Whatever was approaching was ready to reveal itself. As if an invisible raindrop had splashed down, the pools of sand spread out like waves. The fourth spot erupted into a jet of fire that made a candle out of Tirak's little jump. Four huge figures stepped from the show of power as if they were the Elders themselves stepping foot from Maker's hand onto the island for the first time.

As they stalked closer—or no, "paraded" was the *least* dignified way he could ever describe such an impressive gait—Tirak could see that they weren't *quite* as tall as the Elders. But that meant they were still at least half a head taller than himself, his eyes barely reaching their chestplates. The four of them approached until they were perfectly spaced around the siblings, five or six heads away.

Now that his eyes weren't watering, Tirak could see a faint feminine shape to the igni opponent. Something in her features looked vaguely familiar, but he couldn't tell what. The other three all seemed to be brothers based on their faces.

"What do you say, Sikh?" the scrawnier of the brothers asked.

He still had to weigh at least twice what Tirak did. The igni female tilted her head to one side, eyeing the two of them casually.

"Hmm. Daddy's sure going to be interested in seeing what this little one's been up to. Maybe I'll have to drag 'im back to Umbra for a spanking. Sounds like a fun time doesn't it… Tirak, right?"

She winked at him with a maliciously seductive glint to her pink eyes.

"Hey. Don't get too carried away with the twig," another brother teased.

"Awww, don't worry, baby. I'd let you guys join in on the fun too," Sikh replied, dripping with that disgusting tone.

Tirak and Kaleek spent those few moments trying to whisper their plan of attack. Ultimately though, he knew he would just be supporting whatever direction his sister went in the moment. After a short minute, the crowd had calmed enough for Elder Bozrakh to commence the fight.

They were immediately forced onto the defensive and split apart. Kaleek was quick enough that she managed to draw all three of the terrii brothers after her, but even one of these "elderlings" proved to be more than Tirak could handle. The female advanced on him, steering away any attack he sent with an imperious air to her step. He couldn't even conduct a candle flame without her ripping it away from him, turning it back on him.

"Awwww, what's wrong? Hopefully you've got some other tricks up your… well you don't have sleeves, so maybe not."

Even when he tried to molt into his Nature and sprint away, a blazing wolf leaped over him and landed directly in his path. He skidded to a halt on hands and feet before he had hit the edge of her sword-reach. A menacing curved blade swung out to try anyway. Its rose blade swished like fire in the sunlight and left a scorched line of glass through the sand.

"This is going to be so *boring* if you don't come up with *something* soon."

Her tone continued to drip with suggestive mockery. He could try to tap into his other elements and outsmart her that way, but she would see it. A lot of the crowd might, even. If only he'd thought to buy a set of leathers like Kaleek's for himself… He'd always taken that shawl for granted.

A cry rang out. Tirak spun to see a boulder glance off of his sister, get plucked out of the air by another elderling, and sent back toward her. She was full-on dragonfly, but her flight paths were chaotic. One of the four wings flapped limply at her side.

"Wow, they look pretty dead set on paying you back, don't they?"

The elderling dove in close and pummeled Tirak's side until he could break her grip and throw her off.

"What's that supposed to mean?" he spat.

"Vengeance, dear. A sister for a sister is a fair trade, don't you think… *Tirak*? That was quite the vicious stunt you pulled the other day."

His eyes locked onto those pink glowing rings.

"Aw, what? Are you really so surprised that we criminals would stick together? This island might as well *belong* to us. The important half of it at least."

He needed a way to disengage and go help Kaleek! She *needed* him! The elderlings were toying with her at this point. She was trying, but the sand was too tightly conducted for her water to get any purchase against them. As Tirak watched, two brothers raised pillars for the third to run up like a staircase. He leaped for Kaleek and grabbed her behind the neck, dragging her under his cannonball of a body to the ground. There was a sickening rumble as they landed, the male cushioning his fall with Kaleek's body.

"Go on. You should save her before they go too far," the female teased. "Believe me. They can be… a lot to handle. I would know…"

The wistfulness in her voice made Tirak's stomach drop. Could he even trust her? Was this a real moment of battlefield honor? …Did he even have a choice? He stopped thinking and took off in a four-legged sprint. He could feel the trap springing shut around him.

Shrieks of laughter chased his paws, chilling his spine. He had played right into her hand.

Tirak whipped around, but only just in time to gulp. A white-hot column was rushing toward him. In that moment, he knew he was about to die. Almost absently, he heard someone scream his name. He had to block it. Deflect it somehow. Just like every other blow he'd practiced against.

Purple wrapped his left arm as he raised his fists into the right posture. That was a lot of fire for one person to control, after all. Just maybe… he could reabsorb a little of it, or push it away? A crystal in his back snapped and evaporated as he threw his whole will against it.

A gap in the jet stream split just before hitting him. It was razor thin, and was still going to let his sides singe. Worst of all, he wouldn't be able to keep its edges from pinching closed.

Too little, too late. He was so tired.

ELEMENT DETECTED: FURIUM

He blinked as the words from his bracer etched their way across his circuits. He didn't stop to think. He willed Maker's gift to give him strength somehow. Protect him.

Blinding, white-hot light engulfed him, accompanied by a rush of wind that left him deaf. But as it did, the light adopted a violet cast around him, and the gap expanded. It had all happened in the space of nanoseconds.

Energy flooded his veins. Heat built inside, but… not the fiery kind. His muscles felt both overstretched and… invigorated?

Seconds passed. The ache in his body flared stronger and stronger.

The column of fire vanished in a final flash. Tirak's protective bubble disappeared just as quickly without anything to feed it. He stood in the middle of a blackened road that stretched almost the whole length of the arena. In front of him, just beyond the wall of rocks that had deflected the geyser, three elderlings stood stunned.

One of them still had a leather-wrapped leg pinned beneath him.

"E-*nough*—!" he yelled.

Tirak's attempt to gesture threateningly at the brothers sent a bolt straight into one's face. The elderling went down with a scream.

A dagger sank into Tirak's shoulder. The pain followed a few instants after the female's enraged yelling. He spun her off his back with a practiced move. She dislodged easily, and a quick jab on the way down would knock her out for a few…

Her neck cracked with an explosive pop as she landed.

Shards of metal poked through the skin, spurting blood as she tried to rise. The damage traced an outline where his palm had struck. She convulsed one final time, then fell still. Tirak stared down at his hand in shock. He couldn't say he was sorry to see her dead, but…

Silence continued to reign over the arena.

Then, the first voice took up its booing from deep inside the spectators.

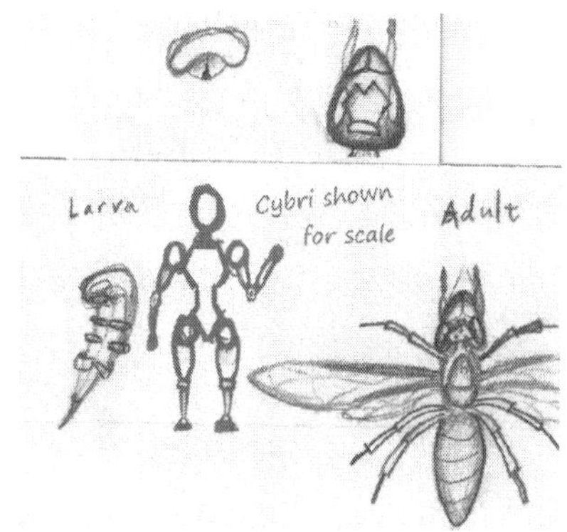

Maker's Log #86301: Introduced the last transplant.

Hopefully this last species will balance out the monolith hive's ecology at last and help keep any one of the others from driving the rest extinct. Fun note about playing with nature: if you're going to try it, maybe make sure you really are, well, ANY sort of macrobiologist first. I'm luckier than I have any right to be the area isn't a wasteland yet.

I mean, this IS a desert already, but… still.

I owe a lot of that luck to Bozrakh too. The guy is infinitely caring, and always seems to know just the right thing to do in any situation. And yet when the situation called for a culling, he single-handedly gave me the extra months I needed to get this queen grub and her drones spreading. Hopefully in a few more days, they can start picking the slack and let him have a break again.

You know… I'm starting to rethink the plan to start with limni for my first batch of mini-heroes. Biri is a great gal, but she can sometimes be a little… temperamental. For a first pick, none of the others even make the list before her even if I put the first-dibs reason aside. Onok and Hakhoz both mean well, but they need a lot of encouragement before they're ready for that much responsibility. I want to say the same for Korma too, but if I'm honest, the guy kind of weirds me out. Like Biri, I can't help wondering if the environment caused the personality, or the personality drew him to such a cold environment. Guy is basically as much a hermit as I am. I guess that makes me the pot and him the kettle…

Bozrakh on the other hand. I can't imagine him doing a poor job at anything. If the mini-versions take after their element anywhere as strongly as the first five do, his chances should be doubled or better. Stalwart, stable, yeah… I can't think of a better combination for the experimental batch. I hope I don't eat my words, but… compared to the alternatives, I don't see what could go wrong.

19

DESERT VIPER

Elder Bozrakh came charging onto the arena floor, arms waving to still the crowd. No one seemed to listen. The uproar only grew in volume. Tirak watched a squad of terrii guards enter from the opposite direction and felt a familiar scene beginning to flash before his eyes.

The Elder reached them long before the guards did. He leaned in close as if to scold them, but shot a wink at them both as he did.

"Just trust me a little, loves. I don't actually blame you. Just ignore what I say next and look remorseful."

His finger had already started waving at them, contrasting the conspiratorial half-smile that only they could see. His voice rose to a boom, and the scolding began. Just before the guards approached, the Elder gave Tirak a mighty shove that landed him on his rear. Rather *firmly* on his rear... ouch. Tirak did his best to not let his surprise take over and, remembering how inappropriate his mask was for a moment like this, did his best to keep his face turned down as Bozrakh's volume washed over him.

His voice grew so loud, Tirak could barely hear what he was saying.

"...*any* idea how that looked?! You call *that* self-defense?! *SPORTSMANSHIP*??? Well? What's your defense for *THAT*, boy?"

As he heard the rhythm of boots approaching, it felt like the right thing to do, so Tirak turned his head away. The crowd was beginning to quiet down, appreciating their Elder's anger.

"Nothing?! Unbelievable! You there, no. Give me that brand. These two don't even deserve the publicity. We are not doing this here!"

The Elder landed a kick on Tirak's legs.

"Get up, boy. Both of you. We're going outside the city to do this. No, captain, you all stay."

"B-but Elder! What if—" one of them started.

"Do you think I can't defend myself? Look at them. They *want* spectators. They *want* to be remembered for this. Don't give them the pleasure."

A hand the size of Tirak's head yanked him onto his foot, leaving him to sway precariously until he could get his numb leg steady under him. After a few more verbal assaults, they were marching away beneath a dead-silent city. Elder Bozrakh muttered frustrated curses to himself, trailing off as the minutes ticked by. Once they had made the first few turns toward Terra's nearest gate, Tirak heard a sound like hushed giggling and whispers behind him.

"Wow. Just wow, Tir. Wasn't Bozzie so amazing back there? You tamed that whole crowd in *seconds*! And… you did a pretty good job too, bro."

By the time he looked over his shoulder, Kaleek already had her arm raised above her head. She squeezed the Elder with a hug, as high around his hips as she could reach. It was all he could to keep swallowing down the bile that was building.

"Ugh… Not this *too*, now. *Please*. Just leave me out of it."

Tirak launched himself from the ground with an effortless jet of fire, ignoring the Elder's calls that he was still under arrest. Either one of them could have caught up with ease if they had wanted to. Instead, the Elder slipped as many heavy sausages between Kaleek's fingers as he could fit and they slowed their pace to a casual stroll.

Fine. Let them have their romantic walk together. He would just go find that tunnel on his own and guard it until they got there.

~~~~~

Tirak glanced at the nicks dotting his arm while he parried another strike. A green ooze bubbled out of each one. He was on borrowed time and he knew it. Fangs snapped inside his guard, just inches away from his chest! A quick pivot kept their tips from landing another strike, then he brought his blade upward as he infused as much heat into its edge as he dared. The head severed with a searing hissss. The rest of the spiny body collapsed into a coil.

But even in death, it left a sickening terror to fester in Tirak's veins. Not defeat. A draw at best.

Bone-chilling images flashed through his mind, leaving him barely able to focus.

He took a step away from its thrashing death throes, and felt his numb leg drag heavily. What in the island…? He looked down and saw another of the things dangling from the mangled calf. A bolt of heat cooked it through, but the damage was already spreading to places he *could* feel.

As with the rest of the brood, the most unsettling part of these things were the way they kept writhing and attacking even after they were killed. He fought back three more of them before the bleeding violet eyes of these two fell still and went dark. Tirak struggled as much against their clever feints and tricks as he did against his own growing horror. And the poison too, but he couldn't *do* much about that yet.

And just as suddenly as the nest erupted beneath him, the vipers turned and disappeared into the sand. That creeped him out, the way they could just do that in solid ground. He wiped off his blade and started clawing his way back up the dune. He regretted getting so far ahead of the others. After taking that spill down the slope, he couldn't even see them anymore.
~~~~~

From the dune's top, sand stretched out in every direction, ending in a watery haze on the east and west sides, and the silhouette of Mount Fulkana rising over the south. But where were Kaleek and that eel, Elder Bozrakh? Had they really not seen anything and just left him behind? He *had* almost reached the access tunnel's entrance, hadn't he?

He scanned back and forth once more. Besides the flurry of bugs around their destination, all he saw were a couple of twisting dust columns.

Wait. He looked east again to the second short twister. It hovered above a perfectly dome-shaped sand dune near the coastline. Even as he tried to puzzle over why that shape looked so wrong, a tidal wave rose over the shore and slammed into it. Two figures popped out as the dune was disintegrated, locked in what had to be either a fight or a desperate embrace: one brown and tan, the other blue.

A pit formed in his stomach. What… what had he been thinking? He should never have left her alone with him! Tirak let his armor bleed to a dull tan and took off at a sprint. His feet left ridges in the sand with each step, propelling him forward, raising him above its surface on an endless supply of springboards.

Even after he had reached an absolutely breakneck speed, the seconds were an excruciating eternity until he had crossed the distance. A final leap sent him cresting mere fingers above the last dune that separated him from the shoreline. His feet dug trenches into the sand as he skidded the last few legs to its base. Forty heads away lay the shore, but the sight in between made his eyes grow wide.

Gashes crisscrossed the beach, big enough for him to stand in. Kaleek was digging herself out of a shallow crater that rose up above the ground in a wide circle. She looked absolutely torn to shreds! Many paces away, a blur of blue was locked in combat with Elder Bozrakh. Writhing arms of sand rose up around the pair and grabbed at the blur, but waves from the shore and the water table beneath crumbled each one in turn. The whole landscape reshaped around these masters and their opposing elements from one moment to the next. The blur's attacks began to build up their effect, driving the Elder backward. Back to the water line.

Walls of water rose in anticipation with each step. Even at a distance, Bozrakh's look of determination made it clear he knew what was coming. And then, a little wave lapped at his foot. Tirak watched a look of horror spread across his face before the boiling mass of gritty water consumed him.

The blur fell still and dropped into the water. Leathery wings folded into the creature's sides as she looked down at her prey. Fangs growled at the churning pool. The massive blade she raised was just about the only way Tirak was able to recognize Kaleek's mother. The temper was a pretty good clue too.

Her blade sank into the water. Tirak jumped. He hadn't expected to ever see an Elder kill one of their fellows! The blade rose again and hacked downward, then again, and again.

Tirak turned away and grimaced as Eldress Biri roared. She'd lost control of herself, reveling in the slaughter. The waves around her were already turning a violet-black. Tirak had to shut his ears off to that direction and focused on his sister. She hadn't moved from her spot. She just shivered there, despite the blazing sun, holding her knees against herself. Sand clung to every part of her. He stepped up to her cautiously, kneeling down to place a comforting hand on her back.

"Kee? Are, are you—"

Steel dug against his throat. If he moved even a hair, it threatened to cut him wide open.

"Touch her and I'll rip every limb from your body and feed it down your throat before I shove your gear shards into your eye sockets!" a serpentine voice hissed behind him.

The blade pinched a little harder.

"Pull the hand away, *slowly*, and leave. Do it, and I *might* spare you."

"...P-please, don't hurt Tirak," Kaleek said weakly.

A long pause followed. Tirak didn't dare try to look up at the stingray-shark of an Elder, so he could only guess at what she might have been thinking. He tried not to think about the drips of blood that were starting to run down his neck.

His vision flashed blue as Biri lifted away her sword.

"Don't hurt my little girl," she hissed with the sort of sneer that could be heard.

She shoved him to the ground and stalked back to what was left of Bozrakh's corpse. Tirak wheezed, coughing up a mouthful of blood while the wound resealed.

"Th… thanks," he said in a raspy voice.

He didn't wait a moment longer to pull his sister into a tight, protective hug. She was absolutely filthy with sand. His hand already stroking strands of her jet-black hair away from the gaps in her mask, Tirak locked a set of shards into his gearbox and began to wash it all away with a trickle of warm water.

She cringed against him as the grit slid across her, but continued to hold tight even after she'd lost her lunch. Other than a few ribbons of purple shirt, bare armor and skin shifted against him with each breath she took. The only thing she seemed capable of was to tremble in silent hysteria. Just what had that snake been trying to do to her? From the freshly re-opened scars up and down her left arm, Tirak could only guess.

The sun had nearly set before Kaleek finally started to calm down. Once she had enough strength to sit up on her own, Tirak extracted himself from around his sister and began to help the Eldress clean up the area. Kaleek was still sniffling when they returned. Biri knelt beside him, and together they struggled to keep a flayed arm held together with new bandages. His sister didn't seem to notice.

Sensing that no good moment would come, Tirak crouched down and offered the ripped bundle he'd gathered up. It took two or three nudges to pull her out of her own head. Tirak closed her fingers around the gift, an image of bloodstains and Umbra cobblestones flashing through his circuits.

"I... found most of its pieces at least. You should still be able to wear it, once I patch the shirt a little."

Her expression changed slightly as she regarded the clothes and his words. In the end, she just shrugged. As if she didn't care anymore.

Tirak balked. "Here. It'll only take me an hour. I can even sew its front back up while we walk. You'll be able to wear it before we've even started climbing the tube. Of course, that's if you even still *want* it, obviously..."

He chuckled uncomfortably. She *did* still want to wear it... right? She'd begged Onok for a set like it for at least half her life. And besides, this one had come from Tirak himself. That alone had to mean something to her... didn't it?

Her hands gripped the shredded clothes and yanked it from him. She ripped strips off it and added them to her forearm, then began pulling the less destroyed pieces on around her torso. The shirt hung open and ruined once the tattered shawl had the top of it pinned safely to her shoulders.

"What for? It doesn't matter. There's no point in hiding anymore. Let the whole island see who I am. I'm not a Limni, I'm not auri—*certainly* not umbri. I'm something better. So, I don't need it."

She didn't need *him*, she meant. Tirak crouched there, stunned by the pain. Finished dressing, Kaleek stood up and regarded him with a flat stare, then shrugged.

"C'mon. We should get this over with and move on. Maker said we're running out of time."

Tirak heard feet pad several steps through the sand and pause. Kaleek sighed.

"Look. I still *appreciate* it. I've just... outgrown it, you know? I'm a fighter that can look defeat in the eyes and walk away the next day, stronger than before."

So, she had "outgrown" him. Did Tirak even have a reason to be here anymore? He snorted at her delusion. Who had been all but catatonic for the last few hours, again? He ground his teeth together and pushed himself onto his feet. A hero didn't cry, a hero didn't complain, so Tirak would bear this too. And yet, his devastation spread as he watched her pull off more tattered strips of the expensive fabric and let them drop to the sand, forgotten. He almost reached for the first bit as he passed, but a teary static kept his eyes from seeing where it was in time. The cloth had been swallowed up by sand before he could turn back to cast a final glance at it.

But… no. He wouldn't let her give him up yet, even if she didn't want him. His hand wiped the last green drop from his shoulder, where two pinpricks finally resealed.

Maker's Log #92340: Contingency plans

Come on, Avoma. Run the numbers again. What are you missing? Why are they ignoring the quest? This can't just be the hybrid girl's fault, Kaylee or whatever. I know things have been different between the Elders ever since, but this level of animosity? To not even show up when called? What's gotten into them all?

Those two KIDS were the only ones to show up. They're new-gen too. Basically no power to start with. They've got so much more ground to cover than I'd planned for. If THEY'RE all we have against the Darkness' army, we're doomed.

Sigh. Stop it. You KNEW this was going to be a low-rate production test from the very beginning. We don't have to put all of our trust in them if I get the rest of this tooling bootstrapped to a full production line. And I haven't gotten the results back yet either. Maybe they've already become two new Elders. Maybe they're the STRONGEST Elders across the island by now. You. Don't. Know. So wait for the data and get more of these produced.

...

Is that?

It can't be...

Oh you star-sent man, Onok. You finally showed up! Yep, that's definitely him on the northwest door monitor. Letting him in now... Time to go see if we can't turn this little arms race back around. End recording.

20

SETBACKS

Kaleek was dying.

Black-violet blood dripped and smeared everywhere as her newly reunited mother laid her on top of a sterile bed. Its blank, padded surface was broken only by the usual gap where a gearbox could rest. Tirak braced his hands against his knees as he tried to suck air into his lungs after that mad sprint through the twisting, winding hallways and chaotic flight over the island before that.

What a disaster. Maker's world seemed like a cruel joke to him in that moment. Why would He let Kaleek finally have the relationship with her mother that she had always been dreaming of, only to rip her life away an hour later?

"Maker!" Tirak bellowed. "Maker, where are you? Kal needs you!"

"Get in here and take your silly device off my daughter *THIS instant,* you old fool!" Biri joined in.

Tirak stopped short, looking at the Eldress with wide eyes. *That* was a far cry from reverent. Her body hovered vacantly above the cot. She looked... crushed, quivering visibly. Finally, she sucked air into her lungs, her head seeming to melt as it took on a new, stubbier, fanged shape.

"MAKERRR!!!"

"Goodness gracious, woman! I heard you the first time. What is it?" Maker said, hobbling in.

The magical sliding door hissed shut as a haggard-looking Maker crossed the room. He bumbled his way past the Elder and finally saw Kaleek. He went stiff, letting out a low, warbling groan.

"Biri... Could you *please* keep your emotions to yourself for even five minutes?! That girl was *working on MY behalf*! Really... you two are exactly alike," He sighed.

Biri blinked at him rapidly.

"You think *I* did this to her?! *YOUR* stupid, dangerous device nearly KILLED my little girl—still IS killing her! Take the silly thing off her RIGHT NOW, Maker. I demand it!"

Maker hesitated, confused.

"You... little girl? Wait. What happened to tearing her bleeding toes off one by one to feed them back into the hellspawn machine that built her?"

"*FIX HER*, Maker! She had already passed out from losing so much blood..."

She began to weep, her voice blubbering less and less coherently with each second.

"Oh, Dark. I... I didn't know the little ones could ever bleed so much! She was... unconscious, unresponsive, but when I tried to pull it off her arm and save her, she woke up screaming! Oh, Maker, you don't know how terrible it was. *More* blood sprayed everywhere! That look in her eyes..."

Maker's own eyes had long been in a flurry of motion as her words spilled out. He looked over at Tirak. Those unglowing orbs looked exhausted behind their silver mask. Sunken twice as far into their slots as normal. Tirak nodded to him, understanding the Man's unspoken plea. He eventually drew the massive Eldress out of the weird, pure white healing room and into a hallway where they could wait.

This place had far less of the polished wood than he remembered from his last visit. Only the highest sloped portion of the ceiling showed any of it at all. The rest was some kind of polished stone. He tried his best to ignore the sound of his childhood hero's sniffling beside him in her moment of weakness. Biri, the mistress of the waters that held up their whole island… was leaning on him like a little girl.

It was only then that he noticed an unfamiliar sound that had been droning in the background ever since they had entered. He tuned Eldress Biri out further and strained to amplify the other noise. It sounded almost like… voices? Either that or water, he guessed. Was Biri doing something to the lagoon nearby out of grief? He supposed they should investigate. Maker said that parts of this home actually went *under* the water. If it had sprung a leak somewhere… He shivered, remembering his and Kal's desperate run from the Scarred. That feeling of his throat being strangled by his element's opposite. But with that came the memories right after as Kaleek saved him. *Her* breath filling his lungs while they hid at the bottom of the river.

Why was it getting so hard to see straight? He blinked, surprised to find droplets forming there.

Ahead, the hallway ended in a wide pair of metal doors. One of them hung slightly ajar. The noise had been growing in volume. He didn't need to amplify his hearing anymore, and even Biri had fallen silent, listening. They pushed the door open to find chaos.

A sea of blue, fear-stricken faces ebbed and swirled maybe fifteen heads down from them. The doors led to a simple platform with glowing buttons. They stepped onto the elevator and Tirak placed his hand on the space where the down button hovered. His stomach churned as they fell gently toward what must have been Limna's entire population!

Voices quieted around the two of them in waves. Excited whispers bled like an aftershock through the crowd. One slim figure pushed through several bodies like a twig in a river as they came to rest at the bottom, a haggard female emerging to meet them.

"Elderess Biri? Oh Maker… you're… you're really alive? They told us you were dead. That you died like a hound while trying to give yourself to them."

Her voice shook. Tirak lurched as he realized who she was. Kaleek's "twin" seemed to have doubled her age in the weeks since they had left Limna.

"Kili? Where is your grandmother, child? Is she well?"

The female shook her head.

"Should you not be tending to her, then? Surely one of the other advisors could be here instead…"

"Dead, Mistress Biri. I have no idea how, but the Scarred knew exactly where to hit us. Your leaf was the first one they destroyed…"

Her eyes had been hollow up till now. She glanced away, cheeks flushing slightly.

"I only survived because… well, I was with… I didn't mean to lose track of time yet again like that."

Biri placed a hand on the girl. A smile of sympathy broke through the sadness that filled each line in her face.

"I understand, Kili, I loved once too you know. I've been more than thankful you didn't leave us for months like we all expected. I doubt your grandmother could have held us all together for so long without you. I'm… even more thankful you took time away at just the right time. Did he at least…?"

Kili sniffled, then shook her head. Biri pulled her into a hug.

"Oh *child*… I'm so sorry."

Tirak shifted his weight uncomfortably. He had no real part in such a candid moment and didn't want to, either. The ceiling brought its answer as it crackled with an unfamiliar sound, like static building before a lightning strike.

"Tirak," Maker said from the air a moment later, "please return to room 441. We need to speak in private."

Biri nodded to him and said something softly about looking after her limnii. He walked back to the elevator they had just come down with a new depth to his growing numbness. He watched the sea of blue refugees shrink. First Terra, now this? So many hopeless faces down there below him. He had glanced down toward Terra City while Biri carried them from the tower. She had been intending to announce their Elder's death before they left.

But the city had been a smoldering ruin. The Darkness had already come and gone, all while the three of them had been busy pumping himself and Kaleek with more *power*. They had become everything Tirak hated about Onok. They had become true *heroes*. What did they need more power for? Kaleek and he already had more than could ever naturally fit inside a cybri.

And still, they weren't enough. This Darkness. It was unstoppable. Ancient. Crafty.Tirak raised his fist toward the open doorway to where he had left Kaleek, about to knock on the frame. Inside, the Maker sat hunched at a table near her, looking across a chaotic spread of bloody tools, glowing devices, and paper scraps. His head hung low toward the empty floor between His feet. His hands were pressed against either side of His head.

He looked… wrung out. Feeble.

Tirak took a step back, wondering if he should come back later, or… Maker lifted His head and looked back.

"Oh! Apologies, I… got lost in thought, I suppose. Comes with old age, you know."

He tried to say the last part with a grin, waving off His previous appearance.

"I… I could always come back, sir," Tirak tried.

"Not at all! Come, son! Come in. I have a lot that we need to discuss."

Tirak swallowed, his throat feeling dry. He couldn't help his eyes flickering toward the pile of stained equipment.

His voice barely worked as he asked, "Is… it about Kaleek?"

"Huh? Oh! No. That was quite the challenge to re-engineer such a flawed design, tendrils worming into all sorts of organs they should never have touched, its receptors focused in all sorts of directions, partially eating her any time she used it... But! Your sister has to be the most resilient girl I've ever met. No no, she's already in recovery now and should be on her feet as soon as the sedative wears off. She takes after her mother for sure. I still feel a little foolish I didn't recognize her the last time you were here... oh!"

Relief had flooded Tirak's head, making it pound, and before he knew what he was doing, he had leaned forward and caught himself against Maker's chest. He let out a ragged sniff, refusing to break down entirely at the good news. By the sounds of another sharp breath, Maker was putting on a more stoic mask than He really felt too. Tirak held himself there for a second until he could collect his emotions again.

Until the acrid smell hit his nose.

Tirak jerked his head up and caught a wincing squint to Maker's eyes. Two blackened burn marks colored His chest, one where the top of his head had rested, the other fitting his palm perfectly. Tirak gasped. Before he thought better, he had reached out a hand again to try and help.

Vents opened in His mask as Maker finally let in a gasp.

"No—please! I'll... I'll be all right, son. I'll heal. Just... *please*. Don't do that again."

"I-I-I'm so sorry, sir! I didn't..."

"You didn't think Light and Dark would actually obliterate each other? Cancel each other out?"

"I...!"

Maker let out a sigh, held up a hand, and controlled His mechanical breathing.

"Enough of all this. It's over now, and it was just yet another distraction to start with. Darkness seems to be worming its way into our plans more subtly than I'd ever thought. No more distractions. Sit."

Tirak obeyed, afraid of causing some other disaster if he so much as didn't blink at the right cue. Smoke continued to curl from Maker's body and He opened his mouth vents to speak. Weird, Tirak hadn't even had any elements in his gearbox ready to use. How had he burned the Man?

Right! Important quest stuff.

"...half the relays now, so how well do you feel you both are progressing?"

"H-half? But there's only three."

"That's what I said, son. 'More than half.' Pay attention. Do you feel stronger now? By how much?"

Tirak winced, deciding to listen better from then on.

"Right, uh, I guess it's helping? Both of us are able to conduct any element we want at *least* as well as a cybri that's native to it. Kaleek is *basically* a water elderling now, and..."

"An elderling?"

"Huh? Oh, um... I think some of the Elders got a little—um, and they... now there's..."

Maker held His hand up again.

"Forget I asked. Hmm... You don't look much bigger, if at all. Either the transfer wasn't anywhere as efficient as I hoped, or it just doesn't work that way. But, no it has to be stored as matter. Far denser than the other two forms... Fascinating. So neither of you can rival Elders Biri or Onok yet?"

"N-no. At least, not without using a second element, I bet."

Maker sighed.

"Worthless..."

"I'm sorry, sir! I keep trying, but it's just so hard to stay focused on doing what's right. And don't even get me started on how many times Kaleek dragged us off onto a side job or decided to beat up some creature just because she could. She keeps saying it's to collect a little more power, but really... We hardly even notice such a little gain anymore.

I'm really worried about what's going on in her head sometimes. Something isn't right with her."

Maker had slumped back in His chair and was staring off into an empty spot in the ceiling. He blinked.

"Eh? Oh. No, I meant Me—My plan. My hail matriarch seems like it's turning out to be a flop. We need another option. The engineer in Me just keeps screaming 'Single point failure!' My old profs would absolutely roast Me alive in a peer review..."

He leaned forward toward Tirak, His hands growing a little more animated with each second.

"We need a way into their center of operations. We've been operating blind since day one, and I'm just so sick of it. We know so much more now from your people than I did two centuries ago, but it *isn't enough*. We need a way for this firestorm of destruction to pass us by. If worst comes to worst, I may have to risk sending some of you into the den itself. The Darkness seems bent on converting any of you to its ranks that it can, so a set of spies may just work. It isn't enough to make my own darkness-based warriors and throw them at the enemy..."

Maker fell silent for a few minutes. He began to look deeply disturbed, and, not sure what to contribute, Tirak waited quietly for Him to gather His thoughts.

"That's the problem, isn't it?" Maker asked into the air. It was a question Tirak knew he wasn't meant to answer. "I'm trying to put out a fire, but I keep dousing it with flames. This whole idea was futile... How could I have missed it? So obvious..."

Well, that wasn't *strictly* true, Tirak noted. He had bested a firestorm of an elderling just yesterday. Fire could beat fire, just like the right measure of violence *could* stamp out a smoldering hate, or a rampant mineshaft fire could be snuffed by one little explosion to starve it of air. After all... according to Biri, the Goldenhearts hadn't been a threat to Umbra since his and Kaleek's little showdown with them.

"What about other plans, Maker?"

Something like a snort buzzed through His mask.

"There are no other plans at this point. I've been so invested in this one for centuries. There is no chance for another."

His despondence didn't last forever though. The barely visible eyes inside the mask's slits squinted.

"I suppose there's the undercover option. I still *might* be able to slip you cybrii in under the guise of a truce. It would be a dangerous move, and I hadn't seriously considered it because I expect most of you to end up lost to them forever. But… we're already losing…"

He looked up at Tirak, eyes grim. Tirak could read a hesitation in them. They held a choice that Maker's light could never allow Him to make, but a choice that needed to be made anyway. That look was a cry for help. A cry to ignore His commands if things came down to it. An unsaid understanding passed between them. Tirak didn't dare break the spell by nodding, but he saw Maker's held tilt once, almost imperceptibly.

"I'll have to keep thinking about this. Thank you, son. I have no more answers than before, but… you've given me a lot to think about. I'll call you back when Kaleek and you are strong enough to continue."

Tirak's circuits churned all the way back to the warehouse room that had become a makeshift Limna. He didn't know much about this Darkness yet, but if its members were anything like the Cybrii, then there had to be a way to trick it. All of them might even be able to fit in, help temper the villain from the inside! It was the story of Onok's Spear all over again. Nothing—*nothing HAD* to be evil. It just needed to be given a different purpose.

He found his way back to Eldress Biri and the small crowd of Limnii that had gathered around her. That advisor girl, Kili, had calmed down and now listened with her arms crossed tightly across her stomach.

Tirak winced. He knew that emptiness. He still felt that emptiness. In fact, as he counted the weeks back, he realized today was his parents' anniversary. A twelve-month anniversary at that. The pain threatened to surge up again like a hot spring geyser. Barely pausing in his strides, he grabbed hold of those feelings and crammed them back down the pipe where they belonged. Now was *not* the time.

He was just approaching the group when they started to turn away from him, a female maybe twice Tirak's age waving toward a side hallway.

"Come, Mistress, there's someone you need to talk to. Maker isolated her in a healing room as soon as we got here, but the poor girl saw everything. She was in a hut on the shore when the first wave attacked."

Tirak raised an eyebrow. Nobody had acknowledged him yet, but neither did they shoo him away, so onward he followed them. Before he knew it, he had found himself falling into step beside Kili. She glanced at him and shuddered.

"For the record," he whispered, "I'm sorry for what happened. I wish I could've been there to save you two again."

A look of shock broke through the girl's empty sorrow, lasting only a few seconds before she retreated back into herself. She sniffed, then her voice came, soft and hoarse.

"Me too. I didn't want him to say anything. I told him how the Mistress would react. She's never even forgiven Elder Onok over that girl. I'm… sorry. For everything he and I've caused… I, understand if you hate us."

"I don't. I think what happened ended up being exactly what Biri needed to help her finally come around. She and Kaleek made it back onto speaking terms with each other yesterday."

"R-really? But when you two left she was so…"

"He's right, child," Biri's voice agreed.

Tirak jumped. Neither of them had realized they were speaking loud enough for anyone else to overhear.

"B-but you hate *anything* that reminds you of those dark days. Even Elder Onok, and you loved him."

"I, um… I suppose I did, didn't I?"

The towering Eldress looked suddenly uncomfortable. Was she self-conscious about the whole group focusing on her own personal life so suddenly?

"Mistress?" Kili asked, "Why *have* you never tried to reconnect with Elder Onok?"

"I..."

A voice deeper than the mountains replied from somewhere behind them.

"A most excellent question, girl!"

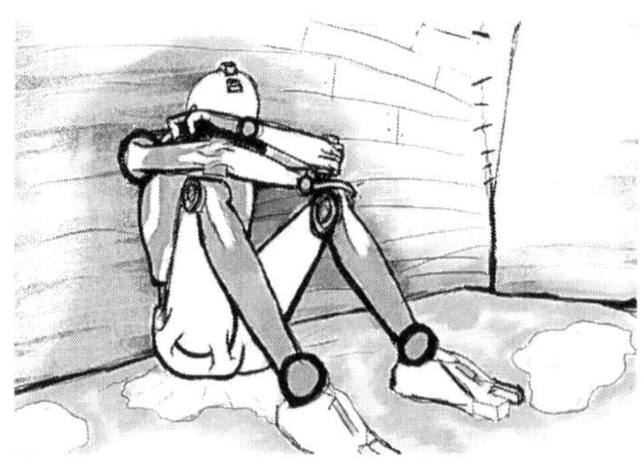

Maker's Log #90310: Villains, every one.

Why do they insist on going back to their old ways? I know I created them from monsters, mechanical villains, but do they really have to be so… monstrous? I can hardly bear to go outside the grove anymore for fear I might stumble onto some new atrocity.

It's not just those Scarred outcasts either. The things that even the most rational, upstanding of the cybrii can end up doing… Do they not see how horrible it all is? Or do they not care?

I can't think which is worse.

Just yesterday I came across this little girl on a visit to see Biri. Her home had been shredded, her parents probably dead. It had probably been an aggravated mudkroc or something, yet no one had come to check on her in days. Neighbors' houses were less than ten yards away, with paths that ran right past the home, and somehow nobody cared that she was dehydrating to death on the remains of a soggy bed?

I don't have the heart for it anymore… I don't want to see another one of my Cybrii again. I'm beginning to regret ever building them in the first place. If this is how they treat each other, I don't dare let them anywhere near humans.

Sigh.

YOU WERE SUPPOSED TO BE OUR HEROES! ACT like it for once!!!

21

UNDER SIEGE

The room fell silent around them. Despite the press of bodies, people found enough space to create a small clearing around their group and its two newcomers.

Onok leaned down and helped Kaleek settle her weight onto two feeble feet. She wobbled against his leg for a second, then started taking steps toward the group. Tirak felt a wide grin split his face as he opened his arms toward his sister. She approached, still swaying slightly.

Before she could reach them, the elegant, refined, and reserved Eldress Biri... *pounced.* Limnii screamed and tried to dodge out of the way, but instead of bowling Kaleek over, she lifted her into a fierce hug.

"Oh my baby girl! You're all right! I'm so, so sorry. If I had known what kind of devices Maker had been *torturing* you with. Strapped to you like leeches... By the time I found out you'd already disappeared across the... the bay... I..."

She went slack-jawed, staring past her daughter for what must've been the first time, and saw the male that had been carrying her. Elder Onok gave them a timid wave that looked more than out of place on someone of his stature and renown. Kaleek raised her arms to return her mother's hug. Her left arm was wrapped from palm to shoulder in a bandage. Even as Tirak watched, fresh spots of black seeped through its thick layers.

"We can catch up later, Mom. Why don't you stay here? Let the rest of us go talk to the quarantined girl for you."

Still rigid, Biri's arms let Kaleek slide to the ground. Tirak noticed she landed much more solidly the second time. Good. That meant her own healing had kicked back in. The process was slower the closer to death a cybri reached, but she had that healing-waters ability. In fact… was that what he had seen beneath the bandage? The stains had vanished when he double checked.

Kaleek gave Biri a short hug as high up the waist as she could reach.

"Go talk to him, Mom. He misses you."

Biri nodded stiffly, eyes still locked forward as her daughter let go and walked over to join Tirak with the rest of the group. Kaleek accepted Tirak's offered hand, leaning on him as they started following Kili toward a side hallway. He felt elated for her, for her mother, for all of them. They all finally had each other again. And with warmth coloring his cheeks, Tirak smiled, knowing that once again he had Kaleek. For another short moment, one short walk, she needed him. And that was enough.

The heavy door snapped open on its own with a hiss at the press of a control panel in the wall. A girl wrapped in a white checkered dress sat on the edge of the bed, knees tucked against her chin and arms wrapped around herself. She was in shock. Tirak imagined he was seeing Kaleek there for a heartbeat. Plain white dress soaked black with blood. He shivered.

Kaleek pushed her way past him and sat next to her.

"She hasn't said much since we found her," Kili said from the doorway. "All I know right now is her name."

"Lingila," Kaleek said.

She rested a hand on the girl's arm, and it seemed to bring a little life back to her empty staring. Her sad, round eyes were the deep color of the far end of a sunset sky. Tirak had never met a limni with such a pretty shade of violet as that before. The girl opened her mouth and began speaking in a voice that had all but forgotten how to talk. Her halting words were hard to follow.

"I… know you. You were… in the village. You were supposed to die. They wanted to kill all the strong ones first. Turn you all into copies of them before they rounded the rest of us up…"

A switch finally engaged behind Lingila's eyes. She let go of herself and buried her face in Kaleek's chest. She began weeping, begging Kaleek to bring her parents back. Words about the Scarred's attack flowed out like a lily vine gushing water. Kili bent down into a crouch next to them and placed a hand on the little girl's back.

"We found two bodies next to her in the hut. They were… mangled beyond recognition, but a neighbor was pretty sure it was, um, *them*. The puncture marks… they looked like hellhound fangs."

Tirak shivered. This girl was young to have watched something so horrible. Even he hadn't had to *watch* it happen. He struggled to shut out his own bad memories as Kaleek continued to coax the girl into talking. Any time she fell silent, Kaleek would fill the gap with a smooth, reassuring tone that he hadn't remembered hearing since…

He could have been listening to his mother telling stories again. Red eyes hung in the darkness outside, right at the edges of his vision. They were waiting to snap at them all. Hungry to eat their throats.

He blinked away several fat tears. Looking around, he realized that the others had already left. Kili was quietly pulling them all down the hallway outside the room's window, toward the crowd of villagers begging for their attention. Soon, the hallway closed its automatic doors. Kaleek's voice was still stabbing into his ears, dredging up those memories he hated to relive. The girl was rocking back and forth, obviously struggling with her own, equally difficult emotions. Oh Maker, Kaleek really did sound just like his mother. He had to get out. He stumbled for the door, resting a hand on his sister's shoulder as he passed.

"I'll give you two some space, i-if that helps."

He stepped into the expansive hallway and sank back against the wall. His mother's colorless face hovered in front of him, surrounded by a pool of black. Accusing him with those unfocused eyes. Defending *him* is what got her killed in the end. She would have been fine if she hadn't needed to protect defenseless little Tirak. He pressed his knuckles into his eyes and finally allowed himself to sob.

He didn't notice how much time passed. He was barely aware of anything beyond the visions of his dying parents until Kaleek's feet began padding calmly toward him. The quarantine door hissed closed.

Eyes still shut against the horrors, he rested his head against the cold concrete and asked into the air, "So, do we have a chance?"

Kaleek didn't respond. Instead, a piercing, discordant wail seized his ears. He looked up in shock. The sound disoriented him, made it hard to think. The limni girl staggered down the hallway with her arms stretched to the sides. Her neck was craned back to an unnatural angle, and Tirak could see from the glow reflected off the ceiling that her eyes shined a brilliant purple.

Fists pounded against the heavy glass behind him. He spun and found a frantic Kaleek yelling something at them in silence. Even tuned to max, he could barely understand more than a garble. That glass must have been incredibly thick.

He whirled back around to the hospitalized girl, trying to understand what he was supposed to do. Time slowed to a crawl before Tirak's eyes. Cracks spread across the ceiling above her head. Her song rose in pitch. Warning sirens erupted, their pulses flashing red, making the girl's voice even more hideous.

The first block struck the floor.

The cracks widened, and a whole area of ceiling folded in above the girl. Dust flooded the hallway, but Tirak didn't need to see to know why her voice had cut off so sharply. Chunks of stone and a wave of dirt crushed him against the wall.

A claw bigger than his face wrapped itself around his torso and ripped him free of the rubble. He was brought face to face with a monster of red scales and absolutely crocodilian teeth. It uttered an unintelligible, high-pitched noise, then twisted its head to put a bulbous eye within a finger of Tirak's nose. Violet lines of light spread across its robotic head, *and the sounds became words in his head.*

You… are another like us. You will join us. Unless your freedom and chaos here is really worth dying over.

Visions filled his head of Terra on fire, of Limna being shredded strand from strand, and then of a million contented-looking cybrii standing in ranks in front of this Shadow and its… brothers? Siblings. There was one among them that felt distinctly female.

Tirak's ears went deaf as a wave of pressure rolled across him, shaking him out of the vision. He dropped several hands to the ground, Kaleek severing the monster's arm in two with a blade of frosted ice. She swept through the hallway like a hailstorm through reeds. Warriors three times her size fell one after the next as she dodged and wove between them, never stopping. She disappeared down the bend without breaking her pace even once. Eyeing the three remaining out of the original death squad of fifteen, Tirak drew his own weapon. He stared them down, waiting for the first attack to come.

The bargain the Darkness offered was obvious now. They were scared. It came to this island expecting one old hermit cowering in fear; instead it found an army that it had no match for.

He smiled. They really *could* win this battle. A dangerous edge emerged from its sheath, already glowing a dull orange as Tirak poured power into his weapon. More. *More!* It brightened to a sharp yellow-white, then further still until it was wrapped in an aura so bright its edges looked blue.

A finishing blow slashed through two of the giants before they could recover. Tirak stared down their dragon-like leader as he approached. The thing was still staring off toward the direction Kaleek had gone. He turned to face Tirak, a chilling smile curling his face despite a long hole running through half of it. Tirak wasn't even sure how the jaw managed to still hold on.

"So much power… That one will be an absolute delight when we finally tame her."

Tirak's blood flash-boiled.

"*Tame* her?! You saw what she just did to you!"

"I *know*, isn't it just wonderful? She will be a queen among peasants, mere *ants*."

It stared him dead in the eye as blackened steel and grey skin closed around the horrid display of circuits and brain matter.

Tirak didn't give it the chance to keep healing. He dove forward, jets of heat sculpting his strike into the very picture of perfect form. His sword swept through its chest, hardly hitting any resistance other than the sputter of evaporating liquid. The cut passed from one side and came out the other, digging almost as deep as the dragon's hardened spine.

Its smile widened. Tirak heard a soft bark like a chuckle.

Come now. Your… sister, already tried that, did she not? But fine, do go ahead and test it for yourself, as long as you don't mind accidentally ending up… dead.

The other giants were on top of him before the dragon had finished speaking into Tirak's brain. They were weaker, collapsing with even one solid hit to any of their vitals. He had soon cleared the room. Except, wait, hadn't that last one lost its head to Kaleek? No, no. Obviously, he had been mistaken. The grunts all looked the same.

He rested his blade point-first into the ground and lifted a triumphant chin toward their leader.

You seem very proud of your accomplishments. Good. We appreciate that in our followers. But… make sure you really HAVE accomplished something first.

The first Shadow corpse stopped bleeding out. It grabbed its missing hips and held them against a bleeding torso, rising to its feet once again. One by one, they all rose to join their brother. Tirak stared, horrified.

You cannot stop us. We are mere Shadows. Weapons pass through us. We are nothing. And we are power itself.

The last of them screwed its head back in place. Tirak's knuckles whitened around his hilt.

Oh, don't worry, little one. We will leave soon enough. My squad was only the distraction. You see, we're here for a debt long owed. I have a sister, too, and where yours is a little angel of death, MINE is an unstoppable goddess. Our goal is but the death of one little thorn in our side.

Tirak's face went cold. No, they couldn't possibly mean... Purple lines pulsed across its head once again.

And my sister is about finished with the task. Too bad you won't get to watch them meet.

Maker's Log #92345: Final—huff—Entry.

Prissi... Keep this running until my vitals are gone or the mask's transmitter melts away.

<COUGHING REDACTED>

Ugh.

This is... Garrett "Avoma" Jones. Last known survivor of... nnNGH! the Atlandia Wildlife Research Center.

This is it.

I can't feel past my hips anymore, my left arm is nothing but a puddle anymore. Their filth is eating me alive. STARS it hurts so much!

I was an idiot, thinking they didn't have a way in, thinking I was safely hidden away. Of course I'm not safe. None of us are as long as we're still on this planet.

I... was trying to rewire Onok's bracer a little better—in the hopes I could give it to him tomorrow—when the door opened behind me.

I didn't even get a chance to turn around.

...My eyes can hardly focus. I keep hearing some kind of scuffle outside, but all I can see is the same leering snake hovering over me.

It isn't fair. We're all doomed. So many plans and details locked away in this head. My children still have no clue what the purpose of all this is for. Stupid. Why didn't I just TELL someone? I knew better. Always, ALWAYS add redundancy!

<PROLONGED COUGHING REDACTED>

Gah. Not like this…
I guess I'll see you soon, my Light, like it or not.
I wish I wasn't. So much unfinished.
So… cold…
<AWAITING SIGNAL STREAM…>
<AWAITING SIGNAL STREAM…>

22

COLDFRONT

Kaleek trudged along ahead of Tirak, her head hung low. She hadn't looked back toward the crags down into Umbra in… at least a few minutes. Yet, she didn't look any less miserable. Tirak felt the pain too, but Maker's death had been weighing especially hard on Kaleek these past few days. He drew up alongside her and nibbled on his tongue. He wanted to rest a comforting hand on her shoulder, but the rough stony terrain would probably make it feel like a punch if he tried.

So instead, he stuck by her side and hoped his presence would be enough. Well, he *tried* to focus on helping her, but the longer they walked, the more Tirak's circuits drifted back to that same burning question. He had to ask it. Next to him, Kaleek's fingers clutched the familiar silver piece. She stared into its empty eye holes, long strands and tubes dangled out the back almost to her knees. He knew opening his mouth might deepen her disgust with him, but …

"Why are we even bothering? How can we ever hope to win this?"

The question floated in the air beside them like a leaf. Sure enough, Kaleek didn't answer beyond the glare she leveled at him as she took a pointed step away. It was a fair question. An important one, even. They couldn't afford to ignore it, not anymore. The ice crystals growing like a snake around her arm weren't lost on him, nor was the tight fist that held its tail. At least he was ready for it this time if she lashed out.

Look, sis, I know. 'Maker planned for this too, and we have to trust this will all work out the way He wanted.' But…" A miserable laugh erupted from his throat. "Maker's *dead*. Gone! Poof! Don't you get it? He can't have plans anymore. So what can we even hope to do?"

Kaleek only pulled her elbows tighter into herself and sped up her pace. Tirak grimaced at the small, shivering picture she cut against the landscape. How badly he wished Onok and Biri could have stayed with them. If only they could let Umbra handle itself for another few days. She *needed* a parent's comfort at least as much as she needed this reality check, and Tirak knew he was being unfair to unload the one on her without the other.

And *he* certainly couldn't offer her that kind of comfort. He still had no idea what he was to Kaleek anymore. Even Biri was more important to her now. He supposed he would always be just Tirak. Just "that boy" that got in the way. Well, "that boy" could sometimes deliver the message she needed to hear. It would have to be enough. Was he distracting himself from his own thoughts of raw loss by thinking about all of this? Absolutely.

Was it working? Mostly. Not really.

They walked a long time before the conversation continued again.

"I still can't believe, after all this time, it was him who…" The words were swallowed in Kaleek's throat along with another choked tear.

"Me neither, Kal," Tirak agreed. "Me neither. He was a great… person, wasn't he? But I should've seen it. I can't believe I was stupid enough to let myself—!"

But Kaleek cut him off, turning toward him and pushing her arms between his. She wrapped his waist in a hug and squeezed tight. Feeling a tear threatening his face, Tirak folded his arms across her back, returning the embrace.

"*No*, bro! You shouldn't have. Don't keep blaming yourself. We're all to blame, but him most of all. I'm glad you didn't know. It makes you're a better person."

That was *provably* false, but he welcomed the comfort anyway. He had seen much worse before. Deep down, he knew he should have done something sooner. How much more death had Tirak caused now as a result? With a final squeeze, she extracted herself from around his torso and they resumed their hike.

The scenery passed in a heavy silence for another few hours as the land changed underfoot from grass to dry brown needles, and then to a crisp white powder he had only heard stories about before: snow.

Tirak noticed a handful of animal tracks as they crossed them, and they even saw a pack of huge grazers nibbling between the growing drifts, but nothing seemed to want to bother them. Well, if not speaking up was the problem before, then he was not going to avoid it now. This conversation was going to suck for her, he knew, but it could be the only chance he'd get before she snapped out of this more receptive mood. He had to keep trying.

"H-hey, Kal?"

She made no sound to acknowledge him, but he knew she was listening.

"Do you think we'll really win this whole thing? Are we going to survive?"

Still no response, but her head became a little more raised. Maybe more thoughtful?

"I-I don't just mean the two of us. We're warriors. We're fighting for a good cause and all that. I'm not as worried about one of us dying, but… but what if none of us can win? What if Maker's plan leads to us dying in some pointless last stand against the Darkness? What would be the, well, the *point*?"

"You're stupid, Tir. Even that wouldn't be pointless."

She turned back to glare at him.

"We're fighting to protect the island. Not just us cybrii, but the creatures who can't defend themselves, *humanity*, Tirak. The sleeping souls of Maker's people."

"You're right! We are. But..."—he struggled to think of how he should put it—"well, what if it doesn't do any good? So what if we manage to actually kill one or two of its Shadows, but all of *us* get wiped out?"

"Then we'll have done what we needed to and denied the Darkness an even bigger legion."

It was true. That attack on Makers Grove had felt overwhelming, but really their forces had been few compared to one of the villages. Tirak knew it was true from his conversation. They had all but admitted it despite not wanting to. That *thing* they did with their minds was far less one-way than they seemed to think. Tirak had *seen* their small factories and camps in the ice tunnels, high above the sky.

But he also knew what he saw when Biri had flown them over Terra. He knew what each of the Limni refugees claimed to have witnessed. This wasn't going to be some simple battle. And then there was the eel of an Elder they both saw during the attack.

"Will we really? That wasn't Maker's plan. He didn't create us just so we could *not* join the Darkness. He wanted us to beat it. But, Kal... you saw the same thing I saw. Your mom didn't leave very much of Elder Bozrakh behind, *but they somehow brought him back!* This is something we don't understand, Kal. We might not have a choice, no matter how much we resist. What if we need to make the tough choice, if only because we won't have one otherwise?"

More silence.

"So, your brilliant idea is, what? Become the villains just so we stay alive? Do you really have that big of a crush on Rekke? Sure! Let's do the same thing the Scarred did! Let's just bow down to the Darkness and do whatever it tells us to. Maybe we can even slit each other's throats and give it something to giggle over."

"What? No. Kal, I'm trying to say that fighting these Shadows head on doesn't seem to be doing any good. They only get stronger with each fight. What if we can't win unless we change the way we attack?"

She gritted her teeth.

"We don't have time to sit around and strategize, Tir! That was Maker's job, but he's dead now! Don't you get it? All we can do is stick to his plan and hope it works! Or are you really so much smarter than the god that created us all, created our island?"

"He admitted that's not true, and He's not perfect either. Just hear me out. They've been preparing for *centuries* to fight and destroy anything that gets in their way. What if they've become so strong that the only way to get past their armor is to hit them from inside? What if someone could join them, and influence them from a place of trust?"

She stopped walking entirely. The land had fallen away from them quickly as the ground started to slope ever more sharply upward. Tirak hadn't noticed the change at first, but now he was out of breath and the pine-coated valley stretched out hundreds of feet below Kaleek's stone perch. Snow caked both of their legs, and a violent shiver racked his bones.

"We're done for today. Go find us a place to make camp," she said curtly.

"Kal, just promise you'll—"

"*NO! YOU* promise *me* you'll never even *THINK* about suggesting that again! We will *not* throw away everything we've worked so hard for and become… whatever it is *they* are!"

Wind howled in a column around her as Kaleek roared. The last few words had been slurred as large mandibles reformed around them. Snowflakes cut into him like chips of sharpened stone. Her armor glowed faintly sky-blue against the dim overcast. At least a dozen eye-points glared at him. He backed away slowly.

"O-okay, sis. Calm down. Please? I just wanted us to make sure we knew *all* our options. I promise I won't bring it up again…"

"Go. Find. Firewood," her unfamiliar voice clicked at him.

He knew better than to disobey. For the next hour or more, he scoured the surrounding cliff for every last ice-soaked twig he could find. Some of them might even be usable, if they tried hard enough. He dreaded going back to their campsite, but finally he couldn't put it off any longer.

Dejected, Tirak sat shoulder to shoulder with his last remaining family member. No matter what was happening in Umbra, he had never been part of those Elders's lives. This was all he had ever had. The tiniest campfire he'd ever kindled fizzled and hissed in front of them with one lethargic flame. A lone, glowing sentry, asleep at the mouth of the tiny cave Kaleek had carved into the snowbank. Surprisingly, sticks that had more ice than wood in them didn't make for very good burning. They watched uneasily as the only other source of heat dropped below the horizon. He drew a blanket tighter around their shoulders to try and shield his exposed side before the wind could bite any deeper into it.

If anything, though, Kaleek's reaction had only proved Maker's backup plan would work. He just wished it wouldn't be up to him to pull it off. Not alone. *Her* plan was guaranteed to fail, though. He knew it. And when it did, they needed something else. He was sure that's what Maker had meant about "having backup plans." This wasn't a pivot at all. Maker must have known from the start this would be an option. Maybe even *the only* option.

But how to pull off such an infiltration? That was the question, and Maker hadn't lived long enough to tell him. Tirak's circuits began to race with possibilities. Most of them died early into their concept. But wherever one thought died, it gave rise to two other options. Better options. Tirak hadn't even noticed himself drift off to sleep until the morning's rays started to rest on his numb cheeks like liquid iron.

Tirak stretched, eyes still closed. He stuck his arms out of the layers of blankets and snapped them back as the chill bit its teeth into them. It was certainly one way to wake up. He looked around in confusion. He and Kaleek were huddled against each other in a pocket of ice.

Snowflakes danced lazily beyond the edge, falling from a dull, overcast sky. A triangle of snow was all that remained of their precious fire pit. Yesterday came slowly back to his cold mind. He smiled, feeling the warmth of her arms around his chest. At least it looked like she had forgiven him… for now.

Time to extract himself from the pile and start thinking of breakfast.

The results were depressing. They had gathered almost nothing between Igna's craggy jungles and these cold foothills, and the rabbits they'd speared while walking had frozen through before having a chance to dry out in the sun. What in the island was *wrong* with this place? So many clouds. So much cold. Who would ever choose to live here? He snapped another red shard of meat off and started sucking on it, waiting until it was soft enough to chew. Being a plain old biological rabbit, its taste wasn't as revolting as a crystalpelt breed would've been. That rotting taste. Bleh.

But it also meant the food would do nothing for him besides keep him on his feet. Keeping his fire reserves charged was going to be a real challenge up here. No latent heat to pull from, and almost no elemental prey worth hunting. Maybe he shouldn't have spent what he did on rekindling that fire…

Kaleek soon stirred, and Tirak offered some lengths of popsicle-meat to help her wake up. She gagged, but after confirming there weren't any better options, she ate it anyway. He listened to her mutter and assumed she was just that grumpy about breakfast. Then, he caught a few of her words. It… sounded like she was talking to someone. Or, to herself. Her eyes darted around as if seeing things that weren't there.

Disturbed, Tirak chose not to get in the way. It wasn't the first time she'd acted like that, and she would probably just tell him to buzz off if he asked about it. Whatever she was suffering from, he knew she would pull through. Kaleek always did. Losing Maker had been a hard blow, and they all had to find their own way to deal with it, he supposed. Hopefully, she wouldn't lose her grip on reality in the process.

After packing up the camp and spending a little time trying out their powers in the new climate in order to warm up, the siblings set off up the path on their last leg of the journey to Aura village. The cold seemed to fit his sister like a glove. Not only did it match her personality, she barely even needed her air element to conduct ice up here.

~~~~~

The village that they entered sat desolate. Tirak's senses were on edge as they passed hut after deserted hut. Only the lack of decay in the buildings gave any sign that it hadn't been abandoned entirely. Things moved at the corners of his vision. Shutters and doors blew slightly in the wind. He couldn't shake the feeling that the whole village was watching them. It was probably true. Aura had always been legendary for its distrust of outsiders, and it hadn't welcomed a single visitor since their Elder died. It was the one place he never remembered his parents visiting during his early months.

"That one," Kal's voice cut through the air. "It looks like an inn. Let's try there. If there's anyone here willing to let us win them over, they'll be inside a place like that."

Tirak scratched his head.

"Why would a place that shuns outsiders have an inn?"

She shrugged. They stepped into the shelter of its porch anyway. An old sign carved with a mug and bed seemed to confirm her guess. Warmth, conversation, and even some singing washed its way across them as they pushed their way inside. All except the warmth died off a second later. Heads from every corner of the room turned to them. They scanned him with critical distrust, but each head that glanced at Kaleek only lingered for a moment before hunching down and turning away.

The siblings shared a look and shrugged. Kaleek decided to try the plump innkeeper first. She approached the serving counter as unthreateningly as possible and cleared her throat.
~~~~~

"E-excuse me, could I ask if there's anything—"

"Ain' givin' nuthin', don' need nuthin' n' don' need trouble neither. Bes' find somewhere else, Missy."

Kaleek sighed and fished out a few shards from her purse, letting them clink against the countertop.

"Well, do you at least have something hot to drink we can buy?"

The keeper frowned, but bit back some comment after looking her up and down a second time.

"Fine..." she muttered.

She shuffled over to a short barrel that was propped above the fireplace. Snippets of whispered conversation slowly began to resume around the place. Tirak still felt like every eye was watching them, but he knew better than to look. Beside him, Kaleek fidgeted with her fingers and cleared her throat.

"So, I guess there aren't very many visitors up here anymore? Uh... with the sunny welcomes and all, I mean."

The plump female kept her back to them as she pulled a handful of red beads from a jar. They hissed and frothed as she poured them into a mug of something that smelled strong.

"You give yer Pa that much lip, too?"

"I—s-sorry... I didn't mean it to sound like that."

Kaleek dropped her head, and he could see an intense blush forming around the edges of her mask. He held back a hiss. The female probably didn't even realize how deep that question would have cut.

"Ah, so you wanted to insult us dumb folk *without* us realizing it. Really not surprising how you got that mask, is it, girl? Y'should go back and tell 'em to switch yours for a jester like your friend's."

She dumped a mug in front of Kaleek and started to move off.

"Wait, can I get one too?" Tirak asked.

"Need more shards than that if you want a second. Fire critters are hard to find this high up."

"That's fine. Here, how much?"

Tirak fished some shards from his own pack and dropped them next to Kaleek's pile. The keeper swiped them off the counter and nodded her thanks. She had swiped *all* of the shards he put out.

He waited for Kaleek to try and continue the conversation, but she sat quietly, staring down. Well, if she wouldn't, then Tirak supposed it fell to him. See? He could still be useful.

"So uh, I hope you don't take this the wrong way, but… your village seems a little… cold? To strangers."

Tirak could practically hear the female's lips pursing.

"And why you think that is, exactly, boy? Tryn'a make a *point*?"

Tirak swallowed. That barkeep's arm really had a ripple to it when she flexed. He decided to backpedal as quickly as he could and drop the subject before he found himself digging a hole.

"Uh. No! Nothing… I… just wondered if it had anything to with Eld—"

The female jerked her head away, looking at Kaleek instead.

"Dear *me*! Your second tone is such a lovely blue, dearie. Kind of a seafoam, right?"

Kaleek looked just as taken aback by the abrupt change as he felt. Her hand twitched, moving toward the tattered shirt as if to pull it closed. She narrowed her eyes.

"Sky blue," she enunciated slowly.

The innkeeper snapped her jaw shut. She shuffled back and forth on her feet for several seconds. Finally, she stopped acknowledging them and continued brewing the second mug. Her face was a little less cold when she turned around, but also more shy. She didn't even slam his mug down like she did with Kaleek's. She hesitated again, as if about to say something.

"Need anything to eat while you're here? Y'look like you've been walking a while," she asked while bustling away.

"Yes, please!" they said together.

With their bellies full, the room seemed to become a little more relaxed. Tirak even tried again to broach the subject of work.

"Hey, Innkeep, is anyone around here looking for help?"

"Nope."

He gritted his teeth. That worked well. He needed to figure out a better way to ask. These villagers were so cold that maybe the best way was not to ask at all.

"Well we're supposed to serve each of the villages—"

"Shame t'be you, then."

"...before Maker will let us take these masks off."

Tirak gestured at their judgment masks, but the keeper gave them a strange expression in response.

"*Please*. We want to be out of your hair just as much as you do. There has to be *something* you need."

"Don' tell me you two *believe* all those fairytales. Ugh, this is why we don't go outside the mountain ranges anymore. The other villages believe the stupidest things. You kids haven't even seen a 'Maker' before, so why should you do anything it says?"

Well, that certainly wasn't an angle Tirak had been expecting. He blinked several times before his mouth caught up to his processor.

"...W-what? But we *have* seen Him. I mean, He's dead now because the Darkness sent its Shadows to attack Him while we were there, and...." His voice trailed off again.

The room was dead silent. Whoever wasn't glaring outright daggers wore an expression that at least said he and Kaleek were the craziest pair to have ever wandered into town.

"Winds help us. They really believe it, don't they?" someone said from a couple tables away.

Tirak rolled his eyes and focused on the innkeeper again.

"Never mind. Tell you what, I saw a nest of glowblood snakes a few thousand heads back down the path we came up. You said you're short on igni beads."

The innkeeper's eyes finally lit up with an emotion besides annoyance. Tirak smiled back. They had their way in. With one job well done would surely come another.

23

SKYKEEP TOWER

The cluster of larva pods melted to slag as Tirak focused his power. His senses cleared as more of the slugs wriggled away, burning. Hallucinations grew more frantic, then vanished in a blink as each one died. Kaleek let out a curse and shot into the air. Her nature form was a blur as it cut between a pair of hawks diving toward the carnage. Tirak had to dodge to avoid being impaled by one metal beak. It wobbled slightly, sticking point first out of the ice. The bodies landed in three heaps soon after. Kaleek landed atop a pile of similar bodies, reforming into her normal shape as she crouched there.

"They're getting more persistent," she called. "How's it going, Tir?"

"They're getting more persistent," scalled. "How's it going, Tir?"

"I think this is the last one."

"That's what you said last time."

He gritted his teeth and chose not to reply to that. His gearbox clicked one notch forward as he summoned a sky-blue shard from his body's reserves. He pushed a wave of air outward in all directions. Kaleek yelped as snow blasted her in the face. The ice underneath was incredibly clear up here. Tirak could see the mountain's rock several feet beneath the surface. No other pockets of eggs were hiding down there. He turned to start walking back to Aura.

"Yeah, that's the last one. Let's go turn the bounty in."

Kaleek nodded, satisfied too.

They settled into the awkward gait needed to slosh through the waist-deep drifts of snow. It was going to be a long walk back. When Tirak glanced behind him, he saw that Kaleek's shoulders were slumped, her head angled at the ground. She wasn't trying to beat back the cold, either. Tirak already knew she barely felt the cold like he did. She was hunched because she *felt* small. He followed her eyes toward a peak that towered above the rest, its highest points disappearing into the hazy sky.

"Hey. You feeling okay, sis?"

Kaleek blinked at him.

"Huh? Oh… yeah. Just thinking about the Aurii."

He waited for her to catch up so he could give her shoulder an encouraging squeeze.

"You'll get through to them. I know you. Some of them already trust you enough that they agree Maker at least might have been real. They'll come around to the Darkness threat too. Just give it a little more time."

Her breath hissed out of a constricted throat.

"That's the *problem*! 'Give it a little time.' We've *GIVEN* it more time than we even HAVE!" she snapped.

The glare Kaleek gave him cut through his skin more sharply than the wind. She waved an arm toward a jungle horizon that was just barely visible through the clouds and snow.

"The whole *island* needs us, Tir, not just Aura. Every day we spend here, more good cybrii are dying down there. More are being turned into monsters…"

"Kee, we can't focus on that. This right here is how we fix that," he tried to argue.

"—and meanwhile, they dump job after *MEANINGLESS* job on us! All to keep us out of their way. I can't even get ONE straight answer about my… about the Elder. I swear to you, Tirak, if I have to look at *ONE* more sweet and smiley face reprimanding me for sticking my nose places…"

He grimaced. Hopefully she didn't blame him for getting them into the laundry list of chores.

"C'mon, sis, it can't be easy for them either. Nobody even knows everything the fallen Elder did. Don't blame them for avoiding it. We can't know how painful it must be for them all to talk about. We just have to keep trying. We just have to find the right person to ask. If nothing else, maybe they can show you where to find some answers for yourself."

Her pace had slowed to a practical crawl. Tirak was beginning to feel as miserable as she was, just by watching her.

"Hey, wanna race back to the inn? No rules barred," he teased.

Instead, Kaleek looked up at the colossal mountain peak behind them again. She gritted her teeth.

"Kal… I don't like that look. You're about to get us into another 'situation,' aren't you?"

She gave him a withering look.

"Those carnivore birds are just going to keep pestering the whole mountain range unless we deal with them. Plus… *He* lived up there. I'm *sure* of it, Tir."

Her preoccupation with Aura's fallen Elder worried Tirak.

"You don't know that, Kee. Unless you've been hanging around a lot more people than I have with that 'sunny personality' of yours, then *nobody* has talked about Elder Korma at all."

She only spared him *one* short glare. Wow. She really was distracted.

"What they're *not* saying is how I know it's true. Come on. I have to know the other half of the story, Tir. I have… have to know what it is I am."

"You… wait. What?"

The logic made no sense, but she didn't give him a chance to object. Thin, webbed wings sprouted from her transforming back and launched her into the air. They left a blast of wind that coated him in a vindictive layer of snow. He sighed and shifted into his own Second Nature, landing on nimble forepaws.

It took him an all-out sprint on all fours to even keep pace with her. She soared straight, unfazed by any swirling gust of wind, but his claws let him grip the jagged ridge line with just enough dexterity to match her.

The footing became more difficult as he went, however. Before long, Tirak was forced to stop and catch his breath after a bad paw placement had sent a small avalanche tumbling miles down the slope. It had almost sucked him along with it. He had nearly ripped out one claw in his effort to avoid that fate. They were hundreds of heads higher than where that nest of psychic slugs had been, and the reduced visibility made Kaleek all but impossible to see up there anymore.

Thankfully, she must have sensed his struggle. She soon circled back around and dove toward him, alighting on a pointy drift next to him. Her elongated legs gripped the snow so gently it seemed as if she hadn't landed at all. She wrapped all four pincers around his waist and lifted him easily into the air. He felt his stomach lurch even worse than the ride from Terra on Eldress Biri's back. She made sense, being so big and powerful already, but feeling Kaleek rip him away from the ground with just as little effort defied all reason. He couldn't shake off the feeling that she might drop him at any moment.

Aside from his breakfast trying to desert him the whole time, the flight was uneventful. Kaleek set him down gently on an unnaturally flat, wide ledge of ice. A cave stretched before them, scattered with feathers, animal bones, and disheveled nests all around. Each nest was a chaotic mess, but it filled a carefully spaced bowl that had been carved into the rock. Just like the smooth-cut edges of this cave's opening, these nests lining its floor couldn't have been natural.

"Well, I guess you were right..."

Tirak noticed that she hadn't moved. Her eyes were locked on the opening.

"Look, we don't have to do this if you're not ready. We can always come back. Some things are better just to not look at, right?"

She gritted her teeth and growled. Her tattered shirt billowed behind her in the wind. The screeches and hisses coming from the cave rose to a crescendo.

"No. No more ignoring who I am. I'm going to cut apart every one of these vultures and then get some answers about the monster that made me."

He nodded to her. "Okay then. I've got your back."

The siblings made short work of the ugly beasts that flapped and hopped around their rows of nests. Somehow, the predators of the sky were much less fearsome when they were waddling around on the ground like drunken midgets. All fell silent after a few gruesome but short minutes.

They looked around, seeing no signs of anything but animals living up here. A fitting description, Tirak guessed, considering the Elder's reputation before he died. Maybe this was just the way he had lived. They were about to turn away when Tirak felt a warm draft tickle his leg.

"Hey wait. Kal! There's a gap in the wall somewhere over here. I think this cave has a second room."

It was true. He realized as he eyed the dark corner that its surface didn't quite look like stone. Sure enough, the corroded plate crumbled into flakes as he pushed on it. Light flooded in from the other side. From the little he could see, it was some kind of laboratory built entirely out of ice. He pushed his way further inside to get a better look…

And he proceeded to eject the remaining breakfast that he had been trying so hard to keep down for the last half hour.

"Ew! Tirak! Get control of yourself. That already smells… so…"

Another sickly draft made him retch again. Kaleek fell silent once she had pushed past him. It really was disgusting. Splatters of black covered almost every surface of the room, radiating out from a lumpy patch of ice in the middle. Tirak wiped his mouth and followed her in.

"Dad once said he had to fight Elder Korma to get Mom back," she whispered.

"It… doesn't look like there was much of a fight," Tirak noted.

"Y-yeah."

She continued to stand there, frozen, so Tirak decided it was best to give her some time to think on her own. He walked over to a workbench of sorts and began sifting through the items littered across it. Some odd tools, old meals—perfectly preserved—and shards of glass mostly, though he found a few scribbled notes as well. He had to scrape some blood-icicles off of them before he could read what any of them said. He did it anyway. Slowly, methodically, trying to not destroy any of what was underneath. He just needed anything at all to keep his mind from focusing on that row of shackles behind him… or the colorful skeletons that were lying in curled up piles below several of them.

Just when he thought he couldn't avoid looking again, his eye fell on a word that drew all his attention back: *tower*. The same word Maker had used to describe His temples.

…really be so bad. Otherwise, Maker wouldn't have demanded I guard His tower among the clouds all on my own. HE gave me these needs, so it can't be wrong to give in to them once in a while. Onok claims the blue one belongs to HIM of course, but he isn't always there to keep…

He let go of the crusty sheet of leather—Dark, he hoped it was actual leather—leaving behind scorch marks wherever his fingers had been. He couldn't read any further. But now he had the knowledge they needed. It made sense, too. Where else would Maker's last tower hide except on the mountain that was already hidden by the clouds? Unless Kaleek needed to absorb the awful knowledge in front of her any longer—she honestly didn't, stuff like this was never healthy to spend time thinking about—they could get on with Maker's quest… *and finally go home!*

"Hey, sis, I think we just found Aura's tower too." He waggled an eyebrow to help his point sink in. "Want to go get a little upgrade?"

That piqued her interest. He showed her the parchment, careful to keep the more depraved sections covered with his grip. It only took a few minutes of searching before they found a second entrance that led deeper into the mountain. Once they had brushed away enough dried flakes of blood, the foreign steel door stuck out clearly. Tirak dry-heaved again at the fresh memory of a finger he had brushed loose from its surface.

It was bolted shut more securely than either of the other two towers' entrances had been. Tirak thought it would only take them a few seconds to get in, but after their third exhausted break from twisting on individual bolts around its edge, he had to admit it was going to take a while. He ran his fingers through his hair, and they came away damp with sweat.

"So… hot. In here," Kaleek grunted as she got up to start forcing her weight against another stubborn handle.

And it was, too. Sweat poured from both of them. Something about that nagged at him as they continued to knock loose the stubborn bolts that held the hatch against the wall. He looked back toward the outer wall of Korma's lair, puzzled. There was more than a simple *lack of* chill in the air on this side of the room. It actually felt warm. Sure, Maker said that big machines produced heat just like a body did, but… just how many machines were on the other side of this wall to make it so warm in there?

The discomfort caused other worries to resurface in his head. On the other side was another vast source of elemental power. The two of them would soon become even more powerful than ever. Tirak, sure, but even after Maker's last tweaks to it, his bracer just couldn't keep up with Kaleek's incredible prototype. The gap between them would be even bigger after today. Her need for him would become that much smaller.

Tirak shook his head, spraying droplets. He channeled the frustration into snapping loose his next bolt. He didn't have to worry. The gap would shrink, but it would never disappear. Their search for Igna's tower had been a bust. He still had more fire than her, and at this point, it seemed like he always would.

She would always need him, ever so slightly.

Kaleek broke through the last bolt and ripped the corroded half-dome from its place. The heavy piece clanged to the ground with a mighty boom. The glow of shining glass flooded the room.

But…

But why was it *THAT color?*

24

HEART OF THE KEEP

Tirak's worst fear had just happened—WAS happening right before his eyes! Lust filled Kaleek's expression as they took their first hesitant steps into the room. Tirak moved to his sister's side and tried to get her attention, but his presence went unnoticed to her. She lifted her bracer, not even a thought spared for their earlier conversations. All that talk of empathy for his fears of becoming obsolete had been a lie, he supposed. He watched her finger the deep, disfigured grooves along her arm as she waited for the device to charge.

The kiss of red light burned against his face and chest. Still he stood there, dumbfounded. Why in Maker's name did the *Air* tower pump *fire* crystals? Kaleek glanced toward him and cocked her head.

"Hopefully the scab holds this time. You gonna start eating? …No? More for me, I guess."

Tirak dropped his half-raised arm. He would have joined in on helping her clear the blockage. It wasn't like he *hated* power. He just… was having a hard time seeing. He blinked away two large beads of sweat that had gotten into his eyes somehow. At least they had stopped stinging. More tears filled their void.

Who was he kidding? Tirak shook his head and took a step back toward the chamber's edge. He obviously wasn't welcome here. The only reason his sister needed him was gone now. She would be able to conduct more fire than Tirak ever could have, probably more than even Elder Hakhoz could. All that was left for him to do now was make sure he didn't get in her way, maybe watch her blind spots as thanklessly as ever, and above all, try his best to keep up when she decided to ditch him. He didn't want to consider the alternatives when that happened.

He turned, wandering far enough down the hall to find a place where he could set up a watch for anything that decided to try and jump them. If all that fireglass was why the tower's insides were so hot, then the whole thing might cool down as his sister gobbled it up. Who knew what Maker had planted around the structure to protect it like he had with the other two? Anything could wriggle its way out once the temperature became a little more bearable.

"Hey. There you are. What's up?"

Tirak started. Had she noticed after all? How much time had passed? A thrill shot through his heart.

"Huh? N-nothing. I just thought I heard something crawling and figured I should check. Wouldn't be good if we got caught by surprise, right? Do you need more time in there?"

He couldn't believe it. She really cared enough about him to wait and make sure he was doing all right? She even made sure to save some for him to make sure he—

"Nah, all done. I got everything I could reach and the pumps are flowing again."

Tirak blinked at his sister, waiting for the punchline and a hint of a smile.

It never came.

"Come on, it looks like there might be a staircase down to the foothills," she said with a shrug.

"Wait, we aren't going back to Aura?"

Kaleek looked over her shoulder at him, one eyebrow raised.

"What for? They want to stay up here and rot. Suits me just fine, so let's go."

Tirak balked at her backside. How could she be so heartless? Maker had wanted as many of them in the fight as possible. Why would she just leave behind half of the remaining villages? She started walking, her armor taking on a strong reddish hue until it looked almost purple. A tongue of fire sparked to life at her fingertip and lit the way before her.

Kaleek was getting away from him. That realization finally snapped Tirak out of his stupor. He took off at a dash, skidding to a stop and falling into step one leg behind his sister. He cringed at the metal-on-metal screech of his feet against the floor. The sound rolled down the curving hallway, on, and on. And on. And on…

Tirak really didn't like how big the place sounded, and Kaleek's candle, held at chest level, was casting shadows so harsh across his path that he could barely see. With a click of his fingers, heat wrapped its way around his arm and formed into a bright candle of his own. He readied a water and earth shard each into his gearbox too. Just to be safe.

"Stop! Put that out. *I've* got the light; I'm in front," Kaleek hissed.

"I can't see," he complained. "And shouldn't we be ready for a fight anyway?"

"I *said…*"

A pocket of solid air condensed around his hand until the flame had snuffed out. They glared at each other.

"At least listen to my suggestions, Kal. I've been doing this my whole life. There's a lot of nuance to conducting fire."

"Pffft, sure your element is sooo special, and only you are smart enough to figure it out on your own."

"That's not what I said and you know it!"

Kaleek bent down and rapped on the floor, ignoring him to listen to its hollow echo returning. Way. Too. Hollow. She grinned at him and ignited her hands, tracing a wide circle around her.

Around them both! Tirak tried to yelp before the floor gave out beneath him. A room opened up as they fell. Circular and seemingly endless. The only floor was a narrow, spiraling staircase around its edge. This wasn't a room; it was a *pit*! Except, no. There was a frail mesh-like floor approaching, and maybe some others beneath it. Tirak sculpted jets of flame to catch himself, eyeing the fragile stuff to make sure he didn't accidentally burn through it and collapse them again. It looked… organic? Haphazard, as if it had been welded together by hand… out of strings.

A mass of red legs vomited itself out of a cavity, each one as thick as Tirak's torso. An engorged body trailed behind them like an afterthought. Pale blue eyes winked to life all across its front. Tirak started to feel sick.

"S-sp-ssspi—!"

Light spread from Kaleek as she charged up yet another attack. Her armor practically glowed molten red as she unleashed a huge arc of magma that cut through the air, splitting both creature and web in two. The web!

Both siblings cried out as the floor caved in beneath them a second time; Tirak with a raw scream, Kaleek with peals of laughter.

"Stop *doing* that! You're going to get us—"

The words were knocked out of him as they slammed through the next steel webbing and into the layer below it. *Hundreds* of dark shapes the size of his head writhed and scuttled around them. As one of them raised its fangs to stab into Tirak's leg, he felt himself growing sick.

A frosty blade stabbed down into its body. Kaleek began burning and slicing apart more of the spiders until they had a clearing big enough to stand in. Tirak struggled to his feet and tried his best to help.

The most frustrating part of it all was the growing wonder Tirak felt at his sister's power. She. Was. Incredible! He barely had *time* to help fight each layer they squashed their way through. Web after web was decimated, their ugly masters left spilling guts from its carapace shell.

Kaleek almost never used pure fire, always grafting with a second or even third element to amplify its effect. In less than an hour, they were standing on a cold concrete floor, molten web and bug juices raining down around them.

Rather, Kaleek was standing.

Tirak was doubled over on the ground, trying to hold his shattered leg together and hoping it would start to heal. Any minute now…

If only he could have landed on his other leg, he would probably be getting back up by now. But his bad leg had always been more than numb. It healed slower, built up less than half the muscle no matter how much he tried to work it over his right side. He glanced an accusing eye back up at his sister's latest jab at his slow reaction speeds.

"Are you happy with yourself? You like seeing me in pain this much? You just *love* seeing me bleed?" He hissed another breath through clenched teeth before he could continue, "Are you *never* going to learn? Power isn't everything if it makes you cut down everyone around you! Have you even stopped to *think* about your body count once this whole quest? And you're this happy to add one more? You're *sick*, Kal! You're as much of a monster as those things up there!"

Her grinning laughter finally began to crack. No, it *shattered.* Her shoulders began to droop before he'd gotten even halfway through. His eyes widened. No. No, he hadn't meant that. He'd meant to wave toward the spiders' remains. Not toward… not toward the mountain's peak. But the damage had already been done. Tirak let out a sigh as a large chunk of kneecap slid back into place and started fusing itself together.

He stabbed his sword into the ground and managed to raise himself up onto his good leg. The other one could heal while they walked. He wouldn't be doing any fighting for a while anyway.

"Come on… Let's just go," he muttered.

The farther they got from the mountain's oppressive heat, the more creatures they found waiting to eat them. But their previous energy was gone. Kaleek fought next to him in practical silence. He could all but feel the steam rising from her circuits. She was *furious* at him. He found out as much when he tried to dodge a venomous fang and stepped a little too close into her personal space. She all but shoved him right back into the thing's leg-filled jaws. He shoved her back once he'd removed enough of the creature's limbs to stop being a threat, and so began the contest.

Two haggard, bleeding siblings crawled their way from a cave's mouth into the open sky once again and collapsed to the ground. Both of them had nearly died at least an octet of times. Tirak glanced over at his sister, regret torturing his numb mind. Her face was pressed into the dirt, her body shaking with what had to be cramps. On anyone else, he might've even guessed they looked like sobs, except… no, that's exactly what they were.

"Uh… I'll set up camp, I guess?" Tirak tried.

Kaleek made no response, so he began arranging the hill around them into a shelter. Even though she'd had it coming, he still found his throat was tied in a knot from seeing her flopped there. The evening's shadows had already climbed halfway up the neighboring mountainside. The glacial valley around them was almost black with gloom. The place had been a forest at one point, though, and dead wood—while a little coated in ice—was more than plentiful. Before the last of the undercast clouds lost its glow, they were huddled into a pocket of dirt under the branches of a needle-filled tree. They lay as far apart as the space would allow, meaning their backs were still pressed firmly together. The tight quarters had been a necessity after his attempt to light a campfire had nearly sent the whole tree up in smoke. On the plus side, his mistake meant they had a cavity tall enough to kneel inside of.

Tirak squeezed his eyes shut and regretted everything he had said that afternoon. If he could only just take it all back… If she didn't hate him before, she certainly did now. He felt his chest constrict under an unforgiving pressure. Would she be gone once he woke up?

He couldn't let himself find out the answer to that.

His mind left him no chance of falling asleep anyway, thoughts running in endless streams through his circuits. He would live. He could defrag some other day. He focused on the sniffling coming from his back, on making sure neither it nor the pressure of her shoulders disappeared. His heart wrenched for her the longer he listened. He could *feel* her trembling, the stifled sobs getting slowly worse instead of softer over time.

A pop startled him. Tirak turned over just in time to watch his sister rip a second chunk of mask from her forehead. She let out a whimper of effort as her hands grasped the next, largest piece yet.

"Kal?! Kal! Stop! What are you *doing*?" he pleaded.

A raw scream finally ripped through her throat as another piece of mask flew free. He turned away, listening to the rest of the horror unfold.

"*Why*, sis? We almost made it home! Onok was going to welcome us back with open arms in front of the whole city. He and Biri are finally together again too. You finally had a real family! You were *that* close to getting it all back… You're just going to throw that away? You were the one that hated the Scarred, Kal. *Why?* Why be like them *now*?"

"Because…"

Her breath hissed rapidly between her teeth, in and out.

"We'll never get that chance. Maker says our home won't be there much longer, if it's still there at all."

Tirak eyed her warily. There she went with voices in her head, again. Should he say something? Another piece was ripped away. He felt he should, but didn't have time to interrupt.

"There's nothing left but the quest now. We either see it through or we die. He says you won't understand, but I think you deserve to know." The emptiness in her voice chilled Tirak's blood. He let out a long, frustrated sigh. Great. So she really was crazy on top of everything else. He opened his mouth to point out the obvious to her when a steadily growing sound finally forced its way into his head. Feet.

Many feet, all thundering on the gravel pathway just downhill from them. What, or *who*, in Maker's name could that possibly be?

~~~~~

Tirak's body rolled, his brow furrowing against a few sharp edges of his mask as familiar images played through his sleeping mind. He was forty moons again, staring into a campfire in Onok's wide reception room, feeling a small, bandaged hand rest on his shoulder for the first time since, his parents… had just…

Howls erupted in Tirak's ears. He winced, and felt another wave of tears run down his cheeks after having felt so numb for days. He was glad the dark hero had left the room, because now Tirak didn't have to embarrass himself in front of such an important Elder. But the blue girl hadn't given up yet. He wished to Maker she would just disappear so he could be alone. Alone forever…

"Hey."

Tirak didn't respond. Why would he bother?

"So what's your name? Mine's Kee… Bleh. I meant, it's Keel—grrr, no. Ka-*leek*. Maker, why is that so hard to say?"

The fire crackled for a while.

"You… look sad. Do, do you want to talk about it?"

Tirak shook his head.

"Can… I give you a hug instead then?"

A… *hug*? What was that supposed to solve? He shrugged, completely unsure of what to say, even if his throat had wanted to work right. Blue Girl leaned closer and put her arms around him. It… felt shockingly nice. He suddenly felt like the thick rind of a fruit, and his sobs became the juice as she squeezed harder and harder.

Unaware of what his hand was doing, he held it against the head that had tilted onto his shoulder. A soft "Ouch!" stirred him out of the endless slideshow of teeth and gory body parts.
~~~~~

Blue Girl—or… Kaleek, he guessed—rubbed at a tan cloth that was stretched across her forehead. A black stain was spreading in a line from its center. It was happening again! Tirak was getting someone else killed! He had to run away, draw the beasts after him, he—

"Ow… Cool."

He paused. Wait, cool? Why cool?

"I-I'm so sorry! I didn't mean to make it worse, I—Please don't die!" Tirak blurted out.

The girl grinned up at him.

"I hope it gets worse. Dad let me see it earlier, and I could barely even tell it was there! I want it to turn into a *wicked* scar. I'm gonna need more of them so I can become the island's best warrior."

She couldn't have been any less than an octet younger than him, but her brimming energy made her seem not even half his age. She ripped the bandage away and demanded he describe *exactly* how it looked. When he hesitated to answer, she started looking around for a chip of stone to "fix" it while the cut was still fresh. Her teasing finally pierced through his numbness and earned a laugh from him. It felt good to do. The wound was actually pretty bad, running right across her eyebrow and cheek in a vertical line that just barely missed the actual eye.

He assured the girl it looked perfectly aggressive on her, and they fell into quiet conversation as they both stared their problems away into the hearth's consuming glow.

"So, you want to be a warrior someday?" he asked. "Pretty big words coming from a girl so small and cute, *Kee*."

A punch landed on his arm.

"Hey, don't call me that! But yeah, so what if I do? Gonna stop me or something?"

Tirak smiled and placed a bruised arm around his rescuer's tiny shoulder.

"Nah, I just meant you'd make an awful sparring buddy for me."

"You too?" Kaleek gasped.

"Absolutely. It's what my p… it's what *t-they* did… before…"

His voice trailed away as fresh tears welled up.

"Hey," the girl nudged him. "Let's help each other become the best heroes this island's ever seen together. I'll promise you if you do too."

He nodded, thankful to be wrenched away from that memory.

"Yeah… promise."

Tirak sniffed, a smile worming halfway across his face. He didn't have a family anymore, but a friend at his back was almost as good.

25

WHERE IT ALL STARTED

The army of Aurii must have been a hundred strong as they thundered into Umbra cavern at a steady march. Tirak and Kaleek led them from the spear's tip, alongside a couple of the decision-makers that the rest of them looked up to. A dumbfounded awe still numbed Tirak's brain circuits. A large part of that number may have been children and other feeble villagers, but the sheer numbers made up for that. He had been *right*! They really had come around to their side in the end.

Kaleek was still resistant to bringing all of them along, but Aura's leaders had made a wise point: No place was safe from an enemy that could fly through the air and cut holes in mountains with a thought. They might as well all stand together.

And to be back in Umbra again? The feeling was surreal! Tirak could hardly believe his eyes. He reached over and pinched Kaleek's cheek to make sure it wasn't a dream.

"Ow!"

She backhanded him—softly—and glared. A full-faced glare. Even with the scars, the lack of a mask to hide her was an amazing sight.

"Sorry." He said, "I had to make sure I wasn't dreaming."

"That… that's not how it works!"

"Sure it is! I pinch you, you slap me, now we both know it isn't a dream."

The glare didn't change. She still hadn't forgiven him yet. Tirak sighed and turned away. Losing her as a sister hurt too much; a pain that was all too familiar, now that they were home. Back, where Tirak had lost so much else. He had nothing here for him anymore. He had nothing anywhere.

Then again, maybe he hadn't lost as much as he thought? A pretty face danced its way back into his mind's eye. There were still some fond memories here, too. Onok was lost to him. Kaleek was. The Goldenhearts. But… that wasn't everyone. Maybe, just maybe… that one glassforge shop was still there, along with a certain girl who always returned his jokes with a smile? Did he dare take some time, once things slowed down a little, and go see her? What could it hurt to finally ask?

Maybe he had things left to protect on the island after all.

Tirak threw himself back into the task at hand with newfound determination. He thought over their logic again as they all crossed the high stone bridge that spanned the city's lower tiers. Together… all together. Something about this felt wrong. Where were all the morning fires? Where were the squad of tunnel entrance guards? Even without the Darkness threat, juvenile chasmhearts and other elementals were always trying to encroach on the place.

And where were Kaleek's parents, for that matter? He figured Onok and Biri would be sitting around, worrying about them. And if not, he would have expected them to be locked in some kind of power struggle down here. So why were there no lights at all except near the city arena? Just because it was *easy* to see the in the dark didn't mean a Cybri wanted to waste that kind of energy day after day.

He couldn't shake the feeling that it was all some big trap. The silent calm, like a hunter holding his breath. As Tirak looked out over the bridge's edge, he grew sick. Grimy streets and shanties sat abandoned, hundreds of feet below. They were walking *right over* the trap!

"Kaleek! Wait, we need to turn back! The bridge is going to—"

He cut off as the stone shook beneath them. Two figures stood silhouetted by the dim glow. One held Onok's familiar staff, its point buried in the surface. Voices cried out behind them as first dust fell, then the end of the bridge began to sag downward. Tirak's armor bled a dark brown as he tapped into his earth control, but it was too late. Cracks laced back and forth between their feet as the bridge crumbled apart beneath its own weight.

"The children! Grab the children!" he yelled just before the plummet started.

Currents of air gushed to life all around him, slowing groups of bodies as he hurdled past them. Tirak focused his attention on switching elements, armor fading grey before finally adopting a pale pearl-blue. Why hadn't he thought to have an air shard readied with his others?

It was his weakest element of the bunch by a hundred heads, and it took him a long series of his most precise jets yet to even start slowing his fall. He *could* use his fire, but he didn't want to cook anyone below him.

Below? Well… that was a much easier answer, wasn't it?

Someone screamed his name as Tirak let go of his air shards and readied an entire set of fire. He tucked his limbs in tight and used the last jet of air to push off a child who had fallen out of their parent's reach, helping to slow them as he rocketed past the lowest Cybri.

White-hot light exploded around him just moments before he slammed into the stony ground. It slowed him in all of an instant. He spent one final jet of heat to touch down just gently enough to keep from re-spraining his bad ankle. He looked up, and wanted to vomit.

The bodies, some still screaming, began to hit. Wet splats were intermixed with sharp, metallic cracks, dragging on for seconds. Tirak screwed his eyes shut, wincing. Most of them were… they hadn't awakened their element yet. Only a few were adults that had been too drained to catch themselves.

Beside him, a silver-haired female knelt and moaned. He blinked. She rocked back and forth, holding a small body against her.

"No… no… my little boy. My precious boy."

The boy's neck was folded backward far enough to stare Tirak in the eyes. Blood trickled from processor cores that had been crushed against his own spine. The pistons that held it up had snapped free and now leaked hydraulics from their ends. Even the skin was ripped in places. He was obviously dead.

Another boy of similar height and colors stood staring beside the mother, his eyes looking haunted. Kaleek stepped up to him and opened her mouth to ask. She closed it again. Her eyes grew hard instead.

Fires blazed around them as voices yelled their ambush. The first was close by too. Kaleek snatched a hand at the attacker without looking. The igni's voice cut off in a gurgle as razor-thin blades of ice shot through him. His head fell backward as his body and shoulders continued running at them. Purple eyes stared at Tirak as they faded black. Kaleek rested a frost-coated hand on the mother's shoulder.

"We'll make every last one of them pay."

He felt a chill. When had they signed up for a massacre? As she scanned the streets around them, he saw a new kind of hatred burning in her eyes.

"Kal, slow down! What do you mean? This isn't just a few Goldenheart thugs anymore, you know."

"You're right," she cut in. "It's an entire element that sold themselves out to the enemy."

"You're pushing yourself too hard, Kal. Think for a minute before you just lash out!"

She looked him over.

"Is there a problem? Maybe something else you want to admit?"

A frosty translucent dagger formed in her hand. Tirak's eyes grew wide.

"W-what? No. Kal… I just mean—"

"Good. Then help me claw our way back out of this *rancid bedpan,*" she hissed.

Her head melted into her Nature, wings sprouting from her back before she shot away to the next group of torches. Tirak trembled as screams and body parts flew in every direction above the rooftops. He gritted his teeth. It was too late to talk her down. There was nothing else to do but try to keep her from wiping out his entire people. If he could just disarm them before his sister had a reason to slaughter them…

A crowd of Aurii had started to gather. Only then did he notice the column of fire raging along his skin. He pointed a burning hand at the ground; at a loose head whose face was at least twelve months younger than Tirak's own.

"This wasn't an enemy! This was a kid! These people aren't themselves. Don't kill anyone you don't have to. Help me push them back. Defend your families. But save the butchering for the real threat!"

He joined the circle of cybrii who had been aware enough to fight off the ambush. Every enemy had the same vacant, purple look in their eyes. They moved expertly, but also… chaotically? As if they weren't even thinking. Tirak got a chilling impression that they were just puppets controlled. As the first attacker came his way, a grey-haired matron with a growl creasing her face, it was almost *easy* for Tirak to parry her ax swing and slip a return strike beyond her defenses.

She dropped like a fruit sack. Her chest now cracked open with a gash far deadlier than Tirak had intended. Oil gurgled from a severed piston and mixed with a spreading pool of blood. Half a gear spilled out, some lengths of intestine wrapped around it.

Tirak stood and stared, forcing himself to remember the face of yet another life on his bloody hands. She was even igni with a similar pattern to his own. Tirak frowned. *All* of these ambushing the group were Ignii. Maybe it was just because this was Low-Tier, but…

No. Some of them were dressed in the unmistakable sashes and garbs of Terra. Both fallen cities' members were being thrown at them, but… only the Ignii. Why them? Why did *his* people have to be the ones this fight threatened to wipe out?

A voice broke his reverie as it roared, followed by a war hammer crashing into the paving stones mere fingers from him. He leaped back, pushing himself on a blast of heat. A young female readied another attack above her head. Golden hair, hands blistered by the heat of a glassforge. Beautiful hands.

"Oh no… please," he muttered.

Aurii danced away from Tirak and the newcomer out of surprise, but a few quickly gathered their wits and moved to join him.

"N-no! Stay back. I've got her! Don't attack her," Tirak called out.

Her hammer slammed down, cracking another paving stone apart where he had been standing only milliseconds before. He waved his hands in a warding off gesture.

"Sara, wait! It's *me*! We don't need to fight!"

Tirak's pleas were drowned out by the girl's roars. Vacant eyes didn't match the emotions in her voice. She almost sounded… in pain. Tirak dove beneath her next swing, trying to get in close enough to disarm her. His hand shot upward toward the handle—

Her leg kicked out, knee connecting with his stomach. Tirak rose helpless into the air as the hammer whipped around faster than he could track. It collided with him, and the next he knew, he was embedded halfway into the side of a clay-brick building. His back screamed with pain. Flakes of shardglass fell around his neck like dust.

Two beautiful arms, as feminine as they were smith-hardened, dragged their weapon toward him along the stones. She stalked closer.

"Sara…" He coughed.

He couldn't keep doing this. Tirak needed to find a way to disarm her, or knock her unconscious, or… no that would all be too dangerous to her.

He peeled himself from the indent. Before she could get into reach of him, he launched himself from the wall and sailed over her head. He landed on the wrong knee, but didn't stumble too badly. He recovered before she had even started to whip around. He might have to hurt the girl a little, but it would be worth it. She would heal from a few nicks on the arm in minutes.

He began his lunge… and his bad leg came down at an angle on the debris-littered street. Only then did he realize how much damage his knee had just sustained. He didn't even feel what had gone wrong until his weight began pitching to the side, the leg twisting completely beneath him. Eyes horrified, he watched the blade sink into flesh between the girl's chest armor and waist. His own weight dragged its edge downward through her in a jagged arc.

It didn't stop until it had torn completely free from her side. The warhammer fell behind her, slipping from stunned hands as the girl Tirak had dreamed of loving collapsed into his arms.

They sank to the ground together. Although the wound started to mend, Tirak knew only one of them would ever stand up again. Blood sprayed against his neck as she forced out a cough. He felt the first tears beginning to fall.

A weak hand reached toward his face. He wept as it stroked his cheek. Gone was the purple haze from those crisp, orange rings that had always sparkled whenever he told a joke. Those gorgeous eyes.

"I used… to dream of resting like this," she moaned softly. "What… what has He made you do? What has He turned you into? Please. It's not too late, Tirak. To… to turn back. Do it for me."

Her voice faltered as the color continued to drain from her face. Memories as far back as his first days running with the Goldenhearts assaulted Tirak's circuits. He had flirted with her that day, and instead of throwing a crucible in his face, she invited him back the next day to learn smithing for himself. And to think it had led to this…

She grew still as the last of any color disappeared from her bonegrey face. Her chest stopped rising. Tirak was forced to watch the lights in her eyes slowly fade to black. He pushed a golden, sweat-streaked lock of hair out of the way and pressed his mask to her forehead. He allowed one, deep sob to wrack his chest. This was what they wanted, he realized with a start. The Darkness had collapsed the bridge on purpose. His people were just pawns to them. They didn't want an easy win against the Aurii. They wanted the Cybrii to wipe each other out!

He gritted his teeth and rose, laying Sara's body to the side as reverently as he could. They couldn't keep doing this. Rage was beginning to boil in his veins. The gear on his back clicked a step forward, releasing another crystal's power with a red flash. They had to stop taking the bait this Darkness was teasing them with. They needed a way back up to the market tier, one that left them with nobody to kill.

One that nobody would ever think to watch.

The answer came no sooner than the thought had crossed his mind. He watched with annoyance as the last glimmer of Kaleek's floating, crystalline banner disappeared beyond the lip of Middle Tier's cliffside. Her ruthless little band would continue killing, but at least he had a chance to prevent the rest of them from killing anyone else. He looked up to his own banner blazing high over his head, carefully sculpted into the burning symbol of Igna with his conduction. He flared it brighter with a powerful yell. It probably looked stupid, like he was throwing a tantrum, but he found he didn't care. It felt good to release his feelings.

Aurii fighters began to fall in around him as they pushed back their attackers and disengaged.

"We can't keep this up. Follow me and I'll explain later."

No one questioned him as he led them back part of the way they had come. They met no resistance either. He led them right up to the cliffside, into a cramped slum's alleyway and up a short mound of dust and rubble that spilled from a crack in the cliff. *His* crack. He had forgotten how narrow it was. The only reason he could still fit through it now was probably because he had grown up climbing its every finger hold. It would take forever for all of them to navigate it in time, but…

Another click. Another crystal evaporated between his shoulder blades. But he had new powers. He rested a hand on the opening and imagined the feel of every crevice and bend. The air began to rumble and dust showered around him. He didn't notice. Several people gasped as the stone rippled and swelled outward. An almost-smooth shaft rose above them when he opened his eyes again.

"Climb in. Two at a time, three if you can fit."

The boldest of them obeyed, stepping onto a concrete-like platform. Hand still against the cliff, he pushed the platform up. Loose dirt seeped into each little crack and imperfection in the shaft's walls, held securely in place as it climbed.

The spectacle of it all helped the rest of them crowd around and join in. Each pair whooped and disappeared as he shot them into the air. In minutes, the band of Aurii had dwindled around him. Then, he was alone. He swallowed the sight of cold forges and ruined homes. Bittersweet. Or maybe just bitter. A pit in his stomach told him this would be his last time seeing it.

"So long, dear friends."

As he reached his palms out to touch the walls on either side, he wondered why it had gotten so hard to see. He barely felt it as his stomach lurched. He shot past his old home in an eye blink. Was he going too fast?

He cried out as purple spikes filled his view overhead. The cavern's ceiling was right there! Then, it exploded. His ears peaked and went silent for several seconds, and he arced to the top of his jump. More thuds beat against his skin somewhere below. He twisted as he began to fall, and found the air above Market Tier filled with battle. The Aurii, true to their element, had used his launches to glide over buildings and streets instead of trying to march their way through. Smart. A straight path and fewer cybrii thralls to worry about. Tirak decided to follow their example, and a few sparing jets of air sent him falling at an angle after them. He would have to be careful, though. He was much higher up, and had a lot less air to spend than they did.

A boulder flew past his head and exploded against the cavern ceiling. More fragments of shadow crystal started to fall with him. He reached out by instinct and lit up his bracer. No reason to say no to a little more power, right?

The device drank up all the free power around him while he planned out his fall. The dust would help him hide, and he thought he had just enough pushes left to cover the gap without using any bright fire.

Someone below him cried out and dodged another blast. It rippled along its edges, crumbling and spraying chips as it rose. Rose directly at him now! Tirak cursed and sculpted a wave of heat downward by instinct to knock it away.

The flash was blinding and obvious. Tirak cursed his mistake instantly. That had been power too. He could have eaten that blast, just like in the tournament, and not given himself away. He shouldn't be wasting his energy like that. Sure enough, a mixture of eyes stared up from the streets, all of them glowing violet. No option now but to grin back down.

His bracer began charging immediately. He waited until the next waves of attacks had almost reached him, trying not to flinch as they approached.

FLASH, FWOOSH!

An explosion of air sent him careening out of the destructive sphere. The attackers were disoriented for a few seconds. Then, someone spotted him, and a flurry of bolts were sent toward his new position. But Tirak was faster and far more nimble. Condensing a boulder beneath his feet, he took advantage of a fire bolt to leap off the falling platform and take flight. These mind-controlled drones couldn't even touch him from this distance. He pressed his advantage and switched from short puffs of air to the brightest jets of fire he could use. He absorbed another wave of shots, and his invulnerability only infuriated the enemy all the more. Even the "smartest" of them couldn't resist the target as the whole battlefield shifted toward him, forgetting the rest of the Aurii.

He dodged and wove his way toward the arena. That was where Kaleek was headed, and he needed to stop her before she got there.

They both knew Onok would be commanding whatever army he had left from there, if he had any defense left at all against the Darkness. If Kaleek reached them before she gave up her rampage… He focused all the harder on that outcrop of stone above the arena's back wall. He would not get there second.

Being the center of all this attention had one other benefit. With so many fast-moving objects just begging to be used as anchors to push off of, Tirak didn't need to spend another hair's weight of Air to maintain his flight. His paws danced across the battlefield, feeling the power and freedom of flight for the first time. He finally understood that blissful look in Kaleek's eyes anytime she spread her Nature's wings. Tirak was surprised when he looked down and realized he had already crossed half of the arena's dusty center. Rows upon rows of purple dots stared up at him, impassive. He winced as debris fell behind him and left patches of dark. Even more needless death…

But he was almost there! The nearer slope up to Onok's judgment outcrop was just ahead of him. He veered to the left to avoid crashing into the side of the wall and braced himself with stone for the hard landing.

Kaleek's banner surged into view from the other ramp on the far end. Tall figures loomed between them. He desperately hoped, for Kaleek's sake most of all, that Onok and Biri were still among them. The platform itself didn't have much room, but the ramps on either side were wide and gradual enough to fit a small army. And his side was all but empty, a perfect landing spot for the Aurii to follow him. A bright bolt from his finger struck the wall just above its edge, marking the spot for the rest of them to see.

He slammed to the ground a moment later, blasting heat outward to clear away any loose footing for the others. If she was right and it was that Shadow dragon instead of the Elders up here, then his and Kaleek's squads would have all of its leaders pinched between them. They wouldn't have anywhere left to go but over the edge. All they had to do next was—

The dim, unlit air went inky black to Tirak's eyes. Even Shadowsight was powerless to help him. A familiar voice boomed with laughter.

"What a welcome sight! Come, come! I've been worried sick over you children. And your mother too."

A tunnel of clarity opened in front of him. It led straight to his father. Tirak approached slowly. He always knew Dad had been the most powerful of the Elders, but something about what he saw in that moment scared him, *deeply*. A glow brightened off to the group's side, and Onok turned to welcome it.

"Ah, and there's my baby girl! Come here and give Father a hug."

The glow became Kaleek, entering from a similar tunnel to Tirak's. They were in a pocket of pure shadow, he realized. A pocket their father controlled completely. Kaleek stepped forward, defensive as she always was, wary. Her movements reminded Tirak of a viper gauging its strike. Lithe, calculating, and deadly in an instant.

"You decided to join them," Kaleek accused.

"Kaleek. That's no way to talk to your father," Biri chided.

Her voice was laced with reprimand, but it had an empty echo to it as well. Her eyes glowed vibrant purple like all the rest.

Kaleek ignored her, still waving a finger up toward Onok.

"So, what, you abandoned everything Maker wanted you to be just to have a little more power? I bet they made you a comfy little officer or something."

Biri scoffed.

"Sweetie!"

Onok held up a hand that seemed to choke off the air from his mate's statement.

"Oh, it's quite all right for her to be angry, love. She just witnessed many of her friends die. Sure, they were rebels, but that doesn't make the pain easier."

He turned back to Kaleek.

"Right, sweetheart? But don't you see? This was all a mistake. I've tried my best to tame those at the edges of my city, but they get away from me sometimes. They weren't supposed to attack *you*. That ambush was meant for the Darkness. There's one last killsquad out there. I've been trying to lure those remaining Shadows in."

The bubble expanded around them to reveal an army of dark soldiers standing in ranks on either side of the two Elders. Their eyes—the ones that had any, at least—were as empty as Biri's.

Kaleek froze. Even from where he stood, Tirak could read tension, anger, and fear in her body language. But her parents wouldn't know that. They didn't know his sister like Tirak did.

Not one to be silenced for long, Kaleek's voice spoke with a soft clarity, "Then why did they keep attacking? Why did *you* try to kill me, Dad?"

"Wha-? Sweetness, I would nev—"

Tirak waited, confused, but Dad didn't finish. His eyes grew wide, knees beginning to wobble, then the hero that had adopted both Kaleek and Tirak collapsed to the ground in a heap. His body had twisted to the left, but his head came to rest facing right... staring directly into Tirak's eyes.

In his sister's hand, a glassy blue sword shimmered with wisps of frost. One streak of black stained its surface, right near its tip. Tirak stared on in horror as she raised her bracer to casually absorb an incoming attack. Blood began to splatter against the stones, and Kaleek lifted her left arm to her face and licked the reopened wound. A crazy look filled her roaming eyes.

She had broken.

And Tirak had just lost everything.

He needed a way to stop her before it was too late! Visions of bloodshed filled his eyes as he imagined the revenge she would rain on the Darkness and anyone else that got in her way. *Especially* on anyone so unfortunate as to get in her way. Anything would be better than a genocide like that! As the grinning maniac opened her mouth to start ranting at the crowd around her, a lone head covered in red scales slowly rotated to look at Tirak.

You see, little one? Your dreams of freedom and safety were misplaced. Where on this forsaken island did you ever have safety before WE arrived? WE offer what you seek. You ran away the first time we offered ourselves to you, and you fought us away the second time. You won't have another chance after this.

Eyes wet, Tirak let himself focus on that dragon's taunting gaze. He nodded. The first quakes began to shake Umbra as Kaleek's fury continued to rise.

Ahhhhh… Well chosen, child. Thank you for giving us the opening we needed. Your people will be protected, don't worry. As for this one… mourn her, but do not restrain us. She must become… an example.

Tirak paled, shaking his head.

She is a lost cause. You must not let your attachments blind you.

"NO!" he found himself yelling.

Kaleek whipped around to face him, eyes filled with murder. Two giant Shadows picked that moment to strike from either side. She let the swings approach, face filling with a dark gleam. A blue light sparked to life on her arm, and a horrifying knowledge spread through Tirak's circuits. She wouldn't. Maker had only been able to tweak the broken bracer, not fix it entirely. If she tried to use it, it would still… Many Cybrii surrounded her. Dark, her own mom was standing in the blast radius if she—

A violet flash sent static through Tirak's eyes. He already knew what he wouldn't see when they cleared. Shockwaves started to rip the cavern city apart, but the end had already come.

Maker's Log #92348: Contingency activated.

Listen. Don't bother with the rest of them. You can't stop the one half nor protect the other half from them. Save the HELPLESS.

You think THESE people are helpless? They still HAVE the chance to fight!

But the others… The others have NO choices. You still have time to reach Terra first. They don't yet realize I never moved them. They're deconstructing the island in their search, but they never thought of the very place they first put them. You can beat them there. You can get them away—HAVE to get them away from here!

They're DEPENDING on you.

Go!

26

GENOCIDE

"How does it feel to be the last Igni alive?"

The question burned channels through Tirak's head, adding a dull pain to the numbness that had swallowed him up. Wind ripped at his hair. A caravan of ugly tube-shaped animals the masters called "train crawlers" carried the survivors through a landscape that was quickly fading from dusty ridges and shrubs to bare sand dunes. Terra was a growing line on the horizon.

Master Hass rested a scaled red hand on Tirak's shoulder.

"Now you understand my people. The sorrow. The hatred we must hold back. Darkness shall smother all, but it must be done… tactfully to have the right effect in the end. We will numb and embrace, even if it's hard to not ruin instead. Your sister out there doesn't understand this. She seeks only our ruin. At any cost."

Tirak nodded. He had seen it. The masters had barely managed to pull him out of Umbra before she collapsed its ceiling. The roar of boulders still made his ears ring above the wind around him. So much death. He tried, desperately… unsuccessfully… to stop wondering if anyone was still alive down there. Would they suffocate in that tomb first? Or starve?

Thunder crackled. The dustbowl that had once been his home flashed into view for a second. Tirak could almost have sworn a face had formed in the storm's underside. More bolts of lightning snaked out from its eyes. They were the only two sources of light in the gloom that was spreading toward them. The illusion was soon gone, and a blackness that tugged at his heart—begged him to drop himself off the side—descended heavier than ever.

Tirak watched ancient runes in his master's skull pulse with waves of light. Hass lifted his gaze to the edge where a new war between the elements was starting. A gust of wind followed soon after. He felt an uncomfortable second of stillness before the rush changed directions, outpacing the train crawler as it howled past.

"The rear units have gone dark," it observed. "She continues to spread her influence. This train must make it to your 'Terra' city *before* the killer does. She is chasing us already. Stay here. Many of the rest of us may have to go slow her down. You are too important to risk on this."

Tirak bowed his acceptance and watched the dragon's wings snap open. Wind billowed through those leathery sails, dragging him away and into the air. He breathed a sigh of relief once the Shadow had become a small red streak in the sky. None of the others were nearby. The Darkness was keeping its smaller followers away from him for the time being. He understood why, but he resented the treatment all the same.

He knew he should be grateful for what the Darkness was doing to save the island's Cybrii. Still, that grin… it made Tirak feel like he was staring a mudkroc down its throat. Like he couldn't even think out of sheer horror for it.

Now though, that spell was distant in his mind, and he began to replay the awful last hour through his cores. He watched another train-crawler, one far back, closer to the storm, lift into the air and get flung away as he remembered Kaleek's sword slashing through Onok's neck. That stain of blood. Blacker than any night.

Maker's designs were cruel indeed. The Elder had survived countless battles against the island's very worst monsters in the great taming wars. He could be the shadows themselves. Untouchable. Yet a thoughtless flick from the girl he'd called a daughter was enough to end him. The amount of *power* the world had lost today. Would things ever recover? All because of one silly element sword.

The sigh he let out sounded more like a sob to his ears. Kaleek had been right all along to fear what her ice could do.

The genocidal dragonfly exploded into view as her battle drifted closer. Blue armor glinted in chaotic thunderbolts. And once again, the terror of seeing her drove any discomfort about the Darkness away from Tirak's circuits. Once again, he felt her control worm its way into his mind. That horrifying loss of himself. Some flying Shadows drove her away to the east. Tirak released his breath again, and only now realized that he had been gripping his handles with enough force to risk popping a piston.

When Master Hass swooped in close again, he was more than glad for the friendly face.

"Master! What news?"

"The girl and her thralls keep attacking the rear trains," he yelled down over the wind. "We lost three already. She keeps snatching up whoever we throw at her. There's more of us fighting ourselves than ever!"

This was exactly what she wanted. Kaleek had always been eager to let others fight her battles. To protect her. Bleed for her so she wouldn't have to. She was going to kill them all, and it would practically be an *accident*.

"Don't kill them, Master!" Tirak blurted.

Let him sound childish. Let the Shadow laugh if he wanted. It needed to be said. They *HAD* to stop letting themselves get tricked into killing each other. Or else… or else they would have nothing left to use when they needed to defend against what lay beyond.

"No, child. I won't strike with anger, but we *will* do what we must!" Hass said in return, though his tooth-filled grin showed he appreciated the selfless thought.

"Just. Just don't kill any Cybrii you don't have to! Try to turn them! Disable them! Anything!"

"I can promise no such—"

The lights wrapping Hass's skull lit up, and his words became easier to hear.

"I must go. I will send a transmitter drone so we may continue discussing this."

With that, he vanished, barely a red smudge across the sky. Not long after, a fidgety skeleton of a creature, more metal and wires than actual body, approached him down the train's length. Violet shards and antennae stuck out from its head in a dozen directions. They pulsed with glowing lines from crystal tip to waist, and Tirak heard the master's voice re-enter his mind.

"Young master..." he started, the softness of his tone warning what would come next. *"The girl killed EVERYONE else."*

"Yeah, I get that. Your butts got whooped by her. Don't underestimate them, but don't *kill* anyone you don't have to. I'm sure I can convince anyone if you can just get *her* out of their heads."

"...There IS no one left to convince. She has but a few corpses fighting beside her on puppet strings. She stole Onok's power—and much more—while down there. The only ones left of your kind are here with us. It's a pity, really. She can't even see what her 'grand rebellion' is really costing everyone. Her loved ones most of all."

Everyone? But her own mother had been there too. Did that mean... that she really had...? Tirak blinked away hot tears and whispered a silent prayer to Maker. Then he felt stupid for doing it. A wave of empathy washed over him across the connection. Compassion for... for himself. His throat tightened. Helpless, Tirak watched more and more of his people—both old and newcomers—die far away, swallowed up by the approaching storm. He nodded, numb.

"Your sister commands an army of HERSELF and enslaved Shadows. And before you bother, no. We will not try to reason with THOSE. Our kind is much more… disposable."

Tirak felt his face turn green.

"Don't call her my sister…"

"As you wish, young one. But you must admit. There has been one constant through her life that she never gave up on. She never gave up on YOU. You are that one thing she will never corrupt. We've seen inside her. It is the truth."

The caravan of remaining traincrawlers started to slow as they finally reached the high walls of sandstone that marked Terra's edges. They had arrived, and only a little too late. The last glimpses he snatched of the towering hive before the storm blotted it out was of a thousand winged creatures slowly changing their glow to a sickly purple and turning toward the ground.

His monster was already here. A lone blue star shooting toward the center. For one last showdown before the end. And Tirak knew it would be him they sent first.

~~~~~

As soundly as their side had lost, however, the army that regrouped inside the city was no small force. They weren't anywhere the size of what the Killer had stolen from the Darkness, but neither were they weak. If both sides were forced to fight, it would likely end in the genocide of the second race that day. Despite himself, Tirak found his heart yearning for a way to turn the Killer back.

"She consumes your thoughts."

Tirak nodded his agreement, speechless. Horrible sounds rumbled and echoed through the streets, radiating from the city's center. rom the arena where Kaleek was making her nest. A tear trickled down beneath his mask. She was building a center of power for herself. A
~~~~~

place from which she could begin terrorizing the island for the rest of their lifetime.

"It's all right to mourn what she plans to do. Even to feel fear. Don't hold those emotions back, young one. Use them like igni fuel to drive you. Let them remind you what we fight for."

Tirak nodded again, but this time he fought to keep his eyebrows from furrowing. They would be able to sense it if he did. But then again, they could sense thoughts like these just as clearly, so why did he bother trying to hide? Yet something inside told him he should anyway. Had the Darkness's lord really just misread him?

But because he had been told to, Tirak let more tears fall as he thought about his lost sister. Even now, she was trying to build an audience of people that would praise her. But something wasn't letting her see the damage it was causing them. If only she could just see. He could practically feel the loneliness and hurt he'd seen in those eyes before everything fell apart in Umbra. If this Master Kalunga refused to see the truth, let him.

Maybe they simply couldn't understand empathy? The Shadow had obviously seen he was in pain, could even feel it alongside Tirak. So why didn't they recognize what was really causing it? He went rigid as a heavy hand rested on his shoulder.

"And so the night of another day falls. May it be her last."

Once the stormfront had dripped its pitchlike edges across the ocean, its true heart broke against Terra's walls. The display was nothing short of awe inspiring. Its fury had grown a hundredfold before catching up to them.

At least, what few parts of it that could be seen were impressive. Even Shadowsight couldn't pierce beyond its very thinnest layers. No daylight in sight whatsoever, no light at *all* except the chaotic bolts that left him blind with each flash.

What a terrible day. Tirak didn't want today to be the last sunset Kaleek ever saw. No, that was dangerous. Too clear. Sorrow filled him anyway. Kalunga's grip tightened.

"Will you still do it, young master, now that you've seen her power?"

He nodded. The masters truly believed she… that monster, of all things… still cared about him. He shied away from thinking about her too directly, lest he lose control. He couldn't show… couldn't show weakness, or else she would seize him in an instant. He looked up at the Shadow towering over him. This one hadn't been in Umbra with the others, and Tirak sensed he was a sort of commander over them all. Maybe he even was the Darkness, and everything else just served him. Each of the others had bowed when he arrived, and Tirak had been forced to do the same before he accidentally offended their lord.

"Y-yes, Master Kalunga. She'll just eat anything we throw at her. But I still think she's hoping, somewhere deep inside, that she can win me back to her side."

"And is she right?"

The hand squeezed him tighter still, the threat clear. It gave the question an air of warning. Fail, and Kaleek wouldn't be the only one who died.

"Possibly, once. But not anymore. Someone that's willing to murder her own parents doesn't have a place for pity," Tirak answered.

"Then you are aware of the danger, small though it may be. This is good. You have our blessing. Go. Meet her in the launch tower."

The name meant nothing to Tirak, but with the command came a flood of information. Mental images of Terra's battle arena, an instinct for which directions to turn at which streets in order to get there, and a hundred less relevant details. He bowed to the Shadow and took his leave.

27

INTERVENTION

Tirak walked through dusty, empty streets. Rare flashes told him when a turn was coming up, or when he had gone too far. Otherwise, he was alone in a dark, infinite world of nothingness. More lightning announced he had reached the arena's outer wall. He passed rows upon rows of docile cybrii, shadow thralls, and animals alike as he approached the entrance. Thunder turned them into looming silhouettes. The glow in their eyes told him that his masters were not the ones who had these enslaved with such a death grip. Such poor souls, to have to be polluted by a monster's touch like this. Like her. A shame indeed, that some might even have to be dismantled before they were pure again. That could be quite a… gruesome process if so.

He passed beneath a crumbling arch, the path dropping off abruptly halfway up the wall. Tirak stared down at the arena floor in awe. Not a speck of sand was in sight. Instead, what lay before him was a complex pattern of metal. Plates, ramps, and walkways divided the messier patches of pipes, vents, and all kinds of machinery that Tirak couldn't even begin to understand. The ground seemed a little lower than it had been, but where had all the pillars and other new features come from? Surely, those would have poked above the sand, if they had been there before. Many of their tops reached all the way to eye level with where Tirak stood. And somewhere down there, his fallen sister worked. Corrupting the very city itself in some new way. She would spread her cancer until the whole island shined chrome like this.

His eyes were drawn through a field of abstract shapes to a partial dome at the very center. Four pillars touched its edges, each ringed with lights of elemental color. Like windows into their core.

Of course, as any insect would do, Kaleek had made an inner nest around which the whole hive would grow. But unlike a hive, her thralls did nothing. They were like standing corpses.

Tirak stepped off the edge, gathering discarded sand behind him as he fell. It snaked its way to the ground long before he reached it, stiffening itself to catch him like an outstretched arm. He smashed right through its center, but it had done its job. He was even more alone now, the gentle touch of his masters barely even present at the back of his cores. There weren't even any thralls here to stare at him with dead eyes.

Finally, the fury began to build inside him. Onok's dying eyes. Biri disappearing in an afterthought of an attack. Friends. Whole families. Those who *could have* become family…

All dead because of Kaleek.

And there she stood ahead of him, her back facing his way. Always consumed by some next goal. Never stopping to think. Never considering the cost. A crystal clicked forward in his gearbox. He watched her carefully as he let his powers mix, quietly growing it into a snake of molten danger. She was eating power from the pillar that had the pale aqua glow.

Thin wings shot out as she flitted over to the next pillar and started drinking the tan from its core. It felt the attack, its lights glowing brighter in protest. Except… no, she was *pressing her own power into it.* The stream flowing between her arm and the window became clearer the closer Tirak crept.

…What? Why would she…?

Now wasn't the time to think. Tirak needed to act! The Killer's reflexes would dodge his first shot, but his second had the best chance to disable her. The recognition of who he was would throw her off balance, even if only for a heartpulse. He just needed to time the hit right. Then, the third would be all he needed to end her.

He felt the heat flow up his arm as he took aim. Magma straightened into a spearpoint. He closed one eye, focusing. Her head twitched toward him, the bug melting into a cybri head for one second.

It was all it took. His hand trembled, and the shot flew wild. The monster didn't even have to dodge as she rocketed toward him.

"Tirak! You're HERE?! You need to leave before I kill you!"

Rage filled her eyes and lips. Her armor started to darken, and Tirak began to feel his processors let go. To give in to her.

"I said *LEAVE*!"

But the change lasted hardly a moment. Her armor lightened again and she dropped to the ground, gasping.

Gooood. Make her try that again. You were right to demand this. She may yet be controlled. You may yet save her.

Tirak had no idea what they meant, but he would certainly try. They believed she wasn't beyond saving. It was enough that he dared to hope again.

Kaleek was back on her feet even before she'd finished rolling to a stop. Her body melted into its Nature, and this time she eyed him with hunger. He had always known he would end up the prey. But still, it hurt to see her be so gleeful about it.

"You gonna kill me and absorb my power like you did to Onok?" he asked.

Faceted eyes blinked at him.

Well, he wasn't going to give her time to answer that. He could still best her in a dual. He was still the better fighter. He was still Kaleek's trainer. He had been gathering sand behind himself during the stand-off, so he was ready to strike before she had started her reply. He straightened his good leg, and launched himself.

Wind rushed by as the sand lengthened to a chain behind him. He took a swing for Kaleek's chest, blade cutting through the air with a whistle.

It missed.

Tirak rolled across the ground and nearly lost hold of his sword. By the time he managed to stop, Kaleek was nowhere to be seen.

"No. Why would I fight you? And you don't really want me to either," she called from above.

Her back was toward him as she clung to a handle halfway up another pillar, her wings folded neatly behind her.

"Traitor!" Tirak roared. "You think you can ignore me? After killing off everyone who mattered to us? Come down here! At least answer for what you've done, you monster!"

"That's what I'm doing," was her simple reply as she continued feeding power into the device.

He locked a set of crystals into place. Footholds and air drafts began to form on nearby surfaces. He may not have had a Nature that let him fly, but he would find the next best way. The next time Kaleek turned all her focus toward the pillar, he began sprinting. If someone had been watching from outside, they might have even thought he was flying as he rose up the sides of walls and tall machines.

He brought his strike down, but at the last second she disappeared in a flash of blue. Ice glanced off his mask and almost ripped one segment off. He fell just a few fingers before his body twisted and spun, stopping abruptly in the air. His wrists burned with pain as he swung from where they had been locked into place. Hands and blade were frozen to the pillar with an icicle almost as long as he was.

"Too slow, big brother. Make up your mind already. Are you going to hit me or not?" she taunted with clicking mandibles.

That disgusting face! His blood *truly* began to boil now. She had murdered their people—*her* own parents even—and this was all still a big *joke* to her? An orange shard evaporated between his shoulders as he kicked a wall of stones and dirt toward her. She dodged again, landing on the side of a third pillar.

"Stop making fun of me and just *FIGHT*!" he roared. "We already know you're better than me. Faster, more nimble, a better fighter. So. Just. Fight! Me! Go ahead and turn your brother into another corpse like Onok."

Yet in the back of his mind, he remembered the passive slaves standing in their ranks outside, and knew he wouldn't survive if she *did* face him with her full force. He still didn't care. This was the job Tirak had been built for. He would protect this once-sister… by putting her down for good.

He pulled his feet up until he could brace them against the cold, slick surface, standing upside down. A flash of steam and he dropped to the ground paw-first.

"That's what you want, right, Kee? You want us all to end up like him and Biri?"

The question finally stopped her cold.

"M-Mom's dead too?"

So she hadn't realized? Oh ho ho, Tirak had some *really* choice words for her now. But he bit them back. Those wouldn't serve his masters' goal. They needed him to seem drawn in by her. *Then* the right time would come.

So instead, he asked, "You didn't even notice it, did you?"

She huffed out dry laugh.

"I guess not. If you hadn't noticed, I was a little busy trying to—"

She laughed. She *laughed*? A shard cracked in Tirak's gearbox, evaporating. He sent a dagger of flames rocketing toward her.

"OF *COURSE* SHE'S DEAD! They're ALL dead, and *YOU* killed every last ONE of them!"

He landed each word with another attack. He began burning through his elements as they turned into a blizzard of ice, stone, and fire too. Some of the hits even landed, but Kaleek had never let a simple wound stop her before. So Tirak chased her through the close network of machines and uneven metal ridges, raining down attacks that she so infuriatingly managed to escape from. Finally, she surprised him by doubling back to attack him.

She stretched out a hand and…

Pushed off his shoulder? Kaleek sailed through the air back toward the four pillars that marked her central nest and ducked behind one of them. The spot where she touched him burned with shame. He had *had* her! He snarled and launched himself toward the same pillar, slamming into its near side, just opposite her hiding spot. He reached around, grabbed hold of something flimsy, and threw Kaleek to the ground by her wing.

She groaned and turned a pleading face up toward him.

"Listen to me, Tir! Can't you see they've been controlling us all along?"

He smirked; of course she would come up with something to justify herself. Some excuse for even murder. It was never Kaleek's fault, even if *she'd* gone crazy.

But the question of Onok came back to him. How had she managed to kill him?

Stop thinking! She's poisoning you. Killing your mind. You'll become a thrall and slaughter any remaining people you know!

But… Tirak's awakening had been eight times more destructive than one small blade of ice, and the Elder had *laughed.* What was one neck wound compared to being pulverized by fire? Between blinks, Tirak thought he saw Maker looking up at him instead of his sister, but the mask was already gone. Something about what she said finally clicked. Kaleek seemed to glow with Maker's light as she continued speaking. And for the first time in weeks, her words *made sense.*

"They're twisting what we see and hear. Just think back, Tirak! Like, back during the championship in Terra, I… I saw you take down that girl at the end, but…"

She swallowed an obviously dry throat.

"Then saw you begin to torture her once she was disarmed. You broke her knee, then jumped on her and pulled the dagger out of your own shoulder and… *Maker*," she sobbed. "You were slashing at her legs while she begged you to stop. And when she wouldn't stop screaming, you grabbed her by the throat, and… and *choked* her. Choked her so hard you nearly ripped her neck in two! It, it made sense at the time because we were so overpowered, but… it was more cruel than I'd ever expected from you. That… never happened, did it?"

He paused his attacks again. No, he didn't remember that. Sikh, he remembered the name. She had been anything but defenseless, but he *did* remember his palm biting into her neck as he threw her off. The feel of her life crumbling under his hand… Shame colored his cheeks.

"N-no. Not like that at least. It was over before I even started. Something about eating that huge geyser attack made me stronger than I knew what to do with. All I tried to do was knock her down, and maybe knock her out of the fight. And suddenly, one jab somehow cut halfway through her neck."

He began to cry as the feel of death clung to his hands. Something still troubled him. It couldn't *all* have been an elaborate illusion. Her parents, both adopted and real, were still dead weren't they? There was no way he was imagining the crater-grave that replaced Umbra out there, past the black horizon.

"But, what about everything you said on our way to Aura?" he asked. "You hated me so much that you almost left me behind!"

That earned a blush from her.

"I-I didn't… Look, I was upset, feeling abandoned, and I said some really stone-headed things. I never meant that I wanted you gone, though. *Ever*, Tirak. You're my brother. Of course I've always wanted you to be around. I *adore* you."

Guilt spiked through Tirak's heart. That… had the sound of a long-pondered apology. Not one that had been rehearsed, one that her head had replayed over and over a hundred times, desperate for a chance to say it out loud. But… surely there was something she still wasn't telling him.

"And your leathers? You threw away almost every piece of it. You said it was just getting in your way. Seeing you do that killed me inside, Kal. It took most of my working wages to save up those shards, but that made you despise it even more! With every piece, you threw away part of *me* too…"

"Throw away…? Tir, I…"

Her bare left arm reached into the folds of her vest that hung open. It withdrew a handful of black and purple tatters.

"Tir, I love you. This gift means more to me than I could ever say."

He gasped as he recognized the thick, hardened leather with its plates of purple bonesteel.

"After Terra, I scoured the whole site to find every piece of this bracer, and even though it was too ripped to wear again, it *still* saved my *life*, Tir."

She unconsciously fingered deep trenches that crisscrossed her skin. They had sharp, square lines to them, like imprints from crude ribbons of leather.

"You saved my life. Again and again, you keep saving me. How could I ever take anything about you for granted?"

"But… but then what about Dad? If you're *so* innocent, how come—"

His voice caught, refusing to let him finish the thought unless he wanted to start sobbing. Her eyes fell, and she began to slump. Before Tirak knew what to do, his people's killer had flung herself against him and… and *was hugging* him! He wasn't stable enough to hold them up, so they sank to their knees together. Tears dripped onto his shoulder, and he realized Kaleek's chest was fighting to its last strength to keep even more violent sobs from belching out.

He held her with one hand while using the other to slip his hunting knife from its sheath. This was just another ruse of hers, he knew… *probably*. He needed to strike before she had a chance to. A voice in the back of his mind whispered that his chance was opening up. Obviously, she deserved it. Her earlier bravado and lies crumbled beneath the undeniable murder of her dad.

"I… I still can't believe that happened."

Tirak had begun to hope. Now for a second time, he felt his throat being crushed by sorrow. Sorrow, because he had been wrong. There was nothing left of her worth saving.

"I told him to duck. Why did he have to stand back up? I wasn't supposed to be able to hurt him! I-I thought I learned my lesson the first time with those street urchins. How could I be so stupid!"

It turned out to be Kaleek who sobbed uncontrollably first, not him.

"P-please, don't hate me…"

The smallness of Kaleek's voice crushed him. As he thought about it, Tirak realized how similar her ice spikes looked to a sword. The thought broke his confidence. Something about the memory started to feel wrong. The voice screamed to end this murderer's pathetic life, but as he looked down, all he could see was a crying, desperate sister.

A sister he loved. A sister that he wrapped his arms around to hug.

His dagger clattered against the steel floor.

"I couldn't hate you, Kee."

Color began to return to her armor as she squeezed him back. Blank, faceted eyes slowly returned to those bright, too-thoughtful blue rings he remembered.

"All I wanted was a way for us all to get out of this nightmare. I—Kal, I'm sorry I made everything go wrong back there. They promised it would be easy. 'No deaths at all.' Now I feel stupid for believing them. Kal, you haven't seen how much they like killing."

"I have. Oh *Maker*, I have. It was a slaughter after you left. Despite everything I did, the aurii broke apart and fled. *They* collapsed Umbra on our heads, and only some of us got out in time. We were hunted like animals for hours, and anyone who got caught was butchered."

His shoulder felt damp.

"Not just killed. *Butchered.* That's when I snapped and began controlling them all. All I want is for this nightmare to end too, Tir."

He snorted.

"Little late for that, huh?" he asked.

"Maybe… but maybe not for everyone."

He raised his eyebrow at her. Rather than explain, she waved a hand that pulsed with a tan glow. A huge metal hatch opened in the ground next to them. It opened into a seemingly endless cavity, columns and columns of storage containers disappeared into the shadowed depths. A small, milky window in the top half of each pod showed a cybri-like face inside. Every face looked almost the same, but also wildly different. *And not a single one had even a flake of metal in its features!*

"This was always about the humans, Tir. Every one of those containers is one of Maker's kind. He built this whole ship to carry them to safety. He built us to power the thing. A starship that the Darkness could never catch up to. He… still wants us to try. The two of us, as long as you're willing. *This* is what the quest has always been about."

Right… he had forgotten about Kaleek's 'Voice of Maker' delusion. The whispering voices suddenly started to sound more reasonable again. This girl was still extremely unhinged. He could possibly go along with her scheme, but if he did, he had a feeling he might end up dead no matter what else happened.

But at the end of the day, what did that matter? He could continue serving the Darkness, they might even give him a cure to his body's stupidly short lifespan. Maybe he would even live forever, like they promised.

Or, he could have one more blissful hour with his precious sister.

"Okay. Then, let's do it. I'm not leaving your side this time, sis," he answered.

The reason didn't matter. She seemed to believe in all this to her core. What kind of brother would he be to stomp that out? The truth was before his eyes. The humans were here. A thrill shot through his veins like ice as a realization hit him: They really had become the heroes of all the stories. Kaleek beamed a smile at him, diving in for another hug before she shot back into the air toward the last lightless generator.

And she had been the one to make it all come true. Pride warmed Tirak's stomach as he watched her go. He stood and started following her instructions on how to prepare the ship.

"Don't leave yourself flameless, but dump *anything* you can afford into that socket there! There too! Maker says they'll balance everything for us automatically. Oh, any air you can spare too! No, not that spot, the white receptacle over there."

Any time she wasn't yanking on crank wheels or plugging things into here or there, Kaleek's hands were a flurry of pointed directions for him to follow. Several times, she reached behind her head and yanked a readied crystal directly from the gearbox, slamming it into a piece of machinery without even pausing to wipe the trickle of blood away. She had to be absolutely *burning* through her charges. But then again… what cybri ever had more to spare than herself, right now?

The gearbox spun a new set into place and her colors bled from a vibrant aqua to more of a pale, golden tan. She slammed kneefirst into the ground, clapping her hands together. A dozen twisters spun away from her as the ground stirred. Huge channels were cut into the remaining drifts of sand. She flitted back toward him, hairthin wings folding into her back and disappearing as she straightened by Tirak's side.

"I… Maker thinks we're ready." Kaleek began to grin as she turned to look at him, excitement building in her face behind the smooth scars. "We just need to jumpstart the first few minutes of launch and it'll handle the rest."

"L-launch? Wait, Kaleek when you say 'Ship,' d-do you really mean…?"

He looked around.

"What did you *think* I meant?" she asked with a snort.

"But… no motors?"

"Down below, or… Maker keeps calling them 'engines,' but they look the same to me. C'mon, how are your reserves?"

Tirak flexed and felt the heat surging through him. He had spent a lot, but the Darkness had pumped him with far more before sending him here. Aura tower had only been a fraction of the fireshards Maker was hiding, from what Tirak's masters had told him.

He shuddered. A feeling in the back of his mind began to sink in as soon as their mention entered his circuits.

"Good. Really good actually! Say the word and I'll get started, sis. You ready to watch my back?"

"Huh? Watch your…?"

That was when the screams started. The horde was coming. The Darkness knew he had failed them.

KILL! KILL! KILL! KILL! He heard his masters rage.

Kaleek gasped, clutching for her chest as she doubled over. Color across her body deepened from their bright near-white to shades so rich they could be mistaken for umbri black. The change pulsed across her several times. Her head snapped up to him, expression panicked and eyes flickering a glassy violet.

"D-do it!" she cried through clenched teeth.

Tirak placed his palm against the panel in front of him and let his element flow out. The first explosion rocked what was left of the city less than a second later. The ground shook and quaked… and the arena began to sink into the sands. Another blast hit, and like the first it kept right on rumbling. Another three blasts shook them halfway off their feet before things had settled down.

But the sinking city—no, *their* rise into the air—wasn't going to deter the masters' hordes. The explosions seemed to shock Kaleek out of her episode, and she looked up at him with crystal blue eyes. The two of them braced for one more fight. Something in the words ringing through Tirak's head warned him it would be his last. A faint, but vengeful scream that echoed his name.

Bodies began to flow over the arena's walls before the "ship" had brought its nose level to the rim, heedless of their fellows propping up their climb. Like a blur, Kaleek shot forward and began cutting through them. Tirak turned all his focus into helping them accelerate faster. The sooner they got up to speed, the less of a chance their enemies would have to climb on, and the easier it would be to get to… wherever it was they were headed.

Where were they headed anyway?

Tirak looked up at the tower-like hive's belly and felt his eyebrows crawl their way up his forehead. The hive had grown teeth! A perfect ring of receding wedges that were slowly fading into its lips. Aura Tower had just become a maw, and they were on a race to let it eat them! For one long moment, the battlefield fell still in awe of the sight.

Panic gripped his throat as he watched pieces of ancient hive break loose and crumble into a freefall. Unable to move from his place, Tirak cried out as one large section hurdled straight toward him.

He was dead.

It was only a few yards from hitting him when a brilliant purple flash left the air clean. Kaleek slid past him, impaling an ice blade into another dark hordling. Her bracer's glow was still fading from the rescue.

"Thanks!" he called after her, knowing she wouldn't have time to hear.

Twisted creatures continued to flood the lip of their platform. Kaleek shot from edge to edge to edge in her Nature form, hurling attacks faster than Tirak could track. All four elements filled the air in every combination he could imagine. And still they climbed. If this ship was flying, then surely the horde had to stop at some point, right?

Tirak watched a boulder crash into the platform and squish at least a hand of enemies. Bug guts coated the area. He snapped his head upward in time to see more bugs and clay chunks fall as another layer deeper into the hive began to split. So this worm had many layers of mouths.

He checked the display on his bracer again. He was feeling drained, and sure enough his reserves of fire were dangerously low. And still they were about to crash through the ceiling. This one was no dark set of jaws. It shimmered like airglass in the sun. A salty drop splashed against his mask. Salty like the ocean.

Three more element pillars lit up with molten colors. More shaking came, then the ceiling began to flow like water. A perfect column formed above their heads.

And suddenly, no more debris fell. They rose, encased in a tube of blue that grew more and more intensely bright with every head they went.

Tirak's wonder was interrupted when a sharp pain erupted in his side. The bite of an arrow, with more to follow.

A voice boomed behind him. Tirak spun out of the way just in time to see a hammer with square edges sing past his head.

BOOM!

He rolled to his feet, and swallowed. The control console was completely unrecognizable now. Elemental cramps raked his muscles. There was nothing more he could have done anyway. His armor was almost colorless. He had no fuel left to give the ship. The depleted ache wanted to consume him.

It was time to help defend.

Grimacing, he ripped the arrow from his side, ignoring the bleeding. The hulking Shadow hefted a hammer at least as wide as Tirak's chest back onto its shoulders. Instinct forced his hand and he tried to send a bolt of thick molten fire into the machine's face. Nothing came except a wave of exhaustion. Dry. Gritting his teeth, he readied one of his other elements instead.

He tried to fire off a stone, but the enemy was faster than it should've been. The rock went wild as he leaped for safety. The floor shuddered beneath another hit from its warhammer.

Tirak nailed it in the back of the head a few times, but it hardly seemed to notice. A small plate had been knocked free, but smooth gray metal bled outward and replaced it in seconds.

"Hey Kee? I think I could use some help here!"

Tirak jumped over its next charge with a jet of air. He came down on its back with his sword. The edge bit in deep, but again the wound healed almost before he could pull his weapon free. He shivered to realize he'd almost been disarmed.

"*Ka*-aal!" he called out.

His opponent spun, grabbing him by the face and sending him flying. Tirak's spine screamed in protest as he collided with a jagged, unmoving wall. Where was Kaleek?

She wasn't coming, he decided. He still clutched the bent arrow. The Shadow was heavily armored, but, like himself, it had its weak spots. All he needed to do was puncture a few hoses and those organs below its chest armor, and it was sure to seize up. He saw his opening and lunged. He didn't have time to wait for another chance. The blow landed true, rewarding him with a spray of coolant and a rotten something that almost smelled like blood. The giant shuddered once. All he had to do now was simply—

It smiled down at him with a cruel expression. Tirak felt a chill. Its hammer swung up from the ground in a blur of impossible speed, catching him in the chest. Something inside him gave, then he was sent flying. He struck one of the elemental pillars and fell to the ground, dazed.

He tried to gasp… and couldn't.

His eyes locked onto his chest. It curved the wrong way now. A jagged void filled what should have been smooth, unbroken armor plates. An entire head could've fit into the cavity. Adrenaline wore off, and the pain made Tirak's eyes unfocus. He tried to scream.

He couldn't.

He couldn't even breathe. His chest wouldn't move! It barely even flexed, fused to itself somewhere beneath that hollow hole.

A body collided with him, her knees sliding beneath him with a careful grace that only sent mild spikes of agony through his core. His sister. Kaleek. She was here, and so were all the enemy. So, he had become the distraction. He would still be the cause of her death after all.

Tirak spread his lips open, but no sound came. His chest tried to heave despite feeling like someone had poured molten rock into it and stolen his conduction. Something inside gave. Only a few hairs, but it was enough! He sucked in the shallowest of breaths.

"kal..." his lips mouthed.

EPILOGUE

The last few shockwaves had finally settled down as the vessel stopped trying to fall back through its tunnel. Everything around her was a hazard zone of wreckage. Kaleek was blind to it all as she conducted more of her healing waters into her brother's chestwound, urging it down her arms like two inky snakes.

But the inflamed skin only grew more sickly.

"kal," Tirak's lips moved again.

She leaned in, eager hope suddenly filling her eyes. His own were growing milky. They darted, searching empty air. Blind.

"go."

She sucked in a gasp, shaking her head violently. His body went rigid in her arms, pain written on his brow and lips. She winced and held him tighter.

"I won't leave you ever again, bro! We're family! We're gonna keep being there for each other. We are family! We always…" she choked, "…always will be."

It seemed to take him every ounce of strength, but a finger reached up toward her. It found her mask's "lips" and pressed against them.

"shhh… it… all right… you…"

A soundless cough interrupted his labored whisper. Those eyes twisted shut again. She redoubled the healing, hoping desperately it would start taking effect.

C'mon, c'mon. Any second now, surely.

"yours… the important mission… now."

His words crushed her. Her body lost all its color as she let go of her elements. She pressed her mask to his, their false foreheads touching.

They didn't even have the decency to help him remove that? Monsters!

"Are-are you s…?" she sobbed.

Tirak tilted his head up a fraction, then down a fraction. The grimace he wore said he couldn't bear to move even a hair more. He… he was still getting worse.

Dying. He's really dying. But-but he CAN'T die! NO!

"go. be… amazing. save…"

He tried, twice more at least. Each time with less vigor than before. The strength to finish his plea just wouldn't come. She looked down at her brother's corpse, numb. Blood as black as the water she'd tried to heal him with still spurted from his stomach, but his eyes were empty, accusing orbs. None of their reddish fire was left anymore. The blood's faint violet glow became diluted as it mixed with hydraulics and blackened water. The mixture ran slick across her hand.

I'm… sorry, Kaleek. You can't save him.

"I *CAN*!" Kaleek yelled into the air. "I just need to use a little more healing and he'll…"

Ice, and fragments of the ship itself continued to fall.

You're just poisoning him further, Kaleek. Look at his face, came the gentle reply.

Discolored splotches had spread all the way to his face now. Maker was right. She cradled his head against her and began to weep.

"I failed you," she whispered.

Me, or your brother?

More liquid threatened to fill the cavities behind the mask's eyeshields, requiring its systems to flush them for her. She was hollow. She wasn't even allowed to feel the small catharsis of hot tears running down her cheeks. Emotion itself was denied her.

Everyone, Kaleek thought back. *All of you. You said I was supposed to beat back the Darkness and carry the humans away to safety. But now look at us. Look at your plan.*

Her mind was silent for a while.

Maybe, but I think there's still a chance, Kaleek. Losing the Cybrii hurts my soul, and it pains me even more to leave my OWN people behind, but there's still time to save SOMETHING. The core of the plan IS still open.

Her body flashed with a yellow glow, comforting her somehow. Visions filled her mind. A grey soda-can shape in the middle of a starry night, then of a hangar of starfighters—

Wait, what ARE any of those? she wondered.

She nodded finally, kissing her brother's cold forehead and letting his body rest on the slanting, broken floor. Planting one leg beneath her, and then the other, Kaleek began to walk.

The image of starfighter bays returned stronger, and with it came a vague sense of nearby-ness. Hidden behind her Maker's mask, Kaleek let a determined grin return. Darkness may have won its war. It may have snuffed out her entire people, but it would never steal her light.

~~~~~

His sister's hands set Tirak down gently, and he heard her feet take shuffling steps away. Her voice continued to sob.

He tried to muster enough breath for one more call to spur her on. His chest tightened further. Further. At last, something gave. A piercing *SNAP!* echoed through his chest, amplified to deafening levels by its hollow shape. Agony blinded him. Whatever it was had been sharp enough to rip his insides apart in the process, and he felt liquid start to build inside.
~~~~~

His glassy eyes watched her leave. Lying there, Tirak died, happy to know he was alone.

Many minutes later, a few final pulses of static flickered across his pupils. The careful observer would have noticed it and known that some final cellular equivalent to a capacitor had just died, releasing its few volts in one final burst. The even more careful observer might have looked a little closer, however. They would have flipped the image, and then reversed it after zooming in as far as they could. They would have been able to read the text that scrolled by.

Reboot failed!

Entering recovery mode…

Recovery failed!

ERROR: missing Boot Sector!

Reflashing sector…

More diagnostic messages flashed unseen across his vision. Reports of corrupted memory cores, disconnected features, error codes, and cellular waste building up. If his ears had still been working, he would have heard an odd skittering approach. He would have felt strong pincers lift his remains and carry them away.

But Tirak didn't feel. He was simply a body, floating in a pool of haze-filled light. A lone object standing with a wall of fog that twisted and curled in every direction. Forever, in an infinite expanse.

"So. Tell us again," the kaleidoscope of voices commanded. "What are you?"

"The… enemy. We… are Darkness. We are Gegnox," Tirak replied.

"GOOD."

The adventure doesn't stop here.
Follow Kaleek's side of the story in:

The Chosen Hero
and the
Villian's Daughter

Delusions of a Cyborg Savior, part 2

Stay up to date with its progress and future announcements at: http://gifthammer.com/book-chvd.html
Or scan the QR Code to go straight there.

POSTSCRIPT

Where did this story come from? Like most things, it had a lot of influences over the years I spent planning it out. The earliest influences came from my highschool attempts at creating new characters from my collection of LEGO Bionicle pieces and trying to think up a place where they could fit into that world's narrative without contradicting the canonical story. Later in college, I learned about the horrors of intellectual property law and had to move myself away from any possible conflicts with the company that was practically my childhood hero. Rather than a fanfic, the flavor that's left is hopefully only enough to inspire readers to go dig up the comics and games from that franchise and appreciate it the same way I did growing up.

In fact, the story that Tirak's mother tells him in chapter 1 is almost a direct carryover of my very earliest fanfic idea from that world.

Next, this was never supposed to be a novel. It's a story that failed to be a videogame. A short adventure game with a handful of story quests. The longer I planned it out, the longer the script for its story became and the more it began to look like a mix of *Brothers: A Tale of Two Sons* and *God Of War* (2018). Once I had a direction for the story and its theme, I knew I needed to include networking for a 2-player co-op feature in order to tell it the right way, and so the complexity expanded. After a few years of barely any momentum, I realized what should have been obvious: my skills were woefully underdeveloped to tackle such a large goal on my own. I had just lost contact with all of my previous indie dev friends, and the few I stayed in touch with had no interest in using a sensible engine or in working on my particular project. I decided to lick my wounds by only working on the story, and then I came across some wise words by Arthur C. Clarke in the preamble to his book, *2001 A Space Odyssey.* I'm not going to repeat him here because I think you should go *read* that book for yourself and his notes about how he came to write it.

One of the gameplay features I wanted from very early on was a two-player coop that would play with character perspective as both a game mechanic and a storytelling device. I wanted the same story to have a completely different path & meaning to the player simply by telling it through a different set of eyes. I struggled with ways to convey this in the early drafts of the game's script, and it was only after the first few novelized drafts that I realized I could achieve that original goal by simply publishing two individual books rather than one messy novel. As soon as Tirak's story was moved out into its own cover page, it had the room it needed to breathe and become its own narrative.

Until too many of my fellow Shut Up & Write peers started complaining about it, I was even planning to have non-sequential chapter numbers to reinforce exactly where the two books are supposed to overlap. I wanted Shadow's Ember and its sequel to still feel like one single story when you placed them side by side. But it's going to be a long time before Kaleek's book comes out, so my friends' complaints were right. Who knows, though. Maybe I'll go change it back again in a second edition… or maybe a deluxe hardback version?

The number one feeling I wanted to convey by telling the story through two different sets of eyes is a need to scream out, "That's not how it happened!" A fact I've noticed throughout my life is that the curse of Babel makes communication between *any* two people fundamentally broken. It's more than just cheesy miscommunication tropes appearing in books, too. It's not a case where someone can just write a Post-It note, stick it on the fridge, and that would've fixed all conflicts between them. We see it in everything from the common disputes that end in a couple's divorce, to the lasting wounds that are the result of well-intended comments between friends. Most of all, I see it day after day in the difference between what my mind thinks and the words that come to my lips any time *I* try to say it out loud. We are all inherently selfish, and can't help assuming that everyone else's intentions are *so much less* noble than our own. When I decided I wanted this to be a two-player co-op, I knew I wanted to play with this idea. I wanted to tell a story where *no* character gets all the details right, where everyone else seems more vile and self-centered because the reader isn't seeing *why* they're doing the things they are. It would be an incredibly fun challenge to make a *satisfying* game that repeatedly pits the "cooperative" players against each other's perceptions.

Lastly, this book, and the rest of *The Humanity Saga* universe it exists within for that matter, comes from a growing pet peeve I have with the entire Science Fiction genre. Every great story I read, my wonder and appreciation is always tainted when I notice it seems to be a desperate attempt to cry out, "See? Look how much better the world would be if only we could get 'God' and those make-believe religions out of the picture! Science is the only thing we need. Get rid of religion and everything could be magical!" Oh, really? The painful part is that I wholly agree with that last part. Religion has absolutely been the most ravaging force of evil throughout our history. But all these authors who try to invent worlds that never needed a Creator's loving touch never seemed to stop and question why our own world hasn't fallen apart yet. They imply that a creator-God need not apply here, but they can't help relying on jewish and christian moralities and themes without explaining why their unrelated world feels any need to obey the rules that He designed us to follow. I find it beyond funny that the question most Sci-Fi authors end up having to grapple with is, "If *this* world is so fundamentally different, then why do the people all act as if what we know as common, christ-like decency is the obviously right and moral thing? Why do even their curses pull from those religions?" They either try to argue that morals based in jewish and christian principles of goodness are really just a common trend across all things (but why though?), or they ignore the problem entirely (and leave us asking the question: *but why though*???). I've watched authors go blue in the face trying to spin networks of logic that always boils down to a simple, "I don't know, just because evolution liked it that way, I guess?"

The result is that even the greatest classics of this genre ring hollow to my ears. I latched onto that annoyance when I started reforming this story to be a part of *The Humanity Saga*. If everyone wants to see what the world would look like if we really did get The Lord to leave us alone, then fine. I'll show them *exactly* what a world built without even the memory of Him looks like. I can promise you the only way to stomach it will be the heavy usage of perception to bleach out just how dark it would truly get. Because when you strip away the One who invented the rules for why our world works the way it does, and the consequences that react to breaking those rules, you don't get another world that's basically the same but a little more fun.

Well, now I've revealed my hand and told you the sinister reason behind why I'm trying to write cool stories. Yes. I am trying to convince you that there really is Someone out there who cares about you. Not the things you have or haven't done. You, yourself, are precious to Him. He designed you just to have the slightest chance to be your loving friend. He loves you enough to have designed you from the ground up, bodily flaws and all. And because He loves you, know that I do too.

Hey, at least I'm honest about my underlying motives. The Scott Cards and Sandersons of this industry will never admit out loud that their dreams of Pretts, Aiúas, and Spiritual Realms are all an attempt to convince you how the world should work, if only our world really did work the way Mysticism claims it does. If only everyone had a slice of eternal godhood inside them.

There's a lot that I could say about the magic system to that end as well. Worldbuilding has been as much a curse in my head for the last decade as a blessing. Almost none of that ended up in this story, by design. The tone just didn't fit. Instead of offering too much of an explanation here either, I'll take the opportunity to plug some of my future projects that will explore its facets in a little more explicit detail. The simplest explanation I can offer here, though: delusion is the basis of how the system works. Whatever Anium crystals are, delusion that a person can control it is what fuels their abilities. The places I managed to weave it into this story were few and vague, but who knows, maybe like some of the plot holes throughout the story that was done on purpose?

ACKNOWLEDGMENTS

As with anything worth being made (and I assume by the fact you made it this far that you considered the book worth reading), the list of people that have been instrumental in making this reach the light of day is longer than I can hope to remember, much less include here.

- My parents, for pointing me towards books at an early age and letting me get lost in what they have to say. You've given me more support and love than I have any right to feel from people that haven't really understood my choice of a hobby these last few years.

- The awesome friends that were willing to stomach my loose scenes and clunky writing at its worst, and had positive things to say anyways:

  - John & Amalee Pruchnic, for being good friends and having an encouraging push or a willing ear to lend when I needed it.

  - Drew Trementozi, for being there next to me when I started rethinking this plot idea into a book. You were willing to trade drafts and offer some encouraging ideas at such a pivotal stage in its process.

  - Ruthanna Witter (go read some of her works too, by the way. She is positively awesome), for swooping in when my drive to go on had almost fizzled out. It's not an understatement when I say you single-handedly relit the fire in my soul that demanded to see this finished. You were the first to actually read it from cover to cover, despite at least two-thirds of it still being an unfinished mash of margin notes. Yet you still managed to sing its praises. You're an absolute Godsend, and I'd be honored to return the favor for you any chance I get.

- The members of my local Shut Up & Write community, for being an amazing resource to lean on, urging me to write *at least a little more* every single week. For being willing to trade story drafts, share ideas around, and give out such a helpful, diverse spread of feedback:

    - Drema Apperson
    - Jay Long
    - Jessica Boyce
    - Indigo Kendzie
    - Tyler Grimsley
    - & the many other regulars, organizers, and off-n-on newcomers whose quiet, focused presence were instrumental in getting this book from 30 pages of snippets and scenes to this final draft.

- The friends online that were willing to lend an ear to this off-tangent idea I kept talking about, and to get excited for my sake… even if they didn't care all that much for the genre.

    - Matthew Smith – Sorry mang, we'd be here all day if I tried to list all the usernames you've switched to over the years.
    - Michael Park – I *will* make sure you and Matt get the first alpha copies if this ever becomes a game. I haven't forgotten, I swear!
    - Emiliohno – You and several others from my Roblox days are a huge part why I keep trying to see this story become something. Your enthusiasm was what made me realize this was more than a neat story I liked telling myself. Thank you.

And tell Hoshpup my starfighters are *still* more fun to fly if you see him.

- The team at Clovercroft Publishing Company, and their amazing list of associates and contractors.

- KAdala S.R.I. for her work on the book's front cover drawing. You really brought my low quality 3D model renders to life.

- And finally, Christian Faber, Greg Farshety, and many other design leads across The LEGO Group, whose works inspired me to start dreaming of more than simple, interesting stories early into my life. They were the first to show me it's possible to craft truly intricate, interactive worlds filled with nuance and deep meanings… even when your medium is a collection of plastic kids' toys and the Adobe Flash webgames used to advertise them.

Above all else though, I thank You, Lord. You know what and who I want this book to point towards. Since it ended up in someone's hands, I trust You to find a way to use it in a way that praises You. I pray that it might bring someone to at least as close a friendship with You as I've enjoyed. May You use it to help someone want You, Lord.